THE FAMILY RECIPE

ALSO BY CAROLYN HUYNH

The Fortunes of Jaded Women

THE
FAMILY RECIPE

A Novel

CAROLYN HUYNH

ATRIA BOOKS

NEW YORK   AMSTERDAM/ANTWERP   LONDON   TORONTO   SYDNEY/MELBOURNE   NEW DELHI

ATRIA
BOOKS

An Imprint of Simon & Schuster, LLC
1230 Avenue of the Americas
New York, NY 10020

This book is a work of fiction. Any references to historical events, real people, or real places are used fictitiously. Other names, characters, places, and events are products of the author's imagination, and any resemblance to actual events or places or persons, living or dead, is entirely coincidental.

First Atria Books hardcover edition April 2025

ATRIA BOOKS and colophon are trademarks of Simon & Schuster, LLC

Simon & Schuster strongly believes in freedom of expression and stands against censorship in all its forms. For more information, visit BooksBelong.com.

For information about special discounts for bulk purchases, please contact Simon & Schuster Special Sales at 1-866-506-1949 or business@simonandschuster.com.

The Simon & Schuster Speakers Bureau can bring authors to your live event. For more information or to book an event, contact the Simon & Schuster Speakers Bureau at 1-866-248-3049 or visit our website at www.simonspeakers.com.

Interior design by Davina Mock-Maniscalco

Manufactured in the United States of America

1   3   5   7   9   10   8   6   4   2

Library of Congress Cataloging-in-Publication Data

Names: Huynh, Carolyn, author.
Title: The family recipe : a novel / Carolyn Huynh.
Description: First Atria Books hardcover edition. | New York : Atria Books, 2025.
Identifiers: LCCN 2024035590 (print) | LCCN 2024035591 (ebook) |
ISBN 9781668033043 (hardcover) | ISBN 9781668033050 (paperback) |
ISBN 9781668033067 (ebook)
Subjects: LCGFT: Domestic fiction. | Novels.
Classification: LCC PS3608.U99 F36 2025 (print) | LCC PS3608.U99 (ebook)
| DDC 813/.6--dc23/eng/20240802
LC record available at https://lccn.loc.gov/2024035590
LC ebook record available at https://lccn.loc.gov/2024035591

ISBN 978-1-6680-3304-3
ISBN 978-1-6680-3306-7 (ebook)

For Charles, for everything. Cảm ơn anh.

All happy families are alike; each unhappy family is unhappy in its own way.

—Leo Tolstoy's *Anna Karenina*

PART 1

MISE EN PLACE, THE GATHERING OF THE FAMILY

CHAPTER I

No matter what, the Fresh Prince of Bellaire, Jude Trần, would be the first of the five Trần siblings to arrive at his father's gated compound. Today was not the day to be unpunctual. His father, Duc Trần, had summoned all of his children home for the first time in a decade, which only meant that he finally finished his will. As the firstborn and only son, Jude would stand to inherit it all—the money, the mansion, and the family business, Duc's Sandwiches.

Jude swerved his leased Audi convertible through the wide lanes of River Oaks, Houston's leafiest and most luxurious zip code, which was protected by oil millionaire Texans on one side and unsavory state senators on the other. He knew the route to his father's McMansion well, because when Jude was a child, his father would take him and his four sisters on long drives through the "nice part of town" in his clunky Oldsmobile. It reeked of cigarettes and there were yellow stains on the carpeted roof to match.

Whenever the children looked up at the roof, they imagined the amorphous stains to be topological maps, reminding them that they'd rather be anywhere in the world than stuck inside the stuffy car with their eccentric father. From behind the wheel, Duc would critique each mansion along the way, a stump of a cigarette precariously hanging from his lips, and proclaim that rich people had no taste. He left the windows rolled all the way down, accidentally ashing the children in the face from all angles. Squeezed together in the back, they swatted away the smoke plumes, unable to escape their father's sermon of the day. Duc had sworn up and down that the moment he became rich, he'd offer an obscene amount of cash to one of these white homeowners, kick them out, and turn it into the prettiest house on the block.

And that was exactly what Duc did. Except their house became the gaudiest one.

Duc always had big, lofty, American, Texas-size dreams of achieving wealth. He made empty promises, which, crazily enough, turned into a harsh reality. He miraculously moved the family out of Jude's childhood neighborhood of Bellaire—or the "Aire"—and into a new zip code that came with its own set of invisible, priggish rules, which none of them had been prepared for. Especially not their mother.

Jude felt a small shiver go down his spine as he allowed himself to think about his mother for the first time all year. He remembered how comically petite she was, how her hair always smelled like rotten eggs, always fresh off a new perm set, and the way she hugged them after they cried whenever they were forced to hug their father. Jude shook his head, kicked out the intrusive thoughts, and straightened the wheel in time, just as an oncoming car honked nervously at him while flashing its headlights. He nodded an apology at the passing driver, a middle-aged woman in a luxury car, face hidden behind sunglasses so large he couldn't tell where her face began and ended. With all the southern hospitality she was raised on, the woman raised her left hand—despite being weighed down with a ring that was at least three carats— and, with a perfect French tip, flipped Jude off. She held the finger at half-mast, slowing down her car, just to wave her finger up and down, side to side, and even diagonally, to ensure he had eyes on it at all times.

He fought the urge to return the gesture, but he'd spent his teenage years attempting to fit into this zip code, so he pretended he didn't see it. Unable to find a resolution with his emotions, and wanting to curb his rising anger, he just blamed his mother for all his troubles, as he usually did. He blamed his mother for making him think of her and distracting him in the moment. His mother's absence made it easier to put all of the world's troubles squarely on her shoulders. She certainly hadn't thought about him in the past two decades since she walked away from the family, so it was only fair all his anger was aimed at her. But the moment the driver was out of sight, he raised his hand and flipped her right back, gesturing to no one but an empty road and his own reflection in the rearview mirror. His dark brown eyes seared back at him. His face was overly tanned from the summer rays with a fresh crop of the wrinkles that appeared when one turned thirty-four.

As Jude pressed down on the gas, his father's mansion appeared quickly on the horizon, sticking out like a weed amid a sea of manicured lawns. It reeked of new money. You could take Duc out of the countryside of south Vietnam, but you couldn't take the countryside of south Vietnam out of Duc. His mansion loomed over Jude as he whizzed past the pièce de résistance of Duc's collection in the middle of the lawn: a replica statue of Michelangelo's *David*, holding up both the American flag and the Vietnamese flag (the prewar version, of course).

Jude knew being on time was important to his father, who had only been late seven times in his life: when he missed out on the births of each of his five children, when he was late to his first wedding, and then to his second wedding. But *other* than those times, Duc had never been late.

Just as Jude pulled into the driveway, he felt sucker punched, and immediately his body began putting up defenses. He wasn't the first of the Trần children to arrive after all. Standing in front of the arched wooden door were his four sisters, looking armed and ready for battle—whether against him or their patriarchal father, or both, Jude hadn't a clue.

But there they were, the Four Horsewomen of the Apocalypse.

There was his oldest sister, Jane, who at thirty-one was still his forever archnemesis just as she had been when she was two years old. She stood protectively in front of his other sisters, always the pack lead, but ironically all bark and no bite. Then there was the second oldest at twenty-nine, Bingo, whom he was secretly afraid of, because her temper issues reminded him of their father. The third, at twenty-eight, Paulina, hovered above all the other sisters, clocking in at exactly 5'10", looking as if she'd just recently hidden a body or two. And finally he was surprised to see the youngest and softest sister present, at twenty-two, Georgia—who perennially lived off the grid yet posted every day on her digital grid.

It was as if someone did CTRL + C on their mother, and then CTRL + V four times to create exact copies of one another: dark roots, strong jaws, big doe eyes, and heart-shaped faces spotted with birthmarks, a near replica of Cassiopeia. Though their faces slightly altered down the hierarchy, a matryoshka doll effect. It was only Jude who looked out of turn, unclear if he looked more like his mother or his father, or if someone attempted to do a CTRL + A and give him a mix of everything. He was stockier in nature and had the thinnest eyes out of them all, eyes set so far apart from each other, there was an immeasurable canyon between them.

Jude screeched the car to a stop in front of his sisters, and calmly got out to face the firing squad. They studied each other. After nearly a decade of coming and going from Houston, a mixture of failures, celebrations, and empty threats thrown at each other, all five Trâns were now in the same place again. The whole band was back together. Jude, Jane, Bingo, Paulina, and Georgia. But no one asked for the reunion tour.

Jude pressed down his gelled hair, adjusted his diamond-plated chain, and greeted his sisters. Despite the dense Houston summer humidity, he had on a matching track suit with knee-high socks and Nike slides. He couldn't tell if the sweat was because of the heat or from the fact that his four sisters were here, ready to challenge his silver-spooned position.

Jane raised a hand, and wiggled her fingers at him like jellyfish tentacles, somehow managing to greet and taunt him at the same time.

"You're late," Jane said, a smirk forming on her lips. "How strange. I thought you'd be the first to arrive so you could permanently hot-glue your lips to our father's ass."

Jude raised an eyebrow. "And you're unusually early for once. How *strange* indeed. I could have sworn you hated our father. Actually, if I remember the exact quote, you told him that you 'will never take a dime from' him because you'd be 'entering into a Faustian pact'?"

"You said that?" Bingo turned to face her older sister and scrunched her nose in disapproval. "Why are lawyers so dramatic?"

"What does *Faustian* mean?" Georgia whispered to Bingo.

"No clue," Bingo whispered back. "Just play along."

"I think the quote was actually, 'screw your draconian ways, I'm never coming back to Houston, just like our mother,'" Paulina said, bored.

"I—just . . . forget what I said before," Jane stuttered, a shade of red starting to settle on her high cheekbones, blending with her blush color. "It doesn't matter. What matters is we *all* deserve a piece of the inheritance. We're here to cash in on all the trauma that daddy dearest caused us."

The repressed anger that Jude had subdued earlier began to rise again, separating itself from his logical side, and like oil from water, blood family from found family, and the DMZ line, Jude could see the divide between him and his sisters clearly.

"Shouldn't you be saving your trauma speech for mother dearest instead?" he retorted. "At least Ba stayed to take care of us. Our mother abandoned us. Evelyn abandoned us."

"Abandoned?" Jane said slowly, as if she was learning a new word. "Our mother didn't *abandon* us. She set herself free and managed to finally crawl out from under our father's thumb. Who can blame her for what she did?"

"What do you call leaving five children behind without a single goddamn note?" he retorted. "Self-care Sunday?"

"Here we go again, it hasn't even been five minutes." Bingo groaned. "You two are worse than feral cats."

"I feel Jude has big 'orchid child' energy," Paulina said. She curled a perfect, acrylic finger and pointed up and down at Jude. Her wrists were stacked with diamond tennis bracelets, and her palms remained uncalloused. Everything about Paulina looked expensive. From the soft waves in her hair down to her logo-less leather handbag. Everyone knew how Paulina made her money, but nobody was willing to say it out loud. Just like how no one questioned how Duc got the money to start the family business. Shadiness ran in their genes.

"What the hell are you on, Paulina?" Jude asked, as he felt his sisters closing in on him, ganging up on him, just like old times. "Are you calling people flowers as an insult now?"

Georgia jumped in, attempting to mediate. "I *think* what Pauly is referring to is this study about kids who grew up in traumatic homes and how they respond to situations. They're either dandelions or orchids—"

"I'm obviously a dandelion—" Jane interrupted.

"You don't even know what the dandelion represents yet—" Bingo said, annoyed.

"—and how kids who are orchids tend to be well, more *sensitive*," Georgia cut back in.

"Sensitive?" Jude bellowed, his face turning bright red. "I'm not some fragile—"

"Dandelions are the resilient ones," Paulina said, finishing Georgia's explanation. "They can thrive in any condition."

"See? *Dandelion.* I'm a dandelion," Jane said, satisfied, to Bingo.

"I am definitely not a dandelion," Bingo muttered under her breath. "I still don't even know how to file taxes properly."

"Basically, what I'm trying to say is that all of us are dandelions . . . except you," Paulina said, looking at Jude.

Jude was gobsmacked. His anger had been hidden behind a dam, but now it couldn't be contained anymore. He unleashed it all at his sisters. "Your little psychological warfare games aren't going to work. You're late by ten years if you're trying to mess with the inheritance," he hissed at them. "Everything is going to me. Serves you all right for siding with Evelyn and not with Duc for all these years. Our father stayed and took care of us while our mother ran off. You've been on the wrong side of history."

All four sisters' eyes seemed to have merged into one evil eye the longer they stared at him. The hair on Jude's arms stood up and he could feel them all have a telepathic conversation with each other, plotting against him.

"You left!" he exclaimed again, still grasping for validation that his anger was justified. "You all LEFT Houston! I stayed behind and kept the old man company. That money is mine. I *earned* it. Do you know how many times I had to go to karaoke and sing Beatles songs, *especially* 'Hey Jude,' and drink Hennessy with him?"

"Earned?" Jane began to laugh maniacally. "You didn't *earn* anything. None of us did. No one *asked* you to stay. Don't pretend like you're some altruistic saint. You stayed behind to make sure you curried favor so he would leave everything to you. But you forget not *all* that money is his."

"ENOUGH!" Georgia cried. But no one took Georgia's outburst seriously and soon a chorus of sonorous voices broke out. Whether it was three sisters against Jude, Jude against Jane, Bingo against Jane, or Georgia trying to keep the peace, the siblings began to argue with one another for the sake of arguing, their voices rising higher and higher until the whole neighborhood could hear them.

The front door cracked open, and a loud gong erupted from inside the house, shattering the siblings' eardrums, rendering everyone immediately silent. From across the lawn, on the other side of the street, they could hear the neighbor telling them to shut up, reminding them that despite how far they had come, from Bellaire to River Oaks, they were still the crazy Asian family on the block.

"Now *that's* dramatic." Bingo whimpered as she cupped her ears. "Why the hell is there a gong in the house?"

An older man wearing an ill-fitting suit walked out, holding the mallet in his hand. The children immediately recognized their uncle, who wasn't *really* their uncle, but they were forced to call him their uncle. It was their father's best friend, confidant, business partner, and the family lawyer, Mr. Huey Ngô. The children didn't know much about Mr. Ngô on a personal level; they just knew random statements, trivia questions about him. Like how they knew he'd been single his entire life and that their father turned to him for everything and that he loved watching sports. Mr. Ngô came and went from their lives without much explanation. He was just always . . . there.

"The gong is an antique your father bought at some pawn shop in Vegas," Mr. Ngô said, shrugging, waving the stick around. "He saw it on a reality TV show and made me go get it. Anyway, come inside, come inside. We have much to discuss."

"Is the gong going in the will, too?" Bingo muttered, still rubbing her ears. "'Cause I low-key kind of want it."

"But why does it also feel kind of racist at the same time?" Paulina bemoaned, rubbing her ears as well.

With throbbing ears, one by one, in a single file line, the Trần children stepped inside the foyer, dragging suitcases and bags behind them. Just as Jane and Jude were about to enter the house, Jane turned to Jude and lowered her voice so only he could hear. "You know, *you* should be the one with daddy issues here, not us," she said, her voice soft yet still cutting.

"And why is that?" he snapped back at her.

She revealed a low and slow grin, peeling back her mouth to reveal something ominous. "Come on, don't make me say it out loud. You ever ask yourself why you don't look anything like our father?" she said, laughing as she went in, leaving Jude alone outside.

His face instantly drained of color. Sweat glistened from his forehead. Those types of rumors had followed him throughout his childhood. But like shoes left at the door, nobody in the family was allowed to dredge up the rumors inside the house. Duc and Evelyn had always denied any verity to them, but something about the way Jane looked at him, it was as if she knew a secret he didn't know.

Duc used to take them down to Galveston Island to catch crabs and throw them into old detergent buckets when they were kids, but he never taught them how to crab. He did it himself. Said that work was for tired men, and not for his kids. Jude used to love watching the crabs pile up, each one scrambling and clawing like hell to get out, fighting each other and themselves. This felt exactly like that moment. Except Jude was no longer staring down into the bucket—he was at the bottom, wondering if he was supposed to be fighting for scraps or if he should be trying to escape.

CHAPTER 2

Jude and Jane sat on opposite ends of the kitchen table, facing away from each other, while Georgia and Bingo sat between them, forced to switch between being referees or bodyguards at any given moment. Silence filled the blank spaces in the dining room. In any other ordinary circumstance, the quiet would have been indiscernible to strangers, but between the oldest daughter and the firstborn son, it was a declaration of war. Though tensions were already running high, the summer heat at noon magnified it. Texas summers were unbearable, and what made matters worse was that the air-conditioning appeared to be broken. Everyone was molting, shedding layer after layer. Even Mr. Ngô revealed a vulnerability, removing his suit jacket and rolling up his sleeves—a rare occasion seeing him without his full lawyer's suit of armor on.

"So! The prodigal Trân daughters have finally all come back to Houston," Mr. Ngô exclaimed, clapping his hands together. He set his briefcase on the table and began to pull out five red envelopes, each addressed individually to the children. Their names, written in haste with a white marker by their father's hand, though all of the daughters' names were misspelled. There was one for his son, Jude, one for John (he meant Jane), one for Paul (he meant Paulina, who sat the farthest from everyone), another one for Ringo (he meant Bingo), and finally, the last one for George (he meant Georgia). "Your father has missed you all very much."

The four daughters stared at Mr. Ngô as if he had just told them that the earth was flat.

"No need to sugarcoat for us. You of all people know how our father is," Jane said to Mr. Ngô. "I'm pretty sure you have to be loved first in order to be missed."

"The man probably forgot he was supposed to meet us here, just like when he would 'forget' to pick us up from school," Bingo said, running her hands through her choppy hair.

"Maybe he's just stuck in traffic?" Georgia asked, her eyes wide and blissfully clueless.

"He's coming. Why else would he call us all back here for the first time in a decade?" Jude said a little too desperately, perhaps needing to believe that he'd have backup soon. "I *know* he's coming."

"Look, apologies for the rush, Mr. Ngô, but most of us traveled from faraway places, and we weren't planning on sticking around for very long, especially not for some accidental family therapy session," Paulina expounded. "May we please just get on with it?"

"I mean, I don't *really* have anywhere urgent I need to be—" Georgia started saying before Bingo hushed her. Georgia's mouth zipped up and she shrank back, physically and emotionally.

Mr. Ngô waved his hands and attempted to calm everyone down. "Now, now. Let's just all take a breather." He shuffled the red envelopes in his hands needlessly, and began to pull out other paperwork from inside his briefcase, almost as if he was stalling. Jane eyed the red envelopes and her eyes thinned, her suspicions palpable to everyone.

"What exactly are in those envelopes—" Jane began before she was interrupted by Paulina, who had left her seat. She opened and slammed the cabinets in frustration. Paulina, who was known for starting world wars over simple miscommunications and impatience, began shoving old newspapers off the countertops and stacking empty take-out containers on top of one another. "I forget how much of a hoarder our father is," Paulina said, commenting out loud to no one in particular, unable to hide the judgment on her face.

While the exterior of the home appeared pristine, albeit nouveau riche, the inside revealed a hoarder who had a strange affinity toward buying in bulk. It was the story of a man who, despite having seven figures in his bank account, suffered from PTSD and war trauma, had a scarcity mindset as an immigrant refugee, and had hints of some kind of mental illness. Though the house belonged to their father, none of them knew it well, especially the four sisters. All around them, piles of toilet paper and soda cans formed a makeshift fort, reaching all the way to the ceiling. Each corner of the house formed a vignette, a trail of Duc's madness as he filled the southwest corner with nothing but kibble and other pet food . . . despite not having a dog. The southeast corner was full of things fermenting in jars.

Paulina continued to pace all over, removing dust with her fingertip from random shelves, straightening things out that didn't need to be, and doing her best to toss out little knickknacks, here and there.

"Also, where's Connie?" she asked with a stiffness. "Where has our favorite stepmother been hiding?" In the corner, Jane gagged at the mention of Connie's name. Though Duc and Connie had been married for over five years, none of the sisters were ever able to recover from the fact that Jane and Connie were the same age.

The Trần girls were notorious in Houston for leaving town the moment they turned eighteen. Gossip used to run wild at the old Buddhist temple about how *sad* it was that Duc Trần and Evelyn Lê had four daughters, and yet not one of them was willing to stay behind to take care of their parents. The gossip grew more vicious after Evelyn had infamously abandoned them all. How *broken* the family must be, for a woman like Evelyn Lê, who came from nothing, to have not only abandoned her children but also her newfound wealth. Rumors, gossip, tattles, whispers around Houston's royal Vietnamese family derived from fear, envy, but worst of all, it stemmed from pity.

What kind of mother would leave in the middle of the night without saying good-bye?

What kind of father would let his daughters leave?

Did you notice how Jude looks nothing like his father or his sisters?

How did Duc become so successful? Where did the money come from?

His sandwiches aren't even that good. The old man has lost his touch.

"Your father went back to Vietnam for a bit," Mr. Ngô responded carefully, still mindlessly shuffling the red envelopes in his hands, flipping and turning them over and over, as if he was about to deal a hand. "He had some last-minute affairs he needed to sort out over there."

"What affairs?" Jude said, surprised. "I saw him two weeks ago and he didn't mention anything to me."

Mr. Ngô stared at the five Trầns, whom he considered his nieces and nephew. There was a brief pause, a slight hesitation in his body language, and he corrected his reading glasses, which had gone askew on his face. "Connie had a bit of a . . . fit last week over some news. So, she flew to her *happy place*. You know how much the Four Seasons on Oahu calms her down. Her reactions can be quite . . . strong."

"Still being a problematic queen, isn't she?" Bingo said with a straight face. "I thought everyone knew to leave Hawaii alone."

"She threw a fit over what?" Jane asked, sitting up straighter, her lawyer persona coming out, interrogating Mr. Ngô. "I thought we were just here to settle the will?" All five siblings looked at each other, then they looked at the envelopes that were still in Mr. Ngô's hands.

"He's not sick, right?" Paulina asked, her voice veering on unsympathetic.

"Wait, he's sick *sick*? Like . . . deathbed kind of sick?" Georgia asked, alarmed and full of concern.

"Oh god, is it cancer?" Bingo asked, more curious than anything. "Stage four, right? Lung cancer? It's gotta be lung cancer. Honestly, though, the way he drinks alcohol like water . . . maybe something to do with the liver?"

Mr. Ngô stared at the children and began to laugh uproariously, breaking the tension. "Duc? Duc Trần *sick*? That man has smoked two packs a day for over two decades, eats canned Vienna sausages like it's crudité, and drinks Hennessy for electrolytes. No, he's not sick. He's just retiring. Which, to Connie, is the same as death. Who will fund her love of designer outlet malls now?"

He looked down at the envelopes, sighed, and, seemingly reluctant, began to pass them out. He leaned back on the creaky wooden chair and popped some nicotine gum into his mouth, his loud smacks filling the air as everyone opened their envelopes and read the letters addressed to them.

"Remember to not shoot the messenger," Mr. Ngô said between chews. "I've known your father since before you were all born, and while he's not perfect, he's always meant well."

Each of the Trần siblings' faces looked as if it was about to go through the seven stages of grief as they read their letter, but at some point, their faces seemed to be stuck in the anger phase.

"Look, I tried to talk him out of it," Mr. Ngô continued, another loud *pop* from the gum erupting. "But he's a stubborn old man."

Duc's words, addressed to each of them, began to sink in, and a murmur of confused whispers escalated into angry tangents. They double-checked what they had just read, and then triple-checked. Their faces turned redder and redder the more they consumed.

"He's always been a *bit* eccentric," Mr. Ngô rambled on. "I guess you have to be a bit of a tortured genius to have acquired all this wealth."

Slammed fists on the tables, spitballed accusations—the siblings tried to understand the "rules" they had to abide by in order to win their inheritance. How long did they have to stay in the city they were assigned to? What kind of revenue did they have to hit? Was it true? That they had exactly one year to play their father's inheritance game, or else they'd lose out on all the money? Forever?

"Look, the rules are simple enough," Mr. Ngô said, in a poor attempt to placate them. "You also *don't* have to play along. But if you do decide to try to win your inheritance, you do only have one year."

"Just because the rules are simple doesn't mean it's fair," Jane said, her face still in shock. "What city did everyone get?"

"Philadelphia," Bingo said, still looking down at her letter. "What the hell am I going to do in Philly? I've never even been to the East Coast."

"I got San Jose," Paulina said, mortified. "Didn't we all go there when we were kids?"

"New Orleans?" Georgia offered up. "I've never been to the South."

"Jane?" Bingo said. "What city did you get?"

"Houston," Jane whispered. "I'm staying here. The old man did me dirty. He's always wanted to trap me here. He's wanted to punish me ever since Má left."

All four sisters turned to look at Jude, to confirm which city he got, but all they saw was how ashen his face had become.

"Jude?" Georgia asked, extending the first olive branch toward her brother. "What city did you get?"

Mr. Ngô coughed nervously as he shifted in his seat, the chair scraping the cold tile, screeching loudly, piercing everyone's ears. "Jude isn't playing by the same rules as you all are," he said. "Your father didn't think he should take over a shop; he wants him to set his goals on something else."

"What are you talking about?" Jane pressed harder.

All four sisters turned to look at Jude, who had been silent the whole time in the corner, and looked more sick than angry. Unlike his sisters, who had scowls carved into their jawlines, Jude looked like he needed a bucket to throw up in.

"Don't tell us you get the money without lifting a finger," Bingo said. "You've gotten everything you ever wanted!"

"Firstborn Vietnamese sons truly are the worst," Paulina whispered.

"I think after all of this, we should try family therapy," Georgia said to no one and everyone in particular. "Do some healing, you know?"

Jude lifted his card for them all to see. "Duc wants me to settle down, get married," he said, his voice hollow.

"That's it?" Bingo howled. "Are you joking? Meanwhile, the rest of us need to uproot our lives, go live in some city we don't know, and revitalize a failing Vietnamese sandwich shop in order to get a chance at the money?"

Again, Mr. Ngô cleared his throat. "Those aren't *quite* the rules. Let me clarify. Whoever is able to turn their Duc's Sandwiches shop around, bring up the revenue *first* before the others do, will get all of your father's fortune. *However*, if Jude manages to marry someone first, then Jude gets it all. It's winner takes all here, not a split. You have a year to figure it out."

Everyone began bombarding Mr. Ngô with questions, then each other, and then aimed at their father, who at least had the common sense to leave the country to avoid dealing with this mess in person. Had the old man gone insane? Was this even *legal*? Hell, was this even *moral*? But had Duc Trần ever been of sound mind or law-abiding?

As everyone continued spiraling, their mother remained in the back of all their minds. They not only wished she was here to stop Duc, but they wished she had also asked them to run away with her, all those years ago.

Out of nowhere, the reverberations of the gong came at them once again. Even Mr. Ngô looked up in surprise as everyone turned to find the culprit. There was young Georgia, holding the mallet in her hand, with a small, sad smile pasted on her face.

"Can we at least argue over food?" she said tentatively. "You know, before we're all scattered across the country again for a whole year?"

CHAPTER 3

Outside Hong Kong City Mall, all five Trần siblings (yes, even Jude was invited) hovered near the crowded swinging doors, hoping to win the lunchtime lottery and the fight against Asian restaurants that don't take reservations. Their ears were constantly perked up, alert, ready for the moment their table was ready to be called. *Trần, table for five.*

"Do you know what's worse than generational trauma?" Georgia asked her siblings forlornly as she attempted to fan herself with a menu.

"What?" Bingo responded as a gaggle of high school kids elbowed her in the face as they packed around one phone screen while walking past. She cursed at them to watch where they were going. "I forget how much I despise the youth. How are they so carefree? Don't they know they're living in late-stage capitalism?"

"Having to build generational wealth," Georgia sighed as she finished her thought, and slumped all the way down into a squat and buried her face between her legs.

"No one has to *build* anything," Paulina scoffed. "Money is fungible."

"Oh shut it, Paulina," Bingo griped. "Not everyone has pretty privilege as leverage. Some of us have to rely on our cheery dispositions to get through life."

"And is that person with the cheery disposition in the room with us?" Jude muttered under his breath, causing Bingo to throw him a dirty look.

"Well, you know what's worse than having to build generational wealth?" Jane snapped. "Having an immigrant father who had the whole rags-to-riches story, only to use his kids as pawns in his sick, twisted inheritance game, purely for his entertainment. Whatever happened to good old-fashioned nepotism? The *one* time we could be like the rich white kids and our father squanders our chances."

"Well," Jude barked, "maybe if you hadn't been such a wet blanket all those years ago to our father, we wouldn't be out here fighting for scraps under the table." Despite lumbering around two hundred pounds, Jude managed to sidestep Jane's hand as she attempted to pinch his arm, just like she used to when they were kids.

"Trần?" A server stuck his head out the swinging front door. "Table for five?"

Two groups of Trầns, side by side, roared at the same time. Jude, Jane, Bingo, Paulina, and Georgia glared at the other group, marking their territory, bracing themselves for a fight. But their staredown was only matched with the same vigor from the other Trầns, including a grandmother who had death daggers in her eyes.

Both groups turned to the server, looking for clarification while also threatening him. He whipped between groups, quickly calculated who would cause the biggest stink, and, to avoid any dramatics, pointed at the Trần siblings, and motioned for them to step forward.

A roar of relief and belts of glee united the siblings. They rushed past the other Trầns, gloating. Like a clown car, they excitedly filed into a single line and followed the server straight into the bustling lunch crowd at Crawfish & Beignets. It was the siblings' neutral zone, a place where no fighting was allowed.

Except this time felt more like the Last Supper.

Seafood boils were a staple of their childhood, reminding them of all the best parts of being Vietnamese American in the South, and none of the bad. Though unspoken, the migration of the Viet-Cajun boil always lingered over them, reminding them of its roots in Louisiana, from other Vietnamese folks who resettled in Houston after Hurricane Katrina, and the resiliency that came with it.

Soon, they would need to channel that resiliency themselves.

After this, they would be scattered to different parts of the country for a chance to win their inheritance. It'd been years since they'd all been in the same room, and now they had less than twenty-four hours to say their good-byes before they shipped off for a year. The last time they were together like this was when they tried to find their mother in Florida and the search ended up fruitless. Evelyn Lê's whereabouts were about as unknown and unexplored as the vast majority of the ocean.

It was as if every Asian in Houston was here now, with plastic gloves on, breaking apart crab legs, crawfish, mussels, and clams in quick succession.

A volcanic eruption of gossip, laughter, parental lectures, and roasts and jabs at their children dominated the restaurant, while garlic noodle slurpers and the squeaky sound of mussels being eaten played in tandem all around them. As the Trâns passed by, they couldn't help but feel envy at seeing how other families operated, how happy they all seemed to be around each other.

Once at their table, the siblings mulled over their father's inheritance game, united for the first time against him. There was a type of rumination in all their eyes that reminded them of the darker periods in their childhood whenever their mother disappeared for long stretches at a time. Everyone used to pretend everything was fine, that their mother's absences were normal, that they were just simply playing a game of hide-and-seek. They remembered standing in the middle of the street, screaming Evelyn's name over and over again, hoping if they were loud enough, she'd hear them and come back home. Ninety-nine percent of the time she did.

Five pounds of crawfish in a metal bucket were soon placed down. The smell of lemongrass, Old Bay seasoning, and fish sauce hit the siblings all at once, and they breathed in the familiar, comforting scent. The coalescent beauty of a Viet-Cajun seafood boil was the magnum opus of the American South.

"Dump it out," Jane commanded.

"Don't have to tell me twice," Paulina said, and she shoved the bucket over, spilling the spicy marinade sauce on the table, accidentally splashing her diamond tennis bracelets along the way. Immediately, a ceasefire was called, and all anger, resentments, and grudges among them were suspended as everyone put on plastic gloves, tucked bibs over their collars, and grabbed a crawfish.

"Remember that period of our lives when Duc would freeze stacks of McDonald's cheeseburgers and we'd have to thaw them out for dinner?" Bingo asked, her mouth already stained red from the house sauce.

"Who could forget? They looked like giant yellow hockey pucks in the fridge," Jane scoffed. "Tasted like them, too."

"Look, honestly . . . the inheritance game doesn't sound so bad," Georgia said, waving a corn around like a gavel. "Wouldn't we split the money between us anyway?"

The tension from earlier seeped back in. "You know if I won, I'd split it among *us*." Jane whirled a finger, indicating just the sisters.

"I'm right here," Jude muttered as he tore a crawfish in half.

"Wake up, grow up, and smell the damn misogyny, Georgia. Not everything can be packed up into a van and posted on Instagram. Life is more complicated than that," Bingo said, slamming her fists on the table, causing the bucket holding the empty shellfish carcasses to go flying into the air and spilling onto the floor. Nobody in the restaurant batted an eye at the commotion. "Why does Jude get a shot at the money just for marrying someone while we have to duke it out among ourselves like NYC sewer rats over a slice of old pizza? It's not that hard to get some sad sack to marry him to split the money. He can *pay* someone to marry him. I'm sick of him getting the easy path his entire life. 'Cause he's the firstborn? 'Cause he's the firstborn *son*? 'Cause he's the *only* son?"

"Still here," Jude said, this time louder, waving around a crawfish. "Still *right* here."

Paulina stared at Bingo, who was only a year older than her, as if she'd lost her marbles. "Actually, is it *really* misogynistic? At least the old man isn't forcing *us* to get married. He's forcing Jude."

"Right, so he can continue the family line," Bingo shot back.

"Okay, your paranoia is getting to you. This is actually very simple, our father is clearly punishing us," Paulina said, crossing her arms. "We all sided with Má in the divorce and told Ba to go to hell—"

"And to take his money and to shove it up his—" Jane chimed in.

"Remember, girls," Paulina interrupted, mimicking their mother's voice. "Nothing is more petty than an angry Vietnamese mother—"

"*Except for a Vietnamese father,*" they all said at once, including Jude.

Regret rained down on them like an unexpected hailstorm, pecking away at their sanity. In between squelches of crawfish, each sister felt a tinge of regret for siding with their mother when, at the end of the day, she had still abandoned them. Was motherhood supposed to be so interchangeable when the sisters hadn't had a chance to grow up?

"Ba became a complete clown when he made it big, didn't he?" Paulina mused as she picked at her plate of uneaten garlic crawfish noodles.

"Remember when he blew his first paycheck on a signed Beatles album instead of paying off his debt?" Jane said.

"For someone who loves Americana as much as our father, it took him a *long* time to realize the Beatles were British," Bingo said, but she couldn't help but laugh a little.

"Or remember when he was convinced he had to collect all the Beanie Babies? That it would pay for our college tuitions?"

"But he started collecting them *after* he already got rich—"

"He spent a *fortune* on the Princess Diana one!"

A tiny bit of laughter caught on and they couldn't help but allow themselves a little reprieve; the laughter soon became tumbleweed, taking hold of everyone.

"Forget the Princess Diana Beanie Baby, remember how *angry* Evelyn was when he bought that album? Till this day, I still don't understand his obsession with the Beatles," Jude said, wiping a tear away after the laughter that had engulfed him.

"Yeah, but remember how much fun we all had, dancing to it in that tiny, windowless kitchen?" Jane said. She cracked a small smile for the first time all day.

"Wasn't there a toilet in the kitchen, too?" Paulina said as she leaned back in her chair, a small smile perched on the edges of her lips.

"Oh god, *remember* when Duc swung Evelyn around so hard, she knocked over that one ugly lamp?" Jane snickered.

"I *forgot* there weren't any windows! Remember that time Jude took the biggest shit and we were choking on the smell for days?" Bingo said, an epiphany kicking in, her mood shifting.

Jude held up his hands, covered in plastic gloves, and pleaded the Fifth.

"Did our mother like to dance?" Georgia asked eagerly, interrupting her siblings as she leaned forward. She'd been silent the whole time, ears glued to these stories, hoping to catch scraps of memories of their mother. Out of all the siblings, she knew the least about her, the least about anyone. Nobody said a word and they looked down at their crawfish, as if suddenly interested in studying its exoskeleton.

Jane coughed, breaking up the awkwardness. "Look, Georgia, our mother was no angel."

"The woman had issues. Big issues—"

"Has. The woman *has* issues—"

"But it's okay to be curious about her, she's still our mother," Georgia said hopefully, breaking with her sisters. "It's our right to miss her. Isn't it?"

"No one has spoken to the woman in almost two decades," Bingo said, with a surprising gentleness in her voice. "The woman doesn't want to be found. Meaning, she doesn't want to be found by *us*."

Everyone grew quiet. Georgia lowered her eyes.

"I should have changed my name a long time ago," Bingo whispered under her breath. "Out of all the names our parents could have chosen to play off of 'Ringo,' why did they choose Bingo?"

The waiter placed five more beers in front of them before scurrying away. Bingo was the first to grab a beer and raise her hand in a toast. "Look, let's just give it our best shot and try," she roared as she turned toward Jude to roast and toast him. "To the sad sack who ends up with Jude."

"Let's not toast to him getting married," Jane said quickly. "To one of the Trần daughters getting there first."

"We'll see about that, sis," Jude said, and though he was smiling, there was a tightness there.

"May the best Trần win the pot of gold at the end of the rainbow," Paulina said, correcting the toast, as she stood up and raised her Heineken sky high.

"And remember it's *just* money. We didn't have it growing up," Jane said, her oldest-sister didacticism kicking in. "We all walked away before; we can easily walk away again."

"Says the lawyer, who doesn't need the money," Bingo shot back.

"Why do you always forget that I'm just an immigration lawyer, I'm not a corporate lawyer," Jane said defensively. "I definitely *need* the money."

"Just toast, damnit!" Paulina said annoyedly, still holding her beer in the air, waiting for everyone else.

"What kind of lawyer is Mr. Ngô, then?" Georgia pondered. "Why has he just always been . . . around?"

"He's a shady one," Jane said, glossing over their uncle, who wasn't really their uncle. "Don't go to him for anything. I still don't really know what he's all about, he's just always . . . there."

"But don't you ever wonder how our father met him? Why are they as thick as thieves?" Georgia pressed on, still eager for any scraps of the past.

Her siblings shrugged and gave the same explanation. "They're two old

Vietnamese guys." As if that was the only explanation their youngest sister needed.

"People, please!" Paulina yelled, still waving her beer in the air. "Let's cheer and move on with our lives."

Jude stood up and raised his glass next to Paulina's. "See you all in a year?"

Everyone reluctantly stood, clinked glasses in solidarity, and murmured and agreed how it was *just* money. But as they each took a swig of beer, not one of them looked any other in the eye. Because Jane, Bingo, and Paulina had already begun plotting how to make sure their shop won, and Jude had already been scanning the restaurant the entire time, checking out every woman's left hand to see if they were single.

Georgia was the only one not thinking or caring about the money: she was still pondering how Mr. Ngô and her father knew each other, where her mother was in the world, and if she was happier now or full of regret, but mostly, the youngest was wondering about the origins of it all and how she got to be where she was, exactly in that moment. She wondered about the thread that wove them all together, creating the illusion of lineage, and whether or not the thread was thick enough to withstand what was to come.

CHAPTER 4

1976, Delacroix Island, Louisiana

Long before Duc was known as the famous purveyor of Vietnamese fare, he was known as Đức Trần, the son of a lowly fisherman from a small village in Vietnam, who had very few dreams aside from following in his father's footsteps. To fit in with the Americans, he bastardized his name to simply "Duc." He wanted to boil his life down to a mononym, something that was easier for Americans to embrace, a name that was *friendlier*. That's how everyone got famous in America, right? Like Cher, Elvis, or Liberace. Being Đức wouldn't get him there, but being Duc would. Duc was ready to leave Vietnam behind in a heartbeat, but Đức would have held him back, reminding him of all the pain and grief that was waiting for him in a country he couldn't call his own anymore.

Duc was determined to become the most American man who ever America'd.

Long before Mr. Ngô was known as Duc's lawyer and eternal sidekick, he was simply Huy Ngô. When Huy arrived in America, immigration kept butchering his name, somehow added an "e" to it, and ended up calling him Huey. Eventually, the name stuck and he went from a Huy to a Huey. Huey welcomed his new American identity with open arms, hoping Americans would embrace the rest of him as well.

Huey quickly learned that everything had to be fast and hot in America. Fast food, hot food, fast coffee, hot coffee. Why did Americans drink coffee in order to wake up, treating coffee as a means to an end? Coffee should be enjoyed slowly, at any time of the day, and always over ice. Despite how strange America was to him, he loved everything about it. He loved the lifestyle more than most Americans—that is, until he met Duc Trần.

Duc was the most American man he'd ever met.

When work began drying up in the northeast quadrant of the country, Huey followed a commercial fishing opportunity down south to Louisiana, even though he didn't want to be a fisherman in America. He'd been a young fisherman with his father back in Vietnam and was seeking a different life here, one where he didn't have to use his hands as much. But boys from his village became fishermen because it was ingrained in their blood to understand how the ocean worked. Reading the currents was like studying a second language. Huey followed his father's advice to always make sure to live by the water. Because even though the ocean could punish you, it could also be generous. It was very much like America.

The fishing boat Huey had been assigned was moored off the coast of Delacroix Island in Louisiana. As soon as he crossed state lines, he knew something was off. His skin started to crawl from all the stares he'd received from strangers. He knew the war had had a bad reception in the country, but he couldn't tell if his presence was a warm welcome or a reminder of so many dead sons who'd died in Vietnam. Did they blame him when they saw his face? Did they blame him for a war that he also wanted no part of? Did they realize that he'd also been displaced and had seen many dead Vietnamese, brothers, sons, and fathers, at his own feet?

The night Huey got into Delacroix, he settled into a sketchy motel off the highway. The sky was pitch-black, and he could barely find the keyhole to fit his key, nor was he able to see the anger in the night clerk's face when he helped check Huey in. It was for the best, because Huey slept soundly that night, despite stained sheets, the room's sour smell, and some motel workers talking shit about the "gook stinking up room 215." The lull of chirping crickets in the distance gave Huey the false promise of peace, because if bugs could sleep well out here without worry, so could he.

In the early morning, Huey set off toward the dock, following a flimsy piece of paper that had blurred instructions. He'd spilled beer on it the night before, and the ink had trailed off until it bled at the edges. But scanning the dock, he spotted the boat easily. There she was, in all her vigor, the *Lady Freedom*. Huey understood patriotism; to a certain extent, he certainly harbored it for Vietnam. Among the row of expensive sport fishing boats, the *Lady Freedom* looked unsanitary and unsanctioned—perfect for immigrants who would do anything for quick cash. Huey noticed rust creeping up from the bottom of the boat, wrapping up around the sides, and cascading outward like rivulets. There was more wear and tear on her than on the other, pristine boats, and there was an odd smell emanating from the deck. Huey climbed on without a moment's hesitation. A job was a job.

He was surprised to see he was the only nonwhite man on the boat so far. The staring was back again. The men stared, and stared, and though Huey had gotten used to all the staring by now, he knew they weren't staring at him like he was a celebrity—more like a parasite.

He went to the captain and clocked in. The captain's eyes lingered a touch on Huey, and though Huey was uncomfortable, he locked eyes right back, squaring his shoulders. The captain took note of the scar that was above Huey's forehead where a bullet grazed him in the war, and Huey took note of how sunken and empty the captain's eyes were, as if life had worn him down. There was something about the moment that unsettled Huey, yet he knew he would have photographic memory when it came to the captain's face. He'd remember it for the rest of his life. Had it been in another lifetime, Huey was sure they would have been friends. But the concept of friendship between the two men was meant for another multiverse, for another timeline, for another century.

For a timeline in which war never happened.

Huey slinked off to the corner to try to shrink himself from being seen. These men weren't just run-of-the-mill men; they were the big, bulky types—working men who needed the money. Huey could smell the desperation on them. Despite being a war refugee, he didn't have the same desperation they did. He didn't have a family to feed, since they had been left behind in Vietnam. It was just him in America and no one else. His desperation was contained to just his own survival.

"Anh ấy," a voice called out behind him.

Huey couldn't tell what made him turn around. Was it the fact that he was hearing Vietnamese for the first time in months? Or maybe he was hallucinating hearing a friendly tone? *Brother.* The young man had greeted him in an informal way, and how he missed it. He turned around and faced a young Duc. They seemed similar in age and both had an air of independence about them—as if they didn't need anyone else in this world. There was an easy gait about Duc, which was highly unusual for someone who'd also just escaped a war. But he looked as if he'd never even seen what war looked like, let alone any troubles. He was slender and short, but his confidence made him taller than all the other men on the boat. He switched to English. "You got a cigarette?"

Huey nodded, mostly confused now. He reached into his pocket and pulled out a banged-up pack, flipped it open, and let one fall out onto Duc's palm. Duc pulled out a lighter, lit it up, and, using the sweat that had gathered from underneath his hairline, slicked back his hair. The weather in the South was scathing and unforgiving, yet Duc looked as if he'd just casually taken a dip in the water. He was handsome in a mischievous way.

"Anh," Duc said again as he blew out a long, billowy cloud of puff, and switched to Vietnamese entirely. "What are you doing here? Where'd you come from, anyway?"

"I needed the money," Huey said, also switching to Vietnamese. He shrugged nonchalantly, as if that was the only conceivable reason anyone would be on a rusted boat in the middle of Louisiana. "Work is dry up north. The family who was sponsoring me to stay with them wanted me to convert to Christianity, so I fled in the middle of the night."

"Where'd they sponsor you?"

"The middle of bumfuck nowhere. Somewhere on the outskirts of Philadelphia. Some Amish town."

"Ah, Philadelphia . . . *Phi-la . . .*" Duc said slowly, scanning his internal Rolodex of cities and Americana facts he'd collected in his short time in the country. "Ah yes! *Philly!* You try their sandwiches? Crazy right? America is wild. So much cheese! Who can eat that much cheese? That stuff will kill you."

Huey stared at the young man before him, who disregarded the fact that he'd escaped to avoid being converted, and who only wanted to talk about Philly cheesesteaks instead.

"Yeah, it was fine," he responded. "But I do miss just a regular bánh mì sometimes. Don't you ever miss it? You know, miss home?"

Duc stared at him as if he were crazy. "Why the hell would I ever miss Vietnam? Why would I miss Vietnamese food? Never go backward, anh. Look where you are! Enjoy all the American food! Enjoy life! Leave your past worries behind you."

"Oy! You two!" the captain shouted over at Duc and Huey. "Why are you two huddling? Y'all conspiring with the Viet Cong?"

At the mention of the Viet Cong, the frown lines on Duc and Huey instantly grew tight, their chests grew even tighter. The casual racism didn't surprise them, but the annoyance on their faces was clear. How could they try to explain to the captain that that wasn't so much an insult, but another display of ignorance? In a lot of ways, Huey was relieved to split the racism with Duc, but at the same time, he didn't know Duc well enough to know if he'd ever help him out if things went awry. That was the problem with being part of the first wave of refugee immigrants to America—would anyone come to help one another in times of crisis?

To Huey's surprise, Duc erased his annoyance with ease, smiled at the captain, and threw him a thumbs-up. "We'll be over soon!"

Duc then slowly turned to Huey and, still with a smile on his face, sent chills down Huey's back. "One day, we're going to buy this boat, and take them all out of business."

Huey laughed and brushed it off. "Just forget it. Let's not cause any trouble."

"You don't believe me? Tell me, what would you be if you had the chance to do anything you wanted? You're in America now. Pick and choose your poison."

Huey stared out into the water. The sun was slowly climbing, its rays starting to hit his face. He thought about it. He thought about all the cities he'd been to in America, and he saw all the respect that men in suits got. Double-breasted suits, three-piece suits, big, fat, thick ties that almost choked them at the neck. Somehow, it garnered deference. Huey wanted that. He wanted the stares at him to not be of disgust, of shame, of curiosity, or of judgment. The next time he caught someone staring at him, he wanted it to be full of respect or fear.

"A lawyer," he said, seemingly surprised by his own answer. "I want to be a lawyer."

"Then you're a lawyer 'cause I say you're a lawyer," Duc responded, winking at him. "See? How hard was that? Now, will you help me—help us—become rich so we can buy this damn boat one day and put those bastards out of business?"

The two men laughed. Huey had heard a lot of empty, grandiose promises from other Vietnamese refugees since he came. A lot of "payback" dreams, of being able to have both money and power one day. For some reason, though, Huey believed Duc. It was the look in his eyes—a hunger.

"Okay, anh," Huey said, still laughing, finally calling him brother back. "Sure, I'll help you. Why not?"

He thought he had agreed to nothing but a mirage that day, not realizing that Duc had meant every word he had said, and would change the course of Huy "Huey" Ngô's life forever. But whether Duc had chartered them down a good path or the wrong one, he couldn't tell. Because the guilt Mr. Ngô carried, all these decades later, still weighed him down more than all the riches Duc had delivered.

CHAPTER 5

Connie

Connie Vũ saw dogs as giant rats, thought rom-coms were for women who suffered from Stockholm syndrome, and hadn't eaten sugar since the 2016 election. Which is why she went immediately into attack mode when she discovered Duc's plans for his children and the twisted inheritance game he wanted to play. Because in all his wild schemes, he'd forgotten one thing: his second wife. What would happen to her share of the money? Didn't he remember there was a prenup? What was the old fool thinking?

She stood waist-deep at the end of the infinity pool at the Four Seasons Resort in Oahu, away from the mass of sweaty, pale, sunburnt bodies that had formed in the middle. A champagne flute in one hand, her cell phone in the other. Her sunglasses teetered at the edge of her nose, as her eyes peered over the rim, judging everyone in their cheap, ugly bathing suits. She watched tourists scream with excitement and take a million selfies with the same exact facial expression that would end up clogging their cloud storage. That was the thing about these big fancy expensive resorts: No one had any shame when it came to tourism. It was as if they were told that an animal was nearly extinct and it made them want to poach it even more.

It was even more terrifying to witness the giant family vacations. Swarms of families rushed past, pushing strollers of crying toddlers, yanking wandering, sticky children's hands. Red-faced fathers wore bucket hats, and mothers in straw hats carried hotel beach towels. It was supposedly their once-a-year vacation, yet they always seemed to be in a hurry, rushing back to their rooms, rushing to their restaurant reservation, rushing to snorkeling lessons.

It was all so *pedestrian* to Connie.

What exactly was so relaxing about traveling with children?

What exactly was so relaxing about *birthing* children?

Connie took a big swig from her glass, emptied it, and motioned for another. She willed her phone to ring. Thank god Duc was seventeen hours ahead, stuck in Vietnam. She never wanted to deal with him directly. Connie Vũ always took the shortcut, just like her mother taught her. Her mother taught her survival skills, and it had gotten her this far in life.

Though she was the same age as Jane Trần, her stepdaughter, Connie looked spryer than Jane. That was the point of having money. At thirty-one, her sleek, shoulder-length hair and wrinkle-free face made her look like Jane's younger sister. Jane's wrinkles came from reading too many law books and fighting for the little people, while Connie haggled over designer bags at the outlet mall.

That was not to say Connie didn't have her stresses. Marriage to Duc the past five years had been one long chess game. She'd been a pawn who had finally reached the other side of the board and was two moves away from turning into a queen. Except her stepchildren were about to prevent her from taking that final step forward.

She never wanted to be the evil stepmother, or even cared if she was liked by her stepchildren. She certainly didn't care how the optics looked, to marry someone nearly thirty years her senior. Because she knew at the end of the day, she'd rather be gossiped about while living in a mansion instead of a studio rental.

Her phone vibrated and she picked up immediately. "Jason? Where the hell have you been," she hissed into the phone. "You know we have a situation here. I'm going to need all hands on deck for this one. What's the status?"

"Good news, Connie," Jason said in his booming voice. "Even if one of Duc's kids gets his fortune you are still entitled to something. The prenup states that they don't get *everything*."

"Yes, but what is included in 'everything,'" she griped. "This isn't the breakfast special, Jason. We've only been married for five years. I wasn't with him when he started his business. I came after."

"Doesn't matter. Anything you two accumulated together during those five years will be taken into account."

Connie paused as she did quick math in her mind, her accounting degree kicking in. Her body turned cold. "But *we* haven't accumulated anything together in five years. The man hasn't hustled in five years; he's been coasting!"

"Well, hasn't the sandwich chain made money?"

"I don't know," she admitted begrudgingly. "He doesn't really talk business with me. He did mention some stores weren't doing well. I think those stores were passed to his daughters. But surely those stores don't affect the entire revenue?"

"Look, you're going to need to dig into his finances and see where he's at. I can't do anything on my end until I see what we're up against."

She pushed her sunglasses up to cover her eyes, shielding herself from curious glances thrown her way. The lone Asian woman shouting into her phone at the end of an infinity pool. A few children on floaties passed her by, shrieking and screaming and splashing water on her. She recoiled, not from the water, but from the children. She tried her best to remember what she learned at her Buddhist retreat in Upstate New York to calm her down. But she couldn't remember a damn thing. *Something, something* about counting her breaths.

"Okay, now tell me the bad news," she whispered into the phone.

Her lawyer paused, already wary of how *strong* her reactions could be. "I did some digging. Look it's not *bad* bad, but it's bad. I mean, on a scale of bad law stuff, it's *bad*."

"Spit it out, damnit," Connie shouted into the mouthpiece.

"Don't shoot the messenger. But, Con, I don't think you are *technically* married," Jason said. She couldn't tell if she could feel him bracing himself or if it was her. Either way, her free hand searched for the pool's ledge to hold on to something until she realized there was none. It was a damn infinity pool.

"What do you mean *technically* not married? We had a whole wedding in Dallas. Over five hundred guests were there. Even your goddamn mistress *and* your wife were there. Lobsters were flown in from Maine. We gave Bluetooth karaoke microphones as wedding favors. What do you mean *technically* not married?"

Jason took a deep breath. "You know Duc's lawyer, Mr. Nope?"

"You mean, *Mr. Ngô*," she said, correcting him.

"Whatever, this isn't a Vietnamese-language class. I don't think he actually ever filed the divorce papers for Evelyn and Duc. I can't find any record of them divorcing," he whispered. "And . . . I can't find your marriage certificate, either."

Connie gasped so loudly she frightened a small child who had floated past her. "But he was the officiant? I saw him sign the certificate!"

"I don't know, I can't find it. Nothing is adding up."

Connie could see her future slipping away. Why couldn't she remember a damn thing from that Buddhist retreat? *One . . . two . . . three . . . something about not thinking about the pink elephant . . .*

She could feel a panic attack coming on. She should have been more prepared, always three steps ahead, just like her mother had taught her. Who'd ever trust a Vietnamese lawyer to actually file paperwork? She should have gone with her white lawyer. She could feel her pawn being attacked on all sides, preventing her from turning into a queen. Was she about to lose the game?

"Mother—" She started to hyperventilate.

Jason prattled on, his voice growing more distant by the second. "Actually, come to think of it, I don't even think he's a real lawyer . . ."

"Fu—"

Connie threw her phone across the pool, dunked her whole head underwater—saw how even uglier the other people's bathing suits were from the bottom half—and screamed and screamed as bubbles came out of her mouth, floating all the way to the surface.

CHAPTER 6

Jane

J ane was the first to arrive at her assigned shop. The journey wasn't as far as it would be for her younger sisters, who were all en route to their new lives in Philadelphia (Bingo), San Jose (Paulina), and New Orleans (Georgia). All Jane had to do was drive twenty minutes from her hotel in downtown Houston, back to Little Saigon. But those twenty minutes felt like twenty years, each passing landmark reminding her of all they'd lost as a family. But it especially reminded her of memories made without her mother.

At 8:00 a.m., Jane walked into the original Duc's Sandwiches shop, located at Dakao Plaza, nestled between a beauty wholesale supply store and a dilapidated travel agency, which was known for shepherding buses full of little old Asian women to Vegas monthly—not to shop or tour the buffets, but to gamble their life savings away. She remembered the plaza well, as much as she didn't want to. She remembered running through the parking lot as a child, and the joy it brought her hiding behind cars, waiting to be discovered. Old faces and lost memories began bubbling up—all those years of watching her parents toil day in and day out at the shop, and the neighbors who would come in to buy lunch from them. There was Thủy from the nail salon supply store, Duy from the travel agency, Xuân from the sketchy CPA's office, and Linh from the refillable, filtered water store a few doors down. Neighboring business owners for over twenty years, who had watched Jane grow from a kid who clung to her mother's skirts to a grown woman who no longer wanted to cling to anyone anymore.

The iconic white pylon sign stood at the entranceway of Dakao, crammed with names of dying businesses in its signature red font. Though every other plaza around them was attempting to be more modern, Dakao was still holding on to the citadel strong, refusing to convert to a sans serif font. It was more than just a sign; it was a sign of resistance and stubbornness from the old guard and gatekeepers of the first wave of Vietnamese refugees who settled in Texas.

"Wow," she muttered to herself as she walked around the barren shop. There it was, the outdated Duc's Sandwiches slanted lettering against a pale green backdrop, which taunted her, reminding her of all they had lost in the pursuit of an American legacy. "Some things really are untouched by time." Vietnamese people were always the last to change but the first to complain. But nothing had truly changed in over two decades. When she had driven through the neighborhood, she begrudgingly noticed how some parts of Little Saigon had relinquished control to the second generation, allowing them to take the reins and breathe new life into the declining area. There was a renaissance happening here, albeit a small one. She just wasn't sure if she wanted to be a foot soldier in that war.

Her mind wandered back to her father's note. She had stayed awake all night, tossing and turning, reading and crumpling his words.

Jane, I hope you remember that once upon a time, it wasn't all so bad. That I wasn't so bad. That we weren't so bad. The things that used to make us want to leave when we're younger can make us want to stay when we're older. Someway, somehow, we always make our way back home.

Since when was her father speaking to her as if he had just discovered Buddhism?

She spotted the same red plastic stools where her parents would sit for hours and prepare their specialty, xíu mại, which tasted just as good as, if not better than, Italian or Swedish meatballs. Diagonal from that corner was the small plastic children's table and stools where Jane first babysat Bingo and then eventually Paulina. Georgia had been born much later, nine years younger than Jane. By then her father had already expanded to several stores in the South, and his empire had grown.

"Jane?" a small voice echoed from the kitchen. "Is that you, con? Mr. Ngô told me you'd be coming."

She turned around and almost lost her footing when she saw a little hunchbacked woman with the whitest thatch of hair. Jane's face lit up for the first time since she arrived in Houston. It was a friction-fire sort of smile because, upon seeing the old woman's face, she remembered the second mother who took care of the eldest daughter, when the eldest daughter in the family was stuck taking care of everyone else around her; an ouroboros of nurturers.

"Bác Cai? I can't believe it!" Jane shouted with glee, and leapt forward. "I *can't* believe you still work here!"

"You almost said 'I can't believe you're still alive,' didn't you?" said Bác Cai, returning the smile. She shuffled her way toward Jane with arms outstretched. Jane drowned happily in her oceanic embrace, burying her face deep in her bosom like a little kid again. Bác Cai's familiar signature scent filled her lungs: Tiger Balm, coconut oil, and a hint of smoke. All things Vietnamese, all things Texas. All the best reminders of childhood. Jane remembered it all. She remembered her childhood in full force again. And for the first time in a long time, Jane missed Houston. She missed home.

I hope you remember that once upon a time, it wasn't all so bad.

Her father's words nipped at her heart again, but she mentally tossed them aside. She almost wanted to shout at her father that now isn't the time. "Seriously, though, I can't believe you're still alive," Jane said, laughing as she pulled away. "You're as ancient as this store."

"I'm still spryer than you, though."

"I don't doubt it."

Jane peeked around the corner, waiting to greet the other kitchen staff. She'd been instantly rejuvenated at the sight of Bác Cai and was waiting for the other three women to emerge. The four elderly women were akin to fairy godmothers of the shop. Because while Jane watched Bingo, Paulina, and Georgia, the four fairy godmothers made sure she ate, brushed her hair, and got dressed for school. When a few ticks of silence went on, Jane remembered fairy tales weren't real.

Bác Cai watched Jane curiously. "Con, what's wrong?"

Jane looked back at her. "Bác Cai, where are the others? Bác Phúc? Bác Trieu? Bác Ping?"

She looked at Jane pityingly. "Not everyone can elude time, con. My time will soon be here, too, one day. Until then, I come into this shop every day at eight a.m. and I leave at seven p.m. All I have left is this shop and my routine. What else is there to live for? One by one, you all left."

How could she not know the fairy godmothers of the shop and of her youth had passed away? Why hadn't her father told her? Jane racked her brain. *Had* he? Had she ignored his calls while she was living her life elsewhere? She was overcome by the difficulty of admitting that this was her fault, and not Duc's.

Jane rarely strayed from a linear path her whole life. And yet, nothing had worked out for her. Here was Bác Cai, still coming into the sandwich shop for the last sixteen years, making the same sandwiches, and she was more at peace with her life than Jane had ever been.

She turned so the older woman wouldn't see the tears welling up in her eyes. "Well, you should take it easy, you're no spring chicken," Jane lectured. She forced herself to bury her reasons as to why she decided to stay behind in Houston and play her father's game. This was neither the place nor the time for her to think of her own concerns. "It's just been you here this whole time?"

Bác Cai shrugged. "Here and there. Mostly regulars, construction crew, and curious tourists. This shop is like a weird tourist attraction for a lot of Vietnamese Americans. You know how people feel about Duc. They look at him like the poor man's Jack Ma. The real rags-to-riches story."

Jane snorted. "Of course. The only people who look up to my father are strangers. They don't know the truth about what an awful father he was."

The old woman raised a brow. "He did the best he could, con. You know he did." There was a slight warning in her voice. The continuous defensiveness of Duc Trần was something that Jane had held her tongue back on her entire life. But as the eldest daughter who escaped, who grew up, and who was standing on the old linoleum floors of her father's old sandwich shop, she wouldn't take it anymore.

"You don't have to defend him anymore, Bác Cai," Jane said. "It's not like he cares about you enough to check in on you or this shop."

Bác Cai raised her other brow, standing her ground. "Perhaps when you are my age, con, you can reflect back on your life and understand that your difficulties were not the same as our difficulties. That perhaps, your father also lived in fear, but a different kind of fear than you're used to."

Jane simply shrugged, unwilling to go into battle. "You know I'm a lawyer, right?"

"And you know I survived a war, right? I have more grit than you do."

Laughter finally erupted from Jane, and she threw her hands up in the air, signaling defeat. "Alright, alright, you win. My father lives to see another day."

"If only you knew . . ." Bác Cai's voice trailed off.

Just then the doorbell sounded. The rusty old bell barely managed to notify the women that they had a customer. An elderly Vietnamese couple came shuffling in, their big sun hats barely squeezing through the door. Jane immediately knew they were from out of town, but she hung back and observed them quietly. They hobbled from one corner of the shop to the other, curiously picking up a dusty branded-green Duc's Sandwiches cup that said "#1 Best Sandwich in Texas," before they left without saying a word.

"Why didn't you ask for their order?" Jane immediately grilled Bác Cai.

Bác Cai scoffed. "Who the hell comes in here to order sandwiches anymore? People from out of town come here out of morbid curiosity. Back in its heyday, Duc's Sandwiches was a phenomenon. Now it's just a decaying shop with food even *I* wouldn't want to eat."

Jane surveyed the shop again, this time with new eyes. She watched as the old Vietnamese couple took a photo in front of the first Duc's Sandwiches in the country, and then walked back to their car. She no longer viewed it with a sentimental lens because tenderness and doing the right thing had never worked out for her. She needed to do right, not for father, or for her absent mother, but for the four women who had turned this shop into her second home and made it more bearable than her actual home. She needed to turn the shop into Little Saigon's crown jewel again. The hub for all passing gossip, the place where everyone ordered their catering from for every milestone in their lives. She needed to preserve the best part of the shop's history. Even when she'd spent the last ten years running away from it.

As her brain churned, so did Bác Cai's words: *Curious tourists. Morbid curiosity.*

"Bác Cai," Jane said slowly as her eyes turned into dollar signs. "I'm going to need your help one last time. We're going to turn this shithole around."

"What do you mean by shi—"

....

For the first time in years, Jane felt lighter. Jane had a plan. And when Jane had a plan, you should expect tsunamis, earthquakes, and lightning to step aside in fear.

The Trần women had to win somehow.

But unlike her three younger sisters, Jane knew she had the upper hand against them. She had a set of skills that only the eldest Asian daughter could wield: Her Vietnamese was better *and* she knew how to talk to old Asian people. Both of which were lost on her sisters, who ran like cockroaches from the light when they had to greet their elder relatives.

Bác Cai and Jane set off in the morning the next day to survey the neighborhood. Jane had compiled a list of recently opened modern shops, which catered to a younger, social-media heavy crowd. The following day, they did the same thing. Jane took notes, photos, and researched. Bác Cai complained heavily. Day after day, the two women, nearly forty years apart, schemed on how to beat out the other Trần children, and turn their shop around.

Jane couldn't help but feel cocky, that the win was hers for the taking. It almost seemed . . . too easy. The more Jane tried to crack the formula, she realized all she had to do was follow the same cookie-cutter recipe as the other stores around her. The new shops were replete with giant neon signs, accented wallpapers, catchphrases on the walls, and diva lights installed in the bathroom mirrors.

Easy.

Their final stop on the modern list was a Vietnamese coffee shop called Cafe Cà Phê. For the past hour, Bác Cai had lodged an onslaught of complaints to Jane about how tired she was, how she needed to sit down in front of the air-conditioning, and how the younger generation was so strange. Jane was only *slightly* losing her mind. They walked into the brightly lit and crowded coffee shop. Bác Cai managed to groan, complain, and collapse into a chair all at the same time. She held out her hand to flag someone down, shaking it vigorously.

"Bác Cai, this isn't a restaurant," Jane chastised her, her face slightly red from the sun and embarrassment as she pushed down Bác Cai's hand. "It's a coffee shop. We have to go *up* to the counter and order."

"Trời ơi, these young kids," Bác Cai whimpered as she massaged her calves. "Don't they understand old-school hospitality? This isn't a drive-through!"

"It's just standard—" Jane began, an annoyance reaching her throat. Just because she was great at talking to old Asian women didn't mean she could withstand it for eternity. Before something ugly came out of her, she managed to swallow it, shoving it all the way down. "Never mind. I'll go up and order for us." Jane turned around abruptly and slammed into the man standing behind her, causing him to spill his coffee on himself. A flurry of apologies and yelps erupted from her.

"No, no, please! I'm the one who should be sorry," he said, his voice deep and smooth, going down easier than discontinued Japanese whiskey. He reached over her to grab napkins on their table. "Didn't mean to hover or stand so close. That's like the coffee-shop version of manspreading on the subway. I deserved it."

Jane also grabbed a fistful of napkins and their hands collided awkwardly in the middle. She furiously began dabbing him all over, apologizing relentlessly and talking a mile a minute. When she looked up, silence overcame her from the sheer surprise of recognizing who it was.

"Henry?" she whispered, her hand frozen on his chest, wet napkin under her fingertips. "Henry Lâm?"

"Jane," he said, a small smile dancing at the sides of his lips as recognition also dawned on him. "You *did* look familiar. How long has it been? Eight? Ten years? You look great."

She gazed into the eyes of the first boy she'd ever kissed and took him in, noting all the differences while celebrating the parts that remained the same. When he was fifteen, Henry had been sharp, rugged in all the wrong places, and highly emotional. Now he looked as if he was rugged in only the right places. She felt an inexplicable pull toward him, like the magnetic north.

He was a composite of all the best parts of growing up Vietnamese American and none of the ugly, generational-trauma parts. Henry was childhood personified: Maggi seasoning drizzled over sunny-side-up eggs, a warm baguette, white rabbit candy, paper lanterns during the mid-autumn festival—but most of all, he was a reminder of what life was like before her father became consumed with money and success, and before her mother was unable to acknowledge her ailing mental health. Henry represented an alternate reality. It was painful to be standing in front of him now, living out the alternative.

"Eighteen years actually," she whispered. "But who's counting?"

Jane remembered that day well. In front of a grocery store over on

Blalock, on an ordinary Tuesday summer afternoon—between freshman and sophomore year—Jane had been sitting in the shopping cart as Henry spun her around like a go-cart. His laughter was maniacal and contagious, her shrieks booming and virtuous. Up until that point, they'd been nothing more than just friends. Just friends. But it all changed within a span of thirty seconds.

One moment he was running and pushing the cart, and the next he was staring down at her as she clutched the sides of the cart. Her bangs clung to her forehead in clumps, sticky from the humidity. He reached down and pushed her bangs to one side, framing her face into a heart shape. She grew quiet under his touch. In harmony, he leaned over and she leaned up, their shadows aligned for once—reaching the perfect symmetry between two very good friends, a rarer occurrence than a hybrid eclipse. She was taught in school never to look directly at the sun during an eclipse. So, she closed her eyes and let him kiss her first.

The things that used to make us want to leave when we're younger can make us want to stay when we're older.

Jane hated that she was thinking of her father in this exact moment, but Duc's letter came back to torture her. She remembered how much she wanted Henry and her to work out when they were younger, how he was the only reason she'd ever consider staying in Houston.

"How long are you in town for?" Henry asked, finally breaking the awkward silence. He looked down pointedly at her hand still firmly on his chest. "Or are you doing your usual sneak-into-town-for-a-few-days-and-then-disappear act?"

"She's here for a while," said Bác Cai, piping up quickly, raising a walking cane and poking Jane with it from behind. An ominous (?) smirk on her face. "Isn't that *right*, Jane?"

"Yes," Jane breathed. "I'm here for a bit."

"She thinks you two should get dinner and catch up," said Bác Cai, piping up again, as she prodded Jane harder. "Isn't that *right*, Jane?"

"Yes," Jane said, surrendering herself over to her puppet master. "Dinner sounds great."

"And Jane will call you soon," said Bác Cai. Her final poke caused Jane to lurch forward into Henry's arms. "*Right*, Jane?"

"Yes, I'll . . . I'll call you soon."

Henry laughed and helped Jane upright. "Perfect. I look forward to your call, then." He gave her a final hug goodbye and walked out.

"I'll be helping you alright," Bác Cai said slowly, as they both watched him leave the shop, walk down the street, and slowly disappear from their view. "But it's not going to be for what you think."

CHAPTER 7

Jude

Word had spread faster than light could travel.

News of Jude's theoretical nuptials made the gossip column in the local Vietnamese newspaper. It had even managed to make a Vietnamese Catholic priest and a Vietnamese Buddhist monk become bipartisan allies, perhaps even friends. Unlike how divided the rest of the community was over anything political, food (northern vs. southern style phở), and religion, everyone came together to exchange information to try to get their daughters in front of Mrs. Vương, Houston's most respected numerologist. So, on a bland weekday, a queue of potential matches had formed outside the dinky coffee shop in a back alley on Bissonnet Street. Vietnamese women of all shapes, sizes, and ages lined up for a chance to play their hand at Duc's inheritance. (And for Jude's hand, of course.)

Son, I look at you and wonder if you will ever find your joy. It's time you discover a different type of joy than what you've been chasing before.

Duc's letter circled over Jude's head, waiting desperately to land. Jude was afraid to acknowledge that his father's letter to him had hurt. It hurt in such a specific way because it was filled with hard truths that he didn't think his father had noticed about him: Jude *was* lonely, and he had no joy. It was not lost on him that even his absentee, eccentric millionaire father noticed that about Jude.

"Nervous?" Mrs. Vương asked Jude, interrupting his thoughts, as she watched him wipe sweat off his forehead, mistaking his sweat for nerves and not because he was in another matching sweatsuit in the middle of summer. "It's okay to be nervous. You could potentially meet the love of your life today. Someone with such a fortuitous birth like yours needs to find a good match."

Jude looked at the old numerologist whom every pregnant mother in the city had sat in front of since time immemorial. Even he had, once upon a time, sat in front of her, flanked by his parents, while Mr. Ngô hovered behind, as usual. He distinctly remembered Mrs. Vương telling his parents that he would grow up to become someone important, someone prominent, someone who would change the course of people's lives. It was the one time he saw Duc be proud of him. Duc had placed a heavy hand on Jude's young shoulder, affirming that he was his son, and Duc was his father. That their bond, though invisible, was indestructible.

But as the years ticked by, Jude became none of those things. Just the laughingstock of the town. Everyone claimed that the only economist anyone needed on speed dial was Mrs. Vương—she could predict more accurate outcomes than Warren Buffett. Her birth chart matches had a 99 percent success rate. The 1 percent failure just happened to be her own marriage.

As Jude observed Mrs. Vương's prehistoric, graying hair, her diamond stud earrings, and her kind face, something about her sincerity seemed too painful for him to bear. She had a motherly quality to her, and it triggered Jude's guilt. Guilt over what he could and *should* have done for his mother, way back then. He hadn't told any of his sisters, but Jude had seen his mother that morning. That fateful morning, twenty years ago, when Evelyn stumbled down the stairs, lugging a giant suitcase behind her.

Jude had seen her walk out the door—and said nothing.

Mrs. Vương patted his arm so lovingly and with such care, it alarmed Jude once again. He remembered faint glimpses of his mother doing that when he was young to help calm him down whenever he was upset or anxious.

Mrs. Vương opened her first manila folder in a stack of thirty, reading off Phoebe Phương's numerology chart so casually, as if she were ordering from a menu. "The first young woman you'll meet this morning is Phoebe Anne Phương. Born in '90 so she's a horse, but her symbol is a tree, so she always needs to be near water," Mrs. Vương rambled on as she put on her reading glasses, letting them fall to the tip of her nose. Jude craned his neck and saw a whole algorithm written down, comparing the two birth charts—his and hers. "She's a nurse over at HCA in pediatric care, and loves dogs."

"Great," he responded lifelessly. "Let's get the paperwork done. Any chance you're ordained? We can get married in this coffee shop."

"Oh come now, don't you want to know more before she comes?" she prodded, teasing him. "She's a *very* impressive young woman. Even runs marathons for fun and sells her knitted creations on Etsy. Beauty, brains, creative, and *strong*! What more could you want in a wife and a mother?"

"Nope, that's all the information I need," he said curtly, shutting her down. "Thank you."

Mrs. Vương, a bit taken aback by Jude's reaction, attempted to keep her cheery disposition. "You know, she's had a bit of a tough life, poor girl. Wouldn't you want to know more to get the whole picture? Don't you want to know why it makes sense for the two of you to marry? Perhaps, you're even fated to marry?"

"We all have trauma, Cô Vương." Jude waved his hand, dismissing her. "We're Vietnamese children of refugee immigrant parents."

A flicker of disapproval crossed the numerologist's face, but she managed to retain the smile on it. "Alright, well, I promised your father I would find a suitable match for you and a good daughter-in-law for him," she said through her teeth. "You know, your father liked Phoebe's profile the most. He said that he enjoyed how close she was to her father and that she knew how to swim—"

Jude's face grew red, then drooped with horror as the realization sank in. "My *father* is involved in this process? Why would he care if she knew how to swim? I barely know how to swim."

"Because she can save you one day in case you are ever drowning," she said, so surprised that Jude *wouldn't* know the answer to the question. "You know he fears the ocean. The Gulf in particular."

"But why has he been looking through the profiles with you? I thought he was unreachable?" Jude asked, still hell-bent on knowing why his father was so involved. "Also, wasn't he a fisherman? How could he be scared—"

"Sit up straight," Mrs. Vương quickly shushed him. "She's heading straight to us."

Phoebe Phương strolled into the coffee shop, not a single hair out of place, with her shoulders pulled back, showing her defined collarbone. Confidence radiated off her. She was in a soft lavender sundress that revealed her curves. Mrs. Vương quickly shuffled the manila folders around, pretending to be distracted. Jude immediately knew that *she* knew Phoebe was too good for him.

Phoebe walked straight to the table, bowed toward Mrs. Vương, and greeted her in a respectful way. It made Jude nauseous. Was her demeanor genuine? Or was she just putting on a show to get a stab at his father's money? Jude took her in, trying to find kernels of truth. She did look familiar to him, but he couldn't tell if it was because of growing up in Houston and every Vietnamese woman near his age reminded him of someone he knew. Was she attractive? Sure, she wasn't hideous. Did she seem kind? Sure, but no one's a saint. Did she have nice eyes? Sure, but most people have two eyes. She wasn't special. None of the surface or internal things mattered, because he couldn't help but recoil at the idea that Phoebe was handpicked by his father as his favorite match for Jude. Just because their birth charts aligned didn't mean it was fated. Jude hadn't grown up to become a "great man of prominence." Mrs. Vương's own marriage ended in divorce. Jude's mother abandoned the family. What was the point in believing in the numbers and stars when everyone always leaves?

Mrs. Vương gathered up her documents, gave Jude a thumbs-up, and tiptoed over to the other side of the coffee shop as Phoebe slid into the empty space. She flashed Jude a smile and extended her hand.

"I'm Phoebe."

"Jude."

"I know."

Coffees quickly arrived for both, and soon it was just the two of them, sitting in silence. Jude felt everyone at the shop staring at them, waiting for a performance. He saw the queue of women outside the window, pressing their foreheads against the glass, peering inside.

Phoebe coughed, attempting to break the silence. "So, did dating apps suck so much it turned you to numerology?" She laughed. "My dad said if I got married this year, it'd be lucky for me. So he put in a word to a friend of a friend, and got my application moved up the stack." Her laugh was so distinct that Jude couldn't help being drawn to it. It sounded like a wind chime on a front porch with a gentle breeze blowing by, soft and pleasing. Jude felt himself loosening up. Her laugh reminded him of his mother's laugh. Jude closed his eyes and cringed at his own cringiness. *Kill me.*

"Hello?" Phoebe tried again, looking for an opening. Her smile revealed tiny dimple pockets. "Anyone in there?"

She really didn't seem so bad. She seemed like a decent person. It dawned on Jude that all he needed to do was get married, sign some papers, and call it a day to please his father. In the grand scheme of it all, it would be far simpler to get married than to try to revive a dying sandwich shop in the middle of nowhere America. Marriages were a sham anyway—might as well do it for the right reasons. At least it would be one step above the reasons Evelyn had for marrying Duc. But certainly not above why Connie married Duc. At that moment, Jude understood Connie a bit more, because Jude now needed his own Connie. He needed a wife to get the money, and he wasn't willing to go through hundreds more of these potential matches.

He cast a leery glance at the growing queue of potential matches outside, their shadows nearly doubling, and he felt claustrophobic.

This one should do just fine.

"So, you want to get married?" Jude asked, finally speaking, as all five senses slowly returned to him. "Let's do this. You and me. Let's get out of here."

"Seriously?" Phoebe responded, dumbfounded by Jude's curveball. "You're not even going to introduce yourself first? Say hello? You're not going to ask me questions about myself? My hobbies? Interests? What is my family like? Dogs or cats? What if I worship Satan and am a serial killer?"

Out of the corner of his eye, Jude could see Mrs. Vương on the other side of the cafe, her eyes peering at them over the daily Vietnamese newspaper, boring into his soul, trying to read their body language. His eyes lowered to see the stack of folders on her table, holding more potential suitors, who were all waiting to take a stab at Duc's money under the guise of love. He could already envision the horrible, awkward wine dates, movie dates, ice cream dates, the job interview–like questions they'd each have to give to each other. All Duc had said in the letter was Jude needed to get married in the next year; he didn't say anything about how long it had to last. He also didn't say he had to love the person.

"No need. Kill anyone you want, worship whoever you want, it doesn't really concern me. Dogs, cats, snakes, manatees, I don't really care, morning person or night person, sleep in late, stay up late, do what makes you happy," Jude said, leaning in closer so no one could eavesdrop around them, and dropping his voice. "Let's be honest here. I know you won't really fall in love with me, and I won't fall in love with you, but we can mutually benefit from this arrangement. I can't give you the whole Prince Charming bit, but if you marry me this year, I can give you a small cut from my inheritance as payment for your time. I just need a warm body standing next to me at the altar. Annulment, divorce, separation, whatever—I'll sign whatever you want. Eventually, you'll go your own way, and I'll go my way. We'll just both be a little richer than before we met."

Phoebe leaned back, her arms crossed, studying Jude. "So you don't even know why I want to get married? Or what I'll do with the money?"

"No. I don't need to know."

He could see her mind churning through a million different calculations, scenarios, and the fateful question: "What's the worst that could happen?" He couldn't tell if he'd offended her, or perhaps surprised her. If there was one thing he'd learned from his father, it was how to piss off women. He braced himself, waiting for her to throw coffee in his face and storm out. To his surprise, she extended a hand toward him, a twinkle in her eyes that matched her laughter.

"*Before* you have yourself a deal," she spoke finally, "you're going to have to ask my father for my hand in marriage, and convince him that *this* isn't a sham. Even if it is a sham. I'm going to need you to convince him that you really do care for me."

He shook her hand firmly, feeling how warm her palm was, and how easily her warmth transferred to his body. Heat rose all the way to his cheeks, as it now dawned on him how beautiful she really was. He took in her balmy brown eyes and her tall cheekbones. She was somehow soft but sharp at the same time. "Deal. Your father will be easier to deal with than my father. I'm sure he'll be easy to convince."

She raised an eyebrow, and he could read her thoughts piling up on top of each other, a game of hangman with easily guessable phrases. "You know my father respects Duc, for all that he's done to 'make it' in America. I don't know if he can say the same about you."

Jude shrugged nonchalantly. It was the same judgment he'd gotten all his life, from outsiders who didn't know what it was like to grow up as Duc's one and only son. "Sure, my father 'made it,' but at what cost? Would you rather be hated by your own family, but loved by everyone else?"

Phoebe tightened her grip on Jude. For the third time that morning, he was alarmed by a woman's uncanny ability to disarm him. She stared deep into his eyes, and for a split second, Jude felt the proverbial walls around him collapse, exposing all his vulnerabilities for this strange woman to witness. Suddenly, Jude felt embarrassed. He was embarrassed by his family, embarrassed by Duc, embarrassed by these inheritance games, embarrassed by what he was wearing (sweatpants in the summer?), but most of all, he was embarrassed for not having grown up to become a man of prominence, as Mrs. Vương had said he would.

"Well, *I* don't hate you."

Jude's chest tightened. There were so many different meanings behind what she just said. Did she mean that he was her family now? Did she mean that she liked him in a romantic way?

"Oh," he stuttered nervously. "Thank you."

"You're welcome," she said, finally releasing her hand from his. Jude squeezed his newly freed hand under the table, feeling the sting of her absence. He tried to ignore the nagging feeling that Phoebe was different from all the others who had tried to come before. "But you're not out of the woods yet. Just remember, you need to win over my father."

....

A week later, Jude found himself up at 5:00 a.m., in a fishing boat in the middle of Lake Houston, staring into the harrowing eyes of Mr. Phương. The entire drive over, Mr. Phương hadn't said a word to him. He just clucked his tongue at the sight of Jude, who was wearing another pair of matching, ill-fitting sweatpants, sporting his usual diamond-plated necklace, yawning loudly, asking if there'll be coffee on the boat. Mr. Phương shook his head, gripping the wheel even tighter. It was the type of nod where one couldn't tell if he was full of disgust, disappointment, or both. Jude once again felt embarrassed. Duc's letter haunted closely behind, along with Mrs. Vương's prediction for him as a child.

Once they were out on the water, it was somehow even more silent between the two men. Though separated by a generation, and by a different set of traumas, the men only had one thing in common: Phoebe Phương. They were the only two out on the water at this time. Jude shuffled uncomfortably on the plastic crate he was sitting on, and tried his best to break eye contact with Mr. Phương, who seemingly never blinked.

Mr. Phương just continued staring at Jude, wearing him down, an unlit cigarette hanging from his lips.

"So," Mr. Phương finally said, breaking the long silence. "Do you know how to fish?" His voice heavy with a Texas accent. Despite the freezing early morning, all the man had on was a ragged sweatshirt that said VIET COWBOY, his stomach protruding over his cargo shorts. He sported flip-flops, and a ratty Astros baseball cap sat on top of his receding hairline.

Jude laughed as if it was the funniest question in the world. "No, why would I?" He immediately stopped laughing when he saw how thin Mr. Phương's lips had gotten, and coughed nervously. "I mean, sorry, no, sir, I don't go fishing a lot. My . . . father used to, though. He was great at catching fish. Used to be a shrimper back in the day, down in Seadrift. I actually wasn't allowed on a boat, growing up. He wouldn't let me."

Mr. Phương raised a brow. "Ah, the infamous Duc Trần. Strange that you weren't allowed on any boat growing up, especially since he was a for-mer fisherman. That life never leaves you."

Jude shrugged. "He said he didn't want us to ever work the way he used to work."

"So, why hasn't he reached out to us yet? You want to marry my daughter, why haven't we all formally gotten together?"

This was the part Jude absolutely hated. How could he explain his ec-centric parents and his upbringing to those who couldn't understand? Mr. Phương looked like the type of father who'd never abandon his family and someone who wanted to be there for every single milestone. Jude ob-served the seemingly endless lake, and felt a sadness for the first time in a long time. Here he was, with a different father, in the middle of a lake, holding a fishing pole, when Duc had never really taken him out fishing like he kept promising he would. Each time the promises were spaced far-ther apart until, eventually, it was never brought up again, lost to the ether.

Jude felt a heavy weight on him. He suddenly wanted Mr. Phương's approval. Not just for Phoebe's hand, but he wanted him to like him. It's not like he was in love with Phoebe or believed in the marriage, but after meet-ing Mr. Phương, he could understand Phoebe a bit more, and why her father's approval meant so much. It was because he cared.

"My father is . . . unreachable. I can't reach him. No one knows where he is, he's somewhere in Vietnam," Jude said. "And my mother left when I was fourteen, so I don't know where she is. My father took me crabbing a few times down in Galveston, but he never taught me how to fish. I mostly just . . . watched him."

Silence overshadowed the boat, despite the sun having risen now. The morning air was crisp. Hidden birds chirped, nestled inside gigantic pine trees that towered over the water.

"Sorry to hear that, con," Mr. Phương said gruffly. Con. The man called him con. There was hope after all. There was affection in the con, almost as if he saw Jude as kin. Jude felt his cheeks flush with unexpected pride.

"Well, we're here now," the old man continued. "I'll teach you how to fish. Learning how to catch your own food is how you'll be able to provide for your family." Mr. Phương reached down to grab two fishing poles and handed one to Jude. "You need to work with your hands, it's a lifelong skill. How do you expect to take care of Phoebe if you don't know how to fish? What if there's an apocalypse and you need to learn how to hunt?"

Jude fumbled the pole as he took it from Mr. Phương, making a joke about how much taller a fishing pole was in person than in photos. Pools of sweat began forming under his armpits as he realized Mr. Phương was expecting him to start fishing immediately. He looked at all the parts of the pole, and tried his best to remember how people did it in the movies . . . or how his father had done it. "You know, my wife left, too," Mr. Phương said abruptly. "But not in the way your mother left you."

Jude looked up quizzically. He watched as Mr. Phương broke character, sadness washing over his face. "She passed away when Phoebe was young. Around the same age as you were when you lost your mother." His voice became gruff. "Cancer."

Jude didn't say anything. He never really knew what to say when it came to death, because he'd also experienced loss, just not in the traditional sense. How could he say "sorry for your loss" when no one had ever really said that in regards to his mother, who was still alive, somewhere out there?

"She's a good kid, you know," Mr. Phương sighed. "She just doesn't know how to relax. Carries all the burdens in her shoulders. I'm sick, too, you know."

Jude looked surprised. "Are you . . . okay?"

Mr. Phương laughed for the first time all morning. "Why does everyone always ask me that question right after I tell them I'm sick? I'm not *not* okay. I have kidney disease."

"Oh."

Mr. Phương laughed again, as if Jude was the funniest person he'd ever met. "I bet Phoebe never told you. Explains why I don't drink, right? She works overtime to help me pay the bills. But don't tell her I told you that. I just need you to help her live a little again. If you're going to marry my daughter, I want her to have the same marriage I had. One full of laughter and light."

Even though he knew the wedding was just a front, Jude began to see Phoebe in a new light. He understood now why she had agreed so easily to get married to him. She needed the money to keep her last parent alive. Both of them would have only one parent in attendance at their wedding. They'd spent the last two decades grieving over their mothers in silence, putting on a mask, and pretending to the entire world that they were just perfect, completely fine.

"I will," Jude found himself saying. "I promise."

Maybe it wouldn't be such a bad marriage after all. Being able to lie next to someone without having to explain your trauma.

Maybe it could even be a great one.

The Lone Star Times

Texas Feud Erupts Between Vietnamese Fishermen and Locals

August 9, 1979

Seadrift, Tex., Aug. 9—Several bombs have exploded since Friday night after the death of local fisherman Billy Joe Aplin, 35 years old. Aplin was fatally shot after a fight erupted between Aplin and two brothers, Nguyen Van Sau and Nguyen Van Chinh.

Tensions have been escalating between the Vietnamese and the local fishermen for some time now. Locals have accused the refugees of overfishing and taking away their livelihood.

With the news of Aplin's death, it was the nail in the proverbial coffin as locals sought vengeance against the Vietnamese. Many trawlers and fishing boats have been set on fire, most belonging to the Vietnamese. The local crab plant was also targeted with a bomb threat, but authorities intervened. The crab plant employs many Vietnamese refugees.

Nguyen Van Chinh was arrested at the scene. His brother, Nguyen Van Sau, turned himself in after the weekend's unrest. Both have been charged with murder and await trial.

It is said that many Vietnamese have left Seadrift, a sleepy fishing town, out of fear, and have scattered to nearby towns—but they have not been welcomed there either with open arms.

Only time will tell if the refugees will ever be able to find a place to call home.

CHAPTER 8

1980, Orange County, California

For the last four years, Huey and Duc were thick as thieves. Often mistaken for brothers, they bounced around New Orleans, Oklahoma City, back up to Philadelphia, even stopping for a brief stint out in San Jose before making their way down south to Orange County and settling there for a brief blip in time. But Orange County's Little Saigon made them small fish in a big pond. In order for them to get to where they wanted in life, they had to be somewhere with less competition.

For money, sometimes they worked as deckhands on fishing boats, but the bulk of their income came from running small scams here and there, some of which came dangerously close to becoming big ones, big enough to get them noticed by local police. Huey and Duc weren't proud when they ran scams on their own people, refugees who had just arrived and couldn't speak a lick of English. But they chalked it up to surviving, and tried their best to absolve their guilt by going to temple more, lighting incense and praying to the Buddha to help them find peace one day. They reasoned that had their victims gotten the chance, they'd have scammed the hell out of them, too, for a little cash and some beer.

Anything goes after surviving war, right?

But after their last scam, which left an old Vietnamese grandmother penniless, they realized they had to change their ways. The woman even knew she was being scammed, and yet she forgave them, blaming herself for her stupidity. That was when Huey knew it was time to stop; he kept seeing his own mother's face. He was never again going to see his mother, who had stayed back in Vietnam, nor would he see the old woman ever again. Instead both women's faces haunted him at night.

On their last night in Orange County, Huey and Duc brown-bagged some 40 oz. and headed to the beach. They often went when no one else was around. Not once had they been able to see the Pacific Ocean during the day.

"We need to do something else for a living. It just doesn't sit right with me anymore," Huey said tentatively, taking a swig of beer—it tasted so cheap it nearly gagged him. It was worse than the Ba Ba Ba beer from back in Vietnam. God, how he missed Vietnam. Even the shit beer back there was better than the shit beer here. "Anh, we can't keep stealing money, only to spend it on *this* shit. It's not even worth it."

Duc laughed and agreed, and the two men sat in silence for a bit. Huey watched as Duc grabbed fistfuls of sand, and let the grains slip through his fingers. The sand somehow formed musical notes in the air and flew gracefully east. Huey imagined the sands somehow landing on the shores of Da Nang, on the other side of the world, where home was. Where his mother was, and where the last remnants of his old life lay buried alongside the sea of dead soldiers. Huey wished he was musically inclined; he would have sent his mother her favorite song.

"Okay," Duc agreed, after he was halfway through the bottle. Before he was even done with the first beer, he pulled out another from inside his jacket. Huey watched as he started it almost immediately, leaving the old one to sink into the sand. "I got a second cousin down in Texas. He said there's work for us if we want it. We won't make a lot, but it's something. For now."

"What kind of work?" Huey asked, but he was afraid of the answer. As much as he blindly followed Duc, he often wondered how far he was willing to go.

"There's a job for us down near the Gulf. A few jobs. A crab factory, a crab restaurant. Or we can join my cousin's shrimping boat," Duc said. "Hell, maybe we can get our own boat one day, go off on our own, and start our own business."

Huey thought about the first time he met Duc, back in Louisiana, on the rusty commercial fishing boat the *Lady Freedom*. They had experienced their first bout of casual racism together, and he remembered being in awe at how easily Duc brushed it off. Duc even promised that they'd become so rich one day, they'd buy that boat and fire everyone. There was strength in ignoring the outside world, strength in dreaming. How did he do it?

"What would our boat be called?"

Duc shrugged. "Is it too on the nose to call it *The Yellow Submarine*?"

Huey let the joke sink in a little bit more, and he let out an uproarious laugh. "Not at all, anh, not at all. Which part of Texas are we heading to?"

"Seadrift."

"Seadrift?" Huey asked. The name felt foreign but familiar, just like everything in America. It suddenly clicked, two puzzle pieces snapping into place. "Hold on a minute. Are you crazy? Isn't that the place where those two Vietnamese fishermen brothers killed that white fisherman? Why the fuck would we head there? They *hate* us down there."

Duc shrugged so casually again, Huey wanted to punch him. "Yeah, but they were acquitted. It was self-defense. What's the big deal?"

"Who cares? It's not *safe* for us to be there."

"Is it safe for us to be anywhere in America?"

"You really think we can make good money down there?"

"They need people at the crab factory and there are jobs on boats," Duc said. "Pick your poison. People are too scared to keep working there."

Huey's stomach dropped. Duc's flippancy toward heading to a domestic battleground unnerved him. As if he didn't care about his surroundings, the politics, or anything current that was happening. Texas was the last unexplored state they had on their proverbial list of states in America. But Huey wasn't immune to what was happening down in Seadrift. Whispers, rumors, word of mouth, run-of-the-mill gossip, and regular tales being shared around the gambling table had told them of how the Vietnamese were being treated in Texas, especially the fishermen. Ever since the two brothers, Nguyen Van Sau and Nguyen Van Chinh, were acquitted of any charges after shooting and killing a white fisherman in self-defense, the town of Seadrift was wrought with racial tension between the Vietnamese fishermen and the locals.

But to head down to Seadrift in the middle of a local, domestic war—after just escaping from one—was madness, suicidal even. But Duc was Duc, and Huey knew he would follow Duc until the end. He was the only family Huey had.

Huey stared out into the pitch-black ocean. The light from the stars couldn't shine enough to see anything. What creatures lurked beneath the waters?

"My father was a fisherman, you know," Huey said, with sadness in his voice. "I remember him telling me he never wanted me to become a fisherman, either."

"So was my father, anh," Duc said, finally letting go of his toughness. "He said the same thing to me, too."

The men lost themselves in the waves, crashing against one another, thunderous but gentle, until they brushed up against the shore and the sound crescendoed and fell. Huey listened and listened to the echoing of the waves, hoping to find his father's voice hidden in there, giving him one more piece of advice. There was a nagging feeling about following Duc into hell, and Huey wondered what his father would think about Duc. But his father wasn't here. Duc was. Huey knew he had no choice but to go back to the ocean. The money was running out, and they needed steady income. He just hoped Duc wasn't a monster hiding beneath the surface.

"To Texas then," Huey said, resigned.

The two of them clinked their beers and tried their best to enjoy their last night in California before heading out in the morning. Though they never talked about the old woman again, they couldn't help but both wonder if she was still at her kitchen table, calling herself ngu ngốc over and over again, until the sun came up, and they began to wonder if they were ngu ngốc for heading to Seadrift and gambling their lives for just a little bit of coin. They'd left Vietnam without a second thought, tired of war, but now they had to prepare for a different kind of war.

CHAPTER 9

Bingo

Like death and taxes, Bingo's nasty temper was accepted as a universal truth.

Bingo and her father shared few commonalities, though if one squinted hard enough, one could see that they might have a similar face structure and the same low-bridge nose. Maybe. Barely. But among the commonalities that they *did* share were recognized by the Trần siblings as the "bad" genes. Duc's "bad" genes happily skipped over Jude, tentatively crawled past Jane, but grew like a weed in Bingo's heart. Both Duc and his third offspring were fueled by rage, spite, and the refusal to be wrong about anything. This behavior instilled a sense of fear among the other siblings, who viewed Bingo as a grenade. Except now the pin had been pulled during Duc's inheritance game, and Bingo had turned into a ticking bomb.

Did you know that Philadelphia has always been my favorite city? I remember thinking I could live here forever. Once you bypass the fear of the unknown, con, this place will become your favorite city, too.

Duc's letter was a complete mystery to Bingo. She was convinced that the letter wasn't anything more than an old man's delusions written down in the form of fortune cookie one-liners. His letter did convince Bingo that he must be dying of something, because she was absolutely positive her father had never spent more than a few days in Philadelphia.

When Bingo landed at Philadelphia International Airport early in the morning, the day after the family reunion, she didn't head directly to the hotel. Instead, she gave the cab driver the address to Duc's Sandwiches in South Philadelphia. She wanted to see the state of the shop and understand what she was working with. Though she had brushed off her father's inheritance game as nothing more than the usual Vietnamese patriarchal clownery, Bingo had yet to tell her siblings that she was desperate to win the money. To her, it wasn't just a game. The windfall would be life-changing.

"Heading to South Philly, eh?" the cabbie asked, a slight chuckle in his voice, as if he could immediately tell she was a tourist. The elderly South

Asian cab driver, whose thick gray hair matched his thick Philly accent, raised his brows up and down at her in the rearview mirror, wanting extra confirmation that she *really* wanted to be dropped off there. The sound of Q102, the Top 40 radio station, served as background noise, the pop music distracting Bingo, who absolutely hated dancing.

"Just so you know, that part of town is overrun with new development," he continued as he took a sharp left to head onto the I-95 ramp. "Go to Chinatown if you want good Vietnamese food."

If there was one thing Bingo hated more in this world, it was unsolicited advice. Her jet lag kicked in, along with a dangerous level of annoyance. She wanted to tell him to keep his eyes on the road and out of her business, but she hadn't reached her usual blind rage. Yet.

"Gentrification is an incurable disease. What can we do about it?" she asked, her tone listless, as she stared out the window at the passing scenery. Philadelphia seemed to her like any other American East Coast metropolis. Steely, cold, lonely, industrial. She could feel her father's mind games breathing down the back of her neck. It was unclear why Duc had sent her off to Philly, or why he was convinced she would love it, but maybe he saw more commonalities between them than she thought. Maybe he also saw her as steely, cold, lonely, and industrious.

The cab driver shrugged. "Don't you want to preserve good food and good people?"

She fell silent for the rest of the ride from the airport to South Philadelphia. As she passed by skyscrapers juxtaposed next to old colonial brick homes, her thoughts became more and more discombobulated as she observed the changing landscape. Doubt began to seep in, finding cracks inside her to hide in and grow mold. The inheritance. The money. The competition among her own sisters. Her father's approval. Jude looking for someone to marry within the next year. Her mother . . . wherever she was.

There wasn't much for her back in Portland, aside from mounting debt and a shared house with four other despondent millennial roommates whom she found from an online ad. They were all forced to live together because the world wasn't economically friendly to unambitious single people. Yet, there was no difference to her between four strangers or her four siblings. Despite the camaraderie she had felt with her sisters over crawfish and beer, she knew it wouldn't last past sunrise. Bingo needed the money more than any of them because she needed an out. The last few years of her life felt like they had been encased in resin, and she had no mobility or control anymore. She wasn't like her other siblings—she had always been the lost one.

As sad as it was to admit, even if she won the inheritance, she wouldn't know what to do with it, which only scared her more.

"We're here," the driver said, pulling her out of her thoughts as the cab lurched to a sudden stop. A broken neon Duc's Sandwiches sign loomed over her, taunting her, reminding her of how far she had to go to get the money. It was all a dog and pony show, and Bingo was more than ready to perform.

Except it wouldn't be as easy as she thought. Her jaw dropped as she took in the dilapidated store. The photos online didn't do it justice, or showcase how abandoned it really was. The sign was broken in half, so only the *Duc* flashed in staccato. Bingo braced herself and scanned the rest of the store. The edges of the front door were rimmed in hard rust, and the signature green color of the store brand had peeled off in splotches, giving the logo an accidental ombre effect. Graffiti coated the entire storefront, and a broken window on the far right somehow had glass on the sidewalk and not on the inside, as if someone from *inside* the shop was trying to break out. Bingo took out a key and unlocked the front door, revealing what looked like an empty sandwich shop masquerading as a money laundering scheme. But it wasn't just the store that was dark and empty; not a soul was walking around the street in the early-morning hours. Where the hell was everyone in Philadelphia?

Bingo could feel the money slipping away from her, like a tsunami reversing away from shore, as if the shore was poisonous. She couldn't help but wonder if her father's schemes had something more sinister behind them, a dying man's last act of cruelty. Bingo had always suspected he liked her the least. Coming out as gay probably didn't help, even though he kept repeating over and over *okay, sounds good* on the day she told him she was into girls. She was not only convinced the old man was dying but also that he had given her the worst storefront because he didn't *want* her to win.

Or maybe it was a fucked-up concoction of both reasons.

"I thought you said this part of town was full of new development," Bingo said, aghast.

"Well, I didn't know you were talking about this old shitter!" the cabbie called out, the car still running. "I can take you to another spot if you want food. You must be hungry after all the travel."

His tenderness almost touched her. But she was too hardened to crack and too selfish to see beyond the horizon. Bingo had never covered five spaces in a row in her life. She'd just been on one losing streak after another. She felt desperation overpower her rage for the first time in a long time and felt incredibly alone. She didn't know what her father was talking about; Philadelphia felt so lonely. How on earth could she ever call this shit city home?

"Where do you suggest then?" she asked feebly, her usual comebacks lodged in her throat. She had to rethink her strategy. It wasn't just the store she had to revive now; it was the entire damn block, the entire neighborhood. If she wanted to win, she had to fish for answers, clues, any scrap of information to help her win over the hearts of Philadelphians. "I know you're not Vietnamese, but you're an Asian immigrant cabbie, which means you're more Philly than anyone else. Where do people go for bánh mì here?"

"What the hell is a bang-meh?" he asked. His left arm rested along the rolled-down window. This time, though, Bingo could feel him really studying her. She could tell she was the most unusual ride he'd had in a long time. Confusion crossed his face as he tried to understand why this strange woman, who just hopped off a flight an hour ago, was chasing Vietnamese food so dramatically in Philly.

"Bánh mì," she said, correcting him. "It's like a Vietnamese sandwich. French baguette? All sorts of mystery meat between it? Paté spread? Julienned vegetables? Usually not more than five dollars when it really should cost at least fifteen dollars? Sir, we are parked right in front of a bánh mì shop right now! You never been inside Duc's Sandwiches?"

"Oh! A *bang-meh*! Of course I know what that is," he said, still mispronouncing it as he slapped his wheel in a moment of flashing clarity. "You mean a Vietnamese hoagie. Love those damn sandwiches."

"But have you been inside *this* shop?" she asked, thumbing the shop behind her.

"Nah, that spot has been empty for years," he said. "I used to go back in the day when it first came out here. But there's better stuff now."

"Take me to your favorite spot for Viet hoagies, then."

He nodded in acknowledgment. Once Bingo was back inside, her luggage taking up most of the seat space, he swerved the cab in a figure-eight motion quickly, knocking Bingo back into her seat. A car honked at them, and a few curse words flew through the air. "I know the perfect spot. It's on the outskirts of town," he said. "Everyone loves this spot. Uppity Ivy kids, broke college kids, old folks, working-class people. I've taken more than a few drunk and sober souls there—either at the crack of dawn, late at night, or for a lunchtime meeting."

Dread. That feeling that Bingo was feeling was dread. She could almost feel time pressed against her neck like a knife, reminding her that not only was she up against the clock, but she was up against her three brilliant sisters and her overly confident brother. She *had* to turn her shop around first. She needed the money more than any of them.

Without putting on his blinker, he merged the car into the next lane and headed for the exit. "Say, how long are you in town for?" he asked. He jerked his head toward her pile of bags. "Seems like you're in it for the long haul."

"Just for a year," Bingo said firmly. "Hopefully less."

"You got stuff waiting for you back home? People and such? Maybe even little people? And little creatures?"

Without hesitation, Bingo nodded robotically and flashed a smile. She knew what the strange man wanted to hear. He wanted to hear that everything was fine in her life. That he wouldn't have to worry about another lonesome, childless, loveless woman passing through on a solo trip. "Yeah, I have a partner, kids, dog, white-picket fence. The whole American Dream. All back in Portland. So I can't stay too long, you know?" She could see the cabbie's shoulders relax, the tension he had held waiting for her answer dissipating into the ether. She would be nothing more than a blip in his life. Just like how she was in most people's lives.

"That's good. You're my last ride of the day. After I drop you off, I'm gonna go see my grandkids," he said, a smile etched on his face for the first time since Bingo got into his car. "We all need to feel needed. Otherwise, what's the point of living?"

Bingo didn't say anything. Exhaustion had finally snuck up on her. She leaned back and watched the unfamiliar city pass her by again, her makeshift home for the year. She let her little white lie envelop them, and she basked in the possibilities of who she could have been in another lifetime, where she really did have people waiting for her. What type of dog would she have? What would she have picked for a career? Would her family have been happier had her father never gotten as wealthy as he did? Would her mother have stayed?

But none of that mattered. She was in this universe. She didn't just want the inheritance money so it could fix her insolvency, but more so that it could make that white lie a reality one day. She'd be able to pay people to love her. Just like how her father got his second wife, Connie, to marry him for money. Maybe that money could find her some company and some friends, at least for a little bit.

She closed her eyes as the cabbie turned the radio volume higher, grateful for the ornate Desi music to be a buffer between them—between reality and her white lie.

....

"Hey lady, wake up, we're here."

Bingo woke up, groggy, wiping the dribble of drool from her mouth. As her eyes began to adjust themselves, disappointment ballooned as she saw what was outside the window: a ginormous line snaking and weaving down the block in South Philadelphia. Three months had passed since she had moved to Philadelphia, and this would be her tenth attempt at trying this sandwich spot. Without fail each time, it had been sold out by the time she reached the front of the line. She watched in awe as human after human, stacked one after the other, like upright dominos, formed an amorphous pattern that could only be discernible from atop a skyscraper. People from all different backgrounds across the sprawling city queued up, waiting to inch a little bit closer to the front of the line. Even from inside the cab, Bingo could smell the lemongrass and the star anise before she saw the smoke erupting from the backyard-rigged BBQ pit. At the sight of all the people waiting, Bingo felt defeated, wondering what it would be like if the smoke would just swallow her whole. Numerous conversations coated in heavy East Coast accents mingled with transplant accents floated all around her, reminding her that she was still a stranger, a transplant to this city that she had not yet cracked. What exacerbated her loneliness even more was realizing that she'd have to stand in line solo. Again. For the tenth time.

The day the cab driver had recommended this place to her seemed so long ago, as three months had seemingly felt like three long years in purgatory. She was awaiting a sentence and wasn't sure she even knew what outcome she wanted.

Her patience wore thin, and her frustrations turned inward. She blamed herself.

She'd made little to no progress on her own storefront. Maybe it would be better if she stopped trying, and just ran out the clock until one of her sisters made it first. Besides, Bingo was used to giving up early; it was something she learned from her mother, after all.

Did you know that Philadelphia has always been my favorite city?

Bingo gathered her bag from the back seat, thanked the driver, and stepped out of the cab to brave the juggernaut line. As soon as she attempted to cross the street, a biker whizzed past her, causing her to stumble backward. She yelped, throwing her bag straight up toward the sun. Her hands scrambled in front of her, frantic for anything to steady herself, and she grasped the side mirror of the parked car next to her at the last minute, coming close to falling an inch off the ground.

"Jesus!" Bingo cried out as she swung herself back up. All the zen she had accumulated in the cab ride over had disappeared faster than a breaking news cycle. Her anger was back in full force. Bingo wasn't just her usual mad; she had reached category four levels. "You could have killed me! Go back to your mother's basement if you can't afford a goddamn car!"

A cold, awkward silence fell on the crowd. Conversations halted in midair. Even the smoke billowing from the BBQ pit looked like it had frozen in time. Everyone stared at Bingo, unsure if they should help the forlorn woman with an untamed pixie haircut and a nose piercing, standing in the middle of the street, yelling like an old man on a lawn.

The biker braked hard toward the front of the line and hopped off. A woman. She moved her bike off to the side, turned around, and began walking toward Bingo slowly. She removed her helmet. The moment their eyes locked, Bingo couldn't feel her rage or her toes anymore. All she felt was curiosity and intense attraction. The biker had bundled-up black hair that was sticky with sweat, thick arched brows, and flushed, red cheeks.

Bingo didn't have to guess her ethnicity. The woman had the same Vietnamese features as her, but they were much softer than Bingo's. It was a softness that felt like familial comfort, almost like laying your head on a cold pillow after a long day.

"I'm so sorry," the woman said with sincerity. She bent down and helped gather all of Bingo's items, which had spilled out of her bag. "Sometimes I push myself to go faster and faster, until I can't think of anything else. Do you ever get passionate over anything like that?"

Bingo was mesmerized by her bright voice, the type that could call cartoon birds to land gently on her fingertips. Was Bingo losing it? She snapped herself out of her reverie before her infatuation could balloon. She knew better than to pursue a woman like her. Rejection from cool Asian women with sleeve tattoos who rode bikes was worse than rejection from straight white men. Not that she would even know what it'd be like to be rejected by a guy. She'd never even kissed one. Rejection just stung more when the call came from inside the house, and Bingo had too many scars from the queer dating scene in Portland, from aloof women who didn't know what they wanted. She could feel her walls coming back up, telling her to hold steady.

"No, I don't have any passions," Bingo snapped. "I don't have time, or money, or resources. We're living in late-stage capitalism, don't be so insensitive." She wouldn't allow herself to become distracted by a pretty woman. That would have been too quotidian of her. She was there for the money. Nothing else. "However, *your* passion almost killed me back there."

The woman threw her a look. "I heard some sharp insults spew out of you that could have skewered me. Words hurt, too, you know."

Bingo raised a brow back. "So *do* you live in your mother's basement . . . ?"

The woman laughed, and Bingo tried to ignore how her laughter sounded like wind chimes, and how refreshing it was, like a cold glass of anything on a porch swing. "Let's start over. I'm Iris," the woman said, winking at Bingo and extending a hand. "Let me make it up to you. Lunch? On me?"

"Sure," Bingo responded. She took her hand, unsure what she was agreeing to. "If you want to wait hours in line to make it up to me."

"Don't worry, the wait time is only ten minutes for you." She winked. She gestured for Bingo to follow her up to the front. "I own this place. You just have to watch me make lunch."

"You . . . own this place?" Bingo asked, both impressed and aghast. Iris was now her mortal enemy, and yet, it turned her on.

"Don't let the gleam of it all blind you," Iris said as she waved her hand toward the crowd. "I'm still poor, haven't broken even yet. Maybe, one day, I'll break even. Maybe, I'll even be able to open my own storefront one day."

Bingo swallowed. She knew she was in trouble. It was the age-old question that no saint, poet, or philosopher ever had the answer to. Money or love? Which did she need more to survive? But most of all, what would bring her the most happiness? It was an endless wild-goose chase to get both. Aside from their horrid tempers, being a fool in love might be the second thing her father and she had in common.

"Philadelphia really is the best city in America," she whispered under her breath as she resigned herself to her fate and followed the stunning Vietnamese woman inside.

CHAPTER 10

Paulina

The moment Paulina stepped off the tarmac at San Jose International Airport, she heard a deluge of complaints in Vietnamese coming from all directions, set against the backdrop of billboards advertising cloud storage spaces from tech start-ups. Vietnamese folks complaining about food, traffic, lines, anything and everything. The noise made her homesick in a weird way, despite swapping one diasporic city for another. It was the same, yet different.

Paulina, I wish I had fought for your mother more. I'm hoping you'll find that fighting spirit for the both of us in San Jose.

Unlike her sisters, Duc's words to her didn't have as much of a chokehold on her; her father in general had little to no effect on her. Paulina had always been good at compartmentalizing. Trauma in one box, family in another locked box, and pleasure in the other box. She didn't need the money as much as she knew her sisters did, but Paulina had always been competitive, and she would not sit out her father's inheritance game.

Paulina went straight to her assigned Duc's Sandwiches shop and immediately began strategizing. She had the self-awareness to know she didn't have any hard skills and she also didn't enjoy labor of any kind—manual or mental. The only skill she had was knowing how to wield her beauty. She had her mother to thank for passing on this type of ethereal beauty. Had she been born back in the Middle Ages, she would have been burned at the stake for the spell she put over men.

Out of the five Trần children, Paulina was the most like their mother, Evelyn—both physically and in mannerisms. Everyone knew it. Especially Duc. Which was why she suspected he sent her to San Jose—because it was rumored to be the place that kick-started the end of Evelyn and Duc's marriage. It was ironic because the Bay Area was also where her ex ended up. Did her father know that? Perhaps he sent her here to punish her for siding with their mother.

Paulina was in and out of her store quickly, no more than five minutes.

She popped her head in, gave a quick look around, realized what she had to do, saw one or two customers lingering, and two workers asleep behind the counter. She walked up to them, introduced herself, and immediately fired them. One woman began to cry and protest, but Paulina said it wasn't personal, it was business. She walked right out of the store and headed to her hotel.

She had never been to San Jose before, San Francisco plenty of times, but rarely did she have any reason to be in the South Bay. Most of her clients worked in tech, which brought her out to the West Coast occasionally. But she preferred her clients to fly to her, wherever she was in the world—whether it was Toronto one day, Montréal the next, or Santa Fe for a weekend. But despite their shortcomings, she knew that the tech guys were her secret weapon. Because if there was one thing she knew she needed to do, it was to upgrade the outdated sandwich shop to match modern society.

Paulina went into the hotel lobby's bathroom, locked a stall, tossed her bags open, and changed immediately from a day to night outfit—a slinky dress with a high slit, paired with a tweed blazer tossed casually over her shoulders. She knew how to hide all the best parts of her, and how to save the reveal until she was able to seal the deal. She quickly brushed her teeth, tousled her hair, spritzed her signature perfume, and reapplied her lip liner at the sink. Her reflection stared back at her: twenty-eight years old, high cheekbones, a cavernous collarbone, and yet none the wiser. Behind her, women of all ages, shapes, and colors came and went in a rush. Some, teeming with envy, gave her the once-over, many ignored her, and a small group admired her beauty. Paulina continued standing still, staring at herself in the mirror, wondering if she should just walk away from it all and disappear. Only one thing—one person—was stopping her from buying a one-way ticket out of the city. Before she made any drastic decisions, she wanted to go and see him first. So, she got back inside her rental car and headed straight into the city.

....

Either Oliver was early, or she was late. She was hoping for the former. But the truth was always the latter. Because by the time Paulina crossed the invisible border into San Francisco from South Bay, she knew she was *very* late. It was the kind of late that could only come with someone so beautiful that things like other people's time were merely suggestions. Paulina wended through the hills until she found herself in the center of the city, in the gentrifying hub of the Mission District. The clock on the dashboard taunted her, chastising her for being late. Her usual cryptic demeanor faltered as she remembered who was waiting for her at the end of the winding road. Would he be irritated at her tardiness? No, he wouldn't. He'd find it charming, like he always did. Though they hadn't spoken to each other in almost three years, the thought of going another year without speaking made her skittish. She zoomed past taquerias wedged between modern new American restaurants and coffee shops crammed with tech workers working late into the night, hoping to discover the next American gold rush.

She swore she wouldn't crack first and come to this city to seek him out or run back into his arms. At least not until one of them changed. She knew it was futile, neither would change for the other. Her father never changed when her mother asked, and her mother hadn't changed when her father asked. It was already coded in her genetic makeup to never change for anyone. But unlike her siblings, she didn't blame her parents for making her this way. She thanked them.

Paulina parked illegally, blocking a row of white electric cars. Despite the valet yelling at her, she opened the car door, extended a long leg, and stepped out into the cold, making yet another grand entrance on an ordinary Tuesday night. The valet was instantly silenced and even began apologizing to her. The infamous rolling fogs of San Francisco crept up her bare legs, causing a shiver to run down her spine. The summers here were brittle and cold, the polar opposite of Houston summers, and she felt sorry for the city and what they were missing out on: long nights smoking brisket, rubbed with five-spice and fish sauce, with her old friends, pretending to cheer on the Texans while convincing themselves that they'd make the Super Bowl this year; and nights so warm, you could sit outside on a lawn chair in a bikini, reading a great book, accompanied by the hum of the cicadas. She was surprised she was so homesick, but she always overly romanticized the idea of home whenever she traveled and knew it wasn't rooted in reality. Just like how she romanticized Oliver.

Her long legs carried her up the tiled steps; men in hoodies with unremarkable tech logos parted for her like the Red Sea. No matter how hard they tried to get her to make eye contact, she only had tunnel vision for the man whose back was turned to her, who sat by himself at the bar. His silhouette grew bigger as she came closer to him, and her heart began beating faster. Paulina had seen it all. She'd traveled far and wide, dined at the finest restaurants, partied in caves, survived alcohol poisoning and an overdose at a 72-hour club in Berlin, but nothing could come close to the thrill of smelling his cologne on her pillow.

New money plagued the city, but this wasn't new. It plagued every city she ever lived in. It was an airborne disease. From Toronto to London to Atlanta, she had seen cities succumb to the same style, catering to only the rich and unattainable.

Rich and unattainable. That summed up Oliver perfectly. Even from behind he was still the handsomest man in the room. He was also the only man left in San Francisco casually wearing a suit on a Tuesday night while everyone else donned white sneakers and Patagonia vests.

"Fuck," she whispered under her breath, and felt a momentary loss of confidence. She was terrified for him to turn around and see that she hadn't changed at all. That she was still the same Paulina Trần who walked away when he had asked her to stay. That she was still the same Paulina Trần when it was her turn to ask him to stay, and he had walked away. The cycle was vicious and toxic between the two of them, and neither could escape the vortex.

"Chen?" she said as she tapped Oliver's shoulder lightly. He slowly turned around, his scotch glass hanging between the rim of his index and middle finger. His hair was slicked back, curled quietly, like a whisper.

"Oliver *freakin'* Chen," she said again with more authority, this time with a smile. His dark brown eyes flashed at her, as if he was acknowledging all their dirty little secrets. There was at least a decade's worth of a dance between them, and yet they still couldn't figure out who was leading. "Still the same pretentious snob as always. I take it that's a heavy pour of Lagavulin in that glass you're holding?"

"Pauly," he responded with a laugh, and raised his glass toward her. Even after all these years, his laugh still made her nervous. "Still the same asshole as always. I take it you broke a few hearts getting here? I estimate it's only twenty feet from the parking lot to here, so you must have broken at least four."

"I heard a few shatter when I walked into the bar."

"Ah, those poor souls. I should have sent a public service warning the minute I knew you were in town," he said, winking at her. His voice was full of jest, but it was a bit more off than normal, more serious, and Paulina could tell things weren't the same between them. "I'm surprised you didn't hear my own heart break from three thousand miles away. All those unreturned calls and texts, and now you're suddenly alive and well in front of me."

The tips of Paulina's ears turned red and she ignored his last comment. "May I sit?" She gestured to the velvet barstool next to him.

"Even if I said no, would that stop you?"

Paulina rolled her eyes, shrugged off her tweed coat, and unveiled her slinky dress, which clung to her in all the coquettish ways. This was her pulling the curtain back before the show began. She knew how to create a moment between them. She waited for Oliver to compliment her, to look at her with hunger in his eyes like he had done three years before, and every year before that when they would meet up once a month anywhere around the world. She waited and waited. But he didn't even turn to look at her. Instead, an awkward lull hovered over them, his eyes still forward, as if he was too busy studying all the alcohol bottles that lined the bottom shelf. Surprised, Paulina tugged her dress down, cleared her throat, and sat next to him. She flagged the bartender and said she'd have the same as Oliver.

"You hate whiskey," he said, still not making eye contact. "Why do you do things you hate?"

"You know I always drink whiskey when I'm around you. I like copying you," she teased, her voice dropping into a kittenish tone. Her two fingers slowly danced across the bar until they came to rest on his elbow. She flicked her heavy lashes up toward him and pouted.

He rolled his eyes, immune to her advances, and brought his whiskey to his lips. "So, how can I help you, Pauly? Why did you ask me to meet you here?"

This wasn't the tone of voice she was used to. Especially not from him. "Is everything okay?" she asked, her voice resuming her normal tenor. Slightly defensive, she pretended to also focus on the alcohol shelves in front of her. "Did I catch you at a bad time? I thought everything was good between us. I mean . . . not good *good* but not bad *bad*."

He shrugged. "Look, I have to be home before midnight tonight. How can I help you?"

"Oh, I didn't realize you had other plans tonight," she said, trying to mask her disappointment. "Who's waiting at home for you?"

"Do you really want to know?"

Her voice caught in her throat. There was no way Oliver had a girl-friend, did he? Impossible. A *wife*? Even more impossible. He was more of a commitment-phobe than she was. But it'd been three years that had passed between them. A mountain of unresponded-to messages lay between them. Cities could have fallen and resurrected during that time.

"No," she said, resigned. "I don't."

"Okay, so, how can I help you?"

Oliver used the same voice with her that he used to speak to his clients over the phone. It was professional yet polite, curt yet attentive. He had a gentle way with words, careful to never judge anyone's ideas, but one word from him could end dreams. Paulina tried to not let her disappointment show again, but her mind began to spiral.

"I need a favor," she said slowly as the bartender placed a glass in front of her. She dipped a finger in, lightly skimming the top, and brought it to her lips to taste, her face curling from disgust. She wanted to spit it out. Oliver was right; she did hate whiskey.

"You need me to hide a dead body?" he asked, raising one brow. He actually looked serious, which only made Paulina want him more.

"That might be easier than what I'm about to ask," she teased. "I need you to help me bring an outdated sandwich shop down in San Jose into the twenty-first century. I need the whole shebang: mobile delivery app, fast checkout, maybe throw in a few robots to make the sandwiches. People here love those gimmicks. Isn't there a robot that serves you coffee some-where downtown? Yeah, I'm going to need a whole crew of those."

Oliver released a chortle, then a guffaw, and then he laughed uproari-ously. When he saw how serious Paulina looked, intrigue settled in. "A *sand-wich* shop? Why? You, Paulina Trần, transitioning to the food industry? Actually, *any* industry that has a paper trail?"

"Do you really want to know the reason why?" she asked huffily. "It's a long story anyway. Do you even care?"

He sipped from his glass quietly. "No."

"Okay then."

After a long pause, he shifted his head and finally met her eyes. The eye contact was brutal. She remembered explicitly telling him never to look her in the eyes during sex, all those years ago—she had lied and said it was the number one rule with her. But the truth was she just didn't want to look into *his* eyes.

"How long are you here for, Pauly?"

"A year, I think. Hopefully less, depending on things."

"Well, okay then," he said, tilting the rest of the Lagavulin into his mouth until it was all gone, every last drop accounted for. "Whatever you need, you know I'm here for you."

A small smile escaped her lips. He still cared *enough*. There was hope, albeit the tiniest sliver of it. It was a small win, and contrary to what her siblings thought of her and her lifestyle, Paulina hadn't had a small win in a very long time, and it meant more to her than the money.

His phone lit up, vibrating on the counter, and she caught a glimpse of a name. *Esther*. There's an Esther in his life now. Esther sounded hot. Maybe even Korean. A hot Korean woman was the stuff of nightmares for her. "I have to get going," Oliver said suddenly, eyeing his phone screen and quickly shutting it off before she could read what the message said. "Text me where to meet you tomorrow and we'll figure out your weird sandwich robots. *Annnnd* I can't believe I just said that out loud."

With that, he quickly got up and straightened out the creases in his pants. She could sense a hesitation, ever so slight, as he hovered. He always kissed her on the forehead before leaving, but they hadn't been intimate since . . . well since three years ago. Instead, he roughly patted her back, his hand brushing against her bare skin, and then just like that he was gone.

She could still feel the reverberations of the phantom touch of his hand. It felt so good, addicting even. Paulina didn't know what to feel. The money was important to her, sure, but she didn't need it. Though she had only begun the fight to win the inheritance money, she had an uncomfortable feeling that her year in the Bay Area would soon become a different kind of fight.

CHAPTER 11

Georgia

Georgia always had a strong sense of smell; it was how she knew her mother was no longer in her life. May rose, jasmine, and bourbon vanilla—she imagined her mother's scent leaving a trail across zip codes, states, rivers, highways, coastal cities, swamps, deserts, hell, maybe even just down the street, because who knew where Evelyn had gone? Later, Georgia discovered empty bottles of Chanel No. 5 hidden behind the second fridge in the garage, where her father kept most of her mother's belongings. He couldn't even bring himself to throw out the trash; he preserved it all, but kept it away from the energy of the main home. Even at the tender age of seven, Georgia felt sorry for her father, who was trapped in a museum of her mother's belongings, while Georgia moved on. She knew her mother was never coming back to claim her belongings . . . or her family.

To my youngest, may you travel the farthest out of all of us. But before you do, I hope you find a bit of yourself, somewhere along the bayou. Just like how I did, when I was your age.

Unlike her siblings, Georgia clung to her father's letter. The letter, which really only had a few scribbled, incoherent sentences, was more important than anything else he had ever said to her in her entire life. She had folded the letter carefully, tucked it away in her wallet, between a loyalty rewards card for a coffee chain and a faded photo of her mother. On the long drive from Houston to New Orleans, a seemingly easy drive along the 10E, whenever Georgia pulled over for food or gas, she carefully took out the letter, seeking scraps, new clues, or hidden meanings, wondering if her father was trying to tell her something coded.

But Georgia's yellow van was on its last legs. What should have been only a six-hour drive took almost a full day. The radiator had cracked, the engine had overheated, and that wasn't even the worst part—she had accidentally killed a spider, which made her pull off the road in Lafayette. She cradled its shriveled body, tears dropped over its curled legs, forming a small puddle in the cup of her hand. She decided that a proper burial was

needed along with a eulogy. After scouring the area, she found a serene
spot under an old willow oak tree, and recited a translated poem by the
poet Du Tử Lê. *When I'm dead, please bring me to the sea.*

The rest of Georgia's drive came full circle as she caught the sunrise
driving toward New Orleans East. Exhaustion circled her, and she bor-
dered on delirium. But she powered through, hoping that once she found
the store, she'd finally be able to rest. She prayed that there was a couch in
the office, or at least two chairs she could turn into a faux couch. Though
she followed her father's handwritten instructions carefully, it was still
hard to parse, and she was unsure why the store couldn't be found on
Google Maps. Duc was notoriously horrible with technology, but surely he
wasn't so bad that not even satellites in space and the world's largest search
engine couldn't find the store's location.

As she rolled through the eastern edge of the city, toward Village de
L'Est, a small yet sprawling suburban area where the roads were wide and
the houses were so far apart, one had to jog to get to their neighbor's, the
van engine began emitting black smoke, clouding the windshield. Through
the gaps, she saw two elderly Vietnamese men leisurely kayaking along a
small body of water, cigarettes dangling loosely from their mouths. Curiosity grabbed her attention, and she diverted away from the instructions,
turned the car around, and slowly began following the kayak until she saw
a horde of Vietnamese people arguing with one another. The men docked,
and just as the sun fully rose, the crowd began circling around people on
the ground, sitting on plastic crates, selling fruits and vegetables laid out on
blankets. That's when it hit Georgia: This was a local Vietnamese farmers'
market.

She pulled the van over and got out of the car to stretch her legs. She
was suddenly craving fruit for breakfast, and she trusted outdoor markets
to have the best fruit in the city. She tucked her messy hair into a low bun,
put on a cap and sunglasses, and headed toward the market, her stomach
rumbling. The sun had now come up, its rays bouncing off the asphalt,
and she walked past rows and rows of men and women squatting, haggling,
gossiping, rolling metal carts, laughing, and Georgia wished with all her
might she spoke better Vietnamese so she could eavesdrop. It was her one
weakness. After her mother left them, Duc didn't speak much to her anyway, and her siblings all spoke to her in English—she never had a chance to

be around the language at all. It was strange to be comforted by familiar phonetic sounds, but not know what any of it meant.

Cutting through the thick noise of chatter, a familiar scent caught her nose, ascending above the smell of sweet melons and fresh basil. Georgia stopped dead in her tracks. Her sense of smell was the fastest out of her five senses and she slowly turned, hoping she was wrong. Because it was the type of smell that didn't belong in a farmers' market; in fact, it didn't belong in her life anymore. But there it was: May rose, jasmine, and a hint of bourbon vanilla.

Georgia searched the crowd, her nose picking up an invisible trail, and her eyes landed on an older Vietnamese woman, with a plastic visor on her head blocking out the sun, squatting next to a cooler. She was trying to attract customers, shouting randomly out into the crowd, hoping her sales pitch would work. "Năm đô la! Chả lụa ngon nhất New Orleans!" the woman cried out. Just like how elusive understanding Vietnamese was, it was strange to smell something so familiar, and to be comforted by it, but not know what it meant.

But Georgia didn't need a translator for this. She had known who it was before she turned around.

"Mom?" Georgia asked so softly that only she could hear. She instantly recognized the seller, matching them up to the old photo she had carried in her wallet for nearly a decade. Despite some obvious differences that came with age, the woman looked healthy, her eyebrows bushy, her hair thick, her jaw sharp, her nose long, her face heart-shaped, her eyes round and large, and the signature look that every woman in the family had: a face littered with birthmarks, forming the familiar pattern of Cassiopeia's constellation that only the Trần women could see, even under the cloudiest of night skies.

The woman kept shouting for prospective buyers to come over, flagging anyone down. She didn't notice Georgia, who was now headed fast in her direction, feet heavy and heart thumping.

"Mom?" Georgia said again.

No answer. The woman kept ignoring Georgia.

"Má?" Georgia said again, louder, trying her luck in Vietnamese. Was she wrong? Had the delirium set in? She must have seemed like a lunatic.

The woman looked up, confused. Georgia quickly removed her sunglasses.

"Evelyn?" Georgia asked again, for the final time.

The woman froze and studied Georgia's face. She took in Georgia's long nose, the moles that scattered across her face, and her big, flappy ears—they were the type of comically large ears that could only have been genetically inherited from one man.

"Now that's a name I haven't been called in a very long time. Má," the woman finally said as she leaned back, tilting her visor up to reveal her full face. "Mother."

Now it was Georgia's turn to freeze up. "Was that a *Star Trek* reference?" she whispered, instantly regretting her first choice of words to her mother after two decades.

Evelyn raised an eyebrow. It was frightening, staring into her eyes, which seemed distant, aloof, but as Georgia looked longer, she spotted a touch of mirth.

"It's from *Star Wars*. But nice try."

"I've never seen a single *Star Wars*," Georgia responded, still in disbelief she was even having this conversation with her mother.

"Well looks like your father didn't do a great job, did he," Evelyn said, aghast. "Speaking of, how'd you find me? Did the old nut finally pin my location?"

Georgia went on autopilot as she reached into her wallet and handed her mother Duc's letter. Evelyn's eyes danced and darted across her husband's words. The changes in her expression were subtle but significant in their meaning. Georgia now wished she could not only speak Vietnamese but also interpret her mother's expressions.

"Looks like your father finally found me, didn't he?" Evelyn chuckled bitterly, handing the letter back to Georgia, without addressing Duc's inheritance game. "So, have you eaten yet? That's something I'm supposed to say, right?"

"No, I just got in—" Georgia began.

Evelyn stood up, wiped her hands on her apron, and took it off. "Great, let's go eat."

"At the sandwich shop?"

Evelyn released another howl as she began packing up her stall. "That old dump? No, I mean let's get some real food."

"Isn't that real food . . . ?"

"Just follow me." Evelyn began wheeling the cooler of pork rolls wrapped in banana leaves behind her, stomping toward the parking lot. Without protest, Georgia began following her estranged mother.

"Don't you dare breathe a word of this to your father," Evelyn said, her voice carrying the thinnest of a threat, thinner than graphene, invisible to the human eye, but despite not ever having had an adult conversation with her mother, Georgia could tell when to keep her mother's secrets.

Georgia just nodded her head, wondering if she was agreeing merely for the sake of it because she was too afraid to not smell her mother's scent again.

....

Three months later, Georgia still felt like she was living in a fever dream.

Strolling through the Quarter in the middle of the day, Georgia didn't know what to do with her hands. Logically, she knew her hands were attached to her body and that her motor cortex was giving her directions on where to direct them, but they felt like foreign objects, heavier than usual, and a burden.

Around her, every tourist seemed to know what to do with their hands. They elbowed their way through swaths of sweaty bodies, grubbily petting the horses that were pulling carriages, which went by every five minutes down the main strip; or they shoved their fingers in the air, pointing at every building, hands coated in sugar and grease from the deep-fried beignets brown bag they'd been carrying around all day. They were so entitled with their hands it made Georgia claustrophobic. She'd always preferred to travel off the beaten path, so being in a high-traffic area almost made her wish her van hadn't made it to New Orleans. But then she'd never have stumbled upon her mother.

It'd been strange, ever since the universe brought her and her mother together three months ago. Per her mother's request, she hadn't said a word to any of her siblings or her father. Yet. They were still strangers to each other, and Georgia couldn't bring herself to address Evelyn as Má. Can a mother still be a mother without the formal nomenclature? So, Georgia awkwardly addressed her as Evelyn each time they met up and hoped for the best.

Evelyn Lê looked very different from the old film photos Georgia would go through in secret as a child. After studying her face for the last three months, Georgia decided the Evelyn in front of her was a much better version than the old stories and photos that framed her. She was warm, sharp, and most importantly . . . happy.

Her mother was so petite in stature next to her, clocking in at barely 4'11", and yet she exuded such a carefree attitude, Georgia felt guilty for interrupting her side of the universe.

Everyone had always said that Evelyn was hard to predict; one moment she was calm and the next she turned into an umbra, instantly becoming the darkness in sunspots. But nothing seemed to be further from the truth. Which is why, despite the niceties and pleasantries between the two of them, Georgia still couldn't solve the mystery.

Why had her mother left in the first place?

Unlike her youngest daughter, Evelyn didn't seem to mind the throng of tourists. Despite most people not noticing the petite Vietnamese woman bulldozing her way through the crowd, she somehow made her presence known. Her confidence and long strides made her appear bigger. Men, double her height and size, even stepped aside for her instead of her having to step aside first. Evelyn seemed unbothered, as if it was just another ordinary Wednesday morning, walking alongside her youngest daughter, whom she hadn't seen since she was a child, on their way to get tea.

Evelyn speed-walked through, not saying much, and Georgia scurried next to her, trying to keep pace. Neither mother nor daughter said a word to each other. Today, Georgia felt like she'd been walking through Hades this entire time, with no end in sight, when in reality it had only been less than fifteen minutes.

Evelyn turned a sharp corner and headed down an old, dark alleyway with sparse stalls throughout. The shop was hidden from the main strip, with not much signage, and there didn't seem to be a lot of foot traffic based on how eerily quiet it was. Evelyn stopped so abruptly in front of a stall that Georgia ran smack into her, almost knocking her over, but Evelyn held her ground. Though Georgia towered over her mother by five inches, that height difference made no impact. Evelyn was weirdly very sturdy.

"We're here!" Evelyn exclaimed, waving her arms in a flourish. Georgia looked up to see a nameless, shabby teahouse. Stacks of loose-leaf teas in old glass jars were randomly piled on top of one another, in no particular order, and there were no labels on any of them. The shop was so small there were no customers allowed inside. Outside, old men were playing games of Go, sitting on red plastic stools, with the board precariously on top of another little red plastic stool between them. White and black stones were separated out in rusty Cafe Du Monde coffee tins.

"Sit, sit, sit." Evelyn motioned for Georgia to grab a plastic stool from the stack and prop it next to the building. She ducked her head inside the shop and ordered for them in Vietnamese. She then perched herself on a stool next to Georgia, whipped out a foldable fan, and began to wave it in front of her face, despite the cool weather.

"What did you get?" Georgia asked shyly.

"You didn't understand?" Evelyn responded, surprised. "I just ordered trà chanh and some finger food."

When Georgia's face still remained blank, Evelyn put down her fan. "You don't speak Vietnamese, do you? Not even a little bit?"

Something in Georgia snapped, and she could feel her left eye twitching. Just as the owner of the shop came out holding two iced teas with limes in them, Georgia could feel the tears coming. The pain was overwhelming, to sit next to a strange woman who shared the same bloodline as her, but nothing made sense.

"What the hell am I doing here? What the hell are *you* doing here!" Georgia yelled suddenly, startling the old men next to them, their Go board toppling over. A sea of black and white stones littered the alleyway, the pitter-patter of the stones hitting the gravel like rain hitting a metal roof. Curse words were thrown at the mother and daughter duo as everyone jumped to their feet to pick up the stones. When Georgia stooped down to her knees to help pick up the tiny stones, she began to cry, and the stones weighed like bricks in her hands.

"Why don't you think for a goddamn second as to why I can't speak a lick of Vietnamese? You left. *You left.* I was a *child.* Who the hell was going to teach me Vietnamese? Duc? Jude? Jane? Paulina? Fucking Bingo? They all crumbled after you left. I had no one. *No one.*"

But Georgia couldn't stop yelling. She got to her feet, and didn't wait for Evelyn to respond to anything she had said. She threw the stones at the wall, creating a firework of white and black. The old men threw their hands up in the air and cursed even more as stones randomly knocked over drinks or pelted into them.

"You sit there calmly, acting as if it's just a friend in town visiting you, for the past three months, and don't address anything? I'm your daughter! Your *youngest* daughter! You haven't told me anything, you just take me all over this city like you're some paid tour guide. You haven't asked me a single question about myself or the rest of us," Georgia screamed, facing her this time. "Don't you care at all? Aren't you even curious why I'm here?"

Evelyn waited for a gap between Georgia's outbursts, turned to the old men, apologized profusely for the trouble, and stared straight into her youngest daughter's eyes.

"Let me ask you something, con," she said, her voice no longer light-hearted and confident. "Would you rather have a dead mother or a living one who feels dead? Tell me what would make you happier, and I'll do it. You want to learn Vietnamese? Translate this: Ngày nào tao cũng muốn chết." With that, Evelyn turned on her heel and walked out of the alleyway toward the main street, leaving Georgia surrounded by a circle of all black Go stones. Though it looked like she had built her surrounding territory, why did it feel like she had lost everything?

CHAPTER 12

1980, Seadrift, Texas

The journey to Seadrift was unceremonious.

The deeper Duc and Huey went into Texas, heading straight down toward the Gulf, the less anyone cared. A few stares here and there, but everyone else around them was too focused on their own survival to see the two lone Vietnamese men who suddenly appeared. Huey and Duc could each feel the other's sense of relief. Perhaps the rumors and stories weren't as bad as they had heard. Perhaps tensions were easing up after the two Vietnamese brothers had been acquitted of murder of the white fisherman, Billy Aplin, last year, on the grounds of self-defense.

Perhaps, perhaps, perhaps.

As soon as they entered the small coastal town of Seadrift, they followed signs until they found a shabby motel with a crooked logo and a burst pipe spewing sewage onto the main parking lot and bleeding into a nearby forest. Duc pulled up into it. They both crinkled their noses at the foul smell. But after all they'd been through, the conditions were still livable.

"I'll call my cousin once we've settled in for a bit," Duc said. "He'll let us know when to show up for work."

In the lobby, a fluorescent pendant crackling above them, Duc and Huey walked up to a middle-aged woman behind the wooden desk. Her hair hung loose in a low bun, and she had not one speck of makeup on her. She'd been chewing on the same piece of gum since 10:00 a.m.; it looked so hardened, it was as if she were chewing on caulk. Yet, somehow, she kept chewing, mauling and grinding away at the piece as if she had nothing better to do.

Duc opened his mouth, and before he could even get a word out, she dismissed him. "No vacancy."

Huey glanced around, staring at the empty lobby, which looked like it hadn't seen another human beside the receptionist in months. The room keys, hanging behind her, had gathered dust.

"Ma'am, there seems to be a lot of rooms," Huey said, careful to hide his accent. "We're just going to be here for a few days while we find permanent housing."

"Do you not speak English?" she snapped, gnashing away at the hard gum even faster. "I said NO VACANCY. Understand? Comprende, amigo?"

Huey turned to Duc, lowered his voice, and switched to Vietnamese. "Let's find another place. I don't want to cause any trouble. We just got here."

"You don't think this woman isn't going to call up every motel in town and tell them not to give us a room?" Duc whispered back angrily. "She's going to drive us out. Have a backbone. You dream of being a lawyer? Start acting like one. Pretend you have a suit on, and fight back. Do something."

"I'm *not* a lawyer. And why are you so damn insistent on fighting everyone?" Huey snapped, letting his voice accidentally get loud. The woman stopped chewing immediately, her mouth wide open, the white gum teetering on her tongue. Her eyes became larger after hearing the men speak in Vietnamese.

"The fuck you reading all the time for then?" Duc shot back, matching Huey's volume. "All you *do* is read all day! You could barely look up from your damn books to help me drive us here! I had to do all the heavy lifting. I *always* do everything for us."

Without realizing it, their volume had escalated higher and higher, unleashing pent-up anger and rage at each other. Ever since Duc and Huey had met on the *Lady Freedom* four years ago, they'd never once fought. Not through any of the hardships—the scams, over beers, cigarettes, sleeping in cars, or taking turns watching over each other sleeping at bus stops—had they ever once yelled. They were more than just brothers now; their roots to each other went deeper than the oldest tree in existence.

"What are you two saying in that filth language?" the receptionist interrupted. Though she whispered, her message was clear. Duc and Huey immediately stopped yelling long enough to see her left hand slowly make its way under the counter. Chills went through their heated bodies as each man blanched from the whiplash and PTSD of the war. Fear—fear is what they felt, running from American soldiers, North Vietnamese soldiers, South Vietnamese soldiers, from each other, away from the bombs, toward the helicopters, and now from this—fear of facing down another barrel of a gun and wondering if this was all life would be.

Their fears were confirmed when she pulled out a gun, aimed steady at them. "Y'all nothing but a bunch of ungrateful commies. Our sons die trying to save y'all over there and then you come *here* and go around killing *us*? You take our jobs, take our resources, take our land, and then you *kill* us? I said *no vacancy*, what part of that y'all don't understand? There are no rooms here, nothing for you in Seadrift. Your gook friends killed that fisherman, you understand?"

Duc raised both hands and tried to placate the woman, dialing up his charm, apologizing profusely for causing a disturbance. But it was too late. She bobbed the gun up and down, aimed so close at them that it would cause a bloodbath at such close range—tearing through every ligament, blood vessel, organ. Whoever she would decide to hit first, the blood would splatter on the survivor's face. Huey even calculated how far the blood splatter would etch on the ceiling, wondering if it was better to be shot from a distance rather than up close.

Huey stole a glance at Duc, saw him close his eyes, like it was agonizing to see another gun. He was tired of surviving, Huey knew that—they both were—and he could even hear his companion's thoughts: *So what? So what if today was our last day? I could use the sleep.*

Seeing Duc, carefree, resilient Duc, back down almost made Huey do the same. Yet a bolt of confidence surged through him, a sense that it was his duty to now stand firm.

"Ma'am, with all due respect, wasn't it in self-defense?" Huey said finally. "Those two Vietnamese brothers who killed that fisherman said it was in self-defense."

Duc's eyes shot open.

"The Vietnamese men were acquitted," Huey continued. "Don't put that on us. That man attacked first with a knife. A local jury decided that verdict."

"You think I give a shit what that jury thought? We don't abide by what some fancy court thinks. And I certainly don't give a shit what men in suits think," she said, a dead laugh escaping her. She spit out the rock-hard gum, aiming it right at the center of Duc's forehead. The gum slid down his face, leaving a snail mucus trail. She reached her right arm behind her, her left hand still aiming the gun at them, grabbed a room key, and tossed it at Huey's head. "Y'all want so badly to have a room here? Go on, then. Go upstairs."

Huey's hands were still above his head, but he slowly stooped down and picked up the room key, ironically relieved, despite having a gun still pointed at him. But his grasp of the English language still had plot holes in it, and he was unable to pick up on her sarcasm.

"Thank you," Huey said, his gratitude genuine.

"You are *most* certainly welcome. Go on then," she said, flicking her gun at them to move along, smiling. "Room 204. Have a restful sleep."

Just as Huey was about to thank the woman again, Duc interrupted him. "Drop the key," Duc said quietly in Vietnamese. "We won't survive the night. I heard they have the Klan patrolling the streets ever since the acquittal."

But Huey continued staring at the key in his hand, churning it over and over in his palm.

All this mayhem over simply trying to get a motel room for one night, he suspected it would only continue to get worse here. Duc had gotten it all wrong. Seadrift wasn't a safe haven for the Vietnamese, it had turned into a battleground since the acquittal of the two brothers, Nguyen Van Sau and Nguyen Van Chinh. In his short twenty-five years on this earth, Huey had already been at rock bottom more times than he could count. So what was one more time?

"Thank you again, ma'am," Huey said, finishing his original thought, ignoring Duc's continuous pleas to leave. "We won't cause any trouble and we'll be gone by the morning."

Huey turned to Duc and spoke to him in English. "Pay her. I'll go get our bags from the car."

The woman laughed at Duc's shocked face. "Looks like your friend is a gambling man with his life *and* with yours," she said.

Duc unfurled crumpled bills and put them gently on the counter.

"See you Chinks in the morning, or whatever you are," she said with a wink. "Thank you, come again," she said in a mocking Sino-accent as Duc and Huey both left for the car.

As soon as they were in the parking lot, Duc turned toward Huey and shoved him. Again and again and again, Huey's body hurled backward, until it hit the hot pavement. A sharp pain ran through his side, and instead of getting up, Huey lay there, sprawled out on the ground.

"Are you insane? We're not staying the night," Duc growled at him. "They're probably calling the Klan right now." From the ground, Duc towered over Huey, looking twenty feet tall. Both of the men's eyes darted over to the lobby window, as they watched the woman talk rapidly to someone over the phone. Their eyes met, and she pulled a curtain over the window, shutting them out.

"We'll take turns, keeping watch over each other, as we always have done," Huey reasoned. "You wanted this, anh. Remember this moment. *You* wanted to come here. *You* started this."

"I made a mistake, maybe my cousin was wrong. He said the work was good, he didn't go into a lot of detail, he just said that folks were scared, but he just glossed it over. I didn't realize a fucking war was happening here," Duc exclaimed, throwing his hands up in the air. "Am I not allowed to make a mistake? Let's just head back to California. Tonight."

Huey slowly sat up. The broken sewer pipe now spit out even more black and brown liquid. The smell more rotten than before. It poisoned his lungs. "Remember that day when we first met?"

"What about it?" Duc responded warily.

"You said one day, we're going to buy that boat. That shitty, rusty boat we were on. And become richer than that captain, and all those men on that boat."

Duc stared at Huey as if he had gone insane. "I think we have bigger problems than buying that damn boat right now. Can you please . . . just focus here?"

"Well, we haven't gotten anywhere the past four years," Huey said, still mulling over his thoughts out loud. "We're both fishermen. It's in our bloodlines. Our fathers were fishermen. Somewhere along the way, we stopped fishing with bait, and began fishing people's pockets. Shouldn't we finally start earning money in a clean way? Like how our fathers have done it? I'm done running, anh. I don't want to keep doing the same thing we've been doing the past four years. Let's just stay here, make our money the real way, and then leave."

A silence hung in the air between the two men. Duc looked around the parking lot, making sure no one was watching them, except, he noticed, the receptionist, who was now peeking out from behind the curtain again, the phone still pressed hard against her ear, her mouth moving a million miles an hour. Duc reached down and pulled Huey up from the ground, and gestured for him to get inside their car. Once inside, he slammed his fist against the glove compartment, revealing a Glock half hidden beneath old hamburger wrappers and paper maps. Huey didn't say anything. He didn't ask how Duc had gotten a gun, when he had gotten it, and why he had one. He didn't ask a single question.

"We may have been born as sons of fishermen, but we won't become bait," Duc said.

Huey didn't say anything. He just brushed off the trash and picked up the gun, surprised that he hadn't been hit with PTSD at the feel of it. Instead, the steel was cool in his palm, and he wasn't sure if he should be afraid of the gun, of Duc, or of where they were. But Huey wasn't a fool. He knew his options were limited in life and that they couldn't go back to being the men they once were.

So Duc and Huey looked at each other, both silently acknowledging that the only way to find their place in America was to live outside the margins and operate in the shadows.

CHAPTER 13

Evelyn

I did not recognize my youngest daughter's face.

Even though I should have recognized how the curves of Georgia's cheekbones are shadows of mine, or guessed from the way her widow's peak sticks out at exactly 3:00—an hour off from my own. Or from the way her big brown eyes appeared like crescent shapes when the sun hits them. You would think that any of these small vignettes would jolt me awake. They didn't. I should have felt guilt, shame, or something, that it took a few seconds for her face to sink in. But I'd been on my own for so long and had forgotten that there were five flesh-and-blood copycats of myself roaming the earth.

I hadn't felt guilt since the day I left Houston . . . the day I left them.

But now Georgia's heart-shaped face made my own heart want to bleed. All I could see was a younger version of myself, and it frightened me to my core. It frightened me so much, I wanted to run away from her, instead of running toward her. I knew someone would find me one day; I just didn't know it would be my youngest daughter. I assumed it would be Duc, with his pretty words, trying to placate me again, or Huey, trying to convince me to go along with the plan again. *The plan.* The ill-fated plan. Their soothing words that tried to convince me, for over thirty years, to go along with it—that it was the only way to protect me, to protect all of us. Thirty years of living the same lie.

I couldn't do it anymore.

And I didn't want to keep lying to Georgia's face, knowing I was responsible for her loneliness, her confusion, and having to force her to grow up without memories of us, unlike the other children. What was it like, to be the youngest daughter of an immigrant mother whose mind had gone feral before her body had? What was it like, to have so many questions, piled up like bodies in a car crash, buried, waiting and waiting for someone to come save you?

My mind had deteriorated so much in those final years living in Houston. I wouldn't have recognized Georgia's face even if I had stayed. I was stuck inside my body; my mind was sentient but not alert. Though I could see my hands, mobile, operational, reaching for the same toothbrush in the morning, eating off the same dinner plates, pressing the same Saran-wrapped remote control, I couldn't feel anything. Not a single emotion could jump-start me. I was comatose. Though I could feel the world around me, and every living organism that passed me by, I couldn't partici-pate in it. I didn't *want* to participate.

This is what it felt like to play pretend. I'd been pretending for so long, I had forgotten what was real. Including how to be a mother. This was what happened when you lived a lie for so long. The lie warps your reality.

In the final week I was in Houston, I could feel the resentment and grief building inside me. It was relentless. The universe must have known something was about to erupt inside of me, because it kept sending me hints. Even the atmosphere changed, despite how stilted Houston summers were. Everything I had eaten turned sour. It was so sour it hurt the inside of my cheeks, sending a tingling sensation all the way up the sides of my brain. I had to leave. The depression was caving in, and the light was disap-pearing.

Duc and Huey were nothing more than men who had robbed me of a life. Men somehow keep robbing me of the many lives I could have had. And I kept having to grieve. But when I overheard them speaking that day, nearly twenty years ago, on that ordinary yet cataclysmic Tuesday, I knew, for the sake of my children, I had to leave. I knew if I had chosen to forget what I heard that day, I'd have sent myself to an early grave.

A forgotten mother was better than a dead one.

I watched Duc and Huey circle around each other out on the lawn, talking loudly, not realizing I was above them on the balcony, within ear-shot. Duc's stupid Michelangelo replica statue towered over them.

I didn't mean to listen in. I just wanted some air. Neighbors sporting polo shirts sped around the bend in their fast cars. Their golf bags stuck out so pompously, a symbol of a class that was leagues out of our own de-spite how much cash we had hoarded around the house. Not all the cash in the world could have given me that type of safety: the type of safety that comes with being able to play golf leisurely on Tuesdays.

I heard Duc's booming voice, once again trying to convince Huey. For whatever reason, I kept listening, instead of ignoring them as I often did.

"Anh, just let it go," Duc said, his voice uncaring and aloof. The sound of his voice was grating. He had an ease about himself that was off-putting to the naked eye; it was his callous way of brushing things off with a joie de vivre that implied that your pain was a nuisance. "Your guilt is starting to show."

"People are starting to talk," Huey shot back, his nerves giving him away once again. He ran his hand through his greasy hair, the stress over the years impacting his hairline. "All the gossip is reaching the kids. They're starting to ask questions. People are starting to question our family dynamic, and Evelyn's mental state isn't the best, can't you see?"

Duc scoffed. "She'll be fine. Just buy her a new bag or some shoes. The kids will also be fine. Buy them some presents, too. The newest Walkman, Gameboy, or whatever the kids want these days. Hell, get a puppy for all I care."

A puppy. The kids would love that.

"That can't be the solution forever," Huey said anxiously, doing his best to push back against Goliath. "Sooner or later, she's going to find out the truth about what really happened."

What on earth were they so worried about? Gossip had been following us for years, from one neighborhood to the next, the more we upgraded ourselves in the small village that was Houston. I wanted to throw something off the balcony and hit the back of Duc's head, but I kept quiet.

"Today's his anniversary, you know, the day he died," Huey said, his words much softer than before. "Should we do something? Go to the temple and light incense for him? I was going to bring Evelyn there later."

I was struck momentarily by Huey's kindness and empathy toward me. Here he was, still willing to honor someone long after their death day. My heart melted for a second, being pulled back in by Huey's gravitational sphere. Was I so angry for nothing? Duc and Huey meant well; they always have, haven't they? In my depressive haze, the gaslighting I had done to myself didn't allow me to see a clear picture.

"Let the dead lay in peace, along with our past," Duc said, his voice getting angry, proving me wrong. He inhaled his cigarette, then spat out the smoke. "I told you that your guilt will kill you one day, and everyone else will be a casualty of our shrapnel."

Huey began to protest, and I lost sight of what he had said, barely making out the rest of their conversation, as another neighbor, whose sports car could be heard from miles away, zipped past us. The roar of the horse engine overpowering the men's voices. I could make out Duc cursing at the neighbor, calling him and his car tactless.

"But it's our fault, isn't it?" Huey asked, his voice clear again. "We killed him, didn't we? All those years ago?"

I froze.

For the first time in ages, I could feel something twitch inside me. I must have been mistaken. What did he just say? I went out as far as I could go on the balcony without being seen.

I've always had my suspicions, but like everyone else during that time, I kept quiet. Quiet was good. Quiet was survival.

"Stop saying that," Duc hissed. "We didn't kill him. It can't be traced back to us. It was his fault. Stick to the story: The man was attacked. He's a martyr. That's always been our story. Why change it now?"

Story? What was the real story, then? My heart began to sink even lower, along with my body, down to the floor, as my fingers turned white, gripping the metal railing.

"Anh, we can't keep lying," Huey said sadly, shaking his head. "We just can't."

"At what point do we tell Evelyn the truth?" I could hear Huey still protesting, but his resolve was becoming weaker.

"Are you stupid? Never. We *never* tell her the truth," Duc sniped back, lighting up another cigarette. "Look how far we've come. What she doesn't know won't hurt her. Look at how she's rotting away. You think telling the truth now about how he died will make her get better? Look at how happy the children are. Look where we ended up. You think telling her now will make a difference? Look at our riches, and remember what we have to protect."

Huey's protests died altogether, and the men changed topics, walking away from where I was hidden. I watched Duc blow another long, billowy plume of cigarette smoke from his mouth and walk toward his car,

Huey, a stray dog at his side, following loyally. They walked around in a crop circle pattern, hands behind their backs. Scheming. Always scheming.

I leaned back and watched the two men finally get into the car and drive off over the horizon, almost colliding with another rich neighbor's brand-new Porsche.

I grew past the point of anger. I just felt numb. Men. Men. Men. I suddenly began to see more clearly than I had the past decade. The loss of Vietnam, the loss of memories of *him*, the loss of a free life, without the lies. Will my children ever know the truth? Will Jude ever know? Where was the little girl I once was? She died the day he had died.

I drew the curtains closed, grabbed a suitcase, any suitcase that was close by, anything that could hold what meager possessions I had chosen at random, and I began to pack. I ignored my children's cries from their rooms, and prepared to leave this life behind.

But decades later, life had finally caught up to me. Here was Georgia, my youngest daughter, standing in front of me. A grown woman in her own right. And here I was, still lying to her. A brutal, endless cycle. Perhaps that is the ouroboros of life, the secrets mothers carry to protect their own, and the questions that children have.

I shouldn't have been surprised that Georgia would be the one to find me. It was always the youngest that is left in the dark. A dangerous and vulnerable position to be in a family. I would know. I am the youngest of four sisters, who were all left behind in Vietnam. I knew Georgia must have made up grand scenarios about me, believing that I'd be back one day, that I had simply "gotten lost," or perhaps I was just in a treatment facility. I knew she believed that I was doing everything I could to go back to her, even when every Christmas or Lunar New Year passed by without my presence. But even if I had stayed, and told her the truth, would she be willing to accept it? Would any of them? That I had to walk away from being a mother because I was afraid that if I didn't, it'd have killed me in the end?

What surprised me was that she called me "Má." Can you believe it? Even after everything that happened, she was still calling me her mother when she found me.

What gutted me was the hope that came into her eyes when she called me Má, as if I would call her con again.

So, I did what any mother would do. It was like remembering how to ride a bike again. Just because I had left didn't mean that motherhood had left me. I looked my youngest daughter in the eye and asked if she had eaten yet.

PART 2

KNEADING, AIRING
OF THE GRUDGES

CHAPTER 14

Connie

After months hiding away at the Four Seasons in Oahu, Connie decided she needed another mini vacation, somewhere quiet to decompress and figure out her next move.

Bali it was.

Not only was Connie able to wrangle information out of Mr. Ngô on Duc's whereabouts and pinpoint a general location, but she also had a plan. Her coward of a husband was supposedly hiding out in a Buddhist monastery high up in the northern regions of Vietnam. She couldn't tell if the old lawyer was lying to her or not, but he gave up Duc's location too easily, which made it even more suspicious. The two of them had always been more in a marriage than Connie and Duc had been, so why'd he spill so easily? He wouldn't tell her which monastery, though, and there were thousands of monasteries and temples scattered across Southeast Asia alone.

The mystery of why Duc was hiding out in a monastery made her veins boil. While she was out here, fending for her life, tracking down legal documents, Duc was *finding himself* at a *monastery*? She wanted to wrap her hands around his wrinkly, thick, rich neck, and watch the life drain from his eyes as he begged for forgiveness. If there was anything she loved more than a good shopping trip, it was hearing the words "I'm sorry." Especially when they came from a man.

But death would be too easy, especially for someone like Duc, who had more than nine lives. She needed to figure out if they were ever legally married and if Evelyn and Duc actually got legally divorced.

Once Connie descended into Bali, she headed straight to the Four Seasons resort in Sayan. Indonesia was close but not *too* close to Vietnam. But even across the ocean, she could smell his deception, and her paranoia was eating away at her. *Were they ever legally married?*

She immediately headed to the pool to scheme. She needed to get to Duc before any of his children got to him. If her lawyer was correct and there was a possibility Connie and Duc's marriage license had never been officially filed nor had Duc officially filed for divorce from Evelyn, she needed to talk to him directly, far away from the eyes of Mr. Ngô. She'd always been suspicious that the man never really liked her, and she suspected he botched the paperwork on purpose.

A knock at the door of her private villa. "Ma'am? You have a message."

"Who's it from?" she shouted back.

"Someone named Duck? Dook?"

Connie quickly jumped out of her pool, threw on a robe, and sprinted to the door, yanking it wide open, startling the poor bellboy. He handed her a note and scurried away. She ripped the envelope open, looking for clues, anything, to let her know that perhaps this was all a sick joke. That Duc wouldn't cut her out like that without *something*.

There was just one sentence on the card, which sent a chill down her spine.

You'll be fine! Stop digging! Go home! Duc

Fine? *Fine? Just fine?*

All she could see was blood. The phantom copper taste of revenge filled her mouth, and she imagined Duc's head on a pike, parading him through the streets. Crowds throwing tomatoes and baguettes at him, yelling *COWARD! DIRTBAG! SHAME!* But no one would ever blame the man; it was always the woman who shouldered the burden. No one was going to come to her aid. They'd drag her through the streets instead, yelling *GOLD DIGGER! SLUT! SHAME!*

But she was Connie goddamn Vũ.

No man was going to toss her aside like she was nothing and the only parading through the street she would ever do was if there was a red carpet rolled out. Duc had been her 401(k) plan, her early retirement, and a way for her to climb out of the hole she was born in. The only type of slut she was, was for a stable and comfortable life.

Among the gorgeous flora and fauna of Indonesia that coated her private villa, draping vines hung daintily all around her. She swatted them away like gnats to get to her balcony and breathe in some fresh air. From high up in the mountains, she could see the infamous rice fields of Bali that curved for miles and miles, as if a giant had etched drawings into the earth. But none of the beautiful views in one of the most beautiful, remote parts of the world could stop Connie from wanting to scorch everything.

Connie had been played. Throughout their entire marriage, she thought she was playing Duc, but Duc was smarter than she gave him credit for. She knew Duc never loved her, and she never loved him back but had assumed that there was a silent understanding between them. Duc never got over his first wife, Evelyn, after she left them all. Connie went into the marriage not caring. She just wanted to survive.

She whipped out her phone and called her lawyer once again. On the fourth ring, he finally picked up.

"Connie! What on earth!" A bleary-sounding voice came out of the speaker. "It's one a.m."

"Well, it's only three p.m. over here. Took you long enough to pick up," she snapped.

"Connie, what is it? How can I help?" Jason responded, yawning loudly.

"Status update?"

She could hear shuffling on the other side of the phone, and a muffled woman's voice cursing Connie's name and telling Jason to hang up the phone and to deal with her "crazy ass" in the morning. But Connie could tell she had won in the marital bickering because soon all she could hear was the shuffling of Jason dragging his feet to his desk, the sound of a light flickering, and the greeting of his laptop being turned on.

"I do have an update," he said, finally settled in, his voice still heavy with sleep. "I got a copy of the will. You're not getting a lot *but* you're getting something. I also figured out the status of each of Duc's kids and what's going on now."

"Speak faster, Jason," she barked into the phone so loudly birds resting in trees nearby flew off, scattering to all corners of the earth. "Don't I get billed every six minutes by you greedy charlatans?"

"So, it looks like the kids have already received part of their inheritance, at least the daughters have. They each inherited a store from the chain, specifically put in their name. Jane got the original store in Houston, Bingo got one in Philadelphia, Paulina's is located in San Jose, and Georgia got one in New Orleans," Jason said, picking up the pace. "But to be honest, we looked into those stores. They're all dumpster fires. Most of them nonoperational. They're playing a losing game. Never bet against the house as the saying goes."

"I'm not worried about the daughters. Those girls have no work ethic," she scoffed, her knuckles turning white as she gripped the iron railing of her balcony. "What about the son? I suspect Duc loves Jude the most."

"He . . . hasn't gotten anything so far," Jason said cryptically. Connie could hear more paperwork shuffling, and the sound of his mouse clicking through his computer. "But he will once he's married. But ultimately, only one kid will inherit everything. Depends on who wins Duc's very odd, *odd* game."

"Who determines who wins? I don't understand. What's the *point* of all of this?"

More shuffling of paperwork could be heard. A stifled yawn. Jason's wife in the background cursing Connie's name. Connie closed her eyes, waiting to hear her husband's name, bracing herself. Quick *clicks* and *clacks* of the keyboard. Connie's impatience grew like a virus, infecting any living organism near her.

"Uh, Con," Jason whispered. "Remember to breathe, okay? Looks like Duc lied to his own kids. It's not about who turns the revenue around first or if Jude gets married first. Ultimately, none of that will factor into the final decision."

"Just spit it out," she screamed into her mouthpiece. "Enough of this meditation crap! It doesn't work! It's a scam! Who decides who wins?"

"Evelyn Lê," he finally responded. "The mother of the kids. It looks like it'll all go to her." She could tell Jason had stopped moving. His breathing was shallow, almost scared.

Connie felt slapped in the face. This whole time she'd been chasing the wrong person, following him nearly six thousand miles across the globe. It wasn't Duc she had to go see. Of course the old fool had never gotten over Evelyn—she had always known that. Over twenty years of marriage, five kids, and one empire together, no one could ever forget their first love, not even if one was hiding out in a monastery on the most beautiful mountain in the world.

While Connie had been chasing Duc this whole time, Duc had been chasing Evelyn the last two decades.

She had two options. She could find Evelyn, her archnemesis, and start from the beginning. Maybe even try to reason with her. Plead with her to see her side. Two scorned women, former lovers of Duc. Maybe she'd understand, woman to woman. Or she could blow up each of the Trân kids, one by one, and make their lives a living hell, and make them want to drop out of Duc's harebrained inheritance scheme.

The ex-wife or the children? Who will suffer the most?

"Con?" Jason mumbled through the phone. "You still alive?"

Connie softened her grip on the balcony railing and went inside to grab her cocktail. She threw out the straw and took a big swig.

"I've never felt more alive."

CHAPTER 15

Jane

Dakao Plaza was teeming with activity: a construction crew doing demolition; hordes of wannabe micro-influencers with their diva lights juxtaposed next to local news cameras; and rubberneckers slowing down their cars, causing more traffic delays in an already clogged city. From the outside looking in, there were more headaches than wins. But everyone was bitten with curiosity, wondering why the hell the original Duc's Sandwiches store had suddenly come back from the dead.

For months, all anyone saw in the decaying plaza was a flurry of action. The once-empty parking lot was now filled with laborers carrying wreckage from the old shop, then carrying in new tiles, neon signs, and mid-century furniture. Cement dust flew between the hours of nine and five, and the constant hammering and drilling echoed down Bellaire, warning of what was to come. A new guard would soon be taking over.

Jane stood at the helm, guarding closely with her clipboard and hard hat. Her hair had gotten longer, and her skin, more burnt, more colored. Summer in Houston had gone by in the blink of an eye, but she looked healthier than when she had arrived—it was as if life had been infused back into Jane's body. One could even argue that Jane Trần was having fun, over-hauling the store. Historically, Jane *never* had fun—it was the curse of the eldest daughter. Her second in command, the elderly Bác Cai, was watching over her. But if Bác Cai thought Jane had gone insane, she kept it to herself and held her tongue. A rarity.

While the recent activity gave the allure of a new renaissance on the horizon, only a handful of watchful, beady brown eyes privately scorned and judged Jane's actions. The neighboring store owners, who had been there longer than the old sandwich shop had been around, and before Jane was born, had a belly full of complaints. For the past few months, the old guard stood watch, arms crossed, clucking in disapproval. Change should be slow, thoughtful, and by those who had been in the trenches. Jane was not one of them. She had become a stranger to the city. She didn't know Houston anymore, and the city didn't know her.

Not once in the past several decades had the neighboring store owners seen their plaza so crowded—not even when the old grocery store across the street had gone out of business, and everything was 75 percent off and a swarm of elderly Vietnamese women ran out of the store, flooding the streets, looking like they'd just committed robbery. Today was more crowded than that fateful day.

And they absolutely hated it. What was the point of change when peace couldn't be achieved in their old age?

The owners stood outside their shops, leaned against the doorframes, watching the chaos around them. Thủy from the nail salon supply store, Duy from the travel agency, Xuân from the sketchy CPA's office, and Linh from the refillable, filtered water store, all hovered, just doors from each other. Despite knowing each other as business owners, they'd never once been to each other's homes. They were businesspeople, not friends, not neighbors, and as America had taught them, they had to learn how to pull themselves up by the bootstraps—and bootstrappers were taught to be divided and not united.

"What do you think is going on over there?" Duy said, a toothpick dangling from his old, dry lips, his sunglasses askew on his nose. He watched the construction crew scurrying around, shouldering large wooden beams, one even hauling a toilet out, while three others rushed in with a frighteningly large plant, seemingly pulled from the depths of the Amazon.

"You think that plant is fake?" Xuân asked, recognizing the oversize monstera plant being shoved through the door by three grown men. Jane shouted at them to be careful, and they shouted back that the plant was too big. "It looks preposterous."

"Everything is fake with that generation," Duy muttered. "You think they're capable of keeping a plant alive? What happened to just having some plastic stools and some lights?"

"That plant looks like it's dying. Why would she have a plant filled with holes?" Linh chimed in, shaking her head. "I feel like that's an unlucky omen to have inside a new business."

"White people love sickly-looking plants." Thủy smirked. "Maybe she's trying to get a new crowd in. She should have gotten orchids instead. Sneak some color in there. All I see is beige. It looks like it's on death's door."

A crowd of people began to grow as the store owners watched Jane argue back and forth with the men about the plant.

"Who is causing all this chaos anyway?" Duy complained. He lit up a cigarette. "There's barely any parking anymore. Being forced to do street parking at *my* age is my version of a fresh hell."

"It's Duc's kid, isn't it? His oldest daughter?" Linh asked as she leaned forward, craning her neck to try to look past everyone. Her crow's-feet sharpened. Her eyesight had been failing her throughout the years, but today was especially bad. "Jane. Or is it Bang? Bong? Bing? Paul? I can't remember. But I think it's the oldest daughter. Definitely not the son, he's got no business acumen. Remember his failed jewelry business? Anyway, one of the daughters has come back to revive the old bánh mì shop."

"Duc? *Đức Trần?*" Duy asked, surprised. "The man hasn't been around these parts in years. Thinks he's better than us now. Why the hell would he send his daughter to revive that old shitter?"

"Speaking of shitter, that little shit still owes me money from the late seventies." Linh glowered. "He thinks because he's Jeff Bezos now, we forget that he owes us? Didn't we loan him the money to open the shop?"

"We loaned him money?" Duy asked, scratching his head, his toothpick falling out of his mouth. "I don't remember this. How much did we give him? I have some gambling debt to pay off. Should I hit him up?"

"Why would she want to revive that old dump? Some things are better left dead. I saw Bác Cai kick out a family of rats from the store last week." Xuân laughed hoarsely, still stuck on the idea of the old sandwich shop coming back to life. His throat was so caked with decades' worth of cigarette smoking that his words could barely make it out. "When's the last time the sandwiches were any good? Since the mid-nineties? Their bread makes the roof of my mouth hurt, it's so dry. It used to be good. Remember when it first opened? We all used to eat there every day, and not once did we ever get sick of it."

Thủy tutted, and tutted some more, while shaking her head vigorously, her hair so gray and glossy, the sun seemed to reflect off it. Though it looked like she was in disagreement, she was actually agreeing with Xuân.

"That shop hasn't been good since Evelyn was running the place. She made the crispiest tofu sandwiches in the entire neighborhood. It was so good she somehow got the white vegans to trek all the way out here, remember? It was Duc who sank the ship the moment she left them. Quality went down."

"Whatever happened to Evelyn anyway?" Xuân asked. Now the men dropped the plant, breaking the pot, causing Jane to emit a shriek that could be heard for miles. "Did anyone figure out why she left?"

Duy, Linh, and Thủy shrugged. "Can you blame her? Look what her children have done to the shop. Desecrated it, really," Duy said.

"Maybe the woman just wanted peace," Linh said to no one in particular. "That's all a woman ever wants, but never gets."

All four of them went quiet as they remembered Evelyn's tofu sandwiches and unanimously agreed that the years when Evelyn reigned were far better. They salivated for the days when Evelyn would be the one in the back, cooking.

Not one person blamed Evelyn for leaving Duc; the two would fight louder than cats and dogs. Their marriage was a cautionary tale for everyone in the plaza to never mix relationships and business. In reality, no marriage was beautiful back then. All anyone knew was hardship; joy was reserved for the next generation. But despite all the deprivation, the owners were nostalgic; they missed the old days. Hell, they even missed Duc, who probably, definitely still owed them money.

So, the aging shop owners of Little Saigon of Bellaire continued watching the crowd, ruminating if they were too stubborn and old for change, or if change was simply not meant for them in this lifetime.

Suddenly, a crusty, beat-up Toyota Tacoma came roaring into the plaza, interrupting their thoughts. They watched as the red truck stopped abruptly in front of the store, braking suddenly, emitting a cloud of black air into their faces, and lurching the vehicle forward, almost knocking into the monstera plant. Out stepped a tall, lanky man, with the blackest and most unruly hair. He pulled a giant bouquet of flowers out of the passenger seat and straightened out his Astros cap as he headed toward Jane and Bác Cai. The neighbors watched as Jane's face lit up, suddenly forgetting all the plant drama from before. Bác Cai shoved Jane toward the man so hard, the younger woman almost fell off the sidewalk and into his arms.

"Well, well, well," Linh whispered. "Is *he* the reason Jane moved back to Houston?"

"I thought she was a lesbian," Duy whispered back, straightening his spine to get a closer look.

"She does give off that energy, doesn't she? So, *who* is *that*?" Thủy was unable to keep her excitement out of her voice. "I'd go anywhere for *that*."

"Maybe we should just get rid of that guy, then," Xuân said. "That way, once he's out of the picture, the parking spaces will open back up, and maybe Jane will stop doing all this renovation and give up."

"What do you mean 'get rid of him'?" Linh asked, suspicious.

"I'm *just* saying! Parking has been a problem during all this renovation!"

"Actually, that's not a *bad* idea—"

"You don't mean, actual murder??"

As Linh, Xuân, Duy, and Thủy removed their eyes from Jane and the mystery man, and began to bicker among themselves, they failed to see how in the afternoon sun, when Jane smiled as big as she did at the sight of Henry, she could have easily been mistaken for her mother, or at least, a younger version of her mother.

And for a split second, it was as if Evelyn never left Houston.

....

Someway, somehow, we always make our way back home.

Her father's words clung to Jane as she watched Henry approach her, carrying a huge, colorful bouquet of perennials. She couldn't remember the last time someone had bought her flowers on a random weekday, let alone that someone being her crush. Her cheeks burned, and she couldn't tell if she was happy or embarrassed, or a wonderful mixture of both.

She gingerly accepted the bouquet. "Are we still on for dinner later?" Henry asked. Her heart bloomed alongside the flowers. "You've been so busy lately with the renovations, I thought I'd drop in to remind you that you still have to eat, you know. In fact, I *know* you haven't eaten."

Jane blushed fiercely, gripping the stems close against her chest, afraid to let go. "I don't know . . . there's just so much work to be done around here—"

"Go! Go! GO!" Bác Cai yelled into Jane's ears. "Take the night off for once. You haven't done anything fun in the four months since you've moved back."

"But opening day is so soon," Jane protested.

"You'll be fine, just *go*," Bác Cai ordered, a threat at the tip of her tongue.

"You did promise me dinner. Then you rescheduled . . . then you *kept* rescheduling . . ." Henry's voice trailed off, but his point was made.

"Alright, alright," Jane conceded. Though she feigned waving a white flag, she couldn't help but be thrilled at the prospect of seeing Henry in an intimate setting again. *Was* it a date? Or just two old friends catching up?

"While he's here, show him your progress, con," Bác Cai said eagerly.

"Okay, but don't judge us, it's still a work in progress," Jane said nervously as she opened the front door for Henry to step into the shop, pulling the plastic curtains aside.

"I'd never judge you. Except when you don't eat."

Inside the half-remodeled sandwich shop, Jane paced around, pointing out all the changes they made while apologizing for all the debris. While her voice sounded confident, her feet anxiously circled. She adjusted shelves along the way, for the hundredth time, making sure all the new merchandise was neatly in order. The tote bags, the plastic cups, the cute baguette plushies.

The rebrand capitalized on an old name: *The original Duc's Sandwiches store*. Jane practiced the pitch that she planned on spinning to all local news stations and influencers next month, giving the sob story of her life. How she was doing all this to fulfill her dying father's last wishes. (Duc wasn't dying.) *The daughter who came back to preserve a bit of Vietnamese American history.*

"So, what do you think?" Jane asked excitedly as she whipped around to face Henry.

She watched as Henry observed the old black-and-white photos of her family all over the store, photos that painted a false image of the Trầns. Photos of Duc and Evelyn, their hands coated in flour, Evelyn behind the kitchen counter, Duc hanging up the original sign with a smile on his face. While all these moments happened, the photos didn't show what happened afterward—how her parents would erupt in anger at each other, at their children, and at the world. Angry that as refugees, the only skills they had to try to make money was through food, and how they had to sell their sandwiches for dirt cheap compared to other American food, despite the labor behind a three-dollar sandwich. But that was how they were seen their entire lives: less than, cheap, economical.

It angered her all her life that immigrant food always *had* to be cheap. Tacos, pupusas, dumplings, phở, gyros, kimchi, pad thai . . . she could keep going. These were all foods worthy of double digits. Of dignity.

Henry stopped in the middle of the shop, surrounded by unplugged neon signs, historical photos, and wallpaper-accented walls, taking it all in.

"Wow," Henry said hesitantly. "It's . . . a lot. It's certainly different."

The smile on Jane's face faltered, and she could feel herself dimming. "What do you mean by *different*?"

"Oh dear," Bác Cai whispered behind her. Before anyone noticed, Bác Cai shuffled to the back room, avoiding conflict, plugging her ears with headphones.

"I mean . . . it's not *bad*. It's just . . . not you?" he said. "I don't see *you* anywhere in this shop. It kind of looks like every other store? I kind of liked the old vibe of the shop, from before. It was homey. Recognizable."

"The *old* vibe?" Jane repeated hollowly. "You mean the *old* vibe when my father would yell at us when he was having a bad day? Or when we struggled so much, we went stretches without any customers except for the roaches? Or how my father put this shop above his entire family and it broke us? Or how my mother's mental health grew worse with each new shop that opened, and she had a nervous breakdown and left? You mean *that* old vibe?"

Henry stepped backward, but the tension in the store grew into a thick fog. "Jane, I didn't mean it like that—"

But Jane couldn't pull herself out. She never could. She scanned the social media–ready store with a different mindset, and though she should have felt proud of herself for getting the store together in just a few months and not let a man's opinion bring her down, she felt empty inside. *Was* it so wrong to hawk a false narrative of her family? She never felt more like Duc than in that moment; nothing more than a used car salesman. But she'd rather be a used car salesman than fail at life. Perhaps, she did have something in common with her father after all.

"Actually, it's getting late," Jane said curtly as she pretended to look at her phone. "I realized I can't get dinner tonight. I have to stay late to sign for some deliveries."

Henry looked taken aback and did his best to protest. "Can't Bác Cai—"

But before Henry could argue anymore, he found himself being gently shoved out the door, with another false promise being made that she would reschedule soon. As she heard Henry's truck start up and drive off into the setting sun, she stared at the colorful bouquet of perennials that lay sideways on the counter, taunting her. Reminding her of a life she could have had if she stayed in Houston.

"How dare he? What does he know about me? How could he possibly know me after all these years?" Jane said out loud to herself. Before she could stop herself, she felt the hot tears starting, and then a panic attack coming on. Why was she really playing into her father's game? Why bother doing all of this?

The sad truth was, she wasn't running away from anything because she *had* nothing to run away from, nor was she running toward anything, because she had nothing waiting for her at the end of the finish line. She was just . . . stuck.

As Jane slid to the floor, tears welling in her eyes, Bác Cai was there in a flash, her arms around her, cradling her, and rocking her back and forth, like she did back then.

"Your mother loved colorful flowers," Bác Cai whispered.

"I know," Jane managed to say between tears. "But the question is, do I?"

CHAPTER 16

Jude

I n the past four months, Jude found himself doing all the obligatory, public-facing things that required +1s. Dinner parties, friends' birthdays, he even went to his first musical, and didn't hate it as much as he thought he would. But why did they have to burst into song randomly like that? It was a jump scare every time. He also didn't even mind Phoebe's crusty, old white dog, who was blind in one eye and had to wear a diaper. For not being a dog person, he found her dog was rather sweet, saccharine even. Jude had never been in a proper, committed relationship before, but he imagined that this was what it felt like, to appear on someone's arm, to smile appropriately, to make the right commentary, and to go to all the dog-friendly breweries. To feel . . . needed. Granted, Phoebe made things easy, especially when there were no real expectations and everything they did was for show.

But again, he didn't hate it all as much as he thought he would.

While Jude wanted to rush into a quick courthouse ceremony and sign the papers, Phoebe's father refused and held firm. Mr. Phương insisted on a proper banquet wedding, complete with the meeting of the families first. Though Jude kept trying to explain that his mother had abandoned them and couldn't be found (correction: didn't *want* to be found), and that his father, Duc, was hiding in Vietnam, only reachable through his lawyer, Mr. Phương was adamant.

Well, what about his sisters?

Well, it's a little complicated, sir. They all hate me and want me to miserably fail so they can cut me from the inheritance. They think my father favors me the most 'cause I'm the firstborn son, when in reality, our father can't differentiate one from the other.

But Mr. Phương pressed him; he must meet *someone* from the family, any representative. Any warm body would do. It was tradition, after all. And for a rather unconventional marriage, wouldn't it be good to maintain some modicum of tradition?

Frustrated, Jude almost chose another file from the stack of other potential matches, someone who would be able to sign the papers today, just to get the marriage certificate. But something about Phoebe made Jude want to try. Maybe it was the way he laughed about how she could crochet while simultaneously being on the treadmill, or the fact that she cared so intensely about a blind and deaf old dog. Or the fact that, late at night, he often found himself calling her, pretending to have a wedding question, and how she would pick up right away, and how they would laugh for what felt like eternity, pretending to be in love.

What was a month or two of waiting? His sisters couldn't possibly turn their dumpster fire of stores around before he got married, right?

Jude decided to try harder than he had for anyone before. Surely, his father would come out of exile to show up for his only son's wedding. He was certain his father would fly out to meet Mr. Phương and his future daughter-in-law if Jude asked. But as the thought of a wedding began to crystallize in his mind, the more the pit in his stomach ballooned, because he realized just how broken his family really was. If the year continued on like this, he was terrified that no one from his side would show up for him. Especially not his sisters.

How far was he willing to go, if that just meant standing in front of the altar alone, with no one by his side?

....

The next day, Jude drove through Bellaire, making pit stops in front of old childhood haunts, like a celebrity tour bus for repressed memories. He narrated each spot in his mind, explaining to himself why it was important to him, and who the key players were. He didn't know why the nostalgia was so heavy on this particular day, especially since he rarely drove through Bellaire unless he was forced to. But as he passed by the old family temple, he pulled over and turned off the engine, staring at the gigantic Buddha statue that sat in the middle of the grounds. He remembered the last day he'd ever attended this particular temple. His mother begged him to go back, but he couldn't stand the people who went there anymore. Evelyn either turned a blind eye to their behavior, or she didn't care—both of which pissed him off at ten years old, validating that his mother was the enemy. The staring and snickering were manageable, but he couldn't stand the fake niceties to his face, only to overhear them gossiping about him later.

Jude's a bastard. Duc isn't his father. Looks nothing like him.
You know his mom's a whore, right?
Once a whore, always a whore.

Jude turned the car back on and headed straight to his father's office, a tiny three-room suite in an old plaza. Nestled at the far end of the neighborhood, it looked nearly abandoned. It was also uncomfortably close to the highway, the sound of cars whizzing past like an F1 race. Since Duc got remarried to Connie, he stopped going into the office, but Jude yearned for the old days, when things were simpler, when his child self would follow his father into the office, and sleep under his desk with his plushies, waiting.

As he pulled into the parking lot, he was surprised to see one car there. Who could possibly be in now? He cautiously approached the office and recognized Mr. Ngô hunched over his desk, poring over papers, puffing on a cigarette. Through the dirty, speckled window, the old lawyer looked distracted, his forehead wrinkled in stress. He watched the lawyer black out large paragraphs with a Sharpie. Just as Jude thought about quietly leaving before Mr. Ngô could catch him, they locked eyes, forcing Jude to awkwardly wave through the window. Mr. Ngô waved for him to come in, but as always, with the neutral lawyer, there was no expression attached to the wave.

"Jude," Mr. Ngô said, setting his cigarette down on his ashtray, its smoke trail snaking all the way to the ceiling. "What brings you here early on a Saturday morning? Shouldn't you be out at a club?"

"Why would you assume I'd be at a club?" Jude asked defensively. "It's ten in the morning."

"Because, well, you're always at a club. I don't know how clubs work, though," he said matter-of-factly, before finally putting down his marker and leaning back. "How is the wedding planning? How is the lovely bride-to-be? Phoebe is her name, right?"

Jude hovered awkwardly at the doorframe, not moving in. He wrung his hands together. He never really knew how to address or talk to his father's longtime associate, someone he informally referred to as "uncle" at family parties. Mr. Ngô was always *around*, but he just didn't *know* Mr. Ngô.

"Fine," he said rather unenthusiastically. "It's going great. We're excited."

"Just fine? Just great? *Just* excited? Is she not the love of your life?"

Jude continued to loiter, unwilling to expose his vulnerabilities to Mr. Ngô. He spotted his father's desk, a few feet away from Mr. Ngô's. The large oak desk sat empty and dusty, untouched by movement for the past few years. Drawn toward it, Jude walked over and traced a finger along the edge, dust clinging to his index finger, leaving a streak. As he circled the desk, he spotted the old fort he had made and realized that his father had still kept it up, even long after Jude stopped coming in. Along with his father's desk, his fort and childhood memories were frozen in time. He was touched. Fond memories flooded in; of him hiding underneath his father's desk as a child and forming a small fort, complete with blankets, a flashlight, comic books, and a rigged curtain fastened with duct tape and old red plastic strings that were supposed to be used to wrap up bánh mì.

"Wow," he whispered. "The old man kept it up."

Mr. Ngô caught on. "Your father loved it when you accompanied him to work, you know."

"I'd never have known." Jude chuckled dryly. "Always thought I was a nuisance. All I ever remember was him telling me to quiet down."

"Well, your voice does carry for miles," Mr. Ngô joked. "Especially when you did your stuffed dinosaur battles."

Surprised, Jude returned a halfhearted chuckle. "Good memory. I forgot how obsessed I was with dinosaurs."

"I remember everything, unfortunately. Perhaps, it's a curse I bear," the old lawyer responded. "So, Jude, what can I help you with?"

Finally loosened, Jude walked over to sit down across from Mr. Ngô and unleashed everything. "Do you know why my father hasn't responded to my wedding invitation yet? It's been months. Mrs. Vương said that my father liked Phoebe's profile the best, so why hasn't he said anything yet? Not even congratulations? Why hasn't he come back to meet Phoebe's father in person? Mr. Phương won't bless our marriage unless someone from the family meets him. And well, you know how it is with my family . . ."

Mr. Ngô sighed and leaned back in his swivel chair, watching the smoke of his cigarette slowly die out, until the cigarette fizzled into nothing but ash. Jude took in his uncle, his receding hairline, his ill-fitting suit, the way his aging, protruding beer belly didn't seem to fit his frame. Jude couldn't help but feel sorry for him. How could a man like Mr. Ngô spend his entire life catering to Duc and his family, and never have a family of his own? But Jude didn't feel sorry in the sense he thought Mr. Ngô was lonely. He felt sorry that Mr. Ngô got stuck with a fucked-up family like his. What would Mr. Ngô's life have turned out like, had he attached himself to a normal family? Jude couldn't shake the fear that he might grow up to be like Mr. Ngô one day—alone with a beer belly, and someone's eternal side-kick.

"I'll go meet Mr. Phương in your father's place." Mr. Ngô finally spoke, and he got up and grabbed his car keys. "Let's go."

"But my father, I need my father—" Jude stammered.

"Yes, he wants to make sure you're making the right choice first. I'll go."

Before Jude could ask any more questions about Duc, he found himself in the passenger seat of Mr. Ngô's beat-up Volkswagen, pushing aside stacks of old newspapers and empty glass coffee bottles. For all the riches that Duc and Mr. Ngô had made together over the decades, Jude couldn't find two more diametrically opposite men. While Duc paraded his riches in front of every neighbor, Mr. Ngô was more subdued, hiding his wealth like a squirrel. But for someone who didn't have a family of his own, Jude wondered what on earth he did with all his money and time.

....

It was almost as if Mr. Phương knew the two men were coming to find him. He had a pack of Heineken, fishing poles, bait, and some cold cuts ready to go in his truck—or perhaps it was just the Vietnamese father's starter sur-vival pack, and he always had this ready to go, at any given notice.

Jude felt that sting again in his heart, seeing a good father come pre-pared. Mr. Phương's face lit up, ecstatic to finally get to meet someone from Jude's side of the family, who would potentially be his family one day. Though Jude and Phoebe both lost their mothers in different ways at a young age, he envied that Phoebe still had a parent who was present—someone who actually cared. Someone who knew what she did for fun, who her friends were, and what she liked to eat. The small drop of envy turned into heartache as Jude watched Mr. Ngô shake Mr. Phương's hand, and Mr. Ngô introduced himself as Jude's uncle. Mr. Phương didn't question if he was his biological uncle or not; he just accepted it as a statement—that Mr. Ngô was family.

Mr. Phương ushered them both into his truck, and he took off toward Lake Houston for a second time. Jude recognized where they were going, the lake where Mr. Phương taught him how to fish. For a while, the conversation was standard between the two men, while Jude kept quiet, feeling like a small child under scrutiny. They asked each other when they both came over to America. *Were you part of the '75 crowd?* And then they asked which refugee camp they ended up in. *Philippines or Thailand?* Eventually, as all curious immigrants do, Mr. Phương asked how Duc and Mr. Ngô got started on the chain, how it was funded, and how it grew to the brand it is known as today. Jude knew the standard story. The first shop did so well that they took a bet on opening up another shop, and then it became a domino effect. But to his surprise, Mr. Ngô glossed over it, changing topics to Phoebe, whereas Duc would have fully launched into a speech for several hours about how he had achieved the American dream. Mr. Phương was more than happy to brag about his daughter.

Once they got down to the lake, Mr. Phương started up the boat, and the three men took off toward the center. To the quieter part, where the waters were darker. Once settled, Mr. Phương whipped out several folding lawn chairs, and the men settled comfortably into position, their fishing lines cast, and the sound of beer tabs being opened filled the air. Jude assumed the two men would continue talking, perhaps even grill each other about the finances, the nuptials, or even going over general elderly Vietnamese men's grievances (the traffic, inflation, and the rising interest rate), but the men instantly grew mute. For the next few hours, not another word was uttered, except for the small ecstatic sounds of reeling in a fish, or asking to pass another can of beer. And when Jude tried to cut the silence, he was met with even more debilitating silence. He was used to Duc being loud, obnoxious, and always talking a mile a minute over everyone, so it was a rather abrupt adjustment to hear his own thoughts again.

Bored, perhaps anxious, Jude got up and walked over to the edge of the boat. He peered into the blackened waters, and wondered how deep the lake was. He lowered and lowered himself trying to find his reflection in the water, wondering if the fish could see him, and wondered what they thought of him, and if they felt sorry for him.

Jude was suddenly yanked back so hard, he fell on his back. Sharp pain shot through him. He cried out in frustration, and as he looked up he saw Mr. Ngô staring down at him, his oval face perfectly blocking out the sun.

"Stay away from the edge of the boat," Mr. Ngô said sternly. It was the sternest Jude had ever heard him talk to him before. "It's not safe. And you don't know how to swim well." Before Jude could talk back, the lawyer was gone and settled back into his lawn chair.

Mr. Phương piped up, giving a half chuckle. "Don't worry, if Jude ever drowns, Phoebe is a certified lifeguard, she can save him."

Mr. Ngô grunted an approval, but did not say anything else.

Rubbing his behind, Jude reluctantly went back to his lawn chair, casting Mr. Ngô an annoyed look for treating him like a child.

By the time the sun set, Jude had elderly-Vietnamese-men fatigue and was ready to go home. As the men silently packed up, and drove the boat back to shore, to head back to the city, he wondered if he had passed the requirements that Mr. Phương needed in order to move forward with the marriage. At the idea of possibly failing the test, Jude was surprised to feel anxiety. The potential of calling off the wedding pained him more than it should have, especially when Phoebe's face came to mind.

To his surprise, before he got into the truck, he felt Mr. Phương's hand on his shoulder. As he turned around to face him, Mr. Phương stuck out his hand.

"Anyone with an uncle like yours, I know your father is a good man," Mr. Phương said gruffly. "I know that your father would have met me personally if he was in town. But you're surrounded by good men, so I know you are a good man for my daughter."

Jude shook his hand back, unsure what to think. In the corner of his eye, he saw Mr. Ngô pretending to be busy, though the corners of his lips were turned up slightly.

A rare, barely noticeable smile.

....

When Jude got back to his car, something overcame his motor functions, and he found himself getting off at a different exit, toward Montrose. Before he realized it, he was soon in front of Phoebe's apartment complex. He'd

only been there once before, when he dropped off a box of wedding invi-
tations, but he'd never been inside. What were her tastes? What movies
was she into? What was her favorite album? Favorite ice cream flavor? He
wanted to know it all. But most of all, he wanted to tell her how great the
day was. How he'd gotten better at fishing, and how great her father was.

How *really* great her father was.

He couldn't wait to tell her that he had gotten her father's approval to
move forward with the wedding. He parked the car and looked up at her
window, suddenly feeling like a creep. Her main bedroom light was on.

Tonight felt different somehow. For the first time in a long time, he felt
like he had accomplished something toward the betterment of his life, and
he had her to thank for it. He worked up the courage to get out of the car,
and found his way to the apartment call box. He scrolled through the
names frantically, missing her name on purpose several times, forcing him
to keep starting over, until he finally pressed the call box for a Phương, P.
Apt. 302.

"Hello?" Phoebe's confused voice came through the call box, dis-
torted. Hearing her voice after a long day made Jude smile. His father's
words from the letter reared their head again at him. Duc's words kept
eating away at him, and Jude couldn't help but wonder if he had finally
found his joy.

Son, I look at you and wonder if you will ever find your joy.

"Hey, it's . . . me," Jude said, his mind unfocused, his words wobbly.
He felt embarrassed for being there so late.

"Who? Sorry, I didn't order any delivery," she responded.

His heart beat faster. "It's me. Jude." Silence. A beat. Perhaps, a mistake.

"Jude? What are you doing here?" Her voice sounded strained, but surprised.

"I . . . I was just driving by. I just came back from fishing with your
father. Again."

More silence. "You want to come up?"

Jude was grateful she couldn't see his face now. A wide grin had
erupted across it. He felt like he had just won the World Series, seen the
northern lights, caught a shooting star, or witnessed a blue moon. This
must be what everyone talked about when they talked about love.

"Yes," he responded. As he recalled the day's events, he remembered how Mr. Ngô had lectured him to stay away from the boat's edge. "I heard you're a good swimmer."

Phoebe laughed. "I am. I can save you if you ever start to drown."

"That's good to know about a future wife."

The gate buzzed open, and Jude walked through without another thought.

CHAPTER 17

Bingo

"**W**here are my boxers? I'm so late!" Iris bemoaned as she scurried all over the back office of the abandoned Duc's Sandwiches that Bingo had converted into her temporary living situation in Philadelphia. Iris rifled through old cardboard boxes, sneezed over dusty white linen that had yellowed over time, yelped when she uncovered a swarm of spiders in one corner, and threw a mighty curse when her knee collided with the metal frame of the spring cot. Though her face tried to contain her disgust, Bingo worried that things were starting to sour between the two of them. Bingo was starting to feel that she was the equivalent of cis men who didn't own bed frames, but who insisted instead on putting mattresses on the floor, while Iris was the "cool Asian girl" who had her life together.

Bingo's face continued to burn scarlet as she saw Iris quickly finger-brush her hair, while throwing another cursory look around the room as she swished some mouthwash around in front of the stand-alone sink. Her anxious attachment style began to rear its ugly head, and though she wanted to scream at herself to shut up and pretend that everything was *fine*, she was unable to stop the car crash from happening.

"So," Bingo began to spill out, her eyes downcast, not able to look directly at Iris. "I know this probably isn't the best time to ask this. But what are we? It's been . . . I mean what is *this*? And I was just wondering what you were thinking—" *Snap*. Iris had slipped on her bike helmet and was hurriedly putting on her jacket. Bingo could tell she was itching to leave faster; the tension in the room was thick.

Somewhere between landing in Philadelphia, that fateful run-in with Iris, spending almost every waking hour with Iris, and learning how to cook with Iris's arms wrapped around hers, Bingo lost track of time, or her purpose for being in the city. When Bingo fell in love, she turned that person into her whole world and forgot how the earth spun. Everyone and everything else were inconsequential—including herself. There was just something so sexy about being with someone from the same background and how they didn't even question putting Maggi on everything. There was no explanation needed between them, no silly argument over food restrictions, what kind of mommy issues they carried, or if they had gone to therapy. They could just simply *be*.

"Look, I'm late, and the meeting is all the way across town," Iris said, almost too placatingly. "Let's talk about this later? You know today's a big day for me."

Bingo nodded solemnly. She walked Iris to the front door, her feet dragging and getting heavier and heavier with each step. They passed by more storage boxes, broken window displays, and crooked shelves—everything still in its same place as the day Bingo arrived in Philadelphia, and in the same place as it was ten years ago, when the shop shuttered.

Bingo hadn't done anything to her store. It wasn't that she didn't want to, she just couldn't find the energy to. Her mother's depression had been passed on to Bingo the most, out of all her siblings. While her sisters were far better at pretending to handle their depression, Bingo couldn't fake it at all.

She unlocked the front door, which was still taped with old shipping cardboard containers to cover up any cracks, and she let Iris out into the nearly empty street. To Bingo, it felt as if the dying neighborhood was somehow managing to die a little bit more every day since she'd arrived. She still couldn't shake off the inkling that her father had sent her here to fail. That, perhaps, she was the one he cared for the least.

"Good luck today, okay?" Bingo said. "Those investors would be a fool if they didn't give you all the money in the world."

Wordlessly, Iris leaned in and gave Bingo a quick peck on the cheek, and Bingo instantly knew it was the kiss of death between them.

"Thanks, Bingo," Iris said wryly. She gave another look around the place. "Maybe you should consider doing something today. Take a walk maybe? Get some fresh air."

"Maybe."

"What about cleaning this place up? What happened to working on the shop?"

"Yeah, maybe." Bingo could feel her voice growing faint, defensive almost. She knew Iris's affection was waning, and she felt defeated. "Are you going to break up with me later? If so, just get over it now."

"I mean, we weren't ever *official* official, so there's nothing to 'break up,'" Iris said awkwardly. "I just think you're a bit lost, Bingo."

"Who isn't?" Bingo's defensiveness was getting stronger. "How are any of us expected to live? Have you seen the rising interest rates? We're all just living to survive—"

"Look, I really have to go. Let's talk later, okay? Meet back at my place?"

Bingo stood there haplessly and helplessly, while hopelessly in love. She simply nodded as she watched the cool Asian girl with the sleeve tattoos— and the self-determination to pull off micro-bangs—hop on her bike and pedal away toward a future without Bingo in it.

She managed to hold it in until she closed the front door, locked it, turned around, and allowed her father's spirit to channel through her. Frustrated, she screamed and began to throw boxes around, trashing the already trashed place. She fought through her hurt, wondering what the hell was wrong with her and why all the girls she'd ever wanted could never see a future with her. And why, oh *why*, did it especially hurt more when cool Asian girls couldn't see her the same way she saw them?

She couldn't stop. She kept taking it out on the store, her father's anger flowing through her, while her mother's depression exacerbated her actions. She wanted love and purpose. Needed to be accepted, to have a reason to wake up in the morning, to not feel so heavy to the point she just wanted to rot away.

Eventually she found a hammer and swung, again and again, until she had nearly completed the half-finished demolition from ten years ago. She turned her focus on the back office and whipped open old boxes, throwing old papers into the air. She kept going until an old black-and-white photo flew out of the box and landed squarely at her feet, among a sea of broken glass and shredded papers. It was enough to make Bingo stop. She reached down and picked up the strange photo.

A photo of her mother, Evelyn, young, nearly the same age she is now, pregnant, and standing with her arms wrapped around a man who was not Duc. A man who—but it couldn't be? Could it?

A young Mr. Ngô—so young, she almost didn't recognize him. They had their arms around each other in a way that implied they were more than just acquaintances, and they were standing in front of the original Duc's Sandwiches back in Houston.

Bingo kept staring. Curious. Questions piled on top of one another. She wondered where her father was and why Mr. Ngô was standing in his place instead. The more she stared at a young Mr. Ngô, the more she couldn't help but think that he looked like Jane when he was her age, and how wide her mother's smile had been. She couldn't ever remember seeing her mother smile once growing up. Her mother's smile lit a fire in Bingo, and she realized just how deeply in love she was with Iris, and how she couldn't go the rest of her life without smiling like that again.

....

It'd been over three decades since Mr. Huey Ngô stepped foot in Philadelphia; he hadn't been back to Pennsylvania since he first landed in America. But Philadelphia wasn't the first city he experienced; it was Lancaster, Pennsylvania. Imagine his surprise at twenty-two, when he had traded in war-torn Vietnam for a town that still used horse-drawn buggies as transportation. His first impression of America was not the advanced promised land he had thought it would be. Where were the *bright lights, rock 'n' roll, give them hell* attitude he kept seeing emanating from the American soldiers? Instead, Lancaster reminded him of home a bit. Farmland as far as the eye could see and involuntary solitude. The men worked traditional jobs, and Mr. Ngô admired their woodworking skills from afar, and he quietly observed the women, who never met his eyes, their heads covered in white bonnets. It was strange indeed that this was where he landed. Out of potentially fifty states, with a width of nearly three thousand miles, he had landed in a town frozen in time—with, ironically, a Christian family who sponsored his resettlement, and who taught him his first English words: *fork* and *spoon*.

Now here he was back in the same state, trying to track down Duc's third-eldest child, Bingo, to check in on her progress, which was a mystery to him and to Duc. She'd gone radio silent, and he knew it was time to show back up in the same city that introduced him to Americana.

Mr. Ngô sighed, and the moment he checked into his hotel, he decided to take a smoke break and walk the streets again out of nostalgia. The familiar stench of the city came roaring back to him. The city was a mash-up of an eternally broken sewer line and sweaty, angry sports fans, even though they had just won. As he walked down Broad Street, he didn't bother checking to see if he was heading in the right direction; time was finite at his age, but in this moment, he simply wanted to remember what it felt like being twenty-two again, and that feeling of sinking his teeth into his first-ever Philly cheesesteak, and wondering why the first two English words he learned were *fork* and *spoon*, yet he was eating with his hands. He wanted to remember the moment he became an Eagles fan, which he still secretly was, despite being a Texan now. He wondered how life would have turned out for him had he not left Philadelphia and followed a commercial fishing job all the way down to Louisiana, where he met the infamous Duc Trân.

As he continued strolling, and the sun began to set, any time he ran into an Eagles fan sporting the comforting colors of kelly green, silver, black, and white, he shouted in their faces *Go Eagles!*, which was shouted back with equal enthusiasm, perhaps even more. It was an instant bond, a shared moment, turning them from strangers into friends. He wondered if Bingo was also making the same memories he had, wandering the same streets and rediscovering her joy. Because out of all the children, Bingo was the one most likely to ignore the rules of society, such as knowing where to properly place a *fork* and a *spoon*.

But he knew better than to worry about Bingo; she always found her way, somehow.

Didn't she?

As the sun set, so did Mr. Ngô's knees, and he began to feel his age, so he traveled to the old Duc's Sandwiches shop. Though spying on all the adult Trân children wasn't exactly what anyone thought of as a good time, he had been excited to watch their progress in secret. It'd been months since he'd explained the inheritance game to them, and it was time to compile a report and update Duc, who was hiding out in Vietnam, getting drunk somewhere and probably gambling away his life savings—even though he had told Connie Vũ that Duc was hiding at an infamous Buddhist monastery outside the city of Đà Lạt, to throw her off his scent. There was no reason to mess with Connie; he just simply thought she was a paranoid woman and liked fueling that paranoia for his own entertainment.

Though there was a pep in his step as he rounded the corner, there was a bit of a fear as well. Call it lawyer instincts, call it being Duc's sidekick for almost five decades, call it some kind of paternal care; he began to walk faster. He couldn't help but allow the *what ifs* to penetrate his mind. He had observed Jude's and Jane's lives in Houston, and though things seemed shiny on the surface, he had that worry in the back of his mind. He was always worried for the Trần children, and whether or not Evelyn and Duc had permanently scarred them. He loved that family dearly; it nearly killed him to do so.

Though Duc had stopped worrying a long time ago, Mr. Ngô never stopped. He worried if he'd made a mistake, decades ago, when he and Duc made that promise to each other, out on the boat down in Galveston, and whether or not the children's traumas were all his fault. But what if? What if everything they had done to bury it all, to protect it all, turned out to be in vain?

With pained knees, he began to hobble faster toward the old shop.

....

Bingo rounded the corner, carrying an obscenely large bouquet of flowers. She wasn't the type of woman to buy flowers, but to hell with it. Desperate times called for desperate measures. Her hair was pinned back, she had on a crisp white button-up, and she looked like someone playing a caricature of a woman who had gotten her life together. She caught her reflection in a nearby window display. Jagged edges revealed her face back to her, and all she could see was a young woman with blank eyes. She shuddered and marched on. Her mother had the same blank look in the days leading up to when she left them. Her mother assumed nobody had noticed, but they all did. Especially the children. It was impossible not to. Her body was there, but there was nothing else behind it.

The idea of losing Iris terrified her. Philadelphia had brought more riches than Bingo could have ever imagined. Bingo had stumbled into the arms of a woman, and she'd finally experienced love in the little moments: having a bottle of MSG around as seasoning, and being able to split food, just to try a little bit of everything. It wasn't until Iris had come into her life, and, one night, crawled into bed at midnight with a plate of sliced mangoes, that Bingo burst into tears, and she realized what she had gained, and what she had lost. Duc had never cut fruit for her, nor had Evelyn. But seeing the mangoes haphazardly thrown onto a plate, by the hands of a second-generation Vietnamese lover, whose cuts weren't neat but conveyed effort, Bingo felt safe for the first time in her life.

Bingo couldn't lose her.

And there Iris was at her store, standing behind the fire as she always did, stoking the flames, which danced in her eyes. Her bangs were coated in the familiar grease Bingo had come to love. The smell of burnt lemongrass filled the air, and she could hear Iris laughing with her employees as they sped through orders with smiles on their faces.

Bingo looked past the flames and all she saw was what her life had been like in Philadelphia. She cared not once for her old life in Portland, or for her father's mindfuckery games. She didn't care about the money or duking it out with her siblings. She didn't care about any of it. She just wanted a real shot at something. She recalled the old photo she had found of her mother and Mr. Ngô, and how it put into question everything. Who was Mr. Ngô to her mother? To them? And why did he smile at their mother like that? But also, why couldn't she allow herself to wear that same smile when it came to romantic pursuits?

Once you bypass the fear of the unknown, con, this place will become your favorite city, too.

Duc's words haunted her. Philadelphia had become her favorite city for one reason, and one reason only. She owed it all to one woman who resuscitated her, who taught her not to hate Vietnamese food anymore, who reminded her that not everyone leaves, and that there could be joy found in the mundane. Hell, she could even become an Eagles fan because of this woman. Maybe.

But as Bingo observed Iris, her feet couldn't move forward. Iris flitted everywhere, from manning the fire, to taking over the till, to joking with customers. Her presence was infectious, and it made Bingo smile. She watched as Iris and everyone took celebratory shots during a lull in service. The investor meeting must have gone well. Though Bingo was excited for her, she acknowledged a difficult truth. She wasn't someone Iris should be with. She had issues, the same kind of issues her father had, that caused her mother to leave. She had to learn how to be the person who cut fruit for their lover instead of waiting for it to come to her. Bingo didn't want to wake up ten years from now, only to watch Iris walk out on her. She'd have to do it first.

She carefully placed the bouquet in the spokes of Iris's bike, chained up outside the old warehouse, and walked away from the white-picket-fenced dream she'd always lied about having.

....

An elderly man was in the middle of Duc's Sandwiches, a broom in his hand, sweeping gently, forming a small mountain of shards and debris. His silhouette was instantly recognizable. But it was his particular smell of off-brand cigarettes and how shiny his receding hairline was that gave away his identity.

"Mr. Ngô?" Bingo asked, surprised, as she walked through the open door. "What are you doing here?"

Mr. Ngô turned around in response, a small half smile on his face. Though Bingo had sworn her entire life that she didn't miss anyone from back home, seeing her uncle's face again, a staple of her childhood, her father's eternal, loyal sidekick, made her feel relieved. A familiar face, in a strange city. It was a piece of home. But the same thought lingered: Who was Mr. Ngô to her mother? Had he been a type of home to Evelyn?

"I was just supposed to observe from a distance, but when I saw all this"—he gestured at all the mess in the store—"I knew you needed my help. What happened?"

Embarrassed, Bingo couldn't find words. How could she explain that her father's anger was in her? That she was frustrated with how her life had turned out? Instead, she just shrugged.

"I was hate-crimed?" she joked.

He threw her a look, serious as always. "Did you hate-crime your-self?"

Bingo scoffed but didn't refute him. She quietly picked up a broom and joined in on the sweeping. Together, the old lawyer and the third oldest of Duc's children worked side by side. They began to take down the broken shelves, removed the rotting cabinets, and swept away the broken glass. Soon it was nearly two in the morning, and the middle of the room had bags and bags of trash piled up. Even Bingo was surprised by how trans-formed the store looked—it looked ready for a new start.

"So, what really happened?" Mr. Ngô asked. They now sat on two old red plastic chairs, in the middle of the store. He took out a cigarette and lit up without a care in the world.

"I just didn't want to play Duc's game anymore," Bingo said, giving a half-truth. "Someone else can have the money. I'm done. I'm out. I'm planning on heading back to Portland at the end of the week. As per usual, I'm the loser of the family, and I'm ready to accept my place." She remembered flashes of Iris's laugh, and she grieved the loss of not being someone who was worthy enough for her, worthy enough for anything.

Mr. Ngô took a long drag from his cigarette, not saying anything. His face flickered with the ghost of an emotion. Disappointment?

He finally got on his feet, let out a small groan of pain, and rubbed his knees vigorously. Before Bingo could stop him, he began dragging the trash out onto the sidewalk, the crisp autumnal freeze sharply hitting his face as soon as he opened the door.

"What are you doing?" Bingo rushed to her feet and tried to wrestle the trash bag from the old man's hands. "You're ancient; you're going to kill yourself."

"I'm going to help you," he argued back. "I'm going to stay and help you get on your feet. I don't think you should give up so quickly."

"Why? Why do you care so much?" she snapped back. "Just leave me alone!" As the two of them bickered back and forth, the old photo came to mind again. A young Evelyn and a young Mr. Ngô, who tenderly embraced each other. The photo burned bright in her back pocket, and as she reached for it to confront him about it, she looked at Mr. Ngô's face again, and the rumors that had nagged them for a lifetime stared right back at her, taunting her.

Her mind began spinning and Bingo released the trash bag, allowing Mr. Ngô to take hold.

"You need help, Bingo. So let me help."

He was just the family lawyer. So why—why was he so keen on helping her? She wondered if she was missing the bigger picture behind all of this, and if Mr. Ngô was the key to it all.

"Okay," she relented out of curiosity. "You can stay. And I'll stay, too."

CHAPTER 18

1980, Seadrift, Texas

Despite how small Seadrift was, and how even smaller the Vietnamese community was, the fishing production setup was a well-oiled machine. Locals called the port "Saigon Harbor," a nickname from the growing list of insults and infractions launched against "the other." The Vietnamese fishermen were known to stay out longer on the water than the locals did, reeling in more catches and selling them to locals for dirt cheap. They broke unspoken societal rules, setting their traps in waters that the local fishermen had claimed for themselves. Invisible lines, which had been drawn in the water for years, a pseudo DMZ, warned each side to stay away. But mounting tensions began blurring the lines between doing the right thing and doing what one had to do in order to survive.

Though Duc and Huey were fortunate to not have any more run-ins with the locals or clashes with the Ku Klux Klan, whose presence cast a darkness over the whole town, not many people were as lucky. Every night, everyone looked behind them to see if another shadow that was not their own was following them home.

But life kept going. And the men continued to go out into the waters in the early mornings and the women would stay back at the local crab factory and prepare and process thousands of blue crabs. They would sort, clean, steam, declaw, crack, and pick the meat to be packed into plastic containers. Some days, they'd gossip while separating out the roe; other days, they'd cry as claws would fly in every direction. They'd cry over missing their mothers, cry over missing Vietnam, and cry over wondering when this life would stop being so hard. But on the rare occasions, on the days they'd be graced with levity, the women would feel content in having repetitive tasks because that symbolized stability.

One woman in particular had caught the eye of all the men, including Duc and Huey. She walked with a nervous gait, but her eyes had a siren call to them, luring men's gazes toward her. Her eyes were sharp brown, distinct, but comforting and wide.

Her name was Điệp, but she went by her American name, Evelyn. Evelyn Lê.

Evelyn rarely smiled, or joined in on the gossip, nor had anyone ever seen her shed a tear. She was quiet, reserved, and diligent in her duties. She clocked in early, and left late, scurrying back to her home and to her husband. Her beauty was somehow gentle and loud at the same time. But she was married, a small ring looped around her wedding finger, thwarting any possible advances toward her. Duc and Huey would stare from afar, envious of her husband, Tuấn.

How fortunate Tuấn was, to have such a good and beautiful woman by his side.

But they also knew Tuấn to be a good man. The only fisherman who had taken in Duc and Huey, two strays from out of town, and allowed them on his boat. A man deserving of a beautiful wife and a beautiful home. He was boisterous but generous. Perhaps too generous, generous with his money, time, and empathy. They saw how Tuấn gave away what little money he had to others who needed it, and how he always took home less than his share of the catch, just so that others could eat more. Tuấn was respected, so they showed their deference back, and only dreamt of Evelyn at night, barely even acknowledging her or looking her in the eye at the factory.

"What if we just lived here permanently?" Duc had said randomly to Huey, one early morning out on Tuấn's fishing boat. "Maybe this is just the life we choose, for the rest of our lives? What if we stop running?"

Huey released a grunt—it was neither confirmation nor disagreement.

Duc tried again. "We could open up a restaurant together one day? A crab shack? Americans love crab. I've seen the way they eat it."

Again, Duc was met with another grunt.

"How about if we open up a—"

Huey interrupted with a grunt. This time it was bigger. More final.

"Okay, how about a bánh mì shop? Americans love sandwiches—"

With an exasperated half yell, Huey turned back around and growled at Duc. "You want to stay here forever and wait for death to come and collect us? We're practically living in another war zone here, anh. Look around, everyone's scared shitless around here."

"Well, we technically didn't lose *our* war," Duc began to tease, but was instantly silenced by the look Huey threw at him. The boat roared to life, heading back to shore. Tuấn was behind the wheel, as usual, a cigarette drooping from his lips, the wind whipping through his unruly hair, making it look as if it had been purposely slicked back.

"You two sisters fighting again?" Tuấn yelled out over the noise, a large grin plastered on his face.

"Convince the coward to stay here," Duc yelled back, jerking his head in Huey's direction. Tuấn said nothing, just cranked the old trawler into full gear and sped faster toward shore, a miracle of a feat since his old trawler was seemingly held together with elementary school glue and gum, yet it somehow managed to keep up with his request. Ocean droplets ran sideways against the three men's faces as they went back to shore.

As the horizon bloomed larger into view, Tuấn spoke up. "You both need a real reason to want to stay in this shithole," he said breezily, wiping off water from his brow. "You know what made me want to stay?" Nearing the harbor, the trawler came to a slow crawl, passing other shrimping trawlers along the way. Other Vietnamese fishermen nodded their heads in acknowledgment, while the non-Vietnamese turned a cold shoulder. Some even spat into the water as they passed. Duc, Huey, and Tuấn avoided eye contact as best they could, even with the slurs flying through the air.

As Tuấn pulled the trawler up to his dock, he took his dying cigarette from his mouth and stubbed it next to the glass jar filled a quarter of the way with old butts, and his smile took over his whole face.

"You want to know what made me want to stay here?" he repeated softly, no longer caring to lecture Duc and Huey.

The three men looked up to see Evelyn staring down at them from high up on the dock, her hair neatly pulled back into a low, soft bun, her face awash with sunlight, her blue linen dress matching the ocean. This time, though, her demeanor was different from what Duc and Huey saw day in and day out at the crab factory.

Evelyn was smiling, and her smile was locked and aimed at only one person.

"See, boys?" Tuấn said, still not looking at anyone else but Evelyn. "You have to have a reason to stay. Find your reason."

Duc and Huey watched as Tuấn docked his trawler, and before he hauled in the day's catch, he hopped over the railing onto the wooden deck and hugged his wife. Though neither man said it out loud, they knew that if they had a woman like Evelyn waiting for them at the end of the dock, they wouldn't ever want to leave—even if they were in the middle of a war zone.

The men laughed and carried about their day, pretending that all was right with the world. Because what else could they have done? They carried on, unprepared for the invisible demarcation line they were all living behind, which was about to topple over into chaos.

CHAPTER 19

Paulina

A s Paulina made her way through downtown San Francisco, she noticed the sea of men in puffer vests with badges hanging from lanyards around their neck. They all looked the same, and her eyes glazed over everyone, even though everyone fought for her to look at them. But Paulina was perpetually bored, bored of mindless workers, bored of the grind culture, and bored of the stories that people made up about her in their minds. The only thing that caught her eye was a young mother in the distance, holding the hand of a small child, their retreating backs to Paulina.

She watched them from a safe distance as the mother protected her child against the crowd, traffic, and the bustle of corporate greed around them, and Paulina felt a sadness wash over her until they disappeared around the corner.

But as Paulina entered the giant office building, which seemed almost phallic, piercing the sky, and made her way up to the sixtieth floor, she immediately forgot about the young mother and her daughter. There was no point in letting sadness win; otherwise she'd end up like her mother.

And that was the last thing she ever wanted.

"Knock knock," Paulina said, rapping her hand against Oliver's office door. Oliver looked up from behind his monitor, visibly shocked. It was a dreary Monday morning in downtown San Francisco, and yet Paulina was on corporate grounds, modestly dressed in a long pleated skirt, cashmere sweater, and a casual logo-less bag dangling off her wrist. Unlike Oliver, who was responsible for over two hundred employees, Paulina didn't seem to have any worry or responsibility, or a wrinkle on her face.

Who was Paulina Trần responsible for, other than herself?

Oliver's office was in a cloister with a few other cookie-cutter tech companies, and she stuck out like a weed in a sea of tech-branded backpacks. Lumped together, the companies were indiscernible to anyone who didn't work in the field. Shapeless logos of start-ups and other tech companies at varying seed stages, all holding empty promises of carving out a utopia one day. But in reality, they were a house of cards whose only pool of money came from bloated valuations and even more bloated egos. Paulina knew a thing or two about a house of cards, especially after having grown up in one.

Corporate America had always made her want to gag. She was certain there was a smell to it. It wasn't just a regular office smell of floor wax and sanitized air; it reeked of depression—like old wet laundry that had mildewed because one had forgotten about it and didn't put the load in the dryer in time. It smelled like no one had any control of their lives.

But Paulina always stuck out, no matter where she was.

She was satisfied watching Oliver's wide eyes, his fingers hovering over his keyboard. He couldn't deny her presence.

"Pauly," Oliver finally said, a warning in his voice, as he folded his arms across his chest and leaned far back in his Herman Miller chair. His face was now blank. His office was freezing in a subtle way that only women could pick up on, so Paulina crossed her arms, mirroring Oliver. "What on earth are you doing here? Also, is this the first time you've ever been inside a real office?"

"Oliver," she responded in a mocking, singsong voice. "What are *you* doing here? A mausoleum has more charisma than this open-floor office plan."

"I believe a mausoleum also has an open-floor plan, but for different reasons," he said sternly. "But you really shouldn't be here. I'm slammed with meetings. How did you get past my assistant? Actually, come to think of it, *where* is my assistant—"

"I've come to hunt you down," she interrupted him. "You've been ignoring and avoiding me. Don't pretend you haven't."

Oliver stared incredulously at Paulina. "I've sent over all the robots, equipment, engineers, and installers necessary to put everything together at your store. What more do you possibly need from me? You have everything you need to set you up for success. Just turn the 'on' switch 'on.'"

"You don't understand, Oliver, I *need* to win this. I need *you* there—"

"Win *what*? I still don't understand what you're winning here. And frankly, I'm concerned your father is doing this as some sort of embezzlement scheme or tax evasion—"

"Oh, get off your high horse. Why do you assume everyone is evading taxes? Is it 'cause we're Vietnamese—"

"Also, it's a *sandwich* shop. No offense, but this isn't exactly dire on my list. And don't take this the wrong way, but shouldn't you be in the kitchen or something? I mean that literally, not figuratively, by the way."

Before either of them could stop themselves, the bickering escalated, as it always did. It always started off softly, even childlike, then it quickly turned into a tornado, an onslaught, and a graveyard for all those in their way. Oliver and Paulina immediately fell back into their old ways, as they had three years ago.

Falling between the nebulous cracks of miscommunication and being misunderstood, but most of all, just missing each other. But neither of them could find the strength to admit it to the other, that perhaps all this pain and hurt boiled down to grief, grief of a different kind—grief knowing that your person is alive and well, but unwilling to reach out first.

Oliver's assistant stuck her head in apologetically for a brief second, murmuring how she had no idea how Paulina got past security, and just as quickly disappeared, just as a few rounds of curse words began to be mounted at one another.

There was a sudden buzzing on Oliver's desk, briefly interrupting their argument. Paulina's heart fell, and she knew who it was before he picked up. Call it a woman's intuition or perhaps being a Virgo, but on the other side of the call was Esther. *Esther.* The name that had haunted her ever since she landed in the Bay Area. Oliver quickly grabbed his phone, read the text, and responded immediately. She hated her jealousy; it was icky, Judas-esque, and irrelevant. She remembered how quickly Oliver got up the last time she saw him and left immediately, all at Esther's beck and call. Who was Esther? But more important, who was Esther to Oliver Chen? Her Oliver?

It pained her to see that Oliver was immune to her now, when three years ago, he'd have dropped everything to be with her. He'd have even quit his job on the spot if she had asked. Had she been nothing more than an experiment? A guinea pig for men to test out, to see if they were capable of commitment?

Paulina, I wish I had fought for your mother more.

Duc's words seared through her. Should she have fought for Oliver more back then? But Paulina at twenty-five was obstinate, unable to listen to anyone but herself. However, Paulina at twenty-eight was starting to feel the weight of time on her, and she was beginning to yearn for something more. Twenty-eight was also the year her mother was pregnant with Paulina. Perhaps that yearning was always ingrained in her, since inception.

"Just so you know," Paulina said as she managed to pull herself together, her jealousy replaced with bitterness as she careened toward self-sabotage. "*You're* the one who left me. You stopped returning my calls a year ago. Don't blame me now for showing up out of nowhere."

Oliver groaned and rubbed his eyes, then his temples. "You really want to do this now? *Right now?*"

"Yes."

"You weren't willing to change your lifestyle, Paulina. You were just flitting across the world. Hong Kong to Taipei to Berlin. You didn't care. You didn't care about *me* or my needs. You just expected me to keep up with you forever—"

"What's wrong with that?"

"People have responsibilities—"

"I have responsibilities—"

"You just care about surface-level—"

"*Surface-level?* Fuck you, Chen—"

"That's not what I meant—"

The slight crack of a door. Oliver's assistant poked her head in again, sheepishly apologized once more for interrupting, and quickly announced that it was time for school. Oliver shut his laptop, got up, and slipped on his coat. He gave Paulina a pointed look that it was time to leave.

"School?" Paulina repeated. As she looked through the glass door, she saw all of Oliver's coworkers, peers, and direct reports walk past his glass office, openly gawking at the two of them post-argument. Their coffee mugs curling steam out of them, their eyes half-awake on a Monday morning, jaws on the ground. Two men almost collided with each other going in opposite directions, too busy being enthralled by Paulina. Her face turned beet red.

"If you'll excuse me," Oliver said quickly, as he began to shove her out of his office. "I have to go do something. Let's finish this discussion later."

"Who the hell is Esther?" Paulina blurted out. "Are you seeing someone?"

"How do you know about Esther?" he shot back, his eyes worried.

"I saw her name pop up on your phone last time we met up, at the bar," she said. "Then you ran out of there with your tail between your legs. Who is Esther?"

He paused, sucked in his breath, his hands turned into fists. She could feel his knuckles behind her shoulders as he steered her out the door. She turned to see the veins expanding on his temples, revealing a side of him she'd never seen before, and she was conflicted on what to do. She was torn between hugging him or continuing to twist the proverbial knife in him even more, left and right.

He sighed. "Pauly, you are so goddamn frustrating. She's none of your business."

"Well, she sounds Korean, and very hot," Paulina sniped back. She felt like being petty for the sake of being petty.

"Well, you're half right, she is Korean, but more half-Korean," he said carefully, eyes cast downward. "But if I were you, I wouldn't call my three-year-old daughter hot." Paulina's face turned pale as she tried to find the words to string together. *Daughter?*

"Yes, I have a daughter," he said, responding to her thoughts. "And don't worry, it's not yours." The joke fell completely flat. "Now if you'll excuse me, I have to take her to preschool."

"Five?" Paulina repeated hollowly as life began to click together. "She's five years old?"

Suddenly, the timeline of everything, and what could have been between them, disappeared in front of her. Before Paulina could ask any more questions, she was thrown into the arms of Oliver's assistant, who held firmly on to her, escorting her out of the building, flanked on both sides by two security guards. Paulina went limp between them as she was suddenly thrown out into the brisk San Francisco fog.

She watched, dumbfounded, as she saw a black car pick up Oliver on the corner, and as he climbed in, she heard the delighted shrieks of a young girl from the inside, greeting her father, and Oliver's smile revealed something she'd never seen before: fulfillment. The car door slammed, and she watched the car pull away, moving toward a future she couldn't comprehend.

She'd never felt more heartbroken—no, grief-stricken—for an alternate life in which she'd be delighted to see her father take her to school, or even for her father to want to take her to school. Paulina pulled the sweater tighter around her shoulders and in the middle of a crowded sidewalk, filled with middle-aged men, badged employees, transplants, transients, and disgruntled strangers, she allowed herself to cry for the first time in years.

....

Back at the Duc's Sandwiches storefront in San Jose, Paulina stood amazed and shell-shocked. *A daughter?* A daughter. Though she was surrounded by mountains of crates and a swarming team of taskers and engineers, assembling all the new equipment for her store, Paulina felt alone. The sound of a thousand drills and hammers, like the crackling of broken headphones, seemed to evaporate into the ether, somehow going nowhere and everywhere at once.

The front door opened, causing the tiny bell to go off.

The nearly twenty-year-old bell, unchanging in an ever-changing enclave, was a symbol of the third Duc's Sandwiches store that had opened. A third pawn in Duc's endless thirst to conquer the chessboard of businesses. Paulina remembered the famous black-and-white newspaper photo of her mother, standing on a stool, hanging up the bell on opening day. It was the first photo she had seen with just her mother in it. It was the one photo where there wasn't Duc or Mr. Ngô crowding it—it was just simply Evelyn. Her mother had framed that newspaper clipping, and hung it up next to her vanity mirror for years. Anytime her mother would spritz herself with perfume or apply red lipstick, her eyes would gaze longingly at that photo. Even long after her mother had stopped spraying perfume or putting on lipstick, or even taking care of herself properly, Paulina still caught her staring at the newspaper clipping from time to time.

Yes, Paulina remembered the photo well.

In walked an elderly woman, pushing a metal rolling cart. A bit wobbly, and still in a fugue state, Paulina stood up and greeted the woman with her best manners.

"Sorry," she said, politely shooing the woman out. "We're closed for renovation. Come back next month."

Confused, the woman looked around, observed all the men in hard hats running around, and gave a wary look at the lone woman at the center of all the commotion. Ignoring Paulina's warning, she steadfastly approached, her cart wheeling faster toward Paulina. "I just want to buy a few loaves. I always buy my bread here. I stock up, you know."

Perturbed, Paulina went up to the woman, firmly grabbed her cart from her, and steered her back toward the door. "I'm sorry, but like I said, we're closed. Come back next month."

"You don't understand, I've been coming here for twenty years—"

Before Paulina could *really* shove the woman out, the bell dinged again, notifying her of another customer coming in. The bell was Paulina's Pavlov's theory—anytime it rang, it triggered an angry response. This time, an unassuming elderly man came in whistling, with a few newspapers tucked under his arm. He looked as if he was ready to park himself in the shop and not move for the rest of the day.

Paulina could feel her temple twitching. She still couldn't get the morning's memory out of her. Oliver. Esther. Daughter. His daughter? Is that why he left her? Who was the mother? A million questions began to swirl, and just as she was about to tell the old man the same thing she told the woman, the bell went off again, and this time, a horde of elderly women came tumbling in, each of their voices trying to outshine the others. Trying to keep up the pace, Paulina rallied the crowd together, assuring them that the shop was just *temporarily* closed, and to come back next month. That things will be better, more efficient. Wouldn't that make their lives easier? She was doing them a favor!

Meanwhile, the first woman was still going around, asking all the engineers and workers where she could buy her loaves for the week. From behind her, she could hear the lead tech engineer advising her to not have all these people in the shop during construction, while other voices began to escalate, asking what happened to Duc's Sandwiches and where was everything as it always had been? What was with all the changes? Why couldn't they just maintain their routines, and get on with their days? Before she could respond, the bell went off again as more regulars flooded in, and this time, Paulina couldn't hold it in anymore. All she could picture in her mind was Oliver and Esther, and the last three years of her losing sleep over him.

The coffee and the everything bagel she had earlier came up before she could stop it. She turned around and slammed into the lead engineer. In the mad rush of it all, she vomited up everything onto him. Specks and flecks of her breakfast could be seen in its chunks. Horrified, Paulina couldn't find a way to apologize. She just watched as her vomit slid off the man's clipboard and down his puffer vest. She silently thanked her mother's beauty for helping her get this far in life. The man gave her a napkin to wipe up her vomit.

For all the unkind moments Paulina had experienced in her life, her mother's beauty was the one privilege that she desperately held on to. But the day in which she couldn't rely on looks anymore was coming faster than she had expected, and more and more she looked in the mirror and saw her mother's face staring back at her: tired, lonely, and misunderstood.

"I said, where's the damn bread?" the first elderly woman repeated, echoing over and over again, frustrated, as she slammed her metal cart. "Where is Chị Mai? She always makes the bread. She's been making bread for twenty years."

"I let her go. I let all of them go. The overhead was too much," Paulina managed to say as she wiped her mouth with the napkin. "It's all going to be automated soon. The bread isn't even that good anyway. This will make it better. More modern. More efficient. Isn't that a good thing? Wouldn't that make your lives easier?"

"You fired Chị Mai?" the old woman said, aghast, ignoring everything else that Paulina had pitched. Promises of a better tomorrow ran in and out of the woman's ear. The woman had learned early on that tomorrow was never guaranteed, but that the only thing that could get her through the days were her routines, and knowing exactly where everything was. But she wasn't the only one who appeared shell-shocked. All the regulars who had come in promptly on Monday morning, and on every Monday for the past two decades, stopped arguing, stopped moving, and looked at Paulina as if she were nothing but a plague that had descended upon their city to disrupt their lives.

Duc's Sandwiches may not have been the best in the city, or particularly very good, but it was their constant. Buying bread was an easy win for them, when life hadn't been a series of wins, but constant chaos, churn, and heartbreak. Buying their daily bread had represented something to them, more than just a bastardized, colonial example of war and fusion, but resilience and hope. That they had turned something so French into something so Vietnamese—it was their pride.

Even if Duc's bread *was* shit.

And Paulina had yanked it all away from them without a thought or care.

CHAPTER 20

Georgia

The sputtering of Georgia's van was often a dead giveaway of her whereabouts, but Georgia was grateful that her faithful van had made a miraculous recovery, practically coming back from the dead. After dropping out of college, and nearly three years on the road, pinballing between the coasts, Georgia's attachment to her van was beyond surface sentimental; it represented a home more stable than she'd ever known. The van offered physical shelter and protection, and hadn't willingly abandoned her like her sisters had.

All Georgia ever had were memories of her family leaving her, one by one. First her mother, then her sisters left the house, each one determined to escape their father and their brother—none of them realizing that they had forgotten her along the way.

As the morning broke, Georgia was determined to keep track of her mother even more. She had lost Evelyn a few days ago, but Georgia managed to find her (her mother's Vespa had dented Georgia's van in an attempt to escape her). This time, though, Evelyn almost made it seem like she wanted to be found. She had even left Georgia a hot plate wrapped in tinfoil outside her van, and knocked a few times on her door before running away to her apartment just a few feet away. It was a plate of chicken. But it was always chicken. Maybe it was a Vietnamese mother thing, or maybe it was a southern thing. Or maybe it was just a stranger trying to remember how to be a mother again.

Georgia pulled back the curtains in her old van, allowing the southern sun to stream in as she enjoyed her mother's chicken. The bayou, blue as ever, greeted her through the window, and she greeted it back with the same warm welcome. New Orleans was starting to grow on Georgia, in a way that no other city had before. Almost half a year into her father's inheritance scheme, and she felt more comfortable living in her van than ever before. She was so secluded from the rest of her family, but she was in the same place as her mother, and perhaps that was all the family she needed now. It was as if she and Evelyn shared a secret that no one else knew, even if all she got was chicken.

Today, Georgia felt that, perhaps, she could find a way to break through to her mother.

I hope you find a bit of yourself, somewhere along the bayou. Just like how I did, when I was your age.

Duc's words murmured in her ear as she put on the coffee, the familiar groaning sound of her ancient coffeepot began to drip, and Georgia set out to get the day's affairs in order. She shoved the mattress back into its corner of the van, took out the composting toilet, refilled the water tank, and air-dried some laundry on a clothesline she had strung together on the roof. She hummed while she put away clothes, washed dishes, and reorganized her tiny spice rack. Everything that Georgia had ever needed was inside that Sprinter van. Though her father or her siblings couldn't understand why she had given up everything to live her life in a van, Evelyn was the one person who hadn't made fun of her when she discovered her youngest daughter's lifestyle.

As the morning turned into early afternoon, Georgia began to feel sleepy. The sun was different here than it was in Houston; a temptress, it was practically urging her to take a nap. Georgia threw a cursory glance outside Evelyn's humble ground-floor apartment and saw that her mother's curtains were still drawn tightly. They'd been drawn for a good few days, ever since their last explosive fight, and her mother hadn't left her complex. Georgia peeked at where her mother's Vespa was parked, double-checking that it was still there. True enough, there it was, rusted, yet sturdy and unmoving. Satisfied, Georgia unrolled her mattress pad and laid her head down, allowing herself to rest, with only the hum of the radio station in the background and the faint chirping of cardinals in the distance. Her mother wasn't going anywhere; Georgia would make sure of it.

But as Georgia let herself go deeper, dreaming of alternate realities and undiscovered poetry books, she failed to see her mother tumbling out onto her patio, complete with a backpack, sunglasses, and a hat. At her age, somehow still spry, Evelyn managed to crawl over the concrete barrier between the porch and the parking lot. She tiptoed toward her Vespa, and wheeled it out into the dirt road before starting it up. She almost threw a fit as the Vespa made a few groaning noises, attempting to quiet it down, until it finally came to life with a roar. She quickly hopped on the bike and snapped on her helmet.

Before she took off, she gave a sad glance at the yellow van that had been parked outside her apartment for days—the van that had been watching her steadily and carefully, that had followed her around for months, trying to get to know her from a distance; the yellow van that had given her a ride home from the grocery store when her Vespa had broken down; the yellow van that housed her youngest daughter, who was so desperate for answers about life, lineage, and for a lost language she would never understand; the yellow van that had been her shadow ever since it arrived in New Orleans. She stared forlornly, wondering if she was making another mistake, or perhaps running away was all she knew. But she could no longer look at Georgia's face without being reminded of her past, of the lies, of Duc, of Huey, of it all. It reminded her too much of a life that had been a house of cards.

Before Evelyn could second-guess herself or dwell any longer, she pulled up the kickstand and sped away from her youngest daughter, and from all the hurt memories that Georgia had brought with her.

....

By the time Georgia woke up, she knew her mother was long gone.

The surrounding woods felt dark, colder than usual, and empty. Her mother had proven everyone in her family right: She simply didn't care about anyone but herself.

How could she?

How could she do this *again*?

Georgia was heartbroken, exhausted, numb. She didn't know why she had slept long after the sun had gone down and through several alarms. The coffee had gone icy and thin, the outside laundry had crinkled and turned stiff, and when she opened up her mini fridge, she saw that there was no food left.

Her mother had disappeared without leaving any food for her, after dangling it in front of her earlier. Georgia felt the pain of abandonment again, and the yearning for a stable mother who actually liked motherhood. The little girl in her curled into a fetal position, too afraid to do anything again out of fear and too hungry to want to do anything.

But Georgia, an eternal hopeless romantic, slid the door wide open and stepped out into the evening, still hopeful that she could be proven wrong. There it was, just a hint of May rose, jasmine, and bourbon vanilla, then it disappeared. Her nose confirmed that her mother was gone, and her eyes confirmed that her mother's curtains were all drawn open, revealing how dark and sparse her home was. Her green Vespa was absent. Evelyn had left no trace behind.

Georgia's fist curled up, and she could feel the tears forming at the corners of her eyes.

"Fuck you," Georgia whispered, barely allowing herself to say the words out loud. Was she being disrespectful? She didn't know. She barely knew the woman, how could it have been disrespectful? Evelyn was a stranger, undeserving of her patience, time, or empathy. "Fuck *you*." She said it louder this time, unafraid. "FUCK YOU!!!!!!!!!!!!!!!!!" She stared down the empty dirt road, daring her mother to show up again to face her. All along the apartment complex row, one by one, lights began turning on as they heard Georgia's scream of anguish, of a young woman trying to understand and make sense of a world with and without her mother.

"Shut up!" someone yelled from the other side of the building. Georgia didn't have the strength to yell back at the stranger, because in that moment, her stomach grumbled loudly, reminding her that she also had to take care of herself, that her body shouldn't be forgotten, either. She gripped her stomach, and slid down, defeated, on the dirt road, wondering what to do next. Should she call Jane and confess? Hell, should she tell Duc? Would anyone believe that she had found their mother? Worse: Would anyone even care? Surely, her sisters would care at least? Maybe they would even fly out to help Georgia look for her. There was still hope. But something in the back of her mind kept nagging at her, telling her that nobody cared at all.

And maybe her mother knew it, too.

Ngày nào tao cũng muốn chết.

Each time her mother and Georgia got into a fight for the past several months, her mother would shout this at her. Their fights remained the same, but escalated in volume: *Tell me why you left us. Tell the truth.* All Georgia could do was memorize the tones each time, hoping to find someone to translate it for her.

Suddenly, the apartment next to her mother's lit up, and the back screen door slid away to reveal a small, middle-aged Vietnamese woman, staring curiously at Georgia. Without saying a word, she gestured for Georgia to come inside. Georgia, polite till the end, smiled awkwardly, and gestured *no thanks*. But the woman was relentless, beckoning at her aggressively. Reluctantly, Georgia did what any dutiful, young woman was taught to—she listened to her elder. She got up off the dirt road and made her way toward her mother's apartment complex, and into the neighbor's apartment.

Georgia took off her shoes and gingerly crossed into the woman's apartment. The woman, frantic, began scuttling around, cleaning up as she went. Towels were bundled up quickly, stacks of fading newspapers were thrown behind a cabinet, the woman apologized in Vietnamese, and Georgia could only surmise she was apologizing for the mess. But the words came out like a gargle, like any time she heard the language.

"I don't speak Vietnamese," Georgia said, shaking her head. "Sorry, but I can't understand you."

The woman gave a pained look, unsure of what to do next. She quickly grabbed her purse and pulled out her wallet, sliding her driver's license to Georgia. *Anne Chau.* Anne.

"Anne," Georgia said out loud. "Your name is Anne."

She nodded.

"Anne, do you know where the woman who lives next door went?" Georgia asked. "She must have disappeared sometime in the early afternoon. Drives a green Vespa? Kinda has crazy eyes? Maybe *is* kind of crazy? Not maybe. She *is* crazy."

Anne, whose black hair was riddled with strands of soft gray, put on her reading glasses and gestured awkwardly for Georgia to sit down. She muttered a few words in Vietnamese again and tried her best to use her hands to talk to Georgia. She mimed drinking. Georgia nodded. The woman disappeared into the kitchen, her head bowing on the way out. The clanging of pots and pans, a cabinet door opening and closing, and the steam of a kettle could be heard in the background.

Georgia took a moment to look around the apartment, trying to surmise who this woman was or how she knew Evelyn. As her eyes roamed, she took note of the yellow-stained ceilings, the orchid plants still wrapped in plastic that lined the patio windowsill, and the many small piles of clutter that crowded the already small apartment. The older woman had wrapped her couch in plastic, recycled every plastic container and used them as storage bins, and saved every newspaper that had ever existed. Georgia felt at home in Anne's apartment. There was a hoarder quality to it, and the inability to keep the dust out—every surface had a layer of film of some kind. To the untrained eye, an outsider would have classified this home as filthy, messy, dirty, dark, crowded, almost depressing. But Georgia knew this home very well; it reminded her of her father's home. She had grown up in this home.

This home belonged to an immigrant refugee woman who was afraid of tossing anything because she had come with nothing.

Anne was a woman who was familiar to her.

And here she was, emerging with a tray of tea and a giant brown bag. She put the bag at Georgia's feet and the familiar smell of homemade Vietnamese dishes curled toward her. There was container after container of food. But it wasn't the type of smells she intimately knew; it was a forgotten childhood smell that evoked old traumas from having grown up without her mother in the house. Duc's cooking was not like Evelyn's cooking; though they used the same ingredients, the outcome was always different. The smell of lemongrass and pork belly—the dish's name a blur in her mind—elicited another stomach rumble from Georgia, and Anne silently handed her some chopsticks and a bowl. Without arguing, Georgia went on autopilot, immediately opened a container, and began to push food into her mouth. She shoveled food until the hunger pain turned into the pain of acid reflux from eating too fast.

Anne just sat back, quietly sipping on her tea.

"Thank you," Georgia said as she finally came up for air, and set the chopsticks down. "I was so hungry. This is delicious; your cooking is so wonderful."

Anne shook her head. "Not me. Your mom. Good cook."

Georgia eyed the bag of crowded food containers suspiciously. "My mom made all of this? You mean the woman who lives next to you? Evelyn Lê?"

Anne nodded, satisfied that they were overcoming their language barrier. "She make. For you. Told me to give to you before she left. Said you are too skinny. Need to eat more."

"Skinny?" Georgia repeated hollowly. "Where did she go?"

Anne shook her head. "Your mom sad. Needed to go away for some time."

"My mom has been sad her entire life," Georgia said, getting angrier. "Why does she get to leave whenever she's sad? She won't *talk* to me. Do you understand what it's like to have a mother who won't talk? Who won't explain anything? That everything just needs to be *accepted*. Doesn't she know that I've been sad, too?

"I've been sad since the day she left. And all I've been able to do is drive around aimlessly, wandering forever in my shit van, looking for a reason to keep going."

But Georgia had hit the ceiling of Anne's language capability, and she was met with nothing more than an uncertain smile. Her ears couldn't grasp Georgia's melancholy.

The woman got up and grabbed an old photo album off the shelf, and a sheet of dust fell in perfect unison. She flipped toward the back and handed Georgia the album. There it was. An old black-and-white photo of Anne and Evelyn, in front of what appeared to be a factory of some kind. Though the two women were smiling, they also seemed tense. Their eyes weren't smiling back.

"When was this?" Georgia asked as she stared deep into her mother's face.

"1981."

Georgia flipped a few pages forward and saw another photo of her mother, and this time it looked like it had been her mother's wedding day. Evelyn wore a loose, cheap red dress, and stood awkwardly between Duc and Mr. Ngô; the three of them had their arms pinned at their sides. Something about the photo made Georgia laugh. "I can't believe my parents have known Mr. Ngô for so long. He even has the same energy here. He's just so awkward. He's just been hanging around with my dad for so long, it's crazy."

"Mr. . . . ?" Anne leaned forward and pursed her lips in concentration. Georgia tapped on Mr. Ngô, who stood tall and gangly next to her mother, in another ill-fitting suit. Both of their faces unsmiling, but fierce and full of life. "That's Huey."

"Huey," Georgia repeated, stamping Mr. Ngô's first name into memory.

"*Huey* Ngô. The family lawyer. My father's best friend. The uncle who isn't really my uncle, but I have to call him uncle. You know how it is."

"Uncle? Huey not your uncle," Anne said, staring at Georgia strangely. Georgia couldn't tell if she understood what she was saying or not. Georgia flipped back to the original photo of Anne and her mother.

"Of course he isn't my 'uncle' uncle," Georgia rambled. "He's like one of those *uncles* you have to call your uncle, you know?"

Anne opened her mouth again, feebly trying to find the right translated words, but Georgia interrupted her. "What are you and my mother standing in front of?"

"Crab factory. Me and her, we worked," Anne said. "Hard times. Very hard, bad times. Your father help us. He helped all of us. He's a good man."

"My father?" Georgia echoed softly, staring at the wedding photo again; this time, her eyes lasered in on Duc Trần—the father she knew on paper, the accolades he had received, the legacy he had built off Duc's Sandwiches. Georgia stared at the larger-than-life figure, hoping that the longer she stared, the more she would be able to understand how Anne could see Duc as this incredible person. But all she saw was someone who had failed spectacularly behind closed doors. Her finger traced his outline, hoping that somehow, magically, her father's soul would transfer to her finger, and she could walk away understanding more.

"Your father isn't—" Anne began. But the roar of an antique-sounding Vespa interrupted both their thoughts. The sound of a dying engine curled up right outside Anne's patio, and Georgia ran to the window, pulled aside the curtain, and saw that her mother was back. Dejected and irritated, her mother got off her Vespa, kicked it in frustration. It emitted a cloud of black smoke back into her face, causing her to cough and recoil. She gave it a final kick, her petite leg full of anger, before stomping back into her apartment. The slam of the back door rattled Anne's conjoined wall.

"Hey, Anne," Georgia whispered, her eyes still glued to her mother's Vespa. "What does ngày nào tao cũng muốn chết mean? Sorry if I butchered that expression. My mother says it all the time, anytime we've fought, she ends it with that. But I don't know what it means."

Anne sighed. "Want death each day." She thumped her heart, two, three times.

"You want death?"

"No, Evelyn. That's what she's saying. *She* wants death."

I want to die every day, Georgia realized.

"That's what my mother keeps saying to me?" Georgia said, shocked. "She wants to die?"

"Death is freedom," Anne said, strained. "But we keep going, con. No choice."

Georgia could hear her mother banging around on the other side of the thin wall, throwing things in frustration, accompanied by loud whimpers of a failed escape. She didn't need to understand Vietnamese to understand her mother.

To understand that Evelyn wasn't just a mother, but a woman who had been in pain for so long.

CHAPTER 21

Evelyn

One of the worst things about living in that gaudy mansion was that it became an echo chamber for the children. The day I had overheard Duc and Huey's private conversation and had begun packing my life into one suitcase, I could hear the children murmuring at the kitchen table, which quickly turned into an argument, a crescendo I knew wouldn't end well. Georgia laughed alone in her room; she was still young enough to need me, my scent, my body, to sleep. But her laugh comforted me; it convinced me that she was going to be okay.

At least, that was the lie I used to comfort myself.

Why do rich people prefer to live in gigantic houses? How could anyone ever see anyone in such a big, empty home? I missed our first starter home, a small duplex off Wilcrest and Bellaire, so much. When we were crammed together in a room, I had eyes on everyone at all times. Life was so much simpler back then.

"Give that back to Paulina, Jude!" Jane's strong voice, demanding restitution. Jane, my eldest daughter. Selfless Jane. Always defending her younger sisters while leaving herself defenseless. I knew she had gotten that trait from me. I felt the failure of motherhood, plunging its knife into my back slowly.

"What's yours is mine!" Jude screamed back with all the might in his lungs. But he was still one against four. Despite being born the exception, the only son in a sea of daughters, the odds were stacked against him in this kind of battle.

I was always awkward with Jude when I should have embraced him more, but it felt safer to hold him at an arm's distance. If Jude came too close, old memories would resurface, and it reminded me of how quickly I could lose everything.

He reminded me too much of him.

"Eat shit, you entitled rat!" Bingo, my second-eldest daughter, and the one I worried about the most. Prone to outbursts and always shunning logic, she was the worst combination of both Duc and me, and I often wondered how she would brave the world as she got older. I knew Duc shouldn't have been around us for so long; his influence was rough and there was a lack of care about the children. I knew he cared, but he didn't *care*.

"I'm telling Má about your dirty mouth!" Jude fought back.

"Go ahead, like she gives a *shit* about any of us. Can't even be bothered to leave her room for weeks. She might as well be dead."

I froze then, midway between shoving some winter clothing into my suitcase. Paulina, the most cutting of them all. Dead? I scoffed. How little they knew.

Meanwhile, Georgia had reached max capacity—her screaming filled her lungs, akin to a cat climbing a tree, unable to find its way back down. She pleaded to be picked up and comforted, her toys too useless to distract her. I was torn between running to her and running away. How could I have possibly ever have prepared for such a life? I never even graduated from high school. Guilty, I let Georgia keep crying.

Once I finished packing the essentials, I proceeded to put on my usual makeup: pencil-thin eyebrows, white-powdered face, and a neatly curled bob. I stared at myself in the mirror, embarrassed by how tired I looked, especially for such a young mother. The deep, dark bags under my eyes revealed my insomnia. Sleep eluded me and was replaced with hallucinations of my childhood in Hà Nội, my teenage years in Oklahoma City, and my twenties spent down in Seadrift. Every place haunted me. I'd been stuck in Houston for over a decade now, wondering if this city was my final resting spot. Vietnamese women were meant to be migratory creatures; it had been a strange adjustment to stay so still. What was I doing, pretending to live a lie so long? Who was I anymore? How could Duc and Huey do it, day in and out, for decades?

But most importantly, what really happened to Tuấn on that boat? What were they keeping from me? What did they not want me to know?

I got up from the chair, walked past my closet stuffed with designer clothes with the tags still on them, and instead put on the same ratty clothes I had on the day I left my parents' home in Oklahoma. I remembered that day well, carving the memory into stone. I had prayed for my life to become biblical, so that I could return laden with the type of stories my mother could only dream of achieving. I dreamt of returning to my mother's arms, rested and fulfilled.

I hadn't seen my mother in ten years, and for the hours leading up to my departure, I wondered if that cycle was doomed to repeat. Would my children be okay if they wouldn't see me for ten years?

As I slowly finished dressing, I saw Duc and Huey through the window on the lawn, in their usual positions. In the past months, Duc and Huey had begun treating me as if I had an incurable disease, that perhaps I should be locked up. I debated having one last conversation, but the thought didn't last longer than flipping a coin for heads or tails. I didn't even care which one it landed on. I wanted out.

I silently crept downstairs, lugging my suitcase behind me. The children didn't even notice me. It seemed almost too easy. It shouldn't be this easy to walk out on your family. But it was. I walked through the arched wooden front door that morning, and the last thing I heard before I shut the door was Jude laughing at the kitchen table. We locked eyes for a brief second, and I was worried he could see right through me.

The moment I made it down the long driveway, in an old pair of ratty slippers, and past Duc and Huey, I didn't look back once. But I allowed myself one more memory: I closed my eyes and preserved my only son's laugh, wondering if I'd ever hear it again. His laugh sounded so sweet yet sickly, like eating so much chocolate you get a stomachache from it. It didn't help that Jude's laugh reminded me too much of *his* laugh.

The ghost I couldn't let go of. Not until I became a ghost myself.

....

The rumor mill let me know that nobody realized I'd been gone for days, not even when the children brought it up the first time, the fourth time, or the sixth time. I had left it all behind. Duc, the empire, the money, the children, the mansion. I had heard whispers, yes; everyone in Houston cupped their mouths in horror, clutching their jade necklaces, and spread rumors faster than the speed of light. They'd all wondered if I'd been possessed by an evil spirit, or perhaps I had found a richer man to attach myself to. Maybe I had gotten greedier when Duc came into money and wanted more. Maybe Duc cheated on me with a younger woman and I went into hiding from shame. Where did Evelyn go?

Yes, where did I go?

Rumors said that I followed the trail out west, to Orange County, like most other Vietnamese immigrants. Others said I went east to Miami, where I started my own empire. The old men who played Chinese chess in the park and smoked their off-brand cigarettes said the local monk had predicted I would move to Australia one day—claimed that I'd always talked about moving to Sydney, and how the Vietnamese community over there was stronger than the one in America.

Something must have been the catalyst for my abrupt departure, because why would an immigrant woman, who came to America with nothing to her name, walk away from a life her own mother would have traded her soul for? Everyone had a fantastical story behind my reasoning, but no one had ever asked the most crucial question, which only needed a binary answer:

Are you okay?

PART 3

SHAPING, FIGURING
OUT WHAT FAMILY
LOOKS LIKE

CHAPTER 22

March 1981, Seabrook-Kemah, Texas

F orty-five minutes south of central Houston, out on Clear Lake Creek, the pier was swarming with families and couples milling about, enjoying the bright blue waters. Children ran down the pier steps, much to the chagrin of their parents, who chased after them, screaming, ice cream melting down the cone and all over their hands. *Jessica! I said stop right now! Tony, you get your tiny butt back here right now!*

It was the middle of March, and spring always brought hope.

Little did they understand how dire the situation had become between the Vietnamese fishermen and the locals.

Everyone on shore saw the boat coming down Clear Lake Creek before it even appeared on the horizon. Some Vietnamese families who were on the pier that day swear they saw the hanging man effigy first before they saw the hull of the boat or any of the white robes. From far away, the white robes could have been mistaken for either white flags or sheets drying in the wind. Either way, they were expecting something a bit more innocuous than what was to come.

Decades later, men would still bolt upright in the middle of the night, sweating from nightmares of the images of the effigy hanging high from the steel beam, which resembled a Vietnamese man.

Chú Bảo, who was there that day, with his wife and three daughters, was the first to realize that the incoming boat was not a friend, but foe. He had thought the hanging effigy was real. Shell-shocked, he prayed it wasn't any of his brothers, uncles, or friends swinging from the beam, their legs dangling, a noose tight around their neck. For a split second, he even prayed it wasn't his father, even though his father was long dead. Who was the man they had? That could easily have been him. How lucky he was that it wasn't him.

But then he heard the laughter rising from the boat, a guttural choir, and he quickly realized they were laughing at him. At all of them. They were laughing and pointing at everyone's shocked expressions. Standing on the shore, their mouths gaping open, their hands covering their mouths in shock. The effigy was a corporeal threat to every Vietnamese left in southeast Texas, a warning of what was to come if they all didn't pack up their lives and move soon. Chú Bảo covered his daughters' eyes as best he could, but he didn't have enough hands to cover all his daughters' and his wife's eyes. He decided right then and there that the minute they got back home, he'd shut down their restaurant and head west to Orange County.

Much to the shock of residents between Seabrook and Kemah, the calm waters were interrupted when a trawler appeared carrying local fishermen and half a dozen Klansmen decked out in their signature white robes. The two groups, proverbially hand in hand, a sign of unity for a growing movement for what was to come if they didn't get their way. At the helm of the boat stood Louis Beam, the Grand Dragon of the Texas Knights of the Ku Klux Klan, reiterating the threat he had made over Valentine's Day. This time, he shouted it again to make sure everyone heard, his voice carried downwind, from Seabrook to Kemah and everyone along the Texas coast: *The Vietnamese fisherman have sixty days to leave town before the start of shrimping season in May; otherwise there'll be hell to pay.*

They shouted, cheered, and toasted one another; their vulgarity against the breezy backdrop of mid-March chilled the onlookers.

"Ba?" Chú Bảo's youngest daughter asked. She pointed to the effigy. "Why does that look like you? Do you think it's a present for you?"

Chú Bảo didn't know how to answer her. All he could do was keep covering her eyes.

A crowd had formed now, half of them began nodding their heads vigorously, vocalizing their agreement proudly. The other side, silent, horrified. How was this humanity? An off-duty reporter, who happened to be there on that fateful day, took out his camera in a rush and snapped the one photo that would forever be cemented in Texas history.

The dirty Vietnamese fishermen have to go.

They're stealing jobs away from local fishermen whose families have been in the Gulf Coast for generations.

They're responsible for Billy Joe Aplin's death.

They don't know the rules of the waters.

They overfished.

Since when did the pier become Saigon Harbor?

Why did they come here?

Off to the side, hidden behind an old ice cream stand, Huey watched in horror as the scene unfolded before him. All his fears from before had now come to fruition. Regret tasted bitter in his mouth, and a million different life paths swirled through his mind. Sixty days? They had sixty days to leave town forever. He watched as the Klansmen waved shotguns in the air. How strange, what freedom meant in this country, how only certain people could wave guns with abandon without repercussions, even though everyone was allowed to own them.

Who would come to their aid now? Huey's faith in the system was gone. Why did Duc take him here? To this shit place? They had to leave. Immediately. But a twinge of sadness crossed his mind. He thought of Evelyn's quiet smile in the moment. Perhaps it was comforting, or perhaps he knew he was going to miss that smile once they left town. But she would never be his. It was quite baffling to Huey, who, in that moment, couldn't stop thinking about Evelyn, instead of his own survival.

CHAPTER 23

Connie

Once Connie entered the airspace of Louis Armstrong New Orleans International Airport, she braced herself. Not only did the atmosphere tangibly change on the descent, but she felt her priorities shift as well. On the entire flight, she rehearsed what she wanted to say to Evelyn. But she felt her stomach lurch the closer they got to the city; phantom bile rose to the back of her throat. Connie hadn't been back to New Orleans in ten years. NOLA, the Paris of the South—monikers of the city, which meant nothing to her. She'd only ever known it as the hometown she wanted to escape from.

Connie had often wondered what it'd be like to meet the infamous Evelyn Lê. She had strange hallucinations during the long journey from Bali. What was Evelyn like in person? More important, which version of Evelyn would she get? The young mother who couldn't get out of bed for weeks to care for her own children? Or the shrewd business entrepreneur who helped Duc crawl their way out of poverty and build an empire together? Or perhaps the ugly rumors were true, and that Evelyn had lost her mind a long time ago, leaving nothing but a hollow shell.

In all her versions of Evelyn, there was still always a crooked halo taped over her head, held with nothing more than straw and hot glue—because despite the trail of suffering Evelyn had caused, her absence had somehow transcended her into a larger-than-life figure. She'd become biblical, the mystery belle of Texas. Audiences loved a tortured woman. They exalted her and she was often the subject of bavardage over coffee by Vietnamese Houston socialites. Her marriage to Duc was used as a cautionary tale by those who attended temple on Sundays—Evelyn was an unsolved medical case, a true rags-to-riches story, who left it all behind for a life of solitude. Was she contagious? Was she patient zero? But Connie saw Evelyn for what she really was, nothing more than a charlatan. If Connie was labeled a gold digger by everyone around her, then Evelyn was the true con artist.

It wasn't fair. None of it was. And yet, the punishment never fit the crime when it came to the public lashing of women.

Connie had always known each location where Evelyn was hiding out. Even when she hid out in Sydney, then moved to Oklahoma City, then Philadelphia, and had a brief appearance back in San Jose. Connie had kept tabs on her. She knew Evelyn had been in New Orleans for years now. Duc wasn't very sneaky, hiring private investigators to keep track of the where-abouts of the mother of his children for the past twenty years. What was strange to her, though, was that he never told his children where she was, despite their own searches and anxieties about their mother. Especially when the searches stopped and the children gave up, he still didn't tell them.

Why would Duc purposely hide their mother's location?

Once she stepped off the tarmac, she stood on top of the ramp and took a deep breath. Long past the dog days of summer, the city of New Orleans was now in the uncomfortable transition of leaving fall and en-tering winter. She remembered how sharp the weather turned in the city, and how locals wouldn't touch the French Quarter with a six-foot pole. Those quiet months were always magnificent, giving the city a breather to recuperate from outside noise and opinions and young white women who made a pilgrimage to Marie Laveau's Tomb, where they would burn photos of their exes. Connie was always removed from all of that.

She shuddered, feeling herself regress to being sixteen, with delu-sional dreams of becoming a pop star one day and never seeing east New Orleans ever again.

Her life hadn't turned out as biblical as she thought it would have. She was just Duc Trần's second wife—who possibly wasn't even really legally married to him. Oh, the anger. The anger. The *unjustness* of it all. Villains only became villains out of desperation. When the world wouldn't listen, they made them listen. Her mind raged on, imagining all the different ways she would sever the limbs off Duc, if she ever saw him again.

But Duc's time would come. Evelyn was up first. Patience.

A black SUV pulled up at the bottom of the ramp, and a driver got out, opening the passenger door for her. She made her way down the ramp, and with each step she conquered, she knew first and foremost, before she showed up at Evelyn's front steps, demanding restitution and for her to put a stop to Duc's insane inheritance scheme, she needed to first see her own version of Marie Laveau in the Crescent City.

She didn't need any voodoo or any of the fake charms peddled to tourists to help them find love or ward off evil. That was amateur hour and for those who didn't understand that there was magic in this world, in the form of a black American Express. She needed to see the most powerful woman she knew, someone she had always been frightened of, to help her take down Evelyn Lê once and for all.

"Where to, ma'am?" her driver asked as he put her suitcases into the trunk.

"Eastern Orleans Parish, please," Connie sniffed. "We're going to see my mother."

....

Mrs. Vũ was a formidable, but frightening and beautiful, woman who rarely smiled. In fact, Mrs. Vũ hadn't smiled since the early eighties, in an attempt to minimize her wrinkles and to avoid conversations with strangers. Also, there was nothing to smile about. Laughter, joy, silliness—those things were reserved for the uber-wealthy, and for those who lived their lives in ignorance and bliss. What was there to smile about, when she had seen the world for what it was? When men ravaged and pillaged the world for causes that hurt those who couldn't fight back and defend themselves? How Mrs. Vũ longed to give her daughter that same ignorance, and then perhaps they both could have a taste for the real finer things in life.

Mrs. Vũ sensed her daughter was back in New Orleans. She was grateful for the invisible strings that tied them together, because at least Connie couldn't cut those strings. She was still able to hold on to her daughter somehow, even if it was from so very far away.

The black SUV pulled into her driveway, and Connie stepped out to face her childhood home: a crumbling one-story duplex that was the size of Duc's entire living room. Connie adjusted her sunglasses, moved her Birkin from one arm to the other, and cuffed her sleeves up, revealing a new tan from her trip to Bali. The house was even more dilapidated since her last visit, ten years ago. The cracks had widened, the small lawn was littered with various trash, and the paint job that Connie had paid for last year was starting to chip. And whatever happened to the rosebush she also gifted? The more Connie stood there, the more she felt claustrophobic. Her humble childhood home taunted her, warned her of what she could lose if things didn't go her way.

The front door opened, and Mrs. Vũ stepped out, in an oversize T-shirt and mismatched bottoms. Mrs. Vũ looked older than ever, tired, and it seemed as if life hadn't been as kind in the latter years to her as it had been to Connie. The smallest difference with money could have been life-changing to her. The most Mrs. Vũ had seen of the world was on the helicopter ride, escaping Sài Gòn. It'd been such a strange moment for her, to see her fallen city, her hometown, from an aerial view. How beautiful it was, and yet how fleeting that beauty was, watching it be torn apart by men, who looked like ants from so high up.

Mother and daughter faced each other. The tension was thick with so many past wrongs, so many lost apologies, so many grudges and miscommunications that had piled on top of one another, until the mountain was too big to climb. But they were never more united than they were when it came to seeking revenge on a man.

"What happened?" Mrs. Vũ asked immediately. No greeting, no "I love you," no "How are you?" It was a blunt knife, straight to the point. "If you're going to get divorced, at least get something. Texas isn't a fifty-fifty divorce split state, you know. It's not like California. I told you, you should have gotten married and moved to California."

"I know," Connie said in an equally apathetic voice, neither one wanting to give an inch or a hint that they cared about the other. "That's why I need your help. My lawyer can't help me anymore. I need to hit Duc where it hurts, or at least, secure *something* for myself."

"Who is the money all going to then?"

"The first wife. The mother."

Mrs. Vũ grew quiet. This situation was dire. She wanted nothing more than to make sure that Connie was taken care of for life. Duc could have dropped dead for all she cared, as long as Connie had the means to live a life better than hers.

"That old fool. Guilt will kill him in the end," Mrs. Vũ muttered under her breath. She opened the front door wider, and gestured for her one and only child to come inside. Connie slowly walked up the steps and into the only home she'd ever known as a child. The four walls and a roof, familiar but suffocating, with a mother who had taught her more about how to survive than to love. "Have you eaten yet?"

"No," Connie said in a small voice, revealing just how very tired she was. "Not yet."

CHAPTER 24

Jude and Jane

An early spring in Houston meant that the city had survived tornado season. No big storms had traveled up from the Gulf this year, and the foliage along Buffalo Bayou had peacefully transitioned from a grayish brown to a jade hue. The sidewalks along the water shined with bursts of bright yellows and greens. People lounged along the park in light jackets, holding hands, talking business, gossiping, or meeting up for the first time from a dating app, asking each other things that only transplants could ask each other. Spring was for strangers who wanted lovers. *What kind of engineer are you? Have you been to the Space Center yet? What are you studying at Rice? Would you ever move back to California?* As Jude walked through the park, his hands in his pockets, deep in thought, he passed by two people sitting on a bench, making their way through "The 36 Questions that Lead to Love." They were still only at the beginning and Jude overheard the young woman, wearing her hair high up in a ponytail, sporting a nose ring, ask her date, "Question number four. What would constitute a 'perfect' day for you?"

"This day," the guy responded, his cheeks flushed red. "This moment."

Jude blanched from the cheesiness. The guy looked too eager to please, with his hair coiffed back with a mound of gel, and glasses too big for the bridge of his nose. The guy leaned in for a kiss, and the young woman welcomed it. Jude couldn't decide if he wanted to vomit or throw himself into the bayou. He had gone through that list of questions as a joke on first dates, never really making it past the first few before giving up. He'd been especially afraid to reach question number twenty-four, and had always ended it early. It also probably explained why there were never any second dates.

How do you feel about your relationship with your mother?

Three seasons into their engagement, and Jude still hadn't kissed Phoebe. Their wedding was in two months, and Jude had meandered through the year, picking out wedding plates, his suit, the seven courses at the banquet, gone cake testing, scheduled the lion dancers. He had dutifully done everything that was expected for the eldest son's wedding. The first to get married in the family—yet, he still hadn't heard from his father, whose silence ballooned his anxiety. As the days wore on, the fatigue of the inheritance game tugged at him.

Son, you should get married because I think it'll help you find purpose. You lack any responsibilities and the desire to live outside yourself. Marriage is hard work, and you haven't ever worked a day in your life. It'll throw you into the trenches.

Also, maybe, stop clubbing so much. It's bad for your health.

Duc's words tumbled around in his mind. They haunted him for almost seven months now, seared into his memory. *Was* marriage the answer? Who was this really for, at the end of the day?

"Jude!" a familiar, demure voice called out, and it was Jude's turn for his cheeks to turn red. That voice—he could recognize it anywhere in a crowd, in a foreign city, on a sidewalk, or in the airport. Phoebe.

He turned and saw Phoebe with a group of friends, scattered atop a picnic blanket, charcuterie board and all, red plastic cups fallen over, and everyone's cheeks were flushed with excitement and inebriated yearning. Another marker of spring. "Come over! Join us!" she called out, her face overly relaxed from too much cheap red wine. The bitter tannins puckered her lips, her shoulders exposed from an off-shoulder blouse, and her hair tousled softly, strands sticking out all over, as if she'd just been struck by lightning. Yet, somehow, her big doe eyes managed to shimmer under the soft sun, even while under towering sycamores.

Jude couldn't pinpoint exactly when he fell for her. The cordiality at first hadn't lasted long. Yes, there was still a layer of mutual understanding between them about the upcoming marriage, but it had grown beyond that, a deeper friendship than Jude could ever have dreamt of. It seemed so easy to explain away to everyone around them that they were getting married for the money. She wanted the money to take care of her father in his old age and his medical bills, and Jude wanted the money to pursue his dreams—whatever those dreams looked like. But sometime in the past seven months, between the beginning stages of learning how to fish with Phoebe's father, to her father bonding with Mr. Ngô—they had grown into a unit. Jude went out on the boat once a month with Mr. Phương, and it turned into weekly Sunday family dinners with him, Phoebe, and Mr. Phương, and sometimes if Mr. Ngô was in town, he'd join them. Somewhere along the way, Jude had broken out of orbit. He'd fallen in love. He didn't need to ask her the thirty-six questions to lead him to love. He just wanted a do-over to ask her the one most important question that he had already fumbled the first time.

He wanted to ask her to marry him again, but this time, do it right.

But as Jude climbed up the small hill, one of the men next to Phoebe suddenly draped his arms over her, and pulled her into a warm embrace. He had dark sunglasses on, a mole on his left cheek, and wore a crisp white shirt. But even behind sunglasses, Jude could tell he was attractive. His cheekbones were high, brows thick, and even sitting down, he was tall. Disgustingly tall. His legs were never-ending, as if he were hiding stilts under his linen pants. The gold chain around his neck matched the one around Jude's neck, yet somehow seemed more expensive, classier. The smile on Jude's face disappeared quickly, and he put his defensive wall back up. Who the hell was this tool? And why did he get the feeling this guy was actually better than him?

"Judie." Phoebe smiled brightly. She somehow was one of those people who when they smiled, their whole body smiled along with them. "What are you doing here? You never come out to this side of town."

"Hey, Jude." The long-legged guy stood up and stuck out his hand. "Oh my god, *Hey* Jude. Hey *Jude.* 'Hey Jude.' Get it? You must get that a lot. I'm Paul. Paul Xu. It's nice to finally meet the infamous Jude Trần."

Jude wanted to punch him, or maybe rip one of his long legs off him. Instead, he smiled painfully and shook Paul's hand. His palm was firm, calloused, and somehow soft all at the same time. The man really was the whole package. Jude hated him.

Jude responded reluctantly, his mouth thinning, "No one has *ever* ever said or sung 'Hey Jude' before to me."

"*And* the man is funny," Paul said, laughing. His grip turned tighter. Jude returned the pressure, squeezing back with all his might. "You got yourself a winner, Phoebe. The whole husband, all packaged up and ready to be delivered in five to eight business days. Are you going to change your last name now to Trần?"

"Oh shut up, Paul." Another girl on the ground, whose cheeks were

more red than everyone else's, spoke up. "The whole town knows the marriage is fake. They're both doing it for the money. At least we're all getting
seven courses out of it."

"Hell, I'll marry you," another guy called out, chuckling. He was leaning back casually on an elbow, drinking deeply out of a red cup with the
other hand. His smirk made Jude feel emptier inside somehow. "No need to
marry Phoebe. Let's split the pot, you and me."

"Back of the line, James," Paul said, finally letting go of the handshake
and breaking eye contact. With a smug smile, he cast a look behind him to
the whole group. "I call first dibs on marrying Jude."

Everyone laughed around them, except Phoebe and Jude. The tips of
Phoebe's ears turned bright red, and soon the apples of her cheeks' color
matched.

"Honey, stop," she said quietly, her voice strained. Jude could hear the
anxiety. "I told you to stop making fun of it."

Paul put both his hands up. "You know I'm just joking."

"Honey?" Jude said out loud accidentally, his jaw dropping. "He's a
honey? Since when?"

"We just started seeing each other seriously," Phoebe said defensively.
"But I've known Paul since college. Besides, I thought it was okay to see
other people? I mean, we never talked about it *explicitly*, but I mean, come
on, Jude, this isn't a real marriage. The first five minutes of when we met,
you said you would never fall in love with me, and I wouldn't fall in love
with you. We'd go our own way after you get the money . . . right?"

Jude knew he looked like a fool. He had said all those words. He could
feel all eyes on him, all of Phoebe and Paul's friends, who looked effort-
lessly cool, sprawled out on a muted picnic blanket. Their eyes bore into
him, clinging to his every word, as if waiting for him to slip up.

"You're right, *honey*," Jude said, faking a laugh, quickly recovering. "I'll
see you this Sunday, yeah? Family dinner as usual with your father? To convince him we're in love?"

"Stick to the plan, right, *honey*?" Phoebe nodded, faking serious. Paul
swooped back down and planted a loud, wet kiss on her right cheek. She
giggled, distracted by Paul, distracted by the sunny day, distracted by happiness.

Jude wondered if Paul was the type of guy who if asked, "What would constitute a 'perfect' day for you?" would respond with "This day, this moment." It somehow sounded even more cringey to Jude, imagining it through Paul's eyes.

Jude said his goodbyes to no one in particular; he didn't even wait to see if Phoebe responded. He just turned his back and walked down the hill. From behind, he could hear Phoebe giggling, her honeyed laughter piercing him. The farther Jude walked away from her, as her laughter became a distant memory, the more he began to wonder if he'd ever know what a perfect day, a perfect life, looked like. His father's letter echoed and rang in his ear. *Son, I look at you and wonder if you will ever find your joy.* If there was one thing he agreed with his father on, it was this.

True joy seemed so improbable now.

He had learned to tune out the rumors his whole life, but something about the way Phoebe's group of friends laughed *at* him, and not *with* him, reminded him of those same kids who snickered behind his back. As soon as Jude got back to his car, he started the engine, unsure of where to go next. He felt an inexplicable tug to find Duc, to find tangible proof that they were still family at the end of the day. His father had been silent for nearly a year now, and even Jude's personal wedding invitation to Duc had gone unanswered. Why was his father ignoring him? Perhaps his silence was just another litmus test he had to pass, but Jude had grown tired. He was done with it all. As Jude took off, he saw Phoebe and Paul, in the distance, hand in hand, walking along the pathway. They were both red-faced, drunk with the intoxication of newly discovered love. That new car smell.

While he felt that with Phoebe, she never had that giddiness with him. He slammed the car wheel, frustrated. Why would Duc like her profile the most? He felt duped. Duped again by his father. The self-pity continued to fester in his mind as he asked himself again: Why *would* he like her profile the most? He tried his best to recall that morning again, nearly a year ago now, and how Mrs. Vương said that Phoebe knew how to swim, and how his father liked that fact the most.

Duc had always been a strange father, an even stranger man, with his eccentricities and his diatribes that went nowhere. But the more Jude remembered more of what the old numerologist had said to him, the more Jude began to grow suspicious.

Why would his father be afraid of the ocean? Of the Gulf?

....

Dakao Plaza was deader than ever.

Jude pulled into the empty plaza and the familiarity of the nail salon supply store, the travel agency, the sketchy CPA's office, and the refillable water store—it all came screaming back. He had purposely avoided this plaza for seven months, ever since Mr. Ngô read Duc's inheritance scheme out loud and Jane had moved back to Houston. Their estrangement was loud and clear; they were both not to disturb each other during the year. Though Duc hadn't responded to his wedding invitation, nor had Jane. And Jude didn't know which one hurt more. The eldest son and the eldest daughter of two Vietnamese refugees—neither one born with a silver spoon. Jude and Jane, mortal enemies since birth. Stuck in a holding pattern of inherited trauma forever.

Jude tentatively got out of his car, and though the plaza itself was recognizable, he could barely recognize the original Duc's Sandwiches storefront. It was a repulsive monstrosity. What had Jane done? He removed his sunglasses and took in the giant, bright pink neon sign, the gigantic tropical plants that had formed a tunnel into the shop. He walked through it and opened the door, the little bell going off.

Bác Cai, who had been fast asleep at the counter, shot right up. "Welcome, welcome!" the old woman exclaimed with a false cheer in her voice. "Don't *Duc* with us, we're the best bánh mì in town!"

Appalled, Jude took a beat to examine the store. The modernity of it was just a Band-Aid on the shop he had grown up in. The walls were lined with a bright floral print, there was a cheap gold finish to everything, and there was a random swing in the middle of the store. It was as if Jane had taken every single trend alive and mashed it all together. What made it all worse were the black-and-white photos of their parents, their childhood, the first years of the shop that painted a rosy American dream, that struggle can turn into a gold mine. Jude felt sick to his stomach. It was all a lie.

"Bác Cai?" he whispered. "What did she do to you? Did she force you to say that line? What did she do to this place? It's *hideous*. It's ghastly."

Bác Cai recognized Jude instantly and threw her hands up in the air in delight. "My Jude! My Judie! I haven't seen you in so long! Not in almost a year. Why haven't you come to see me?" she exclaimed as she left the counter, her creaky knees only allowing her to shuffle slowly toward him. She had somehow aged faster. The bags under her eyes had drooped lower than when Jude had last seen her, and he could see the corners of Salonpas patches on her collarbone peeking out from her shirt. Guilt. Jude felt guilty for not stopping into the store to see Bác Cai. He leaned down and gave her a hug, inhaling the scent of Tiger Balm and mint. Jude didn't want the hug to end. He held on tight, to the woman who raised him when his own mother couldn't, to the woman who packed his lunches, who would sing to him in the back room during naptimes when his parents worked out front. He held on for as long as he could, longing for boyhood again, a time when he didn't have to fend for himself, and he was just simply taken care of.

"She's gone mad," Bác Cai whispered in his ear as she finally pulled away. "I couldn't say a word, I just went along with it."

"It's completely empty out there," Jude said, scanning the store again. "Have there been a lot of customers since the remodel?"

Bác Cai shook her head slowly. "Everyone around here hates it."

Part of Jude relished in his sister's failure. Perhaps there was still a chance he could take it all. Perhaps he wasn't such a fuckup after all, if even she couldn't figure it out, either.

"Typical Jane," he muttered. "She always overdoes it. She doesn't understand how things work around here. She *left*, okay? She doesn't know this city anymore. People here hate change."

"What are you doing here—" Bác Cai began, before Jane appeared in the back, carrying a tower of boxes, obstructing her view.

"Bác Cai, is there someone here? Do we have a customer?" Jane asked, her voice muffled. "Welcome, welcome! Don't *Duc* with us, we're the best bánh mì in town!"

"Jane, please," Jude groaned. "You need to find a new catchphrase. You sound absurd."

At the sound of Jude's voice, Jane dropped all the boxes, allowing them to tumble everywhere, and a burst of plastic utensils slid onto the ground. Huffing, she pointed accusingly at Bác Cai. "You *let* him in here? I told you he's never allowed in here! He's the enemy!"

"Shut up, Jane, just for once, and listen—" Jude shot back.

"Shut *up*?" Jane snarled. "Why don't *you* shut up and just go walk down the aisle and get married, and see how easy it is to run a business—"

The two immediately erupted into a blame game, falling back into their old ways. Their frustrations, their trauma, their estrangement, their pain—it all became too easy to turn on each other. It was so comfortable: Duc, Evelyn, the shop, the games, the wedding, the failure of it all, the strain, yet the necessity of family.

The bread hit Jude first. Then another one came at the side of Jane's head. Then another bread came hurtling at them both, causing both to duck. From behind the counter, Bác Cai began listlessly throwing bread, carrots, cilantro, anything she could grab.

"Don't waste it all!" Jane shrieked.

"Oh hush," Bác Cai said. "No one's coming in, and you know it. You both need to breathe. You've both immediately reverted back to being six years old again."

Jane's ears turned pink. "He started it!"

Jude sighed and stooped down to clean up the mess. "Look, I'm not trying to start World War Three here. I just came here to ask you to come with me to go somewhere. I think the both of us need to start asking questions about why Duc is doing this. I haven't heard from Duc himself, have you?"

Jane shook her head slowly. "No. I haven't. It's been dead silent."

"And Mr. Ngô is no help, he's barely in town these days and refuses to reach out to Duc on our behalf, or if he has, he hasn't relayed any messages," Jude said. "Don't you think it's all strange?"

"Why? You think he's dead? Like, *dead* dead?"

Jude smacked his sister over her head, just like old times. "No, you idiot, I think we're being played like pawns again, just like when we were kids. We're not seeing the bigger picture here. Come with me, I'm taking you to go see someone. Something's been bothering me for a long time. We need answers. Now."

Jude could see Jane's mind going a mile a minute; he knew how conflicted she was. Years of resentment stood between them and a ceasefire, and family grudges were as thick as blood.

After a silence, Jane finally agreed.

"Fine," she said reluctantly. "But you're driving." The two drew a temporary truce and left the shop together, for the first time in years finally in sync with each other.

"Remember, don't *Duc* with us, we're the best bánh mì in town!" Bác Cai shouted behind them.

....

As Bác Cai observed Jane get into Jude's car from behind the window, she waited until they left the plaza before she pulled out her phone and dialed. She pressed her phone to her ear, impatient, until the other line picked up.

"Anh, I think they know," she said without greeting who it was. "They're starting to piece things together."

She nodded vigorously, the other voice muffled, and continued on. "I mean, the shop *really* is very hideous, I don't know how much longer I can do this."

CHAPTER 25

April 1981, Seadrift, Texas

One early evening, when the ocean was warm and inviting, Duc and Huey decided to head out past curfew and into the water with Tuấn, Duc's cousin Vĩnh, and the village clown, Eddie Bùi, for their last boat ride together. Their last hurrah. Duc and Huey were preparing to leave Seadrift, along with a few other folks. The sixty-day countdown the Klansmen had enacted for the Vietnamese to leave Seadrift was ticking down, and though the start of the shrimping season loomed over them all, the ones who stayed, stayed, and the rest had packed their bags, unwilling to see what would happen.

The five of them went out under the guise of late-night fishing. They dreamt of simpler days of just drinking beer, smoking cigarettes, and fishing for the hell of it. Though being out on the water was their source of income, boats were also a source of irony—it was how many of them were able to escape to America, and now they depended on them to make a living. And now, it was all being taken away from them.

"My wife is killing me," Eddie grumbled, his beer gut spilling out over the elastic band of his pants, as he collapsed onto an upside-down crate. Eddie was a hefty man, who had the unfortunate luck of looking much, much older than his actual age. Though he was just shy of turning thirty, he looked near fifty. Life had added twenty years to his face, weathering and leathering him. But as he cracked open a beer, with the sun setting behind him, Eddie accidentally slipped a smile, revealing a missing tooth as well as his hidden youth. The lines on his face spread out wide, joy releasing, despite the complaints tumbling out of his mouth. "We just got married and she can't stop talking about babies. Babies, babies, babies. We can barely afford rent, and she can't stop thinking about having a baby soon. On top of *all* the stress around us, she still wants to bring a child into this fucked-up world?"

Duc, Huey, and Vĩnh couldn't understand his troubles. The three of them roamed Seadrift as bachelors. They had no curfew or extra mouths to feed—even the idea of having to tell someone where they were going and when they would be home was foreign to them. All of them grunted, trying their best to commiserate with Eddie, but all they could do was feel sorry for him and his weighted responsibilities. A wife? A potential baby? A *family*?

Only Tuấn's reaction was delighted, leaning forward and slapping Eddie on his back. Eddie's behemoth of a back merely absorbed the sound, and Tuấn laughed. "Just wait till the day you come home and your wife says she's pregnant," he said. "It's the best feeling in the world. Nothing will ever compare to that moment again."

All the men stared at Tuấn, whose teeth gleamed bright, and their hearts sank. His demeanor was different, lighter, as if he'd been given the keys to a kingdom.

"Evelyn's pregnant?" Huey asked tentatively, the words swishing inside his mouth as if he was too afraid to say them out loud. His beer can crinkled in his hands as he squeezed it. He went through the last time he saw Evelyn at the crab factory, and noticed she was wearing baggier clothes, but that wasn't unusual. She was one of those women who protected their beauty by doing everything she could to avert the male gaze. Huey had also caught Duc and Vĩnh staring at Evelyn that day. Running into Evelyn daily and harboring silly crushes were what kept the men going. Having a beautiful face to look forward to made the long fishing trips go by much easier, and whenever they returned back to shore, Evelyn was a fantasy, a distraction from the banalities of life.

"That's right, boys, I'm going to be a father!" Tuấn exclaimed, sighing, relieved to finally announce the news into the void. "It's a boy. I have a *son*. What luck! Finally, the tides are turning in my favor." While Duc, Huey, and Vĩnh mourned the loss of Tuấn's freedom, only Eddie pulled Tuấn into a rare embrace, held him tightly, and continuously slapped his back in the same rhythmic beat. Duc, Huey, and Vĩnh eventually mumbled half-hearted congratulations.

Huey meant none of it.

"Don't tell my wife this news." Eddie laughed. "Now she'll really never let it go."

Tuấn laughed, staring through the cracks of Eddie's embrace at Duc's, Huey's, and Vĩnh's forlorn faces. "You're all acting as if I'm preparing for my funeral. I'll still be around. When my son is of age, I'll take him out on the boat with us. He'll need his uncles to teach him how to navigate the waters, catch crab, and how to win over a woman's heart. Promise me you'll come back to Seadrift one day, and you'll meet my son."

"Let's just hope he doesn't have to crab for a living." Duc laughed. "We'll be back, when things are calmer."

"Who knows when that'll ever be?" Eddie said.

"Let's just enjoy this moment now, let's worry later," Vĩnh placated. "Now? Now the waters are calm, and it's just us."

Huey remained quiet; he just looked out into the darkening waters and released the idea of ever being with Evelyn. He'd always dreamt of what it would be like to go home to someone like her, and now he would never know. Perhaps it was all for the best that they were leaving. He worried for Evelyn's future, and wondered why she and Tuấn weren't leaving town as well.

Tuấn pulled off fresh beers from the plastic ring, and handed one to each of the four men. "A toast," he said. "To my son, to us, and to this crazy town. May we find solid footing in these waters one day, and may that day come soon."

The five men clanged their cans together, and they all chugged, and kept chugging until they were down to just the last drops. Duc was the first to break the silence. He leaned casually against the railing of the old boat and lit up a cigarette. "Believe it or not, despite everything that's happened here, I feel at peace here, more so than anywhere else I've been so far in America."

"How can you say that?" Huey responded, irritated. By news about Evelyn's pregnancy or by his friend's silly words, he wasn't sure. "We've been pushed out of our livelihoods. We've been threatened to leave or else. What's peaceful here? Nothing."

None of the men spoke up. There was nothing to say.

"Then might I suggest you all settle down when you leave this place," Tuấn said soothingly, a poor attempt at breaking the tension. "It's time for us to move on. Create a new lineage in this country. Start creating babies."

The men groaned and began to throw their empty beer cans at Tuấn, tensions immediately dissipating. "Married with one baby on the way," Duc teased. "Suddenly, he thinks he's Confucius. The man thinks he's better and wiser than all of us."

"It's true! Making more babies will solve everything!" Tuấn laughed, dodging empty beer cans left and right. "I may not have a lot but I'm a rich man."

"Ah, fuck," Eddie said as he teetered back on the edge of his crate, using his feet to steady himself. "Now you're making *me* want a baby. Seriously, don't tell my wife."

"You're making me continue to *not* want a baby," Duc said, chugging beer.

"Same," Vĩnh said, laughing. "No one can convince me otherwise."

Huey didn't say anything; he just stared at Tuấn, who was drowning in so much euphoria. He wondered if he could drown next to him in the same feeling. What must it be like, to be so incredibly fulfilled to the brink of happiness? Is that why they're staying in Seadrift? Despite the odds against them? Tuấn had a family to protect, a reason to stay. But wouldn't that be a bigger reason to leave?

The other men laughed, roasted one another, and continued to make fun of how soft Tuấn had become. They turned the boat back on and decided to head to deeper waters. As the night wore on and more stars came out, the men stopped caring about how many fish they were catching, and instead turned to how many beers they could drink.

"One more," Vĩnh told Duc, who was already swaying side to side, his hands gripping the side of the boat. "Anh, one more, come on."

Duc managed to nod in agreement, despite how hooded his eyes appeared. Vĩnh threw him another Heineken. Duc swigged violently, managing to finish it in just a few gulps. He turned to Huey, burped loudly into his face, laughed into the dark night, and motioned for Huey to drink next. Huey rose to the challenge, grabbed another beer from the cooler, threw melted ice off it, and chugged as well. Round and round, Vĩnh, Duc, Eddie, and Huey challenged each other, one-upping each other, raucous, slurred spit flying back and forth among the men. Only Tuấn remained neutral and temperate. He often looked wistfully back at shore, which appeared nothing more than a dot on the horizon.

"Anh," Duc called out to Tuấn. "Don't be dumb. Drink with us."

Tuấn smiled and shook his head. "I promised Evelyn I wouldn't drink as much." The men groaned and threw empty cans at Tuấn again, but he managed to dodge all of them in quick succession.

"Come on," Vĩnh said slyly. "She's not here, we have hours left. It'll wear off by the time you get back."

"You gotta teach your son how to drink properly, right?" Duc said. "What kind of father would you be if you didn't know how to hold your liquor? Don't be such a prude, your woman isn't here. Look around, do you see a woman for miles?"

Tuấn looked at the men, and there was the tiniest hesitation to him that made all the men jump at the soft chance. Duc quickly opened two cans at once and handed both to Tuấn. "Last one to drink both at the same time has to clean crabs for the other all week."

Leaping up from his crate, Tuấn grabbed the two cans and without saying a word began to guzzle the lager down. Vĩnh jumped at the opening behind the steering wheel and roared the old boat to life, cigarette in his mouth. He moved the boat even deeper out into the ocean. The men laughed, opening another box of cigarettes, and someone took out a deck of playing cards. Cards were quickly shuffled, hands were soon dealt, and more beer tabs were pulled back, breaking the stillness of the water. After a few rounds, as more bad hands were dealt, money lost between everyone, Tuấn had caught up with all the men and more. He was on his fifteenth beer, crushed cans lying at his feet, evidence of his broken promise to Evelyn, and he stood up to go to the edge of the boat to take a piss. Tuấn unzipped his pants and the sound of his piss hitting the water could soon be heard, his body rocking every which way, unable to stand upright.

"Let's turn back soon," Tuấn called behind him, his voice garbled. "I need to go back home."

"What?" Duc yelled back.

"I said let's—"

Out of the darkness, a burst of fire. A noise so loud everyone covered their ears.

Gunfire went off in bursts in the distance, followed by a roar of hollow laughs and howling into the night. The serene waters were no more, and the night sky erupted into vibrant oranges and yellows. The smell of gunpowder filled their nostrils, dripping metallic in their mouths. *One. Two. Three. Four.* Four shots in quick succession. The laughter afterward sent more chills down the men's backs than the gunshots did.

Duc, Huey, Vĩnh, and Eddie lay flat on the deck immediately, beers flying from their hands, sending the cans rolling into the Gulf. Back in the old country, war had trained them not to make a sound, to use silence as a shield, to walk softly in the jungle without breathing and to tiptoe around minefields. Their training immediately kicked in. Vietnam, Seadrift, it didn't matter, they'd been trained their whole lives to survive.

Vĩnh put a finger to his lips and slowly lifted his head. He began to look every which way, attempting to discern where the gunshots had come from. Despite how dark and thin the night was, he saw the hats immediately in the far east, near the shoreline. The silhouettes were unmistakable, even in the darkest of places, the white cones on top of the heads, bobbing up and down, pointing high up toward the sky, ironically trying to pierce the heavens. The matching white robes lit up the sky. Ghosts, living nightmares, floating in the Gulf. Vĩnh's body went cold. He counted the shadows. *One. Two. Three. Four.* Four gunshots were fired, and there were four of them. He lowered himself back down and mouthed the three letters to confirm what everyone else already knew. He whispered it urgently, his lips wrapped around each letter, as if he were trying to suck the venomous poison out of it. He mouthed at them, spelling it out phonetically the Vietnamese way. *Cay-Cay-Cay.* KKK. The KKK were here.

Duc and Huey locked eyes, as they often did. Finding each other in times of chaos had always centered them. They were brothers. But while they had found each other, they were both going opposite directions in their minds. Huey decided that no matter what happened to him after this night, he would never stay here. Huey would never take on a wife, bear children, or have anything that would hold him back like this.

For the first time in their lives, the two men began to pray to Buddha. They closed their eyes and silently called out to Buddha to help them survive the long night. Just as they felt confident they could quietly escape, that was when more gunshots rang out, and the roar of more surrounding boats began to come alive. There were more than just four now; they were outmatched. What little hope they had had been extinguished, the last match against darkness. They stopped calling out for Buddha.

CHAPTER 26

Paulina

The robot arms were malfunctioning. Not in a "there's a screw or two loose" kind of way. More like a "the robots are sentient and are rebelling" kind of way. Though the robots were able to manufacture a sandwich in less than thirty seconds, after assembly, they would fling the sandwich all the way across the room—at a speed of around ninety miles per hour, about the average MLB pitch. Sandwich or baseball, it made no difference; the impact of the pelt remained the same. Paulina, in one of her walk-throughs with some local food influencers, witnessed in horror as one of them was hit in the face with a bánh mì gà. His glasses flew off his face, and his nose began to bleed profusely, gushing a bright ruby hue. Throughout the commotion, between the blood and slices of cold chicken, yelling and crying, Paulina tried her best to assuage the situation.

"Look how futuristic and innovative we are! We even deliver directly into your mouth! What other delivery app offers these types of features?" Paulina laughed nervously as another sandwich whizzed so fast past her head, it fluttered her hair, breaking the sound barrier.

The food influencers never came back. And with each new negative review that had come out, Paulina's desperation grew as the silence grew louder around her.

No one was coming in, and the money was running out. She was afraid that in the rat race toward their inheritance, she was the last one, the fabled rabbit who decided to take a nap, and all the other turtles had hurtled forward. Despite all the buzz and marketing she'd put into a soft launch, no one had come in.

However dire things had gotten, she had refused to reach out to Oliver for help, despite collecting a pile of unanswered texts from him, asking how the store was going, how she was doing. But the worst messages asked if she needed help.

Help? *Help?*

As the third-oldest daughter, Paulina Trần had never asked for help in her life. Her entire childhood, she'd flown under the radar, always living at the margins of the family. *Help* was a dirty word to her. Plus, she'd been actively avoiding Oliver ever since he revealed he had a daughter. *Esther.* Esther sounded cute. Esther also sounded like responsibility. And Paulina was allergic to responsibility.

There was no way in hell she was about to admit she was in trouble.

She didn't want word to get back to her father about how bad things had gotten under her management.

Which was why she was thrown for a loop when she showed up to the shop and saw her father's lawyer, Mr. Ngô, standing outside the doors. Her stomach began churning as she observed him. What the hell was he doing here? His hands were stuffed in his pockets, his forehead pressed against the black window, his eyes squinting, trying to make out the new layout. Though his slouch was familiar and comforting, a small slice of home—even if the idea of home was fractured—Paulina was terrified. Whatever he'd report back to her father could determine how close she was to winning the inheritance. She didn't know enough about Mr. Ngô to determine how to sway him.

Though she had grown up with memories of him walking through the hallways of her home as if he lived there, going into her father's office every day, closing the door behind him, and the hushed tones between the two of them—he was still a stranger to her. She always wondered what her father and he talked about so much. What would an uneducated man turned purveyor of sandwiches and a shady lawyer have in common? Mr. Ngô was a constant, mysterious shadow in her life, and she never thought much of him beyond just that narrative.

"Mr. Ngô?" Paulina feigned delight. "What are you doing here?"

He turned around and waved eagerly. She towered over him, adding two more inches with her black boots, and could see the bald spot at the top of his head. From the aerial point of view of nearly six feet, his baldness could have been mistaken for a crop pattern.

"Ah! Hello, con!" he said, still wearing a big smile. "I haven't been to San Jose in many, *many* years, not since the time your father opened this shop back in the mid-nineties, and before that, not since the early eighties. Your mother loved this shop the most, you know. She opened this shop with pride."

Paulina laughed anxiously, surprised at how talkative and lighthearted he was. She'd only ever known him as Duc's stoic right-hand man. "Here for a nostalgia tour, then? Vacation, perhaps? Funny choice in picking San Jose to come to relax, though."

"Vacation? Me? I've never been on vacation in my life!" He chuckled. "No, no. I'm here to make my rounds, follow up, and report everything back to your father. He wants updates on how you're all doing. And well, it's my job to keep him well informed of progress made on all fronts." His smile remained the same as he gestured for her to let them both into the shop. He was not budging. "And you've been . . . well, *particularly* quiet. May I see what you've done with the place?"

She reluctantly took out her keys. "I'm actually still in the middle of a soft launch you know, so things aren't *quite* up to speed."

Mr. Ngô said nothing. He just simply cleared his throat, lifted his scuffed black loafer gingerly over the threshold, and stepped in. His requisite oversize suit nearly drowned out his small frame, and he began craning his neck in all directions. He pushed his glasses up the bridge of his nose, and whipped out a small green pocket notebook from the inside of his jacket. The sound of his ballpoint pen clicked into action, and it somehow echoed throughout the empty store. His hand began making notes, comments, observations, and at one point, it looked like he'd even drawn a few pie charts, and a life-size map of the store. It felt as if he were carrying a proverbial clipboard, and he'd come to audit her.

After an eternity in purgatory, Mr. Ngô finally spoke.

"Strange direction you decided to go down, huh? All this . . . fancy tech you brought in . . . for sandwiches. You know, your sisters went different directions," Mr. Ngô said, sucking through his teeth. He began to walk up to the automated arms, touching them, and tapped through the ordering tablet, looking at all the options available. "How's business going?"

Paulina put on her fakest smile. "It's going *amazing*. Truly. Everyone here has been so fascinated by watching robots make sandwiches. I have a lot of content creators come in to take photos and videos. Kids love it, you know. Silicon Valley *loves* it."

"Yes, but what about the loyal customers? The locals? The San Jose store has always been a mild success because of the returning customers.

The elderly? They're our biggest base here," Mr. Ngô said, eyebrows furrowing as he jotted more notes down in his green notebook. "Wait, where is Chị Mai? She's been working for us for nearly twenty years."

From her vantage point, Paulina scanned his notebook.

Robot. Sterile. Strange. No life. Happy? Chị Mai?

Why did everyone keep asking about Chị Mai? Who was Chị Mai again?

And *happy*? Why was happiness a criterion in order for her to win a shot at the money? *No life?* What kind of notes was Duc looking for? But mostly, how could her father still manage to insult her from oceans away? She swallowed hard and began to see the money, her future, everything, slipping through her fingers. She decided she had to fake and lie her way through the mess. If her father wanted to see happiness, she was going to give the old lawyer the performance of her lifetime.

"Chị Mai was slowing me down. I've decided to focus on the next generation," she said breezily. "Modernize this place a bit more, keep up with trends."

"You can modernize something without alienating the elderly," he said, almost in a didactic tone. "You know most old people hate technology, right?"

"Of course I knew that," she said soothingly. "I just thought this would be more for 'the kids' than their grandparents, you know?"

"So . . . this is for *children*?" he responded, scribbling more things. "You like kids, then?"

"No, I hate kids," Paulina said absentmindedly, her mind wandering to Oliver and Esther. A daughter. Oliver had a three-year-old daughter. "Can you imagine having a kid? After the way we grew up? A mother who abandoned us, and an absentee father? Talk about repeating the cycle of trauma. Can you imagine what *I'd* be like as a mother? I'd feel sorry for that kid."

Mr. Ngô paused in his note-taking; she could tell he did not like her response one bit. "May I see a demonstration?" he asked, though it sounded more like a command.

"Of course! Happy to give one," she said nervously as she walked up to an open tablet. Beads of sweat began forming under Paulina's brow. Her hands shook as she tapped an order in, and worry began to crystallize in her lungs. *The bugs were fixed, right?* Her lead engineer had sent an email late last night with some code pushes, but she hadn't had a chance to take a look at it yet. She stared at the place order button. What if she just pretended the machines weren't working today?

As if on cue, the robots came alive and made a sandwich without Paulina's command. A loud whirring sound came on as each arm roared into action, the machines sounding like nails on a chalkboard, turned up to the highest volume. With each arm programmed to handle a section of the sandwich, it was as if they were fighting each other to make the sandwich themselves.

"Interesting," Mr. Ngô whispered in both horror and fascination. More notes.

"SORRY IT'S SO NOISY!" Paulina shouted over the metal arms crashing into one another. "WE'RE WORKING ON THE SOUND!" Continuing on their rebellious streak, the arms somehow began to speed up more, causing the screeching sound to go up a pitch. Paulina grinned widely, and weakly gave two thumbs-up to Mr. Ngô, who had now covered his ears.

"HOW FUN IS THIS, RIGHT?" Paulina said, nearly screaming. "IT'S SO NOVEL!"

"How interesting," Mr. Ngô whispered again.

"WHAT DID YOU SAY?"

He just shook his head.

"WE'RE EMPHASIZING THE 'FUN' IN MAKING SANDWICHES! THERE'S JUST SOME SLIGHT KINKS WE HAVEN'T QUITE WORKED THROUGH!"

But it was as if the robots wanted to ensure that she wasn't going to win her inheritance. Just as Paulina went to shut them down manually, a robotic arm picked up the finished sandwich and chucked it at Mr. Ngô so fast, he barely ducked down in time. They watched in terror as it shot out the door and barreled straight into an old woman crossing the street, knocking her shopping bags right out of her arms and causing her to tumble forward. Her hands and knees splayed out on the gravel, for all to see.

The robot arms began to wind down and return to their sleep state, as if nothing had happened at all.

"Don't say anything," Paulina said through clenched teeth.

"I wasn't planning on it," Mr. Ngô whispered. "But as a lawyer, I have plenty to say. Mostly: *that was close.*"

A crowd formed around the old woman as they helped pick her up, then her bags of groceries off the ground. A case of loose oranges eluded everyone's grip and began rolling downhill.

Mr. Ngô turned toward Paulina and clicked his pen again, symbolizing that he was done. "I must ask, Paulina. Have you been happy since you've arrived in San Jose? You've been here what, nearly seven months?"

"Happiness is subjective," she said wryly. "No one is ever really *happy*, it's an elusive fantasy. I'm just . . . doing my job."

Mr. Ngô made another note, then looked back up to her, a hint of sadness in his gaze. "Your father didn't do all of this on his own, you know. He had a lot of help behind him. It's okay to learn to ask for help from time to time."

Paulina was already tired and cranky, and the mention of her father was triggering, a cherry on top of a pile of growing family trauma. "You wouldn't think that from the way he talks about his origin story on how he got started. You'd think the man had gotten bitten by a radioactive spider and gained all this money, fame, and success overnight."

Mr. Ngô stared at all the robot arms behind the counter, then he turned around and pointedly stared at the crowd of folks who still surrounded the old woman, on the corner of McLaughlin Avenue and Story Road, in the bustling heart of San Jose's ethnic enclave.

He closed his eyes and put his arms behind his back. "There's always more to the story than meets the eye, con. You think a refugee, who never graduated high school, had gotten here miraculously on his own?"

Paulina didn't say anything; she just leaned against the counter and folded her arms. "What are you trying to say, Mr. Ngô?"

"You'd be surprised at who will show up for you if you learn to ask for help," he said cryptically. "Also, con, your father cared about you in his own way. It's hard to see now, but maybe one day, you'll be able to understand that he did his best."

Mr. Ngô gathered himself and headed toward the front of the shop, his hand on the door handle, ready to leave. "That guy you were seeing a while back, he lives here, right? Up in San Francisco? It was a bit on and off again between you two for a long time, wasn't it?"

Paulina looked at him, wondering how on earth he knew about Oliver Chen. Without waiting for a response, Mr. Ngô plowed on. "You two seemed to really care about each other, you know."

"How on earth would *you* know anything about my relationship with Oliver?" Paulina asked defensively. "Did my father say something to you?"

Mr. Ngô turned back around to face the second-youngest child of Duc, the third daughter, and the most elusive one, who no one really knew well. They locked eyes and for a microsecond, she could have sworn they had similar features. But it was all eclipsed by the fact of how *tired* he looked. He appeared exhausted, worn down, and Paulina saw him as human for the first time, perhaps burdened by being Duc's sidekick, or perhaps because there was a longing in his face that only someone like Paulina could catch. She knew that look well.

"Con," he said quietly. "I know a thing or two about tipping the scale of love—how one person can love the other person more, and you wait your whole life for the scale to balance out, but it never does. It just never does. But you don't even care, you're just happy to be on the same scale. And all you can do is wait. And you *do* wait."

Paulina watched as he left the store. His retreating back grew smaller as he rounded the corner and disappeared. Tired herself, Paulina wondered which side of the scale she was on when it came to Oliver, and if she missed the entire point of being sent to San Jose.

CHAPTER 27

Georgia

G eorgia's van crept behind her mother's Vespa for the third time all week. Evelyn knew she was being followed, but this time, she didn't care. Together, the two of them formed a tight trail as they went about their days, running errands together, but not *together*. For the past month since Evelyn had come back after her (third) attempted run, they'd somehow grown closer by dancing around each other. Amid the long, sweltering dog days of New Orleans, they let the other into their isolated, small worlds. The two women even began to gift each other the type of empathy that had been missing from their lives.

Once they reached the grocery store, Georgia parked and went inside, following Evelyn down aisle after aisle, meandering from frozen foods to the fresh vegetables. She watched as her mother carefully sniffed each fruit or rolled each lime, dedicated to finding the best one in the stack. She saw her mother press avocados and intuitively, somehow, pick the best watermelon, after passing up six others. Occasionally, Evelyn would call over to her, asking if she had developed any allergies to certain ingredients, and Georgia would respond back, talking over service dogs and crying babies, that no, she wasn't allergic to anything, nor had she become lactose intolerant (yet). Evelyn nodded and wandered over to the meat aisle, where she asked for a pound of pork belly, and barked at the butcher to give her the good cut, not the leftovers.

As the two women returned to the parking lot, bags full, the sun was starting to come down, and Georgia helped her mother load the groceries onto her Vespa before sliding back into her van. She tailgated her mother's Vespa, until she came up the familiar dirt road where her mother turned in to her parking spot. Georgia watched from a safe distance as her mother unloaded groceries into her apartment. Once it was confirmed her mother was safe, Georgia began to settle in for the night, doing her own routines in her yellow van: turning the stove on, unrolling the mattress pad, prepping dinner. Suddenly, a loud slap against the side of the van caused her to yelp. Surprised, Georgia slid open the door and was face-to-face with her mother, who stood awkwardly, and had changed into a pajama set.

"Is everything okay?" Georgia asked, with deep concern. "Do you need me to give you a ride somewhere again?"

Evelyn wrung her hands together and, after some time, worked up the courage to ask her youngest daughter a question that had been plaguing her since Georgia's arrival.

"Would you want to have dinner with me tonight? I'm cooking thịt kho," her mother asked. It almost sounded as if she were asking Georgia if she could play with her on the playground. "I don't know if you've ever had my thịt kho, but it's one of my specialties. You might have been too young to have had it. My place is very small, but there's room. Or I can bring it out here. Whatever is . . . more comfortable for you."

Georgia tried her best to hide her elation, and not scare her mother off. After nearly seven months of trying to get through to her mother, Georgia, with the patience of a saint, simply nodded. She turned off her stove, locked up her van, and followed her mother into her apartment for the first time. She spotted Anne through the window, who'd been spying on them. Anne sneakily gave Georgia the thumbs-up. It was a small win, and perhaps the first win that Georgia had really had ever since she landed in the city. Georgia gave Anne an awkward thumbs-up back, and soon the smell of braised pork belly and fish sauce hit her hard like a sauna when her mother opened the door to her apartment.

Georgia tried her best not to cry as she sat down in front of her mother and accepted her home-cooked meal.

"Con, is this enough?" her mother asked hesitantly, tilting a bowl of rice in her direction.

Georgia nodded. "Yes. Yes, it is."

....

The following week, the roles were reversed. And this time, it was Evelyn who followed Georgia's van into the bustling center of the enclave where Duc's Sandwiches was located. Georgia pulled up to the dilapidated storefront and both women got out, staring down the shop that was the root cause of all their pain. The chain that had caused the chain reaction of unpredictability that brought them to this very moment.

The store stood frozen in time, stuck at the end of the block, far away from the main road. Graffiti tags marred the walls so that neither woman could tell the original color. Georgia didn't even need the key she was given. She simply pushed the door open. The mustiness was foul, but Georgia opened the door wide, allowing her mother and herself to step in. Evelyn didn't speak for a while.

"This store is cursed, con," she eventually whispered, finally allowing Georgia a glimpse into her mind. She rarely offered something about herself, about the past. "All the stores are cursed. Everything Duc has ever touched has been cursed. Do not profit off any of the stores, do you understand me? Don't take a single cent. Don't take a penny of your inheritance, it isn't yours. It was paid for by blood. Do not blindly follow that man off the cliff anymore. Do you *hear* me, con?"

"Blood?" Georgia repeated, shocked. *Blood* was the last word she ever expected to come out of her mother. "What are you talking about, Mom?" Georgia pressed on urgently, preserving every kernel of truth her mother dropped for her.

Evelyn blinked at "Mom." But if it truly bothered her, she didn't let Georgia know, she just shook her head gravely, unwilling to speak more. "Just please, leave all of this behind, con. Move on with your life. Don't give in to Duc's games anymore."

"You need to answer me. What did you mean by 'paid for by blood'? Talk to me, Mom, please. *Please.*"

Her mother's face twisted with something. Was it pain? Did it look like grief? She didn't know. But if grief had a face, she could have sworn it would look like her mother. Georgia stepped forward slowly, hoping that by the time she reached her mother, they might even attempt a hug. Not once in the past year had either woman attempted to hug the other, but Georgia was desperate to curl her head deep into her mother's bosom, and fulfill her fantasy of what it was like to cry while having her mother hold her for once. She wanted to be up close to her mother's scent again. May rose, jasmine, and a hint of bourbon vanilla.

But it was as if Evelyn was suddenly spooked, a stray dog unable to tell if the stranger before her was going to hurt her or save her. Evelyn took a step back, and Georgia could see her physically recoiling. Her mother threw her hands up in the air, spewed profanities, and stormed back outside, unwilling to divulge more.

Georgia was at her wits' end, watching her mother start her Vespa, hop on, and drive off. She left. Again. How much more of this could she take before insanity settled in? She threw a final cry behind her mother's back. "You want me to stop chasing you? Fine. I'm done with this place. I'm done with you. You want to never be found again? You got it. You don't want to give a real answer to any of my questions? Don't worry, I'll make it all up in my head."

Georgia meant every word. She was done chasing a living ghost. A stubborn ghost who didn't want to be found or brought back to life. Anytime she came close to uncovering the truth, her mother would force her back a hundred steps. Now at twenty-three, after a sad birthday spent in her van keeping watch on her mother a month ago, Georgia had spent her entire life wondering what her mother was like. Now that she'd put a face to the woman in her dreams, she preferred the version of her mother in her head to the one before her.

She turned on her heel, furious, and headed back to the Duc's Sandwiches shop. Anger had never once governed Georgia's life or emotions; she saw it as useless and counterproductive. But now, Georgia felt anger. It traveled through her bloodstream, battling every white cell along the way, and it tasted foul and metallic in her mouth. Nothing about this moment was fair, and she suddenly understood how her older siblings carried their anger around like war medals pinned to their jackets. Evelyn and Duc had turned everything into a war zone. She was done with her mother, and done trying to be patient. The pain of the reversal of time singed her. She tried hard to remember how her mother was once a parent to her, and somewhere along the timeline, Georgia became the parent, and her mother, the child. This felt crueler than usual for some reason, considering how Georgia had never known what Evelyn was like as a mother.

But the anger continued to surge out of her, and she relished it. *This must be how Bingo feels 99 percent of the time.* She turned back around, and began chasing her mother again, not allowing her to walk away unscathed this time. Her words became her daggers, aimed right at her mother's retreating back. "They say never meet your heroes, and I wish we'd never fucking met. You want to die all the time? Go ahead."

With that, she headed to her van, wondering where she would go next after this, now that she was free. Maybe she'd drive back west to Baja, camp along the beach, or maybe she'd head to San Diego. Anything was better than this.

But Georgia stopped in her tracks once she saw a figure standing by her van, and it was none other than Connie Vũ, her father's second wife and her stepmother, standing so still, she could have been mistaken for a statue. Beside her was an older-looking woman, who looked like a mature version of Connie. Their faces seemed wry, steely, and unimpressed with what they just witnessed.

"Connie?" Georgia whispered, her mouth agape. "What are you doing here?"

"You Trâns are really something," Connie said in a sinister voice. "All you do is destroy everything in your paths. You really are *all* insane. You all think you can just take me for a ride? You, Duc, Evelyn? *Everyone?* You think I don't deserve a penny? Neither do any of you brats."

Georgia's eye began to twitch at the word *insane.* Unlike her siblings, she'd spent her whole life pursuing a different avenue to release her emotions. She wasn't as removed as Jane, as standoffish as Paulina, or as angry as Bingo. She clung to a different identity; she was the zen one, the peaceful one, the one furthest removed from the drama. But she wasn't immune to the gossip and stories about her family, from the neighbors to her high school classmates to the people at temple. They'd called their family every word imaginable.

Insane, crazy, embarrassing.

Connie took another step toward the Duc's Sandwiches store, and she pulled out what appeared to be a can of some kind. Before Georgia could piece two and two together, she watched in horror as Connie and the elderly woman threw gasoline all over the building. The smell was pungent yet somehow sweet at the same time.

"Wait a minute, what are you doing—"

But before Georgia could finish her sentence, the two women took a step back from the store. The elderly woman struck a match and held it up high.

"You tell me, right now, where Duc Trần is hiding or my mother lights up this store," Connie said, so eerily calm, it caused mountain ridges to form along Georgia's arms, the hairs standing up straighter than they ever had before.

"But I don't know where he is! No one does!" Georgia said frantically. "And why is your mother here?"

"This store is under your name, correct?" Mrs. Vũ spoke up in a stoic tone. Like mother, like daughter. Mrs. Vũ held the match up higher, causing Georgia to panic.

"YES! Yes! It is!" Georgia shouted. She could feel her stomach dropping as if she were on a roller coaster.

"Call up Huey then," Connie said. "Tell him to transfer the deed to this store to me."

"Who the hell is Huey?!" Georgia said, confused.

"Oh for fuck's sake!" Connie said. "Duc's lawyer. Mr. Ngô."

"*Why* the *hell* would I remember his first name?! I just know him as the weird uncle! Also, why is his name *Huey*? That's a bit strange, isn't it—"

"Just shut up! SHUT UP! Call him right now—"

"But *why* do you want this dump—"

"Oh god, you stupid—"

"I don't understand—"

"Insurance fraud—"

"There are better things to ask for—"

"Fire. Payout—"

"This place is a shithole—"

"Duc isn't even your real—"

Back and forth it went between Connie and Georgia. Mrs. Vũ, who stood still next to Connie, grew frustrated and began to yell at her daughter to wrap it up.

Out of nowhere, a cloud of dust and gravel kicked up in everyone's faces as the roar of a Vespa ground to a halt.

Evelyn hopped off her Vespa and began to head toward Connie and Mrs. Vũ, her eyes focused but enraged.

"Evelyn—" Connie sneered.

"Mom," Georgia pleaded. "Help."

Before anyone could say another word, Evelyn shoved Connie and

Mrs. Vũ out of the way, took out a lighter from her pocket, lit it, and threw it against the building. Everyone began scrambling out of the way. Daughters ran after their mothers, ensuring they were safely out of harm's way. Connie grabbed her mother, Georgia grabbed hers, each one yanking them out of the way, back onto the road, far, far away from the burning building. A roar of orange, and before anyone could understand what had happened, the blaze had overtaken the building. The fire reflected back in all four women's eyes and raged on.

"Don't you ever call any of my children insane again," Evelyn shouted as Connie stumbled backward onto the ground. "You haven't seen *real* crazy yet."

"Mom," Georgia whispered as she watched flames engulf the building, swallowing it whole. A burst of orange pierced the sky as the old building cackled under the weight of all of Duc's sins, collapsing the roof inward. "What did you do?"

"Freeing us, con," Evelyn whispered. All four women looked on, watching Duc's Sandwiches burn to the ground, along with Georgia's inheritance, and Evelyn's past. "Freeing all of us."

CHAPTER 28

April 1981, Seadrift, Texas

The Gulf was soon crowded with anchored boats, no more than a few feet apart.

Though shrimping season was months away, the smell of musty netting and acrid fumes lingered. Music rang out into the night, and raucous laughter and trills from the Klansmen—their friends, family, allies, and local fishermen—began to blend together. It seemed strange to hear the other side celebrating, so carefree, while everyone in the Vietnamese community had been living in abject fear for years. Had it been without context, their joy could have been mistaken for a birthday party, anniversary, or any milestone celebration out on the water. The Vietnamese hadn't put on any public displays of joy since they were threatened to leave Seabrook-Kemah. Instead, they were busy putting their homes, boats, and businesses up for sale, as the countdown from sixty days felt like a dystopian New Year's Eve ball drop.

Eddie, Duc, Vĩnh, and Huey were still huddled quietly on the boat's floor. No one had yet spotted their little trawler, which swayed gently side to side, and through a stroke of good fortune, managed to evade the moonlight, granting them peace in the shadows. But their one streak of good luck wouldn't last them forever. Sooner or later, they knew that their trawler would be spotted.

"We need to get out of here," Eddie whispered as soon as he crawled his way to the center.

"How exactly? *Swim* back to shore? *Walk* on water?" Duc whispered back angrily. "Snails are faster than this boat. This piece of shitter is held together by nothing but duct tape and gum."

Huey turned to Vĩnh. "How many guns do you have on board?" At the sight of Vĩnh's crestfallen face, his own face fell. Vĩnh held up one finger, then turned it to where the gun was hidden, in a nondescript box under the steering wheel. One gun, five men, and from the sound of it, nearly thirty to fifty of the Klansmen and their friends, a stone's throw away, and the pitch-black, open Gulf, which could easily conceal a body. No other Vietnamese fishermen were stupid enough to be out this late. No one but the five of them.

Duc pulled himself upright, his breath reeking of alcohol as he attempted to lean against an old barrel, his fear exposed. "What if we just go," he whispered. "They haven't spotted us yet. Maybe if we're fast enough we can get around them."

"They're closer to shore, plus they'll hear us immediately," Huey snapped, almost revealing how hysterical he'd become. "Even if we did try to go around, we'd run out of gas. There's only enough to head back the same way we came." With each new attempt at forming an escape plan, the walls were closing in, and the men resigned themselves to the possibility that they might not make it back to shore alive. It was at this moment when they felt what it was like to be at the end of a fishing hook, waiting to be pierced through.

"Let's just wait it out then," Eddie said hopefully, a childlike innocence in his voice, as if they were simply playing a game of tag. "Maybe they'll head home soon."

The music began to lower, and someone began shouting over it. Some people chimed in, telling others to *shut up* or *lower the damn music* and *they can't hear shit.* A man's deep voice carried toward them, loud, brusque, unflinching. Eddie, Huey, Duc, and Vĩnh looked at one another, looking for confirmation if anyone knew the identity of the man speaking. The four men shook their heads, and though they didn't say it out loud, they looked relieved. Because at least they knew who *wasn't* speaking —the head of the local Klansman chapter, the Dragon himself, Louis Beam. Hope began to seep in again. Though they had seen photos of the Dragon on flyers around town, they were the few left in the Seabrook-Kemah area to have avoided any run-ins with him. It was the type of luck akin to never catching the flu—they constantly lived in fear of the moment they *would* run into the Dragon and they would no longer be immune.

But something about the man's voice still triggered something inside Duc and Huey. They looked at each other, unable to blink as their minds churned through forgotten memories. The voice sounded familiar, but it was a long-forgotten voice, something they had heard once upon a time, in an insignificant blip in their lives. Whoever was speaking still managed to make the hair on all their arms stand up. Even if it wasn't the Dragon himself, it didn't mean it wasn't one of his minions, it was still a voice to help unite the Klansmen and local fishermen who had imparted the sixty-day deadline for the Vietnamese to leave Seadrift.

"Thirty days, gentlemen," the man's voice roared. "Thirty days left before the gooks flee like cockroaches into the night and we take back our land, our waters, our livelihood."

A symphony of cheers, hoots, and clapping erupted. Murmurs of how *close they were* and *well done, boys* and *keep fighting the good fight* and how *Saigon Harbor was as dead as Vietnam* floated into the night air. They proverbially patted each other's backs, as if they had all won prizes given by their kindergarten teacher.

"Huey," Duc whispered urgently, as he suddenly realized who was speaking. His tone, both frightened and yet unsure, waiting for confirmation.

"I'm thinking, hold on," Huey snapped, as he rubbed his temples, praying to sober up, but the world continued to spin faster and faster.

"*Huey,*" Duc said, almost violently, as he found the courage to look up and confirm. "Look."

Huey stuck his head out carelessly. In the distance, the man who was rallying the crowd, late into the night, was none other than the old captain they had worked for long ago, on the fishing boat off the coast of Delacroix Island in Louisiana. The same fishing job where Duc and Huey had met each other and kick-started an inseparable friendship. The man with the sunken eyes no longer looked friendly. It'd been five years since that fishing job, and he looked worse for wear. Time and the crushing weight of capitalism hadn't been kind to him. He looked like every other man in town looking for a punching bag to hit. He looked older and angrier. It was even the same boat that Huey and Duc worked on five years ago. The same captain stood atop that same boat, the *Lady Freedom*, and began to call out onto the open water for the death of all Vietnamese fishermen who dared stay behind.

It was also the same boat on which Duc had made lofty promises to Huey, saying that he was going to be so rich one day, he was going to buy the boat from the captain. All Huey had to do was follow Duc around the country, and they would get there eventually.

Huey quickly shrank back. "What now?" he whispered.

"Let's wait it out till morning," Eddie whispered back. "More people will be out by dawn, and the night can shield us until then." The men agreed and began to settle in for the long night. Huey's eyes wandered over to where the gun lay hidden. He had promised himself after fleeing Vietnam that he wouldn't pick up a gun ever again. But America always seemed to have other plans for him. He just kept trading one war for another, in a vicious cycle, over and over again.

And maybe that was all life really was.

Duc, Huey, Vĩnh, and Eddie huddled side by side, in the dark, their eyes fighting to stay open, but their minds were littered with PTSD from the war. The Heineken began to fully seep into their bloodstreams, and they sat there, grateful to at least be so inebriated that death might not hurt as much if it came knocking for them.

....

Three hours later, Duc awoke to laughter hovering above him. The four men had passed out sometime in the middle of the night, dogpiled on top of one another, a pack seeking comfort and heat, circling each other to ensure no predators could attack one without the others. After succumbing to the alcohol sinking to the bottom of their bloodstreams, the men managed to finally close their eyes, weightless and free of worry.

"Morning, gentlemen." A deep voice emerged next to them. "Beautiful out here, isn't it? Feels like we're on the edge of the world. God, I love Texas."

Fully alert, Duc quickly shoved Huey, Vĩnh, and Eddie awake. Everyone's eyes slowly began to adjust to the harsh sun that felt like daggers in their eyes, and the four men jumped to their feet. Next to their tiny trawler was the massive *Lady Freedom*, rocking gently in the Gulf. Its rusted hull was worse than Duc and Huey could remember, and barnacles clung to the side. Both the boat and the captain looked one and the same, like two stray dogs, both in desperate need of rest, food, and shelter.

None of the men dared to make a noise or respond. In the distance, all the other boats had disappeared and only the captain was left with the men on the *Lady Freedom*. Duc and Huey lowered their gazes, wondering if the old captain recognized them. It'd been five years, but there weren't that many Vietnamese men who traveled to Delacroix for commercial fishing work. They could feel the captain's eyes heavy on them, assessing, but after a few tense breaths, their shoulders relaxed slightly. Their faces elicited no memory for the captain, except for the fact that he hated everyone who looked like them.

Vĩnh made a slow movement toward the tin box under the steering wheel where the gun was, but was hushed by the captain.

"No need for any of that nonsense out here," he said, a strange smile on his lips. "It's just us."

"What do you want?" Duc blurted out. While his face was blank, like all nervous dogs, his knees quaked.

The captain shrugged. He was dressed in military wear, head to toe in a camo print, the type of uniform that indicated that he had also served in the war. But it wasn't real. The four men knew what the American uniform looked like, more than they would want to know, and though it looked as if the captain belonged in the military, it was nothing more than costume jewelry meant to scare off others. The rest of the crew donned the same camo costume, and they looked like a guerilla group, a flint ready to spark a war.

"I just came over 'cause we wanted to let you know, we saw your friend take a swim, way back over there. He must love swimming in the open water at night, facedown." The old captain spoke again. "Strange how you all make us out to be the killers, but you all continue to prove time and time again that *you're* all the real killers. Look at what happened to Billy Aplin, and now look at your so-called friend. What'd he do, sleep with one of your dirty women?" The rest of the men behind him began to snicker.

"What is he saying?" Eddie asked.

Duc's face froze. Huey and Vĩnh suddenly came to the same conclusion together and they both cried out. "Where's Tuấn?" they asked each other frantically.

Duc, Huey, Eddie, and Vĩnh looked around, expecting Tuấn to come out of hiding. As the previous night rolled back into their minds, they all remembered Tuấn standing at the helm of the boat, taking a piss, and then all chaos broke loose with a single gunshot into the air.

"He must have fallen overboard," Eddie gasped. "I—I didn't . . . it was so chaotic after the gun went off. We were drunk. He was so drunk."

"We need to go back," Huey said in disbelief. "What if he's still out there?"

The captain still had a grin on his face as he looked out into the open waters. He started up the *Lady Freedom* and began to steer the boat until it was so close to theirs, the metals began scraping. The captain hovered over them, one leg raised on a platform as he tilted forward, resting his elbows on his knee. "Here's a tip: Wait till early morning the next day, you can use your nets to dredge up the ground for any dead bodies. Y'all competent seamen, right? It's just like combing the floor for shrimp. Like searching for your dinner."

He flicked his cap off at them, and before he sped off into the early-morning hours, they watched in horror as one of his crew members lit up a dirty white rag hanging out of a beer bottle and tossed it onto their deck. The last thing Duc and Huey remembered was how quickly the fire spread—how easy it would be to end it all by throwing themselves into the fire. As they yelled at each other and scrambled for water to put out the fire, they couldn't stop thinking about Tuấn's body out there, either floating or sinking to the bottom of the Gulf.

And Huey couldn't stop thinking about Evelyn, pregnant, waiting patiently for her husband to come home. The more water he tried pouring on the fire, the more it grew, and the more he hated himself.

CHAPTER 29

Jude and Jane

The car ride was deathly silent. Jude and Jane refused to acknowledge or even look at each other. Pride filled their chests, hurt filled in the rest. How could they get over decades of anger, resentment, and being pitted against each other? Jane even attempted to fiddle with the radio to try to add a third party into the mix. It'd been almost a decade since the eldest son and the eldest daughter of Duc and Evelyn were together like this. But this was proof that anything was possible, that if two warring Vietnamese siblings from Houston could learn to communicate with each other, then perhaps the rest of the irate world could follow in their footsteps.

Jude headed east of Bellaire, deep in thought. His thick eyebrows scrunched together as he sat in the awkwardness. *Ding!* A notification. Jane quickly grabbed her phone, furrowing her own eyebrows, her fingers flying across the screen. *Ding! Ding! Ding!* Rapid fire from Jane, and from whoever was on the other side of the screen.

Jude tried to ignore whatever was going on between Jane and her phone, but it was unusual to see his younger sister distressed. She furiously typed another message, heavily sighing.

"Everything okay?" he asked.

"Fine. Everything is just *peachy*."

Silence.

"Are you sure?"

Jane opened her mouth, a slight hesitation holding her back from trauma-dumping on her older brother, someone who she had seen as her enemy her entire life. But then another *ding!* She read the notification, and the tips of her ears turned bright red.

Jane gave in to the rare, tender moment. "Do you remember my high school boyfriend?"

"Henry? Henry Lâm? What about him?"

"We sort of reconnected. But then we got into a mini-fight. *Then* I avoided him. *Then* I told him to fuck off. *Then* I regretted it. *Then* I tried to apologize but, I don't really know how to—"

"Apologize," Jude finished for her. "You don't know how to say you're sorry."

Another silence. This time, it lingered heavy in the air. An apology wasn't just an apology in their world. They'd never heard it between their parents or each other, but they heard it plenty when they would see Duc and Evelyn constantly apologizing to everyone in America who didn't look like them. They weren't taught how to say "I'm sorry" to each other, but were taught how to always appear sorry, always begging for scraps.

"Yes," Jane said, her voice small. "I don't know how to say it."

"But you want to say it."

". . . Yes."

"Then, why don't you just keep it simple and say those two words— *I'm sorry*?" Jude suggested. "Apologies don't need to be long. If they did, then no one would want to apologize."

She didn't reply, but out of the corner of his eye, he saw her thumb hovering over the send button.

"So, who are we going to see?" she asked awkwardly, brushing off his olive branch, attempting to change the topic.

"Mrs. Vương," he responded curtly, also welcoming the pivot.

"*Mrs. Vương? The numerologist? The crazy old bat? Why?*" Jane asked, surprised.

The car skidded to the left as Jude pressed down on the pedal, encouraging the car, and, by extension, encouraging himself to barrel toward the truth faster.

"Mrs. Vương said something to me way back then, when we all started down this crazy journey. She said something very odd. She said that Duc was afraid of the ocean. Of the Gulf. That he liked Phoebe's profile the most because she knew how to swim, that she was a lifeguard. Isn't that strange? Nothing makes sense."

Jane shrugged, leaned back, and put her bare feet up on the dashboard, much to his dismay. "I mean, he's an old bat, too. Why would you take anything he says literally? *Nothing* he says has ever made any sense."

Jude just kept driving, because whatever was nagging him, was nagging him to dig deeper into their family. And he wanted his sister by his side as they got closer to the truth.

....

Mrs. Vương's office had all the hallmarks of a hoarder, like most refugees, but oddly enough, the stench wasn't as bad as the visuals. Stacks of the local Vietnamese newspaper, *The Viet Nam Post*, touched the ceiling, each yellowed, frayed edge revealing how far it went back. Piles of old Chinese texts, maps, and translated works—from Cantonese into Vietnamese, from Vietnamese into Cantonese, from Vietnamese into English, and a true wild card, from Cantonese into Teochew into Vietnamese—formed a fort around the newspapers, preventing them from falling over. Windowless, the small but mighty office revealed a life well lived, with framed newspaper clippings of Mrs. Vương throughout the years, and the lives she'd touched in Houston, Dallas, San Jose, and Oklahoma City.

She had always made sure her track record was pristine, and the proof was in the pudding inside five large rusted metal cabinets, containing the files of every client she'd ever crunched numbers for, dating all the way back to 1957, when Ho Chi Minh City was known as Sài Gòn—the Pearl of the Far East. Mrs. Vương kept her receipts, ensuring that every chart she had ever done was well documented. Just in case.

"So, what brings you both in?" Mrs. Vương said, leaning back in her leather chair, arms crossed defensively over her chest, her expression annoyed at the thought of having to deal with Jude Trần again—especially annoyed at him for his mistreatment of her and her meticulous matchmaking process. "How's the wedding planning going? Isn't it . . . next month now?"

Jude inhaled anxiously, gulping in a thick aroma of grated ginger and notes of stale green tea leaves, which sat moldy at the bottom of skunky mugs littering her desk.

"Cô Vương," Jude said nervously, formally addressing her, his voice shaking slightly. "First, I wanted to apologize to you. I think I might have been too hasty. I have made a mockery of your matchmaking process. I'm sorry. I should have been more serious about it."

A small smirk formed at the corners of her lips. She was relishing his penitence, and it made him squirm in his seat even more, remembering what it was like to be chastised by his mother. Even Jane looked over at Jude in surprise; this was all a first. Perhaps the last several months had done him good after all.

"An apology. I see. Starting to get cold feet?" she retorted. "Too hasty, huh? For picking the first file and thinking you could just have a sham of a wedding *and* then get your inheritance?"

Jude looked surprised. "How did you know I had to get married in order to get my inheritance?"

Mrs. Vương uncrossed her arms, threw back her head, and laughed. It was the first time Jude had ever seen Mrs. Vương display any emotion for anything other than numbers and matchmaking. "Con, the *whole* city knows it's a scam," she said as she managed to settle down through hiccupping chuckles. "The way Duc has made you all scramble, each and every one of you. You think we don't see the monstrosity that Jane has made of Duc's old shop over in Dakao Plaza—"

"Wait a minute," Jane protested. "It's not a *monstrosity*. Sure, I mean, it's gone through some changes but—"

"Not now, Jane," Jude hushed her.

"Oh, don't you shush me—"

"You think we *want* to see the Duc's Sandwiches logo on a *tote bag* all over the damn city? Also, you think we don't know what's going on in San Jose? Or in Philadelphia? Your sisters have also lost their minds. The world is much smaller than you think," Mrs. Vương said, barreling through. She circled her finger around, indicating a group of invisible people. "You forget that *we* love gossip and finding information. We've got all the time in the world. And unfortunately, most of the world hates Duc. He probably, honestly, still owes us all money."

Jude's cheeks flushed red. "Then why did you say my father preferred Phoebe's profile over the other files? Why were you there to help me find a wife if you knew the whole time I had to marry to get the money? Why didn't you *say* anything? Why doesn't anyone ever say anything of worth around here?"

She sighed, resting both arms on the sides of the chair, tapping her fingers slowly. "I've known Duc for a very long time. Perhaps too long. But I did genuinely want you to find love, not for the money, but *love*, or at least have a real fighting chance at it. A good marriage can change *you*. It can be very beautiful, Jude. Phoebe's and your chart were solid together, but there was someone else I had in mind, who was also standing in that line that day—"

Jude stared at the stacks and stacks of folders behind her, regret forming. The last several months could have turned out so differently, had he tried. Somewhere in that stack of folders, cabinets, and mess was someone who was an even better choice for him? It was incomprehensible. He couldn't shake his feelings for Phoebe, but he began to wonder what would have happened had he done it all differently.

"I've always known your chart was never accurate, so I did my best." She turned and grabbed the stack of files off the top of the closest cabinet to her and slammed them down in front of Jude. The label said FOR JUDE.

"What do you mean his chart isn't accurate?" Jane asked, eyeing the stack curiously. "All you need is their birthdate and the time they were born. My mother took me in for this chart, too, when I was a kid."

"I need a bit more than that," she said, annoyed. "This isn't Go Fish. I do complicated family charts, mapping entire destinies out. I chart different lives if one decides to make a different decision, and what that life could lead to. I make out whole different universes, different timelines, and answer the 'what ifs' for you. But in order for me to do this, I need the parents' information as well. Do you understand?"

Jane looked confused. But Mrs. Vương waited for Jude to put two and two together, before she realized she could be waiting for a long time.

"Soooo . . . what you're saying is that Phoebe isn't the one for me?" Jude said, waving his hand along. "And that I should go back to the drawing board?"

Mrs. Vương clicked her tongue and began to rub her left temple in slow motion. "Listen to me carefully. I do not have *your* father's information. I don't know his chart, and because of that, I've never been able to give you a proper assessment of *your* life."

"How can you not know?" Jude asked. But Jane's face turned ghost white. "He's been seeing you for longer than I've been alive! Surely, you would know his birth chart like your own palm lines now. Hell, the man goes to see you anytime the Super Lotto is above five million. Not that he needs it—"

"Yes, I know Duc's chart well," she murmured, looking fed up. She grabbed the pile of files of all the potential matches for Jude and threw them on his lap. "But you are not listening to me. I said that I do not know *your* father's chart."

"Oh my god," Jane whispered as she turned to look at Jude. Suddenly she was one of those school kids, back on the playground, giving legs to the gossip. "I knew it. I *knew* it. Duc isn't your father."

Jude felt the world go cold. He was a dam with a crack in it. Everything he'd been suppressing, wondering if he was actually in love with Phoebe, if he was doing the right thing, winning the inheritance and beating his sisters to the punch, wondering where his mother had been hiding for the past two decades, why Duc hadn't responded to his wedding invitation or reached out—none of it had more weight than the childhood rumors that had followed him all his life, tailing him all the way into adulthood. The rumors had been true all along: Duc wasn't his father. Not only did he never have a chance to get to know his mother, but as it turned out, he never even knew who his father was, either.

Who was he really then, if he didn't even know who or where he came from?

In the windowless office of Mrs. Vương's numerology practice, just east of Little Saigon, in another ordinary, inconspicuous plaza, Jane began cackling. She couldn't stop. Laughter spewed out of her like vomit. Jude sat there helplessly as he watched Jane laugh at the stack of files of potential suitors and matches, with some of the spittle hitting Mrs. Vương in the face. It grew louder and louder, aggravating him to no end.

Between gasps, Jane made a feeble attempt to apologize, explaining that she laughed in times of intense awkwardness.

"You are both clearly not understanding me. Let me be clearer," Mrs. Vương said, wiping her brow with her silk handkerchief. "When I say I don't know *your* father's birth chart, I also mean for all of your sisters as well. Which includes you as well, Jane. I've never once been able to accurately do both of yours, or Paulina's, Bingo's, and Georgia's."

Jane's laughter immediately stopped. Her face turned pale and translucent, and Jude could see her veins throbbing—a million subway lines that kept Jane functioning. Suddenly, it was Jude's turn to burst into laughter.

"Duc isn't our father, either?" Jane said slowly, horrified. "Who the hell is our father then?"

"Who *is* our father then?" Jude echoed Jane's sentiment. He began to feel lightheaded.

Mrs. Vương sucked in her breath, closed her eyes, and though it seemed as if she were praying, it also seemed like she was cursing Duc's name—and perhaps Evelyn's name, too. "Like I said, I don't know who your fathers are," she said, exasperated, as if she were dealing with two unruly children who wouldn't listen to her. "All I can tell you is what I don't know. And I'm telling you both, I don't have any of your fathers' charts."

Fathers. That was the second gut punch to both of them. Suddenly, nothing was funny anymore. Jude and Jane looked at each other as equals, both finding their way to the truth.

"There are two fathers?" Jane whispered, stunned.

"Yes, fathers," Mrs. Vương repeated, for no reason other than to plunge the knife deeper in. "Plural. Multiple. As in, more than one. Two."

Jude's mind began churning. He looked up at her. "Why would Duc send us on a wild-goose chase after our inheritance then? What was the point of all this? Some sort of sick joke to entertain an old man? Is the inheritance even real if we're not even related to him?"

Mrs. Vương looked between Jude and Jane, and simply shrugged. "You're looking at this from the wrong perspective. I'm sure there were lessons learned in all of this. Duc had bigger plans, I'm sure."

"Lessons? We're not in school anymore," Jane shot back, her voice rising. "What was the *point* of all of this?"

"What were we supposed to be chasing then?" Jude asked. He was losing it, like a machine that was overheating from an overcapacity of information.

Mrs. Vương turned around and pulled out their mother's file, and flipped to Evelyn's future chart and began pointing at the numbers. "The only sure chart I have of your parents is your mother. This is guaranteed: She is your mother. Everyone knows Evelyn Lê had bounced around the past two decades. Some people think she settled somewhere on the West Coast or moved back east. But I always suspected she went south. I knew your mother was always a southern girl at heart. It's in her chart, you see?

Born in the southernmost tip of Vietnam, immigrating to Oklahoma City, she was always meant to be in the southern region."

"Why are you showing us this?" Jude stammered. "Our mother is gone, okay? She doesn't want to be found—"

But Jane leaned forward and grabbed their mother's file from Mrs. Vương's hands. Her eyes were furious as her finger traced the lines that crisscrossed a map of America. Houston to Philadelphia to San Jose to New Orleans! She realized that Duc had been in many times to see Mrs. Vương for the past several decades. There was a well-kept log of his visitations and how many times this file had been opened throughout the years. The last entry was the week that he had summoned them all home. New Orleans was circled many times over, drowning in question marks. Georgia's name was next to it, with more question marks. *Send the youngest one in to dismantle her?*

He had pinpointed Evelyn's location, or at least, he thought he did.

"Duc sent us to all these locations because that's where our mother was possibly hiding," Jane whispered. "He wasn't sure of the exact location."

Mrs. Vương clapped her hands, pleased that Jane finally got there on her own. "Just so you know, this session isn't free. I charge two hundred dollars an hour," she said. "And I prefer cash."

CHAPTER 30

Bingo

Long after Mr. Ngô left Philadelphia and Bingo, she began to rebuild by herself. He claimed he was heading to San Jose to check up on Paulina, but something about his mannerisms made Bingo more suspicious of him. But brick by brick, tile by tile, plank by plank, Bingo set out to breathe new life into the shop. As the store transformed slowly, so did Bingo. The more the old sandwich shop was stripped of Duc and his old vision, the more Bingo began to find herself.

Who was Bingo Trần as an individual? What did she want out of life? Bingo saw the store as an extension of her body, a garden of some kind that needed tender care. Never had Bingo cared about anything more. She even got a proper mattress for the back room, with an actual bed frame—an ode to growth and ridding herself of any hetero energy.

But her mind was occupied by thoughts of Iris. What would Iris think if she could see her now? Would she even care?

Though Mr. Ngô and Bingo had bonded while he was here, her father's lawyer stayed mute when it came to questions about his life and background, as he always did. He forever remained a fill-in-the-blank game, always leaving everyone guessing, with minimal clues.

But the photo that Bingo had found, of her mother and Mr. Ngô, and his embrace, stayed pinned to the wall, next to her bed. Every night since, she stared at it, perplexed. It was the *way* Mr. Ngô had his arms around her mother, that look of care and tenderness, that let Bingo know something was very wrong. This was the look Bingo had anytime she used to look at Iris. She knew this look well. She pined to be able to look at Iris like this again. But it'd been months since they had spoken.

And Bingo was no fool or stranger to unrequited love.

Did that mean neither was Mr. Ngô?

Duc's eccentricity was no longer a shield or an excuse to hide behind, because Bingo knew something was very deeply off about her mother,

Duc, and Mr. Ngô. What had the three of them been up to? What were they hiding?

So, Bingo called Jane first. It went straight to voicemail. She then called Paulina, who hung up immediately, not even allowing it to go to voicemail. She debated calling Georgia. But what answers could Georgia possibly have? Georgia, bless her heart, was simply too young to be of help. Bingo almost caved and wrote a text out to Jude. But then deleted it. Individual texts in this family were not for the faint of heart. Group chat it was. Just Jude, Jane, Bingo, and Paulina. She left Georgia out, as they often did. This was a discussion for the adult table only.

Bingo tested the waters with a simple: *we need to talk*

Hours later, a follow-up text, with a word she'd never used before: *please*

The following day: *hello????*

Bingo waited and waited.

While Bingo waited for any signs of life, she kept working and kept her head down. Though the part of town where she was was a ghost town, Bingo began to bring care and joy back onto the sidewalks. She planted wildflowers, built a bench to put outside, and redid the windows. Neighbors looked on curiously, watching her day in and day out. The strange, lone woman with the pixie haircut and the steely demeanor, hammering away, night and day, by herself. Though they refused to approach her, viewing her as nothing more than a visiting alien, they waited and watched from afar. They all knew who she was; of course they did. One of Duc Trần's daughters? He was a living legend, and by extension, so was she.

But not all living legends were created equal. Some had a dark shadow over them.

Bingo wasn't sure what she was building for, or what the vision was. But there was a little voice inside of her that constantly made her think of Iris and her cooking. God, she missed that woman's cooking. The way Iris brought joy back into Vietnamese food for her—when her body had begun rejecting Vietnamese food as a way to remove herself from her father and his empire—was nothing short of medicinal. Her food had healed her. Iris cooked with love and treated every ingredient as part of her community, which reminded Bingo of Evelyn's cooking.

Memories of her mother flooded her, reminding her that once upon a time, Evelyn used to love cooking, and how she used to cook up a storm, both at home and at the shop. The sweet and sour marinades she would make, the way she bit down on chili peppers for a bit of heat, the joy of squeezing lemon juice and mixing sugar into a drink. Evelyn used to love food. And then one day, her mother stopped cooking, and she never came back to it. As a child, Bingo couldn't understand why all of a sudden the food was replaced with frozen dinosaur nuggets or fast food. Why did all that love get suddenly yanked from all of them?

Iris had reminded her of the best parts of it all.

And god, did Bingo miss her.

As spring slowly inched its way into summer, the city of Philadelphia had begun to swelter. Pants were replaced with capris, skirts, and shorts, and Bingo watched the streets slowly come back to life. The days were long, sticky, and somehow, even lonelier. But Bingo had begun to find solace in it. In search of fresh air, she found a red rusted ladder on the side of the building that went up to the rooftop. As she climbed each step, the skyline formed a faux mountain ridge, almost smiling back at her. Once on top of the roof, she saw how much space there was, and the possibilities were endless. The next day, she carried a lawn chair up to the roof. The following day, she brought up some shade. The following day, some planter boxes.

But Iris was always lingering, her smell, traces of her touch.

Did you know that Philadelphia has always been my favorite city? I remember thinking I could live here forever.

For once, Bingo agreed with Duc. She could live here forever.

As Bingo began to place planter boxes all over the roof, a vision began to crystallize in her mind. She saw a vision of the shop in a way that she couldn't before, and the shop had a full, beating heart, akin to her own.

That was when her phone lit up, message after message after message flying in. Her siblings had finally responded, bringing news of something much bigger than all of them were prepared for. Bingo looked down in horror as she read snippets, and she went back to reread the messages just to confirm that she wasn't hallucinating.

Then Paulina came back from the dead and chimed in, exacerbating the urgency. Soon, it was Jude, Jane, Bingo, and Paulina furiously texting each other, confirming all the gossip that had been buried. They had to find their parents. It was the only way. Who did they belong to? What branches of a tree did they belong to?

The truth was ugly: Duc wasn't their father.

But in all of their hearts, they knew. They had always known that they didn't belong to Duc. It wasn't because none of them looked like him, or because of the forced distance that Duc put between them—it was simply children's intuition. Something was wrong their entire lives. All of the children on the playground knew the truth back then. The gossip would seep into their ears, and they could see the truth. It was always the adults who pretended not to see.

Bingo stood on the roof, looking out onto the city, and knew she had to leave right away, to be with her siblings again. There was a sadness to her departure from a city she had been transient in. She was nothing more than an onlooker. There was something to be said about transplants, always observing, unable to find their way in. Perhaps that loneliness of being a transplant was just a constant way to remind her to come home. Bingo hadn't missed Houston since she left when she was eighteen, but now the call of the South was something she couldn't ignore anymore.

Her departure was imminent because she was certain she knew the identity of one of the fathers, and that proof had been next to her bed, nagging at her every night.

But first, she had to say goodbye.

To the city, but also, more importantly, to a girl.

....

In the final days, Bingo finished her shop.

As she took in the full view, standing on the sidewalk, caked in paint and plaster, she acknowledged that something she had created, with her own hands, was beautiful in an understated way. The wood finishes, the crown molding, the sleek marbled countertops. For her final act, Bingo got up on a stepladder, and with a crowbar, she began to remove the letters, one by one, that spelled out *Duc's Sandwiches*. Each letter piled on top of another on the ground, the pile growing bigger and bigger—a Jenga game about to topple over any minute now. The shop now belonged to no one and had no trace of Duc Trần.

It was freeing in a way.

Finding out the last few days that Duc wasn't her father somehow made all the sense and no sense at the same time. It pushed her to finish the shop faster, a final goodbye to the childhood and father figure she had known and had grown to resent.

Because Bingo was done being angry. It was time to move on.

Once you bypass the fear of the unknown, con, this place will become your favorite city, too.

Who was really behind those letters all along? Bingo had always thought it was strange that the tone didn't sound like Duc. Tenderness hid between the lines, but Duc had been incapable of feeling that toward them.

Bingo knew. Rereading the letter with new eyes, from nearly a year ago, Bingo realized who had really written the letters to all the Trần children, and it most certainly wasn't Duc.

One by one, the neighbors slowly came out. They circled Bingo nervously. The CPA who rented the corner office. The owner of the Thai restaurant, who had a 3.5 review rating, which only meant that it was probably the best Thai restaurant in town. And the middle-aged Vietnamese woman who owned the orchid shop a few doors down. But eventually one of them went up to her.

"What will replace Duc's?" the woman asked Bingo, her ears raised for any scrap of information and gossip.

Bingo didn't respond right away. She just gazed at the now empty space where the sign had been, with only the faintest outline of the old name. There was one possible name that would make sense. It was the one name that Bingo held firmly on to, remembering the late nights together, and early mornings. The name that had ridden SEPTA with her, had gone on picnics over at Rittenhouse Square, one too many times, the name that forced her to rent a tandem bike, even though Bingo never learned to bike.

It was the one name that would have made her stay in the city forever.

"A place called Iris's," Bingo finally said, responding to the woman. "Better Vietnamese food is coming to this block. Trust me."

The woman shrugged, not believing her. "Duc's *was* pretty bad. But I'll believe it when I taste it."

A biker zoomed past the small crowd that had formed on the sidewalk, and Bingo looked up a little too eagerly, hoping to see a familiar face. But it wasn't her. It turned out to be just another anonymous biker, in a city full of them.

················

The familiar smell enveloped her. Iris was at it again. The charcoal smoke carried for miles and miles, creating a visible trail that led to the storefront. Bingo was instantly comforted, knowing who the woman was behind all of it. As she rounded the corner, the queue was still standing strong, because everyone knew what was waiting at the end of the line, and that the wait would be worth it.

Bingo knew more than anyone here that yes, the wait was always worth it when it came to *her*.

Bingo spotted Iris immediately. Bantering with a customer, she was able to somehow joke and chop food at the same time—a skill Bingo used to find intimidating, and she'd worry that one wrong laugh would send Iris off to the ER needing stitches. But Bingo worried over her like a lover, when Iris had needed more than just surface-level worry. Iris had kept waiting for Bingo to grow up, and once Bingo did, it was too late.

Bingo saw Iris's bike, locked up in the same spot as it always was. Crowded among hundreds of other bikes, the familiar blue-and-green bike that had brought them together that fateful day stuck out to her immediately. She owed that bike thanks, for allowing her to collide with fate.

The queue grew longer, and Bingo watched on longingly, imagining a life in which she *had* gotten her life together earlier, and they had been able to build something together. She imagined a world in which she had gotten out of her own head, and had allowed herself to be happy. Maybe that would have led to more afternoon naps together, and she'd be curled up in Iris's arms, purring softly as she was showered with kisses. Then no earthquake, asteroid heading toward Earth, or viral pandemic could ever make her get out of Iris's arms.

But reality yanked her back, because it sounded too picture-perfect. All she ever had as an example of a marriage were Duc and Evelyn, and now that the truth had surfaced, knowing their marriage was built on a foundation of lies, there was no point in living in the "what ifs."

Maybe she'd allow herself to pursue real happiness one day. Maybe.

She walked over to Iris's bike and shoved a sealed envelope into the spokes, just as she had done before with the bouquet. It simply said *To Iris.* Inside the envelope was a key, along with a simple note: *Finally got a bed frame. Also, the store is yours. Enjoy.*

She didn't have to sign it. Iris would know exactly who it was from.

CHAPTER 31

April 1981, Seabrook-Kemah, Texas

Rumors had spread all throughout Harris County, down to Seadrift, and all along the coast. Whispers that the Klansmen had killed Tuấn and that he had fought them off bravely, sacrificing himself to save the others. Was Tuấn a hero? He had single-handedly fought off their enemies to ensure a better future for his unborn son and for every Vietnamese in Texas. Tuấn *was* a hero. Right?

Duc, Huey, Vĩnh, and Eddie hadn't spoken since that night, and no one made any motion to correct the rumors. The four men buried their shame and thinned their lips. They allowed the rumors to run wild that Tuấn had been a sacrificial lamb. Because the truth was much more sinister and harder to swallow. That Tuấn had just been drunk and had fallen overboard. And that none of the men had noticed in time because they were also drunk and scared. They could have saved him.

"Let's leave town tonight," Duc said to Huey quietly as they walked side by side down Bay Avenue, swift and rushed. They wanted to avoid the moonlight and eye contact with strangers. There was an invisible curfew in place, because not a soul would chance to be out late ever since the Klansmen set the sixty-day mark. But everyone knew that four walls and a roof couldn't stop the Klansmen's threats from wafting in, invisible and noxious as they were.

"You want to leave? *Tonight?*" Huey responded. He could taste his dinner of expired catfish and fermented fish paste coming back up. But all he could think about was Evelyn, pregnant and alone. In a moment of frustration, he shoved Duc. He'd never laid his hand on him in that way, out of pure anger. He wondered what it'd feel like to push him harder, and the thought seemed so freeing. "You know I never wanted to come here in the first place. I *begged* you not to come down here. We should have left when those racists at the motel threatened us on the first day. And *now* you're ready to leave? After we've killed Tuấn?" Huey's breathing was unstable, and he could feel something in his system. Doubt had begun to poison his mind, wondering why he ever decided to follow Duc around in the first place. Why was he so weak? So weak he couldn't figure out how to be on his own? That he had to rely on a charlatan?

Duc stopped dead in his tracks, shocked that Huey had the balls to get physical. He turned angry and shoved Huey back harder. The impact was harsher and pushed Huey back almost a foot. There was meaning behind that shove and a strange glint in Duc's eyes.

"Don't you fucking say that to me. You *know* it was an accident. Blaming ourselves isn't going to solve anything. Tuấn was drunk. He drank too much. He's always drunk a bottle more than he should have. That's on him if he couldn't handle it," Duc said defensively. "You're beating yourself up over nothing. He might not even be dead. Maybe the poor bastard washed up on shore somewhere and he's just in the hospital with amnesia, like in the goddamn movies. No one found the body. Stop blaming us. Stop blaming *me*."

"You're the one who was fucking around! You kept pressing him to drink when he didn't want to! He's got a fucking kid on the way!" Huey shouted. "What about Evelyn?"

"Who fucking cares?! Fuck him, and fuck Evelyn! We need to look after ourselves now."

"Fuck you!" Huey shouted, blinded by rage. All he could see was Evelyn, cradling her bump, standing on shore, waiting for Tuấn every night since the accident. The image haunted him. He hadn't been able to sleep a full night ever since.

"FUCK *YOU*!"

"You're fucking selfish, always have been. I'm sick of following you around. All you do is cause destruction wherever you go."

"Yeah? Well, you're a spineless fuck. Look how far I've gotten us. Without me, you'd just be nothing but a weak loser. You were weak back in Vietnam and you're fucking weak here! You're a loser, just like your loser father! An uneducated fisherman's son will always be nothing more than an uneducated fisherman's son."

No one knew who threw the first punch.

But in the heat of the moment, no one cared.

Huey and Duc only cared about harming each other, releasing years of pent-up frustration and repressed anger. In a tangle of sweaty limbs, under a clear night sky in Texas, two Vietnamese refugee fishermen recklessly exchanged blows. Huey was thrown against the side of a building by Duc, whose stocky frame served him well as he managed to form a foundation and trap Huey's lower half with his legs. Duc's arms came swinging from each side as Huey felt indents along his rib cage, some deeper than others. Duc's fingers managed to crawl up his thick neck, wrapping his hands around it, squeezing it as if it were nothing more than a condiment bottle, forcing Huey to gasp for spurts of air. In between gasps of air, he rammed his elbows down on Duc's back, trying to throw him off. From afar, it looked as if Duc was winning; his brow was steeped in sweat, and his calves defined and relentless. But he was losing energy. Somehow in all the chaos, Huey managed to wrap his arms under Duc's exposed armpits and lift him off the ground.

With a fierce roar, Huey shoved him as far back as he could, barreling into him like a rocket, until Duc crashed into the rickety wood fencing on the other side of the pier's boardwalk. Losing his footing, Duc nearly tumbled backward across the fence.

Panic bloomed on his face as he shouted in fear. He finally realized what he'd be falling into. The water was black, thick, and foolishly looked like solid land to the ignorant eye.

But Duc knew better.

Even if it was his push, Huey also knew better. He imagined his friend wasn't just seeing his own life flash before his eyes; he also saw Tuấn's life. Fear of tumbling into the Gulf, fear of drowning, fear of escaping Vietnam when Sài Gòn fell, fear of not being able to swim, fear of being gutted like the fish they gutted every day, or perhaps, fear of seeing Tuấn's face at the bottom of the Gulf floor, his expression frozen in time, his hands still outstretched, waiting for someone to pull him out of the water. But Tuấn wasn't just waiting for anybody; he had been waiting for them, his closest friends, to pull him out.

That night on the boat, Huey remembered hearing a splash hit the water. But the sound of the gun going off had put them all into survival mode. In the grand moral Richter scale of the universe, his life was far more important than anyone else on that boat. But he could have checked. Why didn't he notice Tuấn was missing? It was that sick, sinking feeling in his gut, that something terrible had happened, and if he stopped, he'd have to acknowledge it was all his fault.

Duc closed his eyes, and Huey felt maybe he was accepting his fate. His punishment, the freezing Gulf that would soon drag him down into its depths. But Huey couldn't stand it. After all this time together, if Duc were to fall, then Huey should, too.

Huey yanked Duc by the back of his shirt, dragging him back down before he tumbled over the fencing. Together, they collapsed on the wooden planks of the pier, their chests heaving up and down, their sweat dripping down their arms and legs. The brothers in all but blood sat side by side, silently, each one recovering, lost in their thoughts. Huey eventually made the first gesture, and patted Duc on the back, a small semblance of an apology for almost having thrown him over into the water. And Duc being Duc, he merely grunted a response back, took out a pack of rolled-up cigarettes, and handed one to Huey, stuck one in his own mouth, and lit them both up.

"What now?" Huey asked forlornly, the cigarette dangling between his lips.

"Let's sell whatever is left of the boat, take what money we can get, and go," Duc said quietly. "We can head northeast again, back to Philly. I still have some good buddies up there. Hell, we can go even farther north, cross the border. I hear a lot of people have immigrated to Quebec. I have second cousins up there who can help us get settled."

"It was your *other* cousins in the first place who brought us down here to work in the damn crab factory." Huey scoffed, releasing a huge cloud of smoke into the air. There wasn't a hint of a threat or bitterness in his voice anymore; he was simply stating a fact.

"It's not like it's been all for nothing," Duc responded, also stating a fact, though there was some defensiveness behind it. "We've made some money."

"The boat won't even sell for pennies since it's been charred to nothing. Besides, I can't go back to Philly. I can't . . . go backward." Huey touched the cigarette to his lips again. "We're not welcome anywhere else in this country. We've left a trail of destruction in our wake. We either owe people apologies or money, and I don't have either one to give out now."

"But what choice do we have? We need to leave," Duc responded calmly as he rubbed his chin with his free hand, his brow furrowed deep. "I'd rather apologize and face the consequences of our past than face the unpredictability of our future here."

From a few blocks over came a fleet of feet, running the opposite direction from them. The two men stood up quickly. Instinct told them both to flee, but the commotion was running toward the old abandoned seafood restaurant. Up ahead, they saw shadows lurking, huddling behind the boarded-up restaurant. The former restaurant owner was Chú Bảo, who had left town immediately after he witnessed the Klansmen and the American fishermen sail down Clear Lake together, with that hanging Vietnamese man effigy. He had packed up his three daughters, his wife, boarded up his crab shack, and left it to the vultures and to graffiti artists to tag as their playground.

"What's going on?" Huey whispered, watching more shadows appear in the far distance, heading inside the abandoned crab shack.

"Who cares?" Duc hissed. "Let's just leave. Whatever it is, it's not for us to know anymore. We're leaving town."

But something about one of the shadows seemed familiar to Huey. The waif build, the long hair, the stomach bulge seemed larger than normal. He could spot her shadow in any rough terrain, at any hour of the night. Evelyn. What was she doing skulking around this place, so late at night?

"I'm just going to go around the side and peek inside," Huey said, much to Duc's protests. He hunched his body, and inched around the side of the shack, trying to find a way through the boarded-up windows. There were faint sounds coming from inside—nothing he could make out clearly, but he was comforted knowing the main language was Vietnamese, and there were a lot of Vietnamese voices talking at once. Circling the building, he managed to find a broken window, the crack the size of a donut hole, and he perched on his tiptoes, listening in.

Like a magnet always pointing north, he was immediately drawn toward Evelyn. She wasn't hard to spot regardless; she was the only woman in a crowd of twenty or so Vietnamese men of varying ages. Despite her delicate frame, she stood tall, her arms instinctively crossed over her growing, pregnant stomach. Though she appeared normal, grief hung heavy all around her; she was drowning in it, lost in its orbit. Huey's guilt wrapped itself up, tightening its grip around him. The more he tried to alleviate it, the tighter the noose was. He grieved for Evelyn's future son, who would never know how wonderful his father had been.

Huey scanned the rest of the crowd and spotted Eddie and Vĩnh next
to Evelyn. They both hovered around her protectively, their combined
bulk overshadowing her. Huey hadn't seen them since the night on the
boat with Tuấn, but he knew they were avoiding him and Duc. Huey's
guilt was suffocating, observing Eddie and Vĩnh, standing united with
Evelyn in their grief. Though they had all made a pact to never speak the
truth of what really happened that night, Huey knew they were forever
haunted.

He and Duc were nothing more than cowards.

Huey tried to identify the others. There was Old Man Trung and his
son. Tuấn's father and uncle showed up, despite their grief. Huey recognized more faces, but he knew they wouldn't recognize him or Duc. It was
a community they'd recused themselves from. Huey went from carrying
guilt on his shoulders to carrying shame, and he didn't know which was
worse.

As the chatter grew, the crowd parted, creating a narrow pathway for a
man to pass. His back turned to Huey as he walked toward the middle and
silenced the crowd with raised arms. He turned to reveal himself, and
through the small crack in the window, Huey recognized him immediately.
Colonel Nam. He'd seen him around town, and the stories about him had
become almost messiah-like. He'd been elevated as a leader to the people, a
colonel in the South Vietnamese Army. With a taut jaw, gelled, slicked-
back hair, and a strict posture, Colonel Nam was blunt and to the point.
He folded his arms behind him and began his speech.

Huey pressed his ear against the window, attempting to make out bits
and pieces.

Don't lose faith. Fight back. Lawsuit. Lawyer. Mr. Dees.

Believe.

Testify. Testify. Testify.

Huey couldn't grasp the whole speech, but he saw how intensely the
crowd hung on to Colonel Nam's every word. He knew enough of what was
going to happen, all those nights he secretly read up on the laws in this
country. He knew they were going to take the Klan to court. But he didn't
need a law degree to know they were fools in their attempt. No American
court would ever side with them.

His eyes gravitated toward Evelyn, and he saw that her grief needed hope. She cradled her baby bump even tighter, and she hunched over, her shoulders softly rising and falling. She was sobbing. Eddie and Vĩnh both put their hands on her shoulders wordlessly. Huey saw the shame in it all.

Huey didn't just have some schoolboy crush on Evelyn like Duc had; he'd been foolishly in love with the woman ever since he laid eyes on her the first week he arrived. And now the death of her husband, her son's father, was on his hands. Of all the scamming victims they owed apologies to— from Philadelphia, down to New Orleans, to San Jose—he knew Tuấn's face would be forever seared into his memory, until his deathbed. He knew he was trapped in Texas, and that he'd never know peace until Tuấn's body was recovered, until Evelyn and her unborn son were taken care of. The ghost of Tuấn would follow him, like all the soldiers who were never found in the minefields of Vietnam. So many lost bodies and souls—would it ever end?

They said that when the fog settled in for the night in the highlands of Vietnam, ghosts wandered out in the fields, trying to find their way back home. That Đà Lạt was the most haunted place of all of them. Every mother was afraid to go there and find their sons searching for home. Seadrift was Huey's Đà Lạt. Huey knew that Tuấn's ghost would haunt the Gulf forever until Evelyn and her son were taken care of.

When Huey sneaked back to Duc, he wasn't cognizant of his own voice anymore.

"I'm not leaving," Huey said defiantly. "You can leave without me." Duc's face contorted into something Huey had never seen before. "I'm going to stay and help. And help Evelyn."

"Help who?" Duc asked incredulously. "What the hell are you going to do? Pick up a gun? You don't even know how to fire one."

"I'm going to help them gather testimonies and witnesses for court," Huey said confidently. "There's some lawsuit going around to go against the Klan. I want to stay and help."

Duc burst out laughing. "A lawsuit? We're not going to win in a god-damn lawsuit here, okay? The laws weren't made for men like you and me. We're refugees, not citizens."

Huey's face turned red, but he held steady. Facing Duc was harder than facing the barrel of a gun. "Remember what you asked me five years ago when we met? On that shitty fishing boat down in Delacroix Island? You asked me if I could be anything I wanted, what would I be?" Huey asked, his face directly cut in half from the moonlight. "I said I wanted to be respected, and wear a fancy suit one day. I said I wanted to become a lawyer. Do you remember what you told me then?"

Duc's laugh stopped. He stared at Huey as if he was really seeing him for the first time. "Anh, I was joking around that day. Men like you and me don't get to become lawyers here. We aren't the ones who get to wear suits."

"Do you remember what you told me that day?" Huey pressed on, ignoring Duc.

"I said, pretend you're a lawyer and act like one. But we aren't playing pretend here. You're delusional. *This* isn't real. You're going to get killed if you testify or help with the case."

"Then at least I'll die doing something worthy for once," Huey pleaded. "Will you stay and help, too?"

Duc's chest rose, and for a split second, Huey held on to hope, as he always did when it came to Duc. Hope that his friend, his brother, his comrade, would stay for him at least. That he also recognized Huey as more than just a friend, but family.

"Anh, you're a fool," Duc said slowly. "You're on your own. I'm leaving town tomorrow. With or without you." Without another word, he turned on his heel, not giving a second glance back at Huey.

CHAPTER 32

Evelyn

Even after all these years, I still remember his scent.

Tuấn's scent was steel, sandalwood, and fresh soil. But my scent? My scent was so distinctly feminine and expensive, it needed no introduction. May rose, jasmine, and a hint of bourbon vanilla. Chanel No. 5. Why was a woman like me, whose hands were rough and calloused from scrubbing crabs raw for years, wearing Chanel No. 5? What was the point of it?

All the girls around me were obsessed with anything designer, anything that would give us the illusion we weren't living a pitiful life. Were we even *living*? We were women working at the crab factory, stuck in a Podunk town in Texas, where our small lives were made even smaller by the prejudice around us. I didn't want any trouble; I just wanted to keep my head down, and grieve for a Vietnam that would never be mine again.

I'm still allowed to grieve for an alternative life lost, am I not?

How little did I know that I'd continue to grieve again and again, for the rest of my life. A cyclone of sorrow. Had I known that I'd experience even more heartbreak in America, I wouldn't have come.

The girls at the factory and I loved to play pretend with our designer dupes and bootleg perfume. We pretended to be like the women in bigger Texas cities like Dallas who walked around exuding Americana and richness. We cackled about their styles openly, but went home and dreamt about having the same red lipstick as they did. But I had a secret that the girls didn't know. While their perfumes were bootleg copies, my scent was real. Even during the months when Tuấn and I were so poor that we had to comb through the dumpsters behind restaurants, Tuấn had somehow saved up enough to buy me the tiniest sample of Chanel No. 5. It wasn't even a mini size; it was barely longer than the length of my pinkie. I used to cut the sample with grain alcohol to make it last for as long as I could, or I'd spray all my clothes with the scent and store it tightly so the smell would last.

Tuấn would encourage me to use it all up, that he'd get more, but I still lived in fear, as I did for most of my life.

When Tuấn and I lay together at night, our scents would merge, meeting at the bittersweet intersection of young love and poverty. My mother hated Tuấn's smell, and she wondered how I could stand to be around him all the time. Whenever she had to have dinner with him, her nose crinkled so deeply it almost disappeared inside her skull. Her number one insult: She didn't have to season her food with fish sauce if Tuấn was around, because he smelled enough of the sea and fermentation.

I tried to convince her that our scents canceled each other out. I kept pleading with her to stop calling Tuấn "just another dirty fisherman." He was more than that. But she was convinced that Tuấn was never good enough for me. She didn't want me to have the same life she had. But did she know that Tuấn had worked so hard for us to have a stable life that my hands weren't as calloused as hers had been? At least there was still life left in the crevices of my palms. Did she know that he loved me so much, he never once said "I" and only said "we"? Did she know that he bought me Chanel No. 5?

If she saw me in the following years, would she have still felt the same way about Tuấn? Would she see beyond the mansion, the designer bags that Duc kept throwing at me because he thought it'd keep me happy, or the way that Huey grew further away from us, still convinced that he didn't deserve to be around us? Would my mother understand that living a life based on a lie was not a life to live?

Tuấn took my life along with him, the day he never came back from the Gulf.

I knew. I knew something was wrong. When Duc and Huey came to my house that morning, and told me that Tuấn had disappeared off the boat, and his body now belonged to the black waters. They told me that the Klan was there that night. That the fire happened so quickly, they didn't see it coming. That there was *nothing* they could have done. I knew that they were lying, but that one lie stuck out the most.

"There was nothing we could have done."

I looked them straight in the eyes, these two men, who promised me that they would do everything they could to keep searching for Tuấn. They even did the most dangerous thing of all: They gave me hope. They were convinced that he must have crawled to shore, must have kept swimming, must have stayed alive somehow. Even though they knew that Tuấn didn't know how to swim. But I couldn't help myself, I believed them. I believed the charlatans. I believed that Tuấn would have done anything to stay alive, and return back home to me and our unborn baby.

I went out on a volunteer search boat every day. The seasickness and my pregnancy combined were like oil and water. But I stayed. I stayed and combed the Gulf floor with shrimping nets, hoping for something to turn up, then I went home relieved when nothing came up. I called every local hospital, in broken English, giving a description of my Tuấn: 5'9", dark hair, deep-set eyes, thick eyebrows, hollowed cheeks. He was unintentionally funny, loved his Marlboro Reds, listening to the Beatles, Jimi Hendrix, the Rolling Stones, but most of all, he loved coming home to me.

Have you seen this man? He must be there. Has he turned up? Has he asked for me?

Eventually, people around me moved on. The Klan was closing in on their sixty-day threat, so everyone had to focus on their own families. Tuấn became a martyr, a lost symbol. "Don't worry, em," people would say to me. "We'll get revenge for Tuấn's memory." But they didn't know the truth. That Tuấn wasn't a martyr. That something else had happened to him that night. But what really happened?

I kept waiting for Duc and Huey every day, borrowing any boat left, so we could keep looking for Tuấn. But Duc stopped showing up one day. Only Huey tried his best to keep his promises, but eventually, even he stopped looking for Tuấn.

Huey still wouldn't tell me the truth of what happened. He just let me believe the gossip.

That's why now, whenever I looked at Duc, I felt ill. Yes, he was there for us when the kids were growing up. But where was he back then? Why did he lie to me? What really happened to Tuấn that night? But most of all, how could *Huey* keep lying to me? I married Huey out of fear. He was gentle, kind, and I knew he loved me, so I thought I could love him enough. I wanted a father for my son.

Lies. I was still caught up in the swirls of Duc's and Huey's lies, and now I've lost control of my own story.

PART 4

PROOFING (OR PROVING) THAT LOVE EXISTS

CHAPTER 33

Jane

Jane couldn't remember the last time she had woken up in another man's arms. She'd kept to herself for so long, she had forgotten how to seek pleasure for herself in all the intimate, tender ways a woman needed to feel alive. To be able to arch your back, hear whispers in your ear, have calloused hands following the mountains and peaks of your curves, fingers tangled in your hair, and to feel the weight of someone wrapping their arms around you after it was all said and done.

Jane wanted to cry. Why had she denied herself happiness? Why had she spent so much energy in not becoming like her father, that she ended up becoming like her mother? Why did she stay away from the act of love for so long?

The sound of Henry's soft snores reminded her of a life she could have had, had she stayed in Houston for college, had she stayed for law school, and had she continued staying with Henry after high school. But her desire for leaving and going as far away from her family as possible led her down a different path, one she hadn't thought would be so lonely.

If she had stayed, would they have been married by now? Kids? Was that the life she wanted for herself?

Jane lay curled on her side, facing away from Henry. The clock—neon red, bright and unforgiving—spelled out 3:43 a.m. She groaned softly. There was no point in trying to sleep anymore. Hearing the news that Duc wasn't her biological father had haunted her. Why had she allowed herself to be steeped in anger for so long at this man? Her entire life had been dictated by anger. Anger for herself, for her mother, for being born the eldest daughter, at Duc for being absent.

She wasted so much time.

Jane slowly pulled the blanket off her, wrapped herself up in one of Henry's sweaters, and tiptoed around his apartment, her bare feet light against cold hardwood floors.

It was the first time she'd been to his place since she moved back to

Houston, and she finally allowed herself to be vulnerable with him, in more ways than one. Jane needed comfort, now more than ever. She just decided to choose a different kind of physical comfort.

The entire living room wall was covered with photo frames, mismatched ones that almost went all the way up to the ceiling. From the outside looking in, his life was full of people, adventure, and good food—all the markings of someone who was well loved and well lived. She recognized old faces from high school, faces she saw randomly on her social media feeds. Sometimes, if she was in a generous mood, she would like or heart their post, but most of the time she kept scrolling.

If she moved permanently back to Houston, would she be able to fit in seamlessly with all the other squares? Would she be just as loved as Henry by everyone? And would she have the same smile on her face as everyone did on this wall? Jane shivered, hugging herself. She wouldn't be able to fill a wall like this, full of precious, fleeting moments that occupied the time between the mundane. Now that she was grappling with who her real father was, and why Duc would send them on a whirlwind goose chase for the past year, and that her mother was in New Orleans, where Georgia was, she couldn't imagine fitting into any of these squares. Her life couldn't be as neatly summed up as everyone else's.

"Jane?" Henry's quiet voice from behind made her jump, and she turned around, unsure why she looked so guilty.

"Sorry, I was just looking for a glass of water," she said, her voice high-pitched. The lie sounded like a lie, and she flinched from it. He stood there in his boxer shorts and ran his hand through his hair. There was an awkward lull between them, as if they both had amnesia and were pretending they hadn't been intimate just a few hours ago. Funny how two people could find warmth together in bed, but become strangers when their feet hit cold hardwood.

"Are you okay?" he asked, finally breaking the tension.

"Great," she responded quickly, perhaps too quickly. "Yeah, sorry, I was . . . dehydrated."

Jane walked to the kitchen and rummaged for a glass, opening and closing cabinet doors aimlessly.

"Are you thinking of leaving again?" he asked softly, his eyes on the photo wall. Jane found a glass and went to the sink to fill it. She took large gulps, the sounds exaggerated and forceful, and she was thankful for the darkness, grateful that Henry couldn't see all of her face—how guilty she looked.

Again. He had used the word *again*. It landed like a mosquito bite, but Jane was worried that by morning light, the itch would grow worse. But she was contemplating two modes now: fight or flight. She could either curl up like a small child looking for a fort to hide away in, or end the war permanently by blowing it all up.

As always, she opted for the latter.

"You know I was always meant to be here temporarily. I only came back to Houston because Duc set up this obscene scheme for us. And now that he isn't even my father—I don't know. And Jude is my half brother apparently?

"What's the point of being here? I never felt like I belonged here," she continued slowly, her mind beginning to dissociate. She knew this dissociation well. She gestured around his apartment, pointing at random artifacts that screamed bachelor: his Jeremy Lin Houston Rockets jersey, the acoustic guitar in the corner, the giant vintage poster of the NASA Space Center. "*None* of this is me."

"What's wrong with all of *this*?" He mimicked her gesture, hurt splayed across his face.

"Nothing! I didn't say anything was wrong with it! I just said, it's not *me*. You were right earlier. That shop isn't me, this city isn't me. It was never *me*. I don't really see myself fitting in here as an adult," she said meekly. "I've felt that way my entire life, growing up here. That's why I left in the first place. It's not . . . personal."

The moment the last word left her mouth, she knew she had messed up. Henry's face buckled and she realized she'd have to be the one to deliver a lethal blow, not him.

"Are you joking? Of course it's personal! What do you want, Jane?" he asked, exasperated. "All I've done since the moment I ran into you at that coffee shop, almost a year ago, was try to get close to you. I'm sorry about your father—I mean Duc—whoever he is—I'm sorry about everything your parents put you through, but look what you've done with your life so far here. You're *happy* for once. The shop is ridiculous, yes, but look at the life you've made for yourself, the people you've reconnected with. You've smiled almost every day going into the shop. Why can't you just let yourself be happy for once?"

Standing in the middle of the kitchen, Jane could see the sun start to rise. It was now or never. She knew she didn't deserve Henry, not when she had so many issues to work through with herself, her family, and her own traumas. She needed to sever this.

"I just know I won't be happy stuck here with you," she blurted out. What a train wreck. "Your life is just too simple for me. Houston is too simple. I know myself. I'm always going to want more. My mother wanted more—and look what happened. Look what happened to her mental state when she stayed. She's probably been happier out there, living in her truth. I need to do the same."

Henry stood there shell-shocked, his eyes downcast. She braced herself, waiting for him to react negatively, raise his voice, or throw accusations at her. This was the type of ugly love she was used to. This was the ugly love she'd seen her entire life. To push, push, and push people away until they had no choice but to want to leave on their own.

"Well then," he eventually said, blowing out air. There was a tremble in his voice. "I hope you get everything you want, Jane. I hope you get to see yourself happy one day. Because I know I won't be around to see it."

He turned to retreat to his bedroom, and the soft lock of the door confirmed that he was done, leaving Jane alone to watch the sunrise. In the moment, Jane couldn't help but feel anger toward Jude. Had he not encouraged her to say *I'm sorry* to Henry, perhaps all this could have been avoided. Jane could have just simply run away, as she was always prone to do.

Like mother, like daughter.

. . . .

Bác Cai shuffled into Dakao Plaza and the store the next morning around 6:00 a.m.

She was still in her house slippers and her hair was pinned back under a silk scarf. Despite Jane changing everything about the store, one thing that didn't change was Bác Cai's routines. She'd wake up at an ungodly hour, go into the store, water the bamboo plants, and get ready for the day in the store's bathroom. She'd kept the same morning routine for the past thirty years, even using the same old Christian Dior white setting powder on her face.

No one in the twenty-first century had ever seen what she looked like before 6:00 a.m.—until that morning.

The moment Bác Cai entered the back room, she saw Jane crumpled on an old cot, her body shriveled, eyes puffy, and cheeks so tear-streaked, it formed freeway lanes on her face. The eldest Trần daughter had done something once again, she surmised, to prevent her happiness from ever coming to fruition.

They locked eyes, each one disturbed by the other's state.

"Oh my god—" Jane's voice muffled.

"Trời ơi—"

"Is that your real face?"

"What did you do this time, con?"

Jane almost forgot her troubles as she stared at Bác Cai's natural state, before all the primping and priming she did to mask her real age. She saw the dark spots around her eyes, how deep-set her wrinkles were. Bác Cai was old, there was no way around it, and her fragility was on a timer. And there was Jane, much younger, lying in the fetal position, unable to find her way.

"You really shouldn't still be working at your age, you know," Jane said quietly as she sat up. "You should consider retirement. I'll take care of you."

"And how exactly are you going to take care of me all the way from Los Angeles?" Bác Cai raised her eyebrow.

Jane stammered. "I never said I was going to move back anytime soon."

Bác Cai scoffed. "It's all over, is it not? I know you know. About Duc. That he isn't your real father."

Jane looked at her suspiciously. "You knew. You knew this whole time, didn't you?"

Bác Cai laughed, hard. "Con, it's the worst-kept secret in Houston." She then shuffled into the bathroom and began to get herself ready for the day. Jane observed from a distance. She watched as Bác Cai unraveled her headscarf, tucked bobby pins around her thinning hair, and curled areas into bobs to make it look fuller. She took out a thick black liner and began to flick her eyebrows, filling them in, her age somehow disappearing with each new trick she did.

"Why didn't you tell me?" Jane asked softly. "Why didn't you tell us?"

"It's not my life's story to tell," Bác Cai called out. She carefully applied an old, crusty tube of red lipstick to her lips. "It's your mother's story."

"No, it's *our* story," Jane said angrily. "I'm part of that narrative."

"What does it matter? Did Duc not treat you right? Did he not provide a good life for you? Why are you so ungrateful, con?" Bác Cai's voice rose as she turned around to look Jane hard in the eyes. "He gave you everything you needed. His presence shielded you all from the outside."

"He was barely sentient," Jane shouted back. "He *always* confused our names, our birthdays, and didn't know a damn thing about any of us. He always favored Jude, which is crazy, 'cause he's not even Jude's real father, either! What was the point of any of it?" Jane suddenly erupted into tears, there was no weather warning of any kind. Tears fell rapidly, and her chest began to heave, up and down, her breathing shallow, and she could barely get out the next words as her panic attack began to overpower her: "Whataboutourmother?"

"Oh, con, my sweet Jane." Bác Cai rushed forward, and tipped Jane's head onto her shoulder. And just like the day when they realized Evelyn had abandoned them, she held Jane and rocked her back and forth.

Hiccupping, Jane tried her best to get out the next words. "It'snot aboutaboy. It'snotaboutHenry."

"I know, con."

"It'snotaboutHouston."

"I know, con."

"WhatamIsupposedtodonow?"

Bác Cai stroked her hair, and continued rocking her, her sleeve soaked in Jane's tears. "I don't know, con. But perhaps it's time you all end this charade that Duc has put on, find a way back to your siblings, find a way back to your mother, and then figure it out from there. Somewhere, out there, your mother's been waiting for you, for all of you, and only she holds the truth."

Though Jane nodded into her shoulder, she continued to sob, releasing decades of eldest-daughter hurt, crying for the loss of her mother, into the arms of the mother figure who stayed.

....

Jane had entered a fugue state. The thought of opening up the store for the day made her want to hide. She felt like a fraud, concealed inside a Duc's Sandwiches when she didn't know the truth of anything anymore.

Someway, somehow, we always make our way back home.

She reread parts of Duc's letter to her. Almost one year into this journey, and she wondered who was really behind those words. Who had known her so well to know that Houston was her kryptonite? Who had cutting, intimate knowledge about her in that way?

Jane stared at the front door of the shop, expecting another empty day with no customers. What was the point of all of it? Bác Cai had resumed her position in the corner of the store, snoring loudly. It was barely noon.

But to her surprise, the bell rang, not once, but four times. Bác Cai snorted awake, yelling out: "Welcome, welcome! Don't *Duc* with us, we're the best bánh mì in town!"

"No, you don't have to do that anymore," Jane said forlornly, settling her down. "We can cut out that catchphrase."

"Oh, thank Buddha," Bác Cai muttered, sitting back down on her stool.

Like passengers of a clown car, Thủy from the nail salon supply store, Duy from the travel agency, Xuân from the sketchy CPA's office, and Linh from the refillable, filtered water store filed into the store, one by one. Jane was surprised to see the four henchmen of Dakao Plaza, shuffling around her shop sheepishly. They began to poke, prod, and stare at everything in the store, taking in all the new changes. Their eyes settled on the black-and-white photos of Duc and Evelyn, and Jane grew embarrassed at the gaudiness all around her. Now she could see what a fraud she had been, painting a rosy picture of their family, when everyone in town knew the truth. Bác Cai greeted them enthusiastically, perhaps too enthusiastically, asking how business was going for everyone.

Linh muttered under her breath. "It's better than this place, that's for sure."

Xuân was the first to walk up to the counter and order a sandwich. The special, of course. Soon, everyone else followed as well.

Jane, ringing them up, couldn't help herself. "What prompted you all to come in today? Out of all the days that we've been open?" Bác Cai handed them all their food in the familiar *thank you for coming* plastic bags.

Duy, immediately ripping open his sandwich and stuffing his face, began to talk with his mouth full, with absolutely no care about manners. "We got a call."

Linh, Xuân, and Thủy all nodded in confirmation. "Someone told us to come in and order sandwiches from you. Said they would even pay for our lunches."

Perplexed, Jane looked at Bác Cai, who shook her head.

"Who was it?" Jane asked cautiously, her paranoia fueling her into thinking that it all tied back to Duc somehow, as everything always did.

Everyone shrugged. Thủy chimed in, attempting to be helpful. "He sounded young. Probably handsome. Could be dangerous."

Jane's face turned red as she realized who was behind it.

Linh carefully took a bite out of her sandwich. "This isn't bad, you know," she admitted. "It's much better than the old Duc's."

"Could use more paté and cilantro, though," Xuân grumbled. Jane accepted that as the highest compliment that would ever come out of an old Vietnamese man like him. "A bit stingy, if you ask me."

Jane and Bác Cai watched as the four of them finished up and returned to their respective businesses, complaining more about the shop on their way back. The store returned to a comfortable silence as Bác Cai stared at Jane, trying to read her. "You know, con, that was probably better than sending you flowers. He *knows* you, you know. Are you sure you still want to move back to Los Angeles? Don't you want to stay and figure it all out?"

Jane didn't respond.

CHAPTER 34

Georgia, Evelyn, and yes, Connie

Just when Georgia thought her year couldn't get any stranger, she found herself nestled between her estranged biological mother, Evelyn; her estranged stepmother, Connie; and Connie's mother, Mrs. Vũ, outside the burned-down Duc's Sandwiches shop in New Orleans. Hours after the fire calmed down, the women all sat down on the sidewalk, staring at the pile of black ash, each one lost in their thoughts, wondering how life had led them so far from their intended paths.

Connie began to wonder if she had thrown the best years of her life away, in exchange for the life her mother had wanted for her. Had any of it been worth it? Her usual designer attire, blackened and charred, her sleek hair, coated with ash. Money could buy anything, everything in the world, except for the one thing she really wanted—true companionship. It didn't even have to be with the love of her life (if those were even real); she just wanted someone who she could be comfortable with, someone who could laugh with her, from time to time. Her passport was filled with places her mother could only dream of; her bank account, never overdrawn. Do you know how it felt, to look out from your hotel balcony and see the Eiffel Tower, all while drinking a glass of the most expensive, crisp champagne in the world? Connie knew how it all felt. It was exhilarating, but that feeling only lasted for a few minutes. Because she also knew how it felt when she looked behind her and saw that she was all alone.

Marriage had been lonelier than she had thought it would be. But Connie had been lonely her entire life; what was a few more years until Duc kicked the bucket? She'd get her bag, and then some. But as she stared at her lost years, melted down along with the Duc's Sandwiches shop, she realized that her loneliness was going to kill her one day. She looked over at her mother, and wondered if it would be so terrible if she moved back to New Orleans for a while. That, perhaps, it would be nice to be taken care of again, and pretend to be a child.

Mrs. Vũ stared longingly into the black ash, wondering if she, too, had made a mistake in pushing her one and only child into marrying Duc. But he wasn't just any man off the street, he was infamous among their circles. He was Duc of Duc's Sandwiches. That name had weight, it carried with it connotations of gold, the American dream, and a carefree life. Was it so wrong? Connie was young; she could remarry if it came down to it. But Mrs. Vũ should have known most of all why lonely marriages were cancerous—that feeling of being tied to someone who didn't care for your well-being. Mrs. Vũ knew very well how that felt, yet she had encouraged that same pattern.

Georgia stared and stared at the pile of ash. She knew the whole truth now. She knew everything about Duc and Evelyn's history together. In some ways, she wished Evelyn had kept her in the dark. Perhaps her mother should have buried the truth along with the fire. In some ways, Georgia mourned the loss of her innocence, because now that the truth had spilled out of her mother, about Duc, about their marriage, about her past, about Mr. Ngô, she wondered if she could ever see the adults in her life the same way again. If she could ever pine for a lost childhood that was simply never hers to begin with.

Perhaps it was a metaphor or an omen of an empire in collapse that things were starting to collide with one another. But more than anything, Georgia was afraid to face what would come next. She was afraid of losing what little she had left of her family. Her mother, who was alive and breathing next to her, who had been so difficult to get close to for the last several months, but had finally opened up to her, had finally allowed Georgia to call her "Mom." Not even "Má" yet, but simply "Mom." And for now, that was enough for Georgia. Now she was afraid of losing all that progress; of losing her again. Her mother was a frightened stray, who was afraid of anyone coming close. There was a protocol to getting close to her, and only Georgia knew it. Georgia held the key.

And Georgia was deathly afraid that their family would never be able to recover together.

Only Evelyn was the one who saw hope in the ashes. She saw her past, lying among the embers. She saw Tuấn's face, staring back at her: his thick eyebrows, that small scar above his left eyelid he had gotten in an accident, the many shades of brown of his eyes. But most of all, she saw that he was at peace, and that perhaps, after so many decades, it was time for her to find her own peace. Evelyn allowed herself to cry. She finally caved. Her tense shoulders loosened up and she wished with all her heart to see Tuấn one last time, and let him know that she had failed. Life had chipped away at her for so long, she had lost the stamina to fight back. And most of all, she had failed as a mother, allowing external forces to come between her and her children.

Would Tuấn even still love her, knowing how her life had turned out?

The wind came softly at first, and then it picked up speed, creating a swirl of black dust and cinder. The women coughed, covered their faces with their shirt collars or with loose sweaters. The wind pulled more and more away, taking debris to other parts of the country, and releasing them of their anger.

Tuấn's face eventually disappeared altogether from Evelyn's mind. Her grief, after so long, had turned into remembrance. And she remembered him as the love of her life, youthful, generous, and someone who loved her deeply.

Evelyn finally said her goodbye, after being unable to for so long.

To the outsiders who had been hiding and watching in fear, the four women appeared stranger than fiction. Though they were clearly connected somehow, their connection was as loose as a string tied between two tin cans, held together by the memories of a man who had done them all wrong.

"Well," Georgia said, finally breaking the silence. "What do we do now?" She had seen a lot in her short, intrepid life, and was the first to recover.

"We find Duc," Evelyn said, with so much finality that even Connie agreed with her.

"We find Duc," Connie repeated, her eyes glued on the burnt building, still shocked and frightened by Evelyn's unpredictable behavior.

"Okay, let's find Duc, then," Georgia confirmed.

"And once we *find* that son of a bitch," Connie said, her voice now raised, "we're going to skin him alive and then give him a taste of his own med—" Connie's mother put a hand on her daughter's shoulder, to try to soothe her. Even Evelyn wasn't having it.

"That's a bit much—"

"Okay, wait, maybe we don't *skin* him," Georgia said, also trying to tame Connie's anger. "Maybe, use your words?"

"Words?" Mrs. Vũ scoffed. "Who uses words anymore? Do what they used to do to the dictators that embezzled and drank away the money, hiding high up in their ivory towers: Drag them through the streets!"

"I mean, she's not *wrong* wrong," Evelyn said. "But maybe we don't *skin* the man, we just make him bleed a little."

"Men should know what it's like to bleed," Mrs. Vũ affirmed. "I have a knife you can borrow—"

"Wait, wait, *wait*," Georgia said urgently. "Let's just all calm down. Maybe, you know, you can just *talk* to him. *Confront* him. Make him hear us. He needs to hear how much hurt he's caused us, caused *all* of us." Though it sounded like such an innocuous concept, each of the women knew what a milestone that was, to be able to confront someone and let them know how much pain they had been in.

But Connie, Evelyn, and Mrs. Vũ simply stared at Georgia as if she were speaking another language. Perhaps it was too soon to be celebrating growth.

"Let's just focus on finding Duc, then," Georgia muttered, her smile thin. "We'll—we'll figure out the rest once we cross that bridge."

Connie and Evelyn looked at each other. A newfound respect had been planted.

"Should I call Jane? And everyone else?" Georgia asked timidly. "They deserve to know the truth."

But all three women yelled at Georgia to not tell a damn soul, and that they would handle it.

She shut up immediately, though she did not believe them.

CHAPTER 35

Paulina

Though the robot arms were finally operating properly, they were now gathering dust. And though the delivery app had launched (but only for iPhone users), no delivery people walked through those swinging doors at the Duc's Sandwiches in San Jose. Paulina stood in the shop, day in and day out, looking out the window, people watching, willing customers to come in through pure psychic prowess and desperation.

Despite all the promotion, buzz, and the "BUY 2 SANDWICHES GET 1 FREE" plastered on the windows of the revitalized store, the crowd avoided her sandwich shop as if it were the breeding ground of a plague disguised as julienned vegetables, head cheese slices, and a hearty spread of paté, all nestled within a warm French demi baguette. But the more people walked by, without giving a second glance at the modern Duc's Sandwiches, the more Paulina felt like a failure. It reminded her of all the ways she had failed in her life. Of all the times in which she couldn't see or understand her audience. But especially, of all the times she couldn't recognize when her mother needed help.

Her siblings' group chat lingered on her mind. A week had passed since then. Who was Duc Trần? Who was this man who had been parading as her father—as *their* father—for so long? Who was their real father?

But most of all, who was Paulina without all of *this*?

Paulina kept tossing and turning at night, wondering who their father was, where their mother was, and what was the point of defining family, when family was just one giant escape room.

You'd be surprised at who will show up for you if you learn to ask for help.

Mr. Ngô's last words to Paulina pierced through her. To Paulina, asking for help was akin to asking for money. Both were embarrassing, and she'd rather go broke than ever admit she needed help.

Paulina's eyes narrowed. Everyone outside pretended the store was just a giant sinkhole, and they had to go around the edge. Everyone around her marched on with their lives, going from point A to point B, strangers kept being strangers instead of customers, and it all drove Paulina mad.

Paulina hated how right Mr. Ngô was. The old lawyer had warned her that the impatient old-timers hated technology or change of any kind and that she would be alienating her biggest customer base in San Jose. From the tiniest drop in the weather, down to having to get a new pair of socks, any minuscule changes in their rigid routines turned them off forever.

The store felt like a mausoleum. She'd automated the hell out of Duc's old sandwich shop, replacing human workers with robot arms to make the sandwiches. The firing of Chị Mai had rippled through the community, and everyone knew to avoid Duc's, and to follow Chị Mai wherever she had gone next.

Out of the corner of her eye, from across the street, Paulina saw signs of life; and they were walking straight toward her. But it wasn't the sign she wanted to see. She swallowed hard, a lump at the back of her throat. The roughness of Oliver Chen's scruff and his crisp white button-down shirt stuck out in a crowd of elderly people and their wool knitted vests. Clinging to his right hand was the smaller hand of a little girl whose hair was pulled back into two neat, low pigtails. Her eyes were wide and curious, radiating innocence, reminding Paulina that once upon a time, she was her age.

Esther. The little girl must be Esther.

Paulina scurried away from the window, and pretended to be busy wiping down the countertop, as she heard the *ding* of the front door open behind her.

"Pauly." Oliver's voice trailed behind her. "The store looks . . . great." His voice sent vibrations throughout her body, despite his hesitation. His tenor crashed against her shores, reminding her of their past. The constant push and pull between them, the humiliation, the never-ending "will they or won't they" tug-of-war, which turned into a real battle between them.

For ages, Paulina had thought she was winning the war in proving that she didn't need Oliver to live, but now she realized she'd been losing the whole time. Oliver had just simply let her believe she was winning. She didn't *need* Oliver; she wanted him.

God, how she loathed her father for sending her to the Bay Area. She hated San Jose. She hated the tech bros. She hated the locals. She hated all the transplants even more, including herself. She hated the tourists. She hated the 405N. She hated Silicon Valley. She hated this dumb shop. She hated herself for even playing along with her father's insane inheritance scheme. (When he wasn't even her real father!) She hated how stubborn old Vietnamese people were. She hated how those same old Vietnamese people refused to embrace her or her store. She hated that her sisters wouldn't call her back, even though they promised each other they'd stick together during all of this, especially after the truth about Duc came out. She hated being so close to Oliver's hometown, yet being so emotionally distant from the man himself.

Most of all, she hated how she didn't know where her life was going. She thought all of this would simply be just another blip in her story, but she was stuck, in the very middle of it, with no way to move forward.

"Oliver," she responded, whipping around to face him, sarcasm stuck in her voice like crystallized honey. "No need to lie. I know you know the store is shit—"

"*Language!*" he said hastily, quickly covering the young girl's ears. Paulina quieted. "Pauly, there's someone I want you to meet. My daughter, Esther. Esther, what do you say to the nice lady?"

Composing herself, Paulina took a sweeping, awkward step forward and thrust out her hand in front of Esther, as if she were a business deal she needed to close. "Nice to meet you, Esther. I'm . . . Auntie Pauly."

"Hello," Esther responded shyly, her voice barely louder than a whisper. The girl timidly took her hand, and upon holding the world's smallest palm, Paulina felt a sudden emotion come over her. It was almost . . . maternal. She examined Esther's palm in hers, so tiny and unscathed, and she wondered what her own hand must have felt like, at Esther's age, grasping her mother's hand. But Paulina had only reached for empty air. She wanted to shelter Esther forever from the outside world. Especially young children whose faces looked like hers.

"Are you hungry?" Paulina asked, her voice softening and contorting itself into a voice she didn't recognize. She squatted down, so she was eye level to the mini-human in front of her. "I have an army of giant robot arms, ready at my command, to make you the world's *best* automated sandwich."

"You're really not selling this," Oliver whispered to Paulina, shaking his head.

Esther giggled, delighted at the thought of robots, and nodded. Paulina led her toward the tablet and instructed her on how to order a custom sandwich, and she stepped back, watching Esther order with ease. Kids her age were much better with tech.

Just in case the robot rebelled and readied to launch baguettes, she stood in front to shield the girl.

"It's incredible how technology is so ingrained in children's lives these days. They don't even second-guess it," Oliver said, reading Paulina's mind. "It's just so natural to them. Imagine what it'll all be like when she's older."

"Honestly, I'm kind of jealous," Paulina said, also enthralled, watching Esther's delighted reaction to the robot arms. "Imagine growing up in a world where all the world's information is seconds away at your fingertips."

"I'm not jealous," Oliver said. "I'm happy for them. The whole point is to watch each generation evolve . . . even if the technological revolution is through sandwich-making robots." He smiled.

The tips of Paulina's ears singed red. "What are you doing here, Chen?"

"Well, we haven't spoken since you bombarded my office. You haven't returned any of my calls, even when the robots were installed. I've . . . I've stopped by a few times, but you weren't in the shop."

"Why would I return the call of a complete stranger?" she said, lowering her voice so Esther couldn't hear. "In all the years we've known each other, you never once told me you had a kid."

"You think I wanted to bring my kid up any of the times we met up around the world? Why the hell would I haul a kid around for cross-continental booty calls?" he scoffed, running his hand through his hair nervously. He leaned against the counter. "Also, I didn't know I had a kid until recently."

"Oh yeah? How recent?" she said, crossing her arms, not believing him.

"Three years ago."

"Oh." Around the time when he'd stopped responding to her calls and messages. "Shit."

"Shit indeed."

Silence. A nervousness between them. Oliver had blamed her for not responding to his call; she had blamed him for not responding to a text. Now, none of it mattered. They had both stopped responding, and dropped off the face of the earth for each other, forcing lovers to become strangers—straddling the line between reality and insanity.

"What happened to her mother?" she asked softly, not wanting to hear the answer out loud. She could guess.

"She—she didn't want to be a mother anymore," he said, defeated. "So she quit. I have full custody now. I'm still new to all of this."

This time, Paulina took several steps back, her triggers flaring up, her ears ringing. She had felt gut-punched at the news of Oliver being a father; now she felt as if someone had thrown her off the Golden Gate Bridge. Maybe it was the idea of another mother quitting that triggered her, or the fact that there was now shared trauma between the two of them, but something possessed Paulina. She was pulled in two directions: wanting to run up to Esther and hug her tightly, or grab Oliver and kiss him. Perhaps this was what Duc felt like, pulled from all directions when Evelyn left.

She hated to admit how Duc had stepped up, despite not being their biological father, and had financially cared for Paulina. How he had done the same for Jude, Jane, Bingo, and Georgia, in his own way, when their mother was long gone.

"You know, you're operating at an extreme loss, Pauly," he said, quickly changing the topic, noticing her sudden reaction. The absence of Paulina's own mother hung in the air between them, possibly contagious, and it was as if the longer they were on the topic of absent mothers, the more it would spread. "At this rate, you might go bankrupt."

"Heh, so much for the 'if you build it, they will come' mentality," she said ruefully as she paced back and forth, also avoiding eye contact.

"Please don't tell me you were following the advice of Silicon Valley swindlers," he said, laughing.

Paulina said nothing. She just stared at the back of Esther's head, admiring how neat her pigtails were. Knowing how new of a father Oliver was, she was struck by how there was not a single strand out of place.

Once Duc had tried to braid her hair when Evelyn had left them. After several poor attempts, Jane stepped in to finish the braids because they were late to school. Duc never attempted to braid her hair again after that. She wondered if Duc knew that low pigtails were also an option back then, or if he wanted so badly to replicate how their mother used to braid their hair, and prove that they didn't need her.

She admired the simplicity in how Oliver tackled fatherhood. There were no grandiose promises of a perfect French braid, or a fishtail braid, or something to show off for others. There was simply the promise of someone showing up for you, no guarantees with how life will turn out, but that they'll always be there. Paulina looked around at her cold, lifeless store, and saw all the life that was now bustling in front of it. She felt claustrophobic. This wasn't her at all. Duc's legacy wasn't the life she'd ever wanted to maintain. All she ever wanted was a simple unfussy braid, and none of the theatrics of a more complicated one.

Through the window, Paulina spotted an elderly woman shuffling across the street—the same woman who had come into the store during renovations, the same woman who had asked repeatedly to buy her weekly loaf, and who Paulina had callously brushed off, nearly a year ago. She was with a group of other elderly women, flanking each other, side to side, front to back, each one dragging behind them a metal cart on wheels.

"One second," Paulina said suddenly. "Watch the store for me."

Oliver called behind her retreating back as Paulina dove out of the store, the little bell dinging. "There's nothing to watch! It's all automated, remember?"

"Wait!" Paulina cried out to the old woman. "Wait, please!"

The woman turned around, and looked Paulina up and down. There was a notable disdain on her face as she recognized who Paulina was.

"Yes? What is it?"

"Please, I just want to apologize for my behavior a year ago," Paulina said, a bit out of breath. "I . . . I didn't know what I was doing."

"Well, don't apologize to me," she huffed, and stepped aside. "Apologize to her." She revealed Chị Mai, the woman Paulina had fired. It'd been so long since she fired her, Paulina barely recognized her. But there she was, a head full of gray, who reminded her of all the aunties back in Houston, who watched her grow up when Evelyn disappeared. She realized that not even Duc would have been as callous as she had been. In all the years she'd been inside a Duc's Sandwiches, it had been mostly female workers behind the scenes. Duc had always made sure these women's livelihood was guaranteed.

Paulina was worse than Duc, and that made her feel like shit.

"I'm so sorry," Paulina said quietly. She fumbled in her pocket for a bit, and then pulled out the store key and gave it over to Chị Mai. "Here. It's all yours. Do with it what you want. It's time for me to leave."

Before she could wait for Chị Mai's answer or any of the shocked women's expressions behind her, Paulina turned on her heel. Watching Oliver and Esther interact through the shop's window, she knew it was time to say goodbye to them, too. With a heavy heart, she walked back into the store, the infamous bell dinging again.

"Hey, you want to get out of here?" she said suddenly.

Surprised, Oliver looked at her. "What do you mean?"

"Let's play hooky," she said mischievously. "You, me, and Esther. Let's go have some fun. The robots don't need us here. You're right, they can watch after themselves. We can . . . go have a picnic somewhere."

She could feel his hesitation, his defensive wall starting to go back up, his shoddy attempt to keep her at arm's length. But she could also feel how tired Oliver was, being a single father, and struggling to always make sure the little girl in front of him was cared for. The scales—she remembered Mr. Ngô's words—were starting to move, finally, and Paulina began to see them even out between them. Perhaps having Esther on the scale helped.

"You're about to go bankrupt and you want to abandon your store in the middle of the day?" he said incredulously, but a small smile danced on the edge of his lips. "And you want to abandon ship to go have a picnic somewhere?"

"What's a few more negative losses today anyway?" She could feel him lowering his wall, or at least stopping the drawbridge from coming back up.

"I don't know, foreclosure? Filing for Chapter 11 bankruptcy? The loss of everything, your inheritance, your father's disapproval—"

"There are worse things in life," Paulina said. Before Oliver could finish another sentence, Paulina had already stuffed a few sandwiches into her purse, grabbed his hand, grabbed Esther's hand, and pulled them out the door. The bell dinged again, and Paulina knew that it would be the last time she would ever hear that bell.

Because Paulina knew it was time to go home. But she wanted one last chance, one last shot, at the real prize.

CHAPTER 36

Bingo

Bingo knew something was terribly wrong when all her siblings were suddenly thrust into a group chat, but even more indicative of the world ending was that Jane had added Jude. She couldn't remember the last time when all five of her siblings were in a group chat—without any snide side texting going on—or a time when all four sisters weren't ganging up against Jude, or a time when they weren't forced to pick sides between Duc or Evelyn. While her siblings' names began to pop up on her screen, one by one, rapid-fire responses flooded the screen and pushed the others' messages down the queue.

They were starting to finally communicate with one another. Really communicate.

The dark horse appeared: Georgia finally entered the chat. No one had heard from Georgia in almost a year, besides sporadic messages that provided proof of life. She had presumably dropped out of the rat race, and was living her granola lifestyle off in her van somewhere.

[Georgia] we should go to vietnam. confront duc in person. face him. together.

It was a strange proposition, but they didn't have a lot of options; in fact, no one had a better idea. A series of ellipses appeared, disappeared, appeared, disappeared, until their phone screens were still. Jude was probably wringing his hands about how far the trip would be, and all the amenities he needed to bring to survive. Jane hadn't been back to Vietnam since she was a teenager, and probably had trauma from her last trip there with Duc. And Paulina probably didn't give two shits; she just wanted a plan of some kind, her Type-A personality was in disarray. But to Bingo's surprise, everyone began to warm up to the idea. It was the first thing any of them had agreed on in a long time.

[jane] agreed. meet back in houston first? then fly from here? Or fly out from where we are?

[jude] i don't care as long as i'm flying first class

[paulina] can't wait for our "family" reunion

[georgia] so excited to finally get to go to vietnam!! do u think we have time to go to ha long bay??

[jane] this isn't a vacation, georgia. also ha long bay is overrated.

[jude] where is duc anyway? which part of vietnam. does anyone even know?

[georgia] i have it on good authority that he's hiding in the town of sa pa, at a buddhist temple at the top of fansipan mountain

"What the hell," Bingo said out loud.

[paulina] how do you know this

[georgia] a few locals in new orleans here confirmed it, he still talks to them about the store

[paulina] locals? Like who?

[georgia] someone just told me ok. trust me.

[jude] to sa pa it is then

After a momentary pause in conversation, the real question emerged, the one that everyone had on their mind. That had weighed heavily on them when the truth had finally been revealed.

[jane] who do you think our real father is?

[jude] forget you guys, who is *my* father?

This time, it was a painful type of silence. To her siblings, it remained one of the biggest unsolved mysteries of the universe. Who was their real father? And to whom did they belong? Was he kind? Had he loved them at all? Did he even care? Half of who they were belonged to these two mysterious men, their shadows haunting them their entire lives, without any of them realizing it. The whole time, they'd been focused on their mother, splitting themselves up, the girls with their mother, Jude with Duc. Each one approaching the jury box with their own arguments. The whole time, they had never questioned who Duc was.

[paulina] does it really matter in the end, does anything really change?

Bingo remained silent, not ready to contribute to the conversation. Because she had a suspicion about who their father was. As she watched her siblings plan their trip to Vietnam and plot their confrontation with Duc, she began to hatch her own plan. First, she wanted to take in the view. She looked out the train window. Nearly thirty hours had passed on the train, and she found herself in Tennessee, watching the Great Smoky Mountains pass her by. Summer was starting to creep up on them, and how strange it had been, coming up on a year. Bingo had experienced (and survived) her first East Coast winter, and she had fallen in love in Philadelphia, and with a woman.

Wildflowers bloomed tall and feral, nearly scraping the sides of the train car. The forest was lush, vibrant, and bursting with green. The mountain range seemed like it belonged to another world. Bingo had never been to this part of the South, nor had she ever laid eyes on the Smoky Mountains before. A first of many firsts.

The train ride from Pennsylvania to Texas was a little over two days long, but Bingo didn't care. She had never taken a cross-country train before, and she suspected she wouldn't be back on the East Coast for a long time. She imagined Duc and Mr. Ngô, train-hopping in their youth, when they first stepped foot in America. Philadelphia, New York City, New Orleans, San Jose, Orange County, Houston. How had these two Vietnamese refugees seen more of the country than she had in her entire life? The two men had been seeking more than just work; they had been seeking a city to call their own. It wasn't too far off from what Bingo had tried to do. Jumping from Houston, to Portland, to Philadelphia.

Bingo removed the photo from her back pocket. The black-and-white photo of her mother and Mr. Ngô. It was the one thing she had taken with her from Philadelphia. The answer had been in front of her all along. She knew the identity of one of the fathers. But why? Why did he pretend to just be their father's lawyer for so long? Always lurking in the background? How could he have lived with this lie for so long?

But the photo told no lie to her. She saw how much yearning Mr. Ngô had in his eyes when he stared at Evelyn.

She took out her phone and began to put her own plan in motion.

She thought about the one constant male figure in her life, who was always lurking in the shadows, watching closely but never interrupting. Though he wasn't at the forefront of their lives, he was in almost every childhood memory—and his presence became even more fortified when their mother left. She remembered when Duc couldn't pick them up from school, he'd be there, in his ill-fitting suit, carrying a worn-out briefcase, dabbing his forehead with an old handkerchief to mop up the sweat. She especially remembered the day she had come out to her parents, to Duc and Evelyn, and Duc had merely grunted a response back. But every Pride month since she had come out, Mr. Ngô had made sure that Duc's statue of *David* replica on his front lawn, in front of his McMansion, held up three flags: the American flag, the Vietnamese flag, and the Pride flag.

It had taken more than a village after Evelyn left, to raise five children, and two men had tried their best.

He picked up immediately. As he always did. "Hello, con? Everything okay?"

And Bingo asked for help for the first time in her life.

CHAPTER 37

May 1981, Houston, Texas

I n a nondescript courthouse in Texas, an unusual case had gripped both the locals and the state. On May 10, 1981, the trial began—many even placed bets on the outcome, wondering which way the winds would turn. Crowds formed in clusters outside the courthouse, jostling each other, on the off chance they'd be able to listen in. After all, it was a Black female judge presiding, with a Baptist attorney named after a Jewish friend representing the plaintiffs, the Vietnamese fishermen refugees, against the defendants, the Ku Klux Klan. That synopsis alone caused anyone from any side of the dividing line to want to listen in.

In five days, the shrimping season would begin, and everyone held their breaths wondering if they'd ever be able to go back out into those waters again. It was a battle no one had ever seen before. A battle over the Gulf, over shrimp, and the right for both. Perhaps it was also the most American court case that the town had seen in a long time.

Huey sat in the back of the court for four days, his face half-covered in a hat, wearing an ill-fitting suit he had managed to pull from the Salvation Army dumpster—a puke-green color that was three times as large as his frame. Huey sat quietly, listening in as both sides of the courtroom intertwined with each other, people setting aside their differences to claim empty seats. Side by side, shoulder to shoulder, locals, reporters, Klansmen decked in white robes, and Vietnamese families dressed their best to look more American, sat together, faces intense, listening in on testimonies and cross-examinations.

Duc was long gone at this point. Where he had gone, Huey didn't know or care. He could be on his way to Quebec or perhaps he had worked up the courage to go back west to Orange County. Evelyn also never showed up to court at all, but Huey stopped by to check in on her every day after the trial ended, to see if she needed anything. If she didn't come to the door, Huey would mow her lawn or leave food out on her front steps, not leaving until he saw her stick out her arm and pull the food inside her house. Neighbors said that she had been consumed by her grief; she couldn't get out of bed for days, or go to the courthouse. But still, Huey kept watch, as best he could, from a distance.

Huey Ngô was never one to carry hope around. He had lost it a long time ago, back in his childhood home in the south of Vietnam, watching it dissipate forever when he witnessed chaos at such an early age. But as the son of an uneducated fisherman, Huey felt the tiniest iota of hope begin to fill his chest again as he witnessed friends and the Vietnamese fishermen approach the stand, and recount their stories of living in fear, intimidation, and with the threats they received from the Klansmen. Even Huey had to recognize the miracle it took for any Vietnamese to step forward and testify.

On the final day of the trial, Huey settled into his usual corner seat in the last row, far away from anyone. Just as the doors were closing, he saw Evelyn sneak in and someone quickly give up their seat for her. She slowly lowered herself, burdened by the heaviness of her belly. Her face was red, puffy, and raw, and he could tell that she had been crying herself to sleep. She was due any day now, and his guilt compounded. He was consumed not by the idea of Tuấn's body still somewhere out in the Gulf, but by the fact that Evelyn still didn't know the truth—that the rumor mill still pointed the blame toward the Klansmen and not at the real truth. That it had been five men on a boat, full of drunken, infallible logic, scared out of their minds that night. And that they had simply forgotten about Tuấn.

Huey turned his head forward, back to the front of the courtroom, where a young Judge Gabrielle Kirk McDonald sat on the bench, her eyes poring over notes from the previous day. Once the gavel sounded, she cleared her throat and began speaking.

Over the years, members of various Klan organizations have engaged in acts of racial intimidation, harassment, and terrorism . . .

Huey didn't remember much after that. He just remembered that as the judge continued speaking, the room erupted into chaos. Translations began from English to Vietnamese and then it quickly reversed. The Klansmen burst into fits of anger, some even removing their white hats, while locals were torn between cheering or booing, depending on which side they were on.

All Huey remembered was when everyone rose from their seats and began congratulating one another, he and Evelyn locked eyes across the courtroom. Her eyes were black and empty, knowing that the justice served today wouldn't ever take away her pain, because it wasn't her justice to take. The justice served today, in favor of the Vietnamese fishermen, would not make her life better in any way. Because Tuấn's body was still out there, and Evelyn would never see him again.

It was all Huey's fault.

Bodies blended as everyone cried, congratulating one another, thanking the lawyer, thanking the judge. A beautiful mix of English and Vietnamese could be heard from every corner of the room. But all Huey could see was Evelyn, still sitting there, heavily pregnant, and he got up and began making his way toward her. She made no indication for him to stop. He slid onto her bench and sat next to her silently, his hands folded in his lap, respectful. Huey and Evelyn sat side by side as the rest of the world moved on without them.

....

Months after shrimp season had officially started, the world righted itself. The Gulf had finally lived to see peace again. The waters seemed blue again, instead of red and black. And the locals and the Vietnamese were able to shrimp without any harassment, and as the sun rose and set each day, one could see trawlers of all shapes and sizes off in the distance, swaying side by side.

Huey, whose chest had felt tight for years, even long before coming to Texas, had allowed himself to relax a bit. He saw glimpses of what life would be like, if he just continued living for others, and not for himself. Though Evelyn had only just started inviting him into her life slowly, Huey was grateful. Grateful for a chance to make it up to her, somehow, some way. If Evelyn couldn't love Huey in a romantic way, it didn't matter. Huey would still take up arms for her. He would protect her forever.

One night, on his way to Evelyn's house to help with the newborn baby—a son—he was whistling. He'd been hit with a sudden bout of nostalgia for the days with Duc, the days of bonding over Beatles' tunes and shitty beer. As he followed the familiar path lined with old palm trees to Evelyn's house, he thought fondly of the palm trees during his days in Orange County with Duc. He whistled "Yellow Submarine."

Their old trawler had burned so that it was unsalvageable; it'd be the Devil's work to bring it back to life. Perhaps it was a blessing in disguise, a chance to burn their friendship as well, before Duc brought Huey to the end of the world.

As Huey walked the half-constructed dirt road, his shoes made no sound against the soft mud. The woods were unusually quiet, and not even the cicadas were out. Only Huey's whistling indicated that he was the only sentient creature out there, roaming the night. Evelyn's dilapidated house soon appeared, next to a row of mobile homes with crooked blinds. Huey had begun studying for law school every night, and often came over to Evelyn's to learn in peace. Just like at court, they sat side by side, while Evelyn knitted and Huey pored over his books. She would cook them dinner. It was a friendship of sorts, a bond between two people grieving in their own different ways. Huey grieved the loss of Duc's friendship, the only family he had ever known in America. And Evelyn grieved the loss of her son's father, forever lost to the Gulf.

Through the half-open shutters on the windows, Huey saw Evelyn pace back and forth, carrying the baby in her arms, cradling his head against her chest, and Huey felt that pang of guilt again. Tuấn's ghost hovered close by, watching his every move.

As he got closer to the house, a chill ran through him as another voice creeped out of the woods and began harmonizing with his whistling. They were both now at the bridge of the song. Huey stopped walking, and the other whistler stopped as well.

"Who's there?" Huey called out.

"Is that how you greet an old friend?"

Huey's body turned cold. The same familiar deep voice that woke them up the morning after the fateful night Tuấn died, the same deep voice that greeted him when Huey walked onto a commercial fishing boat down in Delacroix Island, and the same deep voice that laughed at them when they realized that Tuấn had died. The old captain emerged from the woods, the moonlight casting a glow across his face, revealing it to be more haggard than the last time they had met. He was emaciated, the bags under his eyes had expanded, and the smell of alcohol emitting from him instantly hit Huey's nostrils. Life had been cruel to him, and Huey immediately knew that the old captain was looking to hurt him. Cursed men often become cruel men.

"You got a nice wife and kid. Didn't take you for a father. Didn't seem to have it in you."

Huey's face turned white, his eyes quickly darting to where Evelyn was in the window, ignorant and blissful of what lay beyond her front door.

"She's not my wife," Huey said lamely, unsure what to do next. "She's just a friend. I help them sometimes. That's not my son."

The old captain laughed. "Still spoken like someone willing to protect them, no matter what. You know my father was an evil son of a bitch. He was tough, hard on us. Hard on my mother. He was also a drunk."

Huey didn't try sympathizing because no matter what he said, he knew the man wouldn't believe him. "What do you want?"

The captain took a giant step forward, and in the glow of the light, Huey could see a flash of a gun in his holster. "You know you're on the Klan hit list, right? I saw your name on it," he slurred.

Huey cocked his head to the side and raised his hands up in a placating way, taking a step back from the captain. "I don't know what you're talking about or what that Klan list is for, but I don't want any trouble. Whatever you think I did, I didn't do it."

The captain reached down below his belt, gripping what Huey now saw was the sheath of a knife. "Are you not Huey Ngô? Did you not help bring evidence to the case?"

"I barely helped—" Huey started helplessly. "I just talked to people, it's just testimonies, nothing more—"

Nothing Huey said was getting through. The alcohol wafting from the old man grew stronger with each forward step—a mix of cheap whiskey and beer for the colder nights.

"You're on the list," the man kept repeating, his incoherence slipping through. Two different liquors mixed together could ruin any man's spirit. "You're on the list. You and your family. You're on the list—"

Huey began to beg. "Please, you don't understand, she's not my wife, that's not my son, I'm not—" He cast a quick glance again at Evelyn in the window. He was nothing more than just a friend, a helping hand for her to get on her feet. That was all he would ever be, and that was what he was okay being. The scales of love had never been balanced in his favor anyway. Perhaps this was the closest he could come to it.

"You're on the list," the captain continued repeating, slurring. "The kill list."

"Anh," a familiar voice called out from behind him. "It's going to be okay. I'm here now."

Before Huey even turned around, he had already forgiven him. He looked at Duc, his one family member and friend in America. Sheepish and apologetic, Duc crawled out of the woods, hands also raised, attempting to pacify the intoxicated captain.

"That's my wife actually," Duc called out, his hands still raised. "Not Huey's. You got it all wrong. That's my wife and my son. Huey just comes by from time to time."

"Your family? That's *your* family?" the captain repeated slowly, his breath foul, as he shifted his hand away from the head of his knife, and instead to his flask, hidden behind his jacket.

"Yes, they're my family," Duc whispered, nodding at Huey to play along. "I had nothing to do with that trial, I skipped town. I'm—I'm a coward, you know."

"Your family," the captain repeated again, staring at Duc.

"My family." Duc nodded.

"Yes, that's his family," Huey managed to say. "Please, leave them alone. Just go after me, okay? It was all me. All those testimonies, it was me, I was the one who helped. Not Duc. I have no family."

"Okay." The captain closed his eyes, pulled out the flask, and took a long swig. He stared at Huey one last time, studying him intensely. "Okay."

The captain memorized him—Huey's floppy black hair that looked like it could recede later on in life, his dark brown eyes, the smattering of birthmarks that lined his face, the ill-fitting suit he wore. "When you least expect me, you'll meet yours one day. And when you turn around, it'll be too late. Understand?"

"I understand," Huey said, with finality. He continued to let the captain study him as Duc silently slipped toward the house, where Evelyn and the baby were, to stand guard at the front door. Huey felt his chest loosen again, knowing that no matter what happened to him, Evelyn and Jude would always be safe with Duc watching over them.

CHAPTER 38

The Trần Siblings and Two Shadowy Figures

U p in first class, a stewardess in a red sarong kebaya for Singapore Airlines delivered an Old Fashioned to Jude, who was half-asleep, sunglasses crooked on his face, his seat partition halfway rolled up. She tapped his shoulder gently, and he jerked awake, wiping a bit of drool from his lips.

A soft groan escaped him as reality began to set in. He hadn't been to Vietnam since he was a child. It was surreal that they were doing this just to track down a man who wasn't even their biological father.

"Sir," she said softly. There was just the tiniest hint of a Singlish accent. "I am sorry for disturbing you, but here is the drink you ordered."

Jude grunted a thank-you, managed to sit up while still hunched over, and downed the entire drink in three gulps. The whiskey churned through his body, instantly warming him up, and his only note was that he wished it burned more. He gestured for another one, quickly changed his mind, and gestured for two more.

"You know we haven't even left the ground yet, right?" Paulina's voice called out from the next partition over. "Economy class is still boarding you know."

Jude rolled his eyes and waved her off. "Can't you save your judgment for when we're up in the air, then? Also, how are you able to afford first class? Aren't you broke from your failed shop? Go to the back of the airplane with the rest of the peons."

"Don't worry about me, I'm savvy with my savings," she shot back. "You're the one who should be a bit more economical these days with your cash flow. Haven't you considered that perhaps Duc was lying about the 'inheritance' the whole time? He's not even our real father, so who knows where the inheritance is really going or if it even belongs to us."

It pained him to admit how right Paulina was. He hadn't thought about the consequences of finding out the truth about Duc. Did Duc and Evelyn plan on hiding the truth from them for the rest of their lives? Questions upon questions piled up, but the truth was lost in the haystack. The mystery of it all continued to fuel his paranoia that they were all still missing something: *Why* would they go through all this trouble?

And even if they confronted Duc in Vietnam, would he even tell them the truth? *Was* he capable of the truth?

Jude thought about Phoebe, back in Houston. He still reeled from the fallout of a public breakup, while Phoebe walked away unscathed. The unanswered emails in his inbox from the banquet hall about catering and dietary restrictions, the thousands of decision-making details left on the final wedding touches, and the enormous guest list, which somehow had gotten ten times bigger since he last looked at it. It had all been so easily extinguished with a simple email, the subject line: WEDDING OF JUDE TRẦN & PHOEBE PHƯƠNG CALLED OFF.

But Phoebe had simply nodded her head along as Jude explained why the wedding wasn't going to work. And it broke his heart to see how nonchalant she had been. How *understanding* she was, and how he had seen photos of Phoebe and Paul on social media, hanging out afterward. Jude had confirmed his fears: that he was not important to her. She promised to maintain a friendship, but even in the moment, Jude could see how easily her attention flitted. That all the women he had been chasing his whole life mimicked his mother's shadow; simply put, no one wanted him.

What added more poison to the wound was how easily Phoebe's father had cut him out. Mr. Phương had removed any traces of Jude from his life. How easy it was for parents, or parental figures, to snatch away love so fast, dangling the idea of unconditional love. Perhaps Jude should have been better equipped to handle it, after how easily their mother left.

Looking back, it all seemed so fruitless. But now, he wondered why Duc even cared in the first place if he got married or not, when he wasn't even his real father. What was the point of all that? The stewardess set down two more drinks in front of him. The second glass went down easier than the first, but the third began to taste like water, and he knew he was drunk.

But Jude kept drinking. Drinking and drinking, hoping that it would numb the pain.

As more economy passengers began filing past him, haphazardly dragging their cheap carry-ons behind them, he slowly raised the partition all the way up to block out the rest of the noise. Just as the partition was about to close, he caught the eyes of Bingo and Georgia as they filed past him, also lugging ginormous suitcases behind them. Bingo, who looked distracted, gave an awkward nod toward Jude, but Georgia, being her usual young, sweet self, waved and attempted to make small talk, forcing him to lower his partition again.

"I can't believe we're going to Vietnam!" Georgia squealed at him as the economy line ground to a halt behind her. Jude groaned. They had twenty-one more hours of travel time to go. Georgia was between Jude's and Paulina's pods in first class. "This is so, so exciting. I wish my Vietnamese wasn't so shitty, you know? I wish I knew more so I could speak there. You think it'll be okay?"

"Don't worry, you have us as translators. Also, this isn't a vacation, Georgia," Paulina reminded her again, her older-sister persona kicking in automatically. "We're going to find Duc and confront him. About everything. The marriage. Why he pretended he was our father our entire lives, the inheritance, the games, everything. *Why* did he put us all through that for the past year? And *who* is our real father?"

"Also, we're not staying long, either," Jude said, slurring his words slightly. "So don't get used to it. Vietnam isn't all that it's cracked up to be, you know. Don't let those travel influencers and all the rebranding fool you. I used to go with Duc all the time back when I was a kid, and hated it."

"Speak for yourself." Paulina scoffed. "You've got an archaic view of the country. A lot has changed since when you were a kid, and when Duc and Evelyn escaped Vietnam during the war. It's sexy and modern now."

"When were *you* last there?"

"Last year, dummy. I go quite often."

Frustrated, the economy passengers began to inch forward a bit more, attempting to shove Georgia forward. Tired travelers bickered among themselves to hurry up and store their carry-ons faster before all the good bins were taken.

"I've never been to Vietnam before," Georgia said forlornly. "I've always dreamt of it, but my Vietnamese is the worst out of everyone in the family. I never got to go with you all on all of Ba's trips. Am I not allowed to be excited? I get to see the country where our parents came from."

"Duc isn't your real parent—"

"He took care of us, didn't he?"

"When Evelyn couldn't?"

The line suddenly began to spill forward faster, and before Jude and Paulina could say anything else, Georgia was carried away like a swift current, all the way to the back of the plane, near the bathrooms.

"We could have been more excited with her," Paulina said quietly to Jude. "I forgot she's the only one who has never been to Vietnam."

A stewardess handed Jude two more drinks, and he managed to down another one quickly before answering. "She's not our responsibility, Paulina. When would any of us have had the time to take her on a trip to Vietnam? We can barely even eat dinner together as a family; what makes you think we'd survive an international trip abroad?"

"Well, we should have been better older siblings," she snapped back. "We failed her. When Má left and then Ba couldn't handle being a single parent, we all went our separate ways."

"Stop calling him Ba," Jude sniped. "He's just Duc. He's not our father."

With that, he pressed the button to roll up the rest of his partition and drown out Paulina. But as the partition began to close, an older Vietnamese woman walked past him, wearing a baseball cap low over her head. She made eye contact with him, her stare intense, as if judging him for everything he had just said to Paulina.

Jude squinted. He wasn't sure if he had seen a mirage, but the partition shut before he could second-guess the image. The woman almost looked like his mother. But it'd been too long, two decades, and he wasn't sure he would be able to recognize her in a police lineup, on the street, or in line at the grocery store. Still, though, it was something about the woman's eyes. But also the faint scent she left behind in her wake. May rose, jasmine, and a hint of bourbon vanilla. He quickly pushed the button to roll the partition back down, but by the time he was able to stick his head out, the woman was long gone, far down the aisle, way out in the boonies in economy.

Next to him, Paulina also seemed confused by the woman. For she had also turned her head to look in her direction.

They both had the same thought but refused to say it out loud, afraid to get their hopes up.

....

Over in premium economy, Jane was crafting an email. Or at least, she was trying to. It wasn't about a boy, but there was a boy she didn't want to hurt.

The last time she ever expressed her feelings to a guy was, ironically, Henry, back in high school. Funny how love is often doomed to repeat itself with the same lovers, over and over again, in a vicious cycle.

> Dear Henry.
> Hey you.
> What's up?
> Hey friend!

She couldn't get past the greeting. All she could think about were the last ugly, parting words she had said to him. Tears began to well up in the corners of her eyes, and she closed her laptop on the tray. He must hate her. She laid her arms and head on the laptop. She hated crying in public. She hated crying in general, but nothing was worse than having people watch her cry.

She could feel snot coming out of her nose, and her breathing became ragged. She could feel her seat-neighbor inch away from her, and she could tell he'd rather be seated next to a crying baby for an international flight than a crying woman who kept making mistakes, over and over again, at her age.

A hand brushed against her shoulder, and she looked up, thinking it was a stewardess telling her to put her tray table away for takeoff. But as she looked around, all she saw was an older Vietnamese woman, wearing a baseball cap, shuffle away from her.

....

A few rows behind Jane, over in economy, Bingo was in a nightmare situation.

Wedged in the middle seat between two straight white men, who rested their arms on the armrests on both sides of her—the equivalent of a manspreader on a subway—Bingo felt a disturbance in the force. Before she had left, she had promised everyone that she would take a deep breath, think first, and then open her mouth. She would *not* blow up. She had also made a secondary promise to even *not* speak in *some* situations. But whipping her head between both men, and looking at the projected flight time ahead of her, Bingo thought she might break that promise.

Correction: She did.

"Don't either of you have any etiquette? Manners? Were you raised in the basement?" she snarled at the man to her left, and then to the man to her right, "everyone knows the middle-seat person gets both armrests because we're stuck in the middle. You sweaty, foul miscreants."

"Who made up *that* rule—? That's like the 'women and children first' argument," the man on her left began to protest, his chest hair exposed and red. Bingo counted four unbuttoned buttons on his paisley shirt and wondered what was the point of even wearing a shirt.

"Foul? Miscreant? BASEMENT—?" The man's face on her right burst into flames.

"Besides, I don't see any *ladies* present—" grumbled the other man.

All three voices began to rise, each one trying to overpower the other, arguing beyond the topic of etiquette for sharing armrests. Bingo was now arguing for equality. The stewardess was alerted to the rising argument and stampeded toward them, a forced smile on. In the middle of the stewardess telling Bingo to calm down, and the two men gesturing wildly, and Bingo drawing on her napkin a graph of who gets entitled to what for each seat—even if it's not written out in FAA regulations—no one saw what came next.

The man in the aisle seat yelped in deep pain. It took Bingo a few seconds to realize that his water glass had been poured all over his lap, and she quickly denied throwing water at him. He began rubbing the back of his head vigorously, bewildered, his eyes enlarged and confused.

"I didn't do anything," Bingo said quickly. "I didn't throw that water or knock it over on purpose."

"I know, ma'am," the stewardess responded, also looking confused. Passengers continued to file past and around the stewardess.

"Someone *hit* me," the man claimed, still rubbing his head. "Someone walking past *hit* me!"

The stewardess diverted her attention to now mollifying him, as his voice escalated even higher than Bingo's. Bingo turned around and caught the eye of an older Vietnamese woman wearing a baseball cap, who was in the very last row. Why did that woman look so familiar to her? There was something about the curve of her face . . . and her scent. A trail of May rose, jasmine, and a hint of bourbon vanilla.

But also, why did the woman just wink at her?

....

After a rough two days of traveling, all five Trần children descended into Nội Bài International Airport in Hà Nội. It was the first time they had all been on a plane ride together in nearly two decades. The last time they had attempted to fly on a plane was for Georgia's ninth birthday when they tried to go to Disneyland in California. But when Duc got to the airport he realized he was ill equipped to take five children to Disneyland on his own, without Evelyn handling everything. The children witnessed Duc's very first public meltdown, and Mr. Ngô canceled the trip and took them out for ice cream instead.

The transfer from Singapore to Hà Nội was smooth and eerily quiet. Quiet could be both a good and bad thing for a flight. Jude, Jane, Paulina, Bingo, and Georgia continued to sit in separate rows, in separate classes, and in separate tiers, far away from each other, revealing the different gaps between them. As the plane began to descend closer to the tarmac, all the distractions that had followed the siblings for a year were no longer there.

Here, they were back in Duc and Evelyn's homeland, naked, vulnerable, and exposed. Diaspora children were oxymorons; they belonged but also didn't belong, and no matter which way the pendulum swung, they were still tourists at the end of the day, visiting a country they had no real connection to.

Duc isn't our biological father.

They couldn't admit it, but their anger and quest for the truth was what brought them together. The enemy of their enemy was their friend? And for once in over a decade, the Trần children were united in fighting a common enemy.

CHAPTER 39

Jude and Georgia

The heat hit them immediately. Jane's glasses fogged up the moment she stepped off the tarmac, her vision blurred yet her regret clear. Jude's gold chains felt heavy on his neck, as if the gold had suddenly spun into brick stones held loosely with wire. Paulina's heavy designer knitwear and leather heels suddenly shrank a thousand times in size. Bingo began heavily panting, shedding layer after layer, bemoaning the weather and how hot it was. Meanwhile, Georgia took everything in, her eyes enchanted, enthralled by the prospect of finally seeing the motherland, the country that was embedded deep in her DNA—a history that flowed through her veins, a living, invisible organism that she knew nothing about, but somehow it was the reason why she was standing there now.

Evelyn and Duc had always talked about how the weather along the Gulf Coast was similar to Vietnam, but they could never really prove that it was the same until this very moment.

From the moment they stepped outside the airport, all five Trâns realized they were in Vietnam. It was an inception of realizations, as it was also their first sibling vacation in two decades. Duc had taken a couple of kids back and forth, but he didn't have the capacity and mental energy to take all five at once. Though he had kept dangling it over their heads for years, the promise of one day showing them their roots.

One day, we'll all go to Vietnam together and you'll see why I miss it so much.

Georgia could hardly contain her excitement. She tried to rein it in, but she quickly unfurled a spiral notebook in front of them, full of places to eat, direct translations, and a cheat sheet for money conversions. Her hopefulness lined up like a grocery list.

"Okay, I have a whole list of places for us to hit up," she started prattling on, taking the lead. "Hà Nội, Sa Pa, Hạ Long Bay . . . does anyone know how to ride a scooter? The Hà Giang Loop? It doesn't seem that hard to ride a scooter here—"

"Georgia," Jane's voice, tired and jet-lagged, warned her.

"—and what about Central Vietnam? Will we have time to go to Huế, Hội An, and—"

"Georgia!" Paulina and Bingo began shouting from the middle seat of the van.

"—but I really want to go to Da Nang? Is this too much for the first time? Should we cut back on—"

"GEORGIA!!!" Jude, Jane, Paulina, and Bingo shouted all at once. Even the taxi driver was startled, swerving the van, almost hitting scooters to the left of him. Angry curse words were thrown in all directions, including from the driver himself. Georgia didn't speak any Vietnamese, but road rage was universal and didn't need any translation. Embarrassment took hold, and Georgia's face turned red, going all the way down to her collarbone.

"Georgia, please, just stop," Jude growled. "We're not here for some happy family vacation, okay? If we wanted that, we wouldn't be on our way to confront our fake father, who has been hiding away in some damn temple, wasting our time all year."

Georgia shrank into her seat, quietly folded her notebook up, and tucked it away in her backpack. She didn't say a word for the rest of the drive to Hà Nội, and instead, just turned her head to look at the road and scenery passing her by. No one else said a word, either. Despite how noisy traffic was all around them—a sensory overload of Vietnamese, cars backfiring, mass hordes of scooter drivers zipping through the cars—and how unbearably hot and stuffy the taxi was, none of the siblings spoke again for the rest of the trip into the city. Each sibling was lost in their own thoughts, their minds fixated on how it all went so wrong.

Not just for them, but for everyone.

Including Duc and Evelyn.

....

By the time they got into the center of the old capital city, it was a mix of exhaustion, delirium, and fluctuating anger toward both Duc and themselves. (Though, more toward Duc.) Jane's impeccable Vietnamese went on autopilot, and she began to negotiate a deal with the cab driver. Her Vietnamese was pristine, with just a hint of a Texas accent. All those years of having to step into the role of becoming a second mother forced Jane to become more fluent than her siblings. From being able to negotiate pickup times and day care for each of her younger sisters with older aunties, to being able to ward off nosy neighbors inquiring *Má con đang ở đâu? Where is your mother?* Flying to Vietnam to confront Duc over his deception fell into the same long laundry list of Jane's responsibilities to protect her sisters, even Jude. Maybe.

She only wished she had someone to protect her.

As they each received their hotel key card, one by one, Jane, Bingo, and Paulina silently retreated. Only Jude and Georgia were left standing in the lobby, stomachs rumbling so loudly even the receptionist could hear it. An awkward lull lingered between the oldest and the youngest Trần as they realized they had no choice but to pretend to be a working family unit. Beyond the years between them, the emotional distance was tangible, thicker than the humidity itself. Who was Jude to Georgia, and who was Georgia to Jude? They didn't know much about each other beyond the fact that they shared the same blood.

"So, you want to go get some food or something?" Jude asked awkwardly, rubbing the sweat off the back of his neck, though his attempts were futile, as his sweat continued to expand to all parts of his body.

Georgia, trying her best to contain her excitement, nodded her head casually. "I'm starving. I was stuck in economy, so the food wasn't that great down there."

Jude didn't say anything about the fact he had fresh seared tuna and caviar bumps up in first class. "So, what are you in the mood for—?"

Before Jude could even finish his thought, Georgia had already whipped out her notebook again, to a hand-drawn map of the Old Quarter with areas marked where she wanted to go. "STREET FOOD," she nearly shouted, her excitement spilling out. "Let's go find some late-night barbecue! There's a couple of places I researched that have whole streets closed off."

Jude didn't protest this time or quiet her excitement. He didn't want to admit how out of touch he was with Vietnam. It'd been almost a decade since his last visit, and too much had changed for him to pretend he knew what he was talking about. So he followed behind Georgia like a puppy with his tail between his legs, unwilling to admit he was grateful for her research.

As the two walked out together into the Old Quarter, they were as comfortable as two acquaintances could be traveling in a foreign country. Strangers who had quickly turned into companions, who just happened to be older brother and younger sister.

Despite how late the night was, the city was still very much alive. Busy tourists wearing bucket hats brushed past them, laughing and drunk with wonder. Travel agencies were still trying to sell last-minute day trips or trying to convince people to do money exchanges with them instead of at the bank. The churn of the city was a never-ending hamster wheel. The sound of street food vendors clashed with one another—some began packing up for the day, while others began to set up for the night. Mothers yelled at their children to get ready for bed, while the *tuk tuk tuk* of scooters racing home—with their handlebars full of plastic bags carrying takeout and groceries—drowned out the children's cries and pleas to stay up a bit longer.

"Found it!" Georgia yelled, her voice full of delight. She scrambled toward a bustling food stall, crowded with a mix of tourists and locals, sitting on red stools with metal tables covered between them, entire tables with overflowing plates of barbecue, chicken feet, chicken thighs, pork skewers, and pressed honeyed baguettes drizzled with cinnamon. The smell was intoxicating—a mix of charcoal smoke braided with remnants of branded Hero cigarette smoke. Despite it being so late, many people were still drinking coffee. Georgia's excitement was contagious, and soon Jude had caught some of it. He mimed for two bottles of Bia Saigon.

The vendor nodded and gestured toward them to grab any two empty stools. As they sat, he automatically brought them plates and placed them down. Georgia mimed with her hands, attempting to say she hadn't ordered yet, her face growing redder with embarrassment as her grasp on Vietnamese was worse than a fetus's understanding of the world.

"Oh, Georgia." Jude began laughing, watching his youngest sister fail so badly. "Your Vietnamese really is atrocious. You're basically speaking an alien language."

He looked up at the vendor and began speaking on her behalf, confirming that they hadn't ordered the food placed in front of them. "Anh chưa gọi món." The vendor shrugged him off, and explained how there was no order system; he just brought out the specials of the day, and that was that. Jude thanked him on their behalf, grabbed more plates from the vendor, and began chugging his beer.

"Well?" Georgia asked helplessly. "What did he say?"

"He said for you to go back to America, American scum."

She punched him hard on the shoulder—so hard he yelped.

"Since when did you know how to throw punches? I swear you've been in diapers the entire time I've known you." He groaned, rubbing his shoulder.

"What did he really say?"

Jude explained how the stall worked and for her not to worry. "What are you getting so worked up over anyway? We're just eating, it's not a life-or-death situation."

"You don't get it, Jude," Georgia said, emotions bubbling up, despite her mouth full of food. "It's embarrassing, okay? I never got the chance to learn Vietnamese. Mom left before I realized I even had a mom, and Dad was never around to speak to me in Vietnamese. I feel like I've lost something, even though I've never had it. Out of all of you, I've lost the most in all of this. I have no memories with anyone, and I know the least about being Vietnamese. None of you taught me. I don't even feel comfortable calling them Ba and Má. It feels like I'm not allowed to call them that."

Jude chewed quietly, eyes lowered onto his plate, pretending he was focusing all his energy and concentration into eating. But all he could taste was Georgia's pain. It was the first time he'd heard Georgia's distress about their parents, about her inability to speak Vietnamese.

"You know, for the longest time, I only knew how to say negative things in Vietnamese," he said finally. "It took me a long time to learn the actual language and not just the bad things."

"What do you mean?"

"Well, Duc and Evelyn fought so much, I only ever knew how to insult someone," he said quietly. "I only knew how to say things like *I hate you, You're crazy, You're the worst thing that's ever happened to me.* So in a lot of ways, you should be grateful that you didn't pick up Vietnamese from our parents."

Georgia fell quiet, picking at her food. "You said 'our parents,'" she said finally, sticking a skewer in his face, and moving her brows up and down.

"Sorry, I mean—"

"You can say 'our parents.' I still think of them as Mom and Dad. Even if no one else does."

Jude didn't correct her. "Also, it's not a competition, you know. You don't get some diaspora trophy for being able to speak Vietnamese the best out of all of us or whatever."

"Not a competition, huh?" Georgia nearly choked on her beer. "Sure seemed like we were in one, fighting one for the past year. Seems like all we did was try to beat everyone else to the finish line. And for what? Money that might not even be ours at the end of the day?"

While laughter filled the air around them, Georgia and Jude withdrew from each other, and finished the rest of their meal in silence as they people-watched. In front of them, they saw a family of seven, finishing up their meal. Two parents with their five bubbly, raucous children. The incomprehensible part to Georgia and Jude was how happy and comfortable they felt, sharing a meal together. Neither of them could remember the last time everyone—Duc and Evelyn included—had sat down for a full meal together.

They lost so much time. Had they known the truth, perhaps they could have sat down for a family meal, with all the fathers or father figures, or parental figures, who had raised them throughout the years. They could have just simply acknowledged each other as family, instead of avoiding it.

As the nightlife around them continued, Jude and Georgia were the only two still stuck in the past.

CHAPTER 40

Everyone and More Shadowy Figures

"Okay, so it's almost six hours by bus to Sa Pa. I suggest we leave on the midnight bus and arrive in the morning," Jane said, studying the bus timetable. All around her, people were milling about, lugging suitcases, and shoving giant cardboard boxes full of dried food, fruits, and vegetables, taped up haphazardly with duct tape. "It's a sleeper bus, so we'll be able to stretch our legs for the duration."

"Are we sure we trust Georgia's information? Is Duc really in Sa Pa?" Bingo asked nonchalantly, her eyes shifting unexpectedly. "No offense."

"None taken," Georgia responded.

"What choice do we have? All we know is that Duc is living in a monastery, in the mountains, somewhere in the north. The locals in New Orleans confirmed it. All roads lead to Sa Pa," Paulina said. "It's our only shot."

"Sounds like he gave us video game directions," Jude said suspiciously.

"Forget the directions, the real question we need to ask ourselves is, are we chasing a ghost who doesn't want to be found?" Jane mumbled under her breath.

Nobody responded, in part because no one knew what to say. Perhaps it was two separate things or the same thing. Duc had become a ghost who didn't want to be found.

"Well, we have a full day in Hà Nội left until we get on the bus then," Georgia broached nervously. She adjusted her bucket hat and shifted her body. "Should we at least try to do some sightseeing? Instead of just staying inside the hotel?"

Everyone else looked at each other, too defeated to stamp out Georgia's optimism, energy, and eternal fountain of youth.

"Please . . . ?" Georgia begged, her littlest-sister's voice whining. Groans were let out. Despite how angry they all were with each other and with their father, something about the baby sister begging was always gutting.

"Sure, fine," Jane said, sighing heavily. "You win. Where should we go?"

"But try not to have that stupid smile on your face all day," Bingo growled. "At least pretend for our sake that you're not having a good time."

Excitedly, with the face of someone who had struck gold, Georgia whipped out her notebook and a map of Hà Nội. "Well, I was thinking we first start with a walk along the lake Ho-on Ke—wait, how do you pronounce this lake's name?" she said.

"It's pronounced *Hoàn Kiếm*," Jude said gently, correcting her.

Georgia repeated it back slowly, and Jude took the time to explain which parts she needed to enunciate more. Jane looked at their brother in surprise. Georgia repeated it a few more times until she got it perfect, and Jude approved.

"To Hoàn Kiếm Lake we go!" Georgia exclaimed, and began to follow the map, leading the charge. Bingo and Paulina shrugged at each other and began to follow closely behind, Paulina's giant sun hat nearly knocking into the surrounding people.

Jane looked at Jude curiously as they fell behind the group. "Why did you do that?" she asked, her voice neutral for once. There didn't seem to be a hint of anger directed at Jude, just mostly confusion. Even a tone of respect.

"Do what?"

"Help Georgia with her Vietnamese like that. I've never once heard you ever try to correct anyone's Vietnamese, *nor* have I seen you actually try to help anyone in our family."

Jude shrugged and brushed past her, the tips of his ears turning a soft pink. "Why do you have to turn everything I do into a *big* thing? It's not that serious, Jane. She . . . she wants to learn, and you and I are the most fluent, so we might as well teach her. Right?"

Jane watched as Jude jogged to catch up to the others. Did she just witness Jude do something nice? For someone other than himself? She began to walk toward her siblings, her shoulders loose for the first time since landing in Vietnam, and out of the corner of her eye, she saw a familiar-looking woman whose face was also half-covered by a sun hat. Almost like the woman she saw on the plane coming into Vietnam.

Jane blinked twice, and looked again, but no sooner had she opened her eyes than the mysterious woman was gone into the crowd, as an onslaught of tourists and tour buses filled in the empty space.

·················

The siblings didn't bicker or try to outshine each other. They just stepped back, allowing Georgia to fulfill her fantasies of traveling to Vietnam, and they did all the tourist things that one did when visiting Hà Nội. Together, they walked the cobblestones of the Old Quarter, ate northern-style phở, drank egg coffee, walked alongside the hidden alley where a train ran through, sat underneath centuries-old banyan trees, and as night fell, they decided to get some beers together before boarding the sleeper bus to the mountainous region of Sa Pa.

They walked into a wooden shack with vines draped all over. The bar was crowded with a mix of tourists, locals, and expats, all elbowing to try to find an available plastic stool to sit on. A server walked past, carrying an ice bucket full of Bia Saigon, and Jude managed to grab five bottles.

"Am I allowed to say I love Vietnam?" Georgia asked tentatively as she opened her beer, turning 360 degrees, taking everything in.

"Look, Georgia," Jane said slowly, trying to rein her back in.

"Okay, sorry, forget I said anything. I know I shouldn't be so excited—" Georgia interjected.

"No, Georgia—"

"I just have always wanted to come here—"

"Georgia—"

"—and I was always so jealous that you all got to come here—"

"Chrissakes, Georgia," Jane yelled. "I'm trying to apologize to you!"

In any ordinary bar back in America, Jane would have gotten looks and stares from fellow patrons, but here, not one single person batted an eye at her outburst.

"Apologize?" Georgia asked meekly.

"*Apologize?*" Bingo gasped. "You?"

"Don't get used to it," Jane said sarcastically. "I—I shouldn't have been so quick to dismiss what you wanted to do during the short time that we're here. I often forget you've never been here, and that Duc never took you along on one of his business trips. You were always too . . ."

"Young." Georgia finished the sentence. "I know."

"Well, let's not be weird and sentimental, then," Bingo said gruffly. "Let's just drink, okay? Let's not get all into our *feelings*."

"Look, I also want to say something," Paulina said as she stood and held up her beer.

"Oh god," Bingo whispered, setting her beer back down. "Why is everyone acting like it's someone's wedding?" The bar was packed as everyone laid eyes on Paulina, whose beauty was even more exaggerated through drunken, rose-colored lenses. Tourists from Spain, Germany, and Australia looked immediately lovestruck as the whole bar went quiet to listen to her speech.

"I know I've been giving out weird compliments all day. About the coffee, the food, the environment, the people, whatever," Paulina continued. "But, I have to say, this is the nicest day we've all had together in probably a decade. It felt like we're . . . a family. Even crazier, it feels like we . . . like each other?"

Though Jude, Jane, and Bingo all groaned and protested, their walls had begun to soften.

"So, what I'm trying to say is . . . 'to family,'" Paulina said, though it came out as a question. As she raised her glass up high, the whole bar followed suit, cheering along.

"It does feel like we're a family, doesn't it?" Georgia said softly after a while, as her eyes wandered toward the crowded street. Night fell quickly, and even though the sun had disappeared, the air somehow remained the same. It was a dizzying mix of all types of people parading in and out through the streets.

Though they all shared the same thought, they were too afraid to say it out loud. Because in some weird, crazy way, Duc was responsible for bringing them all together like this, and they didn't want to admit that maybe they were all there in Vietnam for something more than just chasing Duc, the truth, or the money. That they were here chasing something far more elusive, and that was to belong again to one another, to be able to tell strangers that they had four siblings, and that they, in their own flawed ways, loved each other.

Once everyone was settled onto the sleeper bus, and Georgia's selfie stick was finally put away, no longer whacking every passenger in the head, everyone roughly closed their respective curtain, shutting out the world and each other. Jude, Jane, Bingo, Paulina, and Georgia lay on their backs or turned on their sides, and took out their phones, lighting up their beds. Their legs magically stretched out, despite how cramped the sleeper looked from the outside. In a lot of ways, it was roomier than a New York City studio nestled in the East Village.

They had roughly six hours to go before they reached Sa Pa, which meant six more hours of constant stewing. Inside each micro-cabin, each Trân privately grieved or celebrated their milestones.

In Jude's makeshift cabin, he mourned the loss of Phoebe. In fact, he was relieved to be so far away from Houston. The glow of his screen comforted him as he scrolled through old photos of himself and Phoebe. He wanted so badly to message her, and tell her everything that had happened so far, and how strange it was that he was bonding with his baby sister, but he was too afraid to make first contact. And can you believe he was in Vietnam? With all his sisters? But all he saw instead were more and more photos of Phoebe and Paul together, at group events, restaurants, bars, concerts. He missed her, or perhaps he missed the idea of her. That maybe Duc's letter wasn't wrong, that Jude needed something more to live for.

In the row across from Jude, Jane was scrolling through photos of Henry. She had also accumulated hundreds of photos somehow, each square piling up on top of one another, giving a documentation of what she had built since moving back to Houston. She was haunted by her last interaction with Henry. She began to have phantom conversations with him, practicing how to say the two hardest phrases in the world: "I'm sorry" and "I love you." Jane allowed herself to cry quietly, so no one else could hear her, thankful for how loud the engine was. Jane didn't know how to allow someone to love her.

Underneath Jane, Paulina was huddled in a pool of her own mess. Her usual austere exterior had melted in the harsh Vietnam climate. Gone were the days of heavy makeup, the designer outfits, and blow-out hair. She was naked in more ways than she could count, open for a hit from any assassin. Paulina stalked Oliver over social media, checking all his socials to see if she could figure out where he was currently and what they meant to each other. Now that Paulina had met Esther, she felt a yearning. A draw to be part of them. Paulina looked back on old photos of the picnic they had had on her last day in the Bay Area, and she began to yearn for their time together again, to start over, and to try to build a different type of family, one that wasn't steeped in trauma.

Meanwhile, in the next cubby over, down the world's tiniest ladder, Bingo contemplated sending a text to Iris. But she stopped herself. What would be the point? Bingo had been observing her from afar on social media, and watching Iris slowly take over the old Duc's Sandwiches space. There was no point in bothering her. Then Bingo sent a different text to the man she suspected was their father, to see if he had fallen for her bear trap. And he had. He'd just landed in Vietnam, and would meet them at Sa Pa. A small smile formed as she relished the fact that she was the one carrying a family secret now.

Unbeknownst to Bingo, she wasn't the only one plotting that night. In the cubby diagonal to hers, her baby sister, Georgia, stuck her head out of the curtain, waiting for the final two passengers to get on. As two women approached, passing Jude, Jane, Bingo, and Paulina's cubbies, they tightened their wrapped scarves around their shoulders, shoved their plastic visors even farther down, and pushed their big sunglasses up the bridge of their noses. They subtly each gave Georgia a nod before heading to the very back of the bus.

While some of the Trâns cried themselves to sleep that night, some stayed awake, listening to the sound of both tourists and locals snoring, or others rudely blasting YouTube videos without headphones. An Australian couple was having a heated argument about whether they should divorce or go to couples therapy. But no matter who was on that bus, everyone could feel how broken and bumpy the road was underneath their thin cotton pad. No one slept like princesses or princes that night.

CHAPTER 41

Everyone. Yes, *everyone.*

"**S**omeone please explain to me why there are so many damn temples and steps in Vietnam," Jude said, breathing heavily as he stopped climbing the steps, catching his breath. He leaned over, holding on to the ledge, and he made the mistake of looking down. His fear of heights mixed with paranoia began to settle in as he finally realized how steep the steps were. "Haven't they heard of escalators? Isn't Asia beating America in the technology race? They can't just airlift people to the top or beam them up somehow?"

Bingo was close behind Jude, her breathing also ragged. "I think that defeats the purpose of visiting a Buddhist temple. You're supposed to suffer to reach the top. Something about reaching nirvana. Enlightenment."

"Yes, but do you think Duc will ever reach enlightenment?" Jude muttered.

"Also, the cable car is broken," Jane said. Her chest was also heaving up and down as she rested her hands on her hips. "You can blame all the tourists around here."

"There's a cable car?!" Paulina's raggedy breath behind all of them floated down the mountain. Heels in hand, she had trailed so far behind everyone, she appeared like a dot on the horizon. "Are we *sure* Georgia is right? What if Duc isn't here? What if he lied to us?"

No one replied; they just kept following Georgia begrudgingly to the top. Once again, the youngest Trần irritated them all. Georgia's youthful spirit and energy was noninfectious, as her four older siblings heaved, dragged their feet, and complained all along the way. But it wasn't Georgia's youthfulness that propelled her; with each step she took on the stone marble, she knew she'd reach a different kind of inconceivable nirvana: the idea of a happy, united family.

At the bottom of the stairs at Fansipan, Connie was circling like a vulture, waiting for the clear to attack. She puttered about in a nonsensical pattern, and the cable car attendant to her right moved a few steps back from her. In the far distance, she could see the five siblings slowly inch their way to the top, struggling, out of breath, and slowing down. At one point, she even saw Paulina take a tumble. Though she had grown and evolved, she couldn't help but relish in their suffering.

Satisfied, she turned to the attendant, who immediately rushed forward. She handed him a wad of cash and thanked him for putting the lift out of operation. She barked orders to restart the lift again, and when a car came down from the mountain, they opened the door for her. With a pointed ballet flat, Connie stepped into the lift. The whirring sound of the tourist trap began to come to life, and she set out to the top of the mountain, where the temple was—and where her husband had been hiding for the past year.

"Nowhere else to hide, husband," Connie said to herself as she glided over large patches of the forest, heading toward the top of the legendary mountain.

....

At the very top of Fansipan, all five Trần siblings collapsed onto the final steps of the temple, making more of a ruckus than the four-hundred-year-old temple had ever seen in its lifetime. Old monks in orange robes stared horrified while younger monks in gray robes rushed to carry trays of offerings, nearly sending the blessed fruit flying into the air. Even tourists began to look down on them. The audacity! The disrespect! But everyone stopped in their tracks, curious as to why a group of five people who looked similar to one another seemed to be entering the sacred mountain with such aggression. They debated whether or not the siblings were tourists or Vietnamese diaspora on their identity journey—either way, it was the same to them, because diaspora will always be tourists. Though the monks had seen it all in their lifetimes, this time, they knew something was strange.

"We're looking for someone. Anyone know a Duc?" Jane called out hoarsely in Vietnamese. "Duc Trần? Owner of Duc's Sandwiches? Parading around for the past thirty or so years pretending to be our biological father?" The monks all looked at one another, confused, trying to figure out who Duc was. Bingo whipped out a photo of Duc on her phone and began showing it around. She was met with blank, puzzled faces.

"Just so you all know, Duc's Sandwiches aren't very good," Bingo called out. "It's a bit unseasoned."

An older monk stepped forward, his hands tucked inside his robes, giant wood beads adorning him. "There is no one staying here by that name," he assured them all, in perfect English. "No one outside is allowed to stay here unless you commit your life to the Buddha, and we have not had a new person in a very long time. Please, you must all leave, you're causing a disturbance."

"What?!" Jude yelled. "He's not here?"

"I fucking knew it," Jane whispered. "I knew he was lying. That old lying piece of—"

"Mom?" Bingo said, shocked, interrupting Jane.

"Okay, look," Jane said, her voice full of indignation. "I know I was like a second mother to you, but please don't call me your mother. It's disturbing—"

"Má?" Paulina now repeated hollowly, her eyes looking past everyone, to the lone woman who stood in the middle of the temple grounds, her petite body frozen, her shaggy gray hair pinned neatly, wearing all linen, so loose it drowned out her frame. Her arms hung awkwardly.

Evelyn took in all her children, whom she hadn't seen in over two decades. Her children represented her past, present, and future; each one had come out of her body, and she carried a part of them with her—including all her invisible demons. Each child looked like her in one way or another.

But Jane especially looked like her.

"Mom?" Jude's voice shook as he stared down the woman who had abandoned them all. Jane saw how ghost white Jude's face had become. It was whiter than the clouds around them—clouds that huddled together like cotton balls in a children's art project, haphazardly glued without rhyme or reason, but still joyfully.

All five Trần children were soon looking into the eyes of their mother, Evelyn Lê, who stood there as if it was nothing more than an ordinary Wednesday afternoon.

"I guess we're all here for Duc, aren't we?" she finally said, breaking a twenty-year silence. The siblings took in her aged appearance. Aside from Georgia, who slid herself out of frame, out of her siblings' purview, while also pretending to be shocked at seeing her mother in person.

"May rose, jasmine, and a hint of bourbon vanilla," Paulina said softly. Her eyes were adjusting themselves to the light as if they'd been in the dark for so long. Her mother had gotten old. Remnants of her beauty stood the test of time, but she looked thinner, exhausted, after hiding for so long. "I should have known. There was a faint trail of it on the way up."

"I smelled it on the plane, but figured everyone who was going to Vietnam was wearing the same scent," Jane said quietly.

"I smelled it on the bus," Bingo chimed in. "But I also figured every old Asian lady loved—"

"Chanel No. 5," everyone said at once.

Jude looked as if he was about to faint at the sight of his mother. He imagined Jane whispering *mommy issues* into his ear. It wasn't really mommy issues; he was only trying to make sense of seeing a stranger again, a stranger who was responsible for all this pain, just standing before him, as if the past twenty years of pain never transpired. But something in him made him step forward. He didn't know what kept him going, but he was the first to break out. One foot in front of the other. He didn't know how to stop, but he needed that reassurance in the way only a mother could give. He brushed past his sisters, walked toward his mother, and embraced her, pulled her close to him. His face burrowed into her shoulder and he began to cry, much to the shock of all his sisters. They watched as their mother awkwardly stood there, arms tight at her sides, until they could see her eyes softening up, and then eventually, she reciprocated.

"I think it's actually you who we've been looking for the whole time," Jude whispered into the crook of her neck, still holding on tight.

One by one, Evelyn's daughters began to step forward, their defensive walls coming down, moved by this unexpected reunion. The next one to hug Evelyn and Jude was Georgia. Paulina came soon after. Bingo nearly tripped on herself as she ran with her arms outstretched toward the growing mass, until only Jane was left. Jane continued standing on the other side of the temple, her mind in its own torture chamber as she grew resentful at the reunion before her.

Somehow through the tangle of all the arms and bodies around her,

Evelyn was able to lock eyes with her eldest daughter, and she silently pleaded with Jane to understand why she had to leave them. Both women's eyes were wounded, but Jane made no movement forward. Everyone with eyes and ears knew that Jane had always been the one with real mommy issues, the one who stepped into the role of mother far too early, the one who shielded her siblings from their mother's depression and anxiety, the one who had to give up any modicum of a childhood in favor of making sure everyone else would turn out okay. Jane wondered if her mother knew how much damage she had inflicted on her and her inability to find her own happiness.

But Evelyn knew. She didn't need anyone to show or tell her. She knew so much that she stepped away from her four other children and began walking across the long, cobbled temple grounds, making her way toward Jane. The rest of the Trần children, monks, tourists, nuns, volunteers, tour guides, and those who had come to the temple seeking refuge and answers watched in awe as a Vietnamese mother approached her eldest daughter, as if she were approaching a timid stray and didn't want to spook it. Evelyn eventually reached her destination, and took Jane's hands into her own calloused, rough ones. The younger woman's hands were diametrically the opposite of Evelyn's: perfect, smooth, the hands of an immigrant's daughter who had the privilege of going to law school, was a voracious reader, and who had traveled the world and had seen more places than Evelyn ever would in her lifetime. She might have been alone on these trips, but she still had freedom.

Evelyn proceeded to say the two phrases that Jane had had trouble her entire life saying:

"I'm sorry, con," Evelyn said. "I love you more than you know."

It was the two phrases that Jane couldn't say to Henry. To anyone.

Behind everyone, the young monks in the gray robes dropped the baskets of blessed fruit, not from shock or surprise, but because they were overwhelmed with gratitude for being alive and present to witness the rare beauty of generational healing, which was just simply another step toward nirvana of a different kind, the kind that could be achieved here on earth.

Jane began to cry, dropped her mother's hands, and wrapped her arms around her. They both stood there, swaying from side to side, Jane towering over her petite mother. Georgia, ever the optimist, started clapping and jumping, her eyes brimming with tears, but Bingo put her hands over Georgia's, doing her best to silence her.

"Wait a minute, is that . . . Connie over there?" Paulina whispered to her siblings.

Out of nowhere, Connie Vũ came bursting up the steps, pushing monks out of the way, her eyes feral, her designer bag glistening in the sun, the repetitive, tacky logo on display for all to see. A sea of orange tunics went flying in the wind as monks scattered in every direction, attempting to avoid being touched by the rabid woman. Despite having taken the lift to the top of the mountain, she was drenched in sweat, unaccustomed to the country's heat. She raged toward Evelyn and the siblings, a fire pouring out of her, adrenaline coursing through her veins. Just like everyone else, Connie was also looking for answers.

"Where is he?" she roared, birds scattering from the trees. "Where is my so-called precious husband?"

She stared into the faces she'd been chasing for the past year. Jude, Jane, Bingo, Paulina, and what's the youngest one's name again? Georgina? Whatever.

"Connie!" Georgia snapped. "Remember the plan? I told you to be *patient*."

Jane looked at her in alarm. "What do you mean, 'plan'?"

"You're wasting your breath. We don't know where he is," Bingo said, interrupting, shrugging.

Everyone turned to look at Evelyn, including Connie. The manic desire for revenge suddenly seemed harder to achieve for everyone. She also shrugged. "I don't know where he is, either, I was just following you all."

"We *both* were trailing you all. We flew here together," Connie said gruffly. "You're all not very observant."

Jane grew impatient, her voice growing louder. "Georgia, I just asked you. What *plan* were you talking about?"

Georgia stood meekly, trying to make eye contact with Connie and her mother for help, but both dropped their gaze. "I invited Connie and our mother here."

Soon all their voices began to mesh together, so much so that no one knew who was talking.

"What do you mean *you—*"

"Invited? Like a birthday party invited?—"

"You were in contact with our *mother*—"

"This whole time—"

"*Twenty* years—"

"Look, forget Duc. Who is my real father, Má?" Jude suddenly burst out loud, his voice overpowering everyone else's. He turned toward Evelyn, putting aside their beautiful moment. "Why did you lie to us for so long?"

"Forget Jude's biological father, who is *our* biological father?" Jane asked, pushing forward, as she pointed toward all of her sisters.

Evelyn opened her mouth and closed it quickly. Her hesitation drove everyone around her mad. "I knew this day would come eventually. Look, your father has always loved you," Evelyn said carefully. "And Duc has loved *and* cared for you all, too. You are all Duc's children in a way."

"That's not the question I asked," Jude bellowed. "I waited my entire life to ask you this question. Everyone knows he isn't. *I've* always known. *Who* is my real father?"

"Oh just tell them," Connie shouted, throwing her arms in the air. "Just tell them so we can all focus together and track down Duc."

Jane could see her mother withdrawing into herself. Like the lie she had worked so hard to maintain had become so embedded in her, and she didn't know how to utter the truth. "Má, why did you lie for so long? Why keep the lie going if Duc wasn't even your real husband or our real father?" Jane asked gingerly. "What was the whole point?"

"It was complicated back then," Evelyn said as she began twisting her hands together. "You don't know what it was like, what was happening to all of us back then. We were so scared someone would come after your father. There was a list, with your father's name on it, for the Klansmen to seek revenge on. Your father testified in court, he helped gather evidence and testimonies. He took on that risk, but he wasn't a father back then. So Duc stepped in and pretended to be your father so nobody would take revenge on you all. He made sacrifices to make sure we'd all be safe."

"Don't make him into such a saint, okay?" Connie groaned. "Duc may be a saint to you all, but he's no saint to me. He wrote me out of his will!"

Behind everyone, there was a commotion and all the monks and tourists began backing away again, making yet another clear path.

Mr. Ngô soon came bobbing up the steps, sweat pouring out of him as he loosened his tie. His suit jacket hung over his arm. Unlike how graceful Evelyn was in the heat, the top of Mr. Ngô's shiny, balding head had been fried scarlet by the overbearing sun.

"What the hell?" Paulina said suddenly. "Mr. Ngô?"

"Jesus Christ," Mr. Ngô said, gasping for air. "Why is the lift broken today of all days?"

"Language," the monk closest to him said warningly.

"Oh sorry, I mean . . . Buddha?" Mr. Ngô said as he turned toward Bingo. "Okay, I'm here, what's the emergency? Why is this temple suing you all?"

"Anh?" Evelyn whispered. "What are you doing here?"

Mr. Ngô's face fell instantly when he realized Evelyn was standing there in front of him. A lifetime of secrets standing between them. Her disappearance wrecked him. But here she was, alive, flesh, bone, and all. She looked exactly the same, save for a few more gray hairs. Her beauty still standing the test of time. The tiniest spark of *something* passed between them, and Mr. Ngô dropped his suit jacket on the temple ground.

"Em? Is that really you?" he whispered. "What are you doing here?"

"For god's sake," Connie cried out as all the monks angrily stared at her. "Sorry, sorry. Who else is going to come up those stairs? It's like a clown car."

Everyone at the temple had fully stopped doing whatever they were doing to watch the saga unfold before them instead. Some even began pulling out plastic chairs and setting them down in the courtyard.

Bingo beamed proudly and pointed at Mr. Ngô. "Ladies and gentlemen, our biological father."

Jude, Jane, Paulina, and even Georgia looked shell-shocked as they began to connect the dots and looked at Evelyn for confirmation. But her thinned lips and her anxious expression confirmed it all for them.

Observing Evelyn and Mr. Ngô side by side, the daughters saw the resemblance. They stared at the old, crusty lawyer, who had been by Duc's side since they exited Evelyn's womb, who had always been there for them in the shadows, who had picked up the kids from school when Duc couldn't, who made sure everyone's teeth were brushed when Duc was too busy with the sandwich chain, who made sure they never went to bed hungry, and who had helped Jude build his fort under Duc's desk.

Mr. Ngô began protesting. "What did you just say? I don't have any children, I'm no one's father."

"Wait," Jane began as she really began observing Mr. Ngô's mannerisms and how closely he resembled all the daughters. "You were the one who convinced and mentored me to go to law school, for immigration law."

"Oh my god," Paulina whispered, still processing. "But the letters? The ones Duc wrote to us that kick-started this? Did you write those . . . ?"

Soon every voice began to pile on, accusing Mr. Ngô of moments of true fatherhood, the kind of moments that went unnoticed and were often taken for granted. Mr. Ngô's face remained frozen as he inched toward Evelyn, seeking shelter from the onslaught.

"Sorry about lying, I had to get you to come here somehow," Bingo said to him. "The temple isn't suing us, that'd be crazy. I just said that 'cause I knew you'd come. You . . . you always come when we need you."

"Would it be crazy, though?" a monk behind them whispered to their fellow monk. "*We* could sue for emotional distress."

"I'm not—I'm not your . . ." Mr. Ngô's face turned beet red. Now he was really cowering behind Evelyn.

"Give it up, anh," Evelyn said, exasperated. "They caught us."

"Why the fuck are we in Sa Pa, then?" Jane yelled. "Who told us that Duc was here?"

Connie turned angrily toward Mr. Ngô and all but shoved Evelyn out of the way. She thrust a finger against his chest. "You told me Duc was hiding out in a temple, doing charity work and finding inner peace."

Mr. Ngô gave a weak smile. "I did say that, didn't I? I mean, it was clearly a lie."

"Who told us to come here, then?" Jude joined Jane in the witch hunt. "Speak up!"

Georgia whimpered, a strangled noise came out of her, and she raised her hand. "I'm the one who said Duc was here even though I knew he wasn't."

"Why would you do that?" everyone shouted, including Evelyn, Connie, and Mr. Ngô.

"Because Fansipan has always been on my list?" She released a small, awkward smile. "I thought it'd be cool to see this as a family, especially the rice paddy fields. Look where we are, look how beautiful it is. We did it, didn't we? My first real family vacation. *Our* first real family vacation."

Everyone groaned. Curses flew through the air as chaos erupted even more. Everyone began chiding Georgia, then they all turned on each other. Evelyn and Mr. Ngô began arguing about where she'd been the last twenty years and why did she leave them? But why did she leave *him*? Connie took out a vape and stood in the corner, and all the sisters naturally began ganging up on Jude, for absolutely no reason at all except that old habits die hard. Even the monks gave up trying to get everyone to settle down, or to watch their language. Instead, they began to pray for the family.

In the middle of the chaos, Evelyn turned to Jude, and only Jude. "I'll tell you about your father one day. Just know that he loved you. His name was Tuấn."

With that, no other explanation was needed. Jude could see the grief on his mother's face. Jude kneeled, collapsed under the weight of a type of grief he didn't know he could ever have. The grief of something in the "past tense," knowing that that person, whoever it was on the end of that, was gone from this world. He grieved for a father he would never know.

PART 5

BREAKING BREAD

CHAPTER 42

September 1983, Seadrift, Texas

There was another baby on the way.

Call it motherly instincts, or perhaps it was the constant craving for bún bò Huế—the satisfying rich spicy red broth, the mountain of fresh bean sprouts, the way one had to work their teeth around the pork knuckle to remove the tiniest bit of meat, and of course, the wide, paper-thin vermicelli noodles, which soaked up the broth so beautifully. Evelyn craved it almost every morning for the past two months, so much so that she began to have phantom tastes of the flavors the moment she woke up, till the moment she went to bed. That was when she knew she was pregnant. She hadn't had such an intense craving since she was two months pregnant with Jude.

She walked barefoot around her tiny mobile home, less than four hundred square feet. Her feet were swollen to the size of unripe melons. She could hear Jude crawling about in the living room, clanging his wooden toys together. The sound of it both comforted and terrified her. She was a mother, but a mother carrying a terrible secret. The sound of two wooden toy horses clashed against each other, going into battle, crossing the rough terrain of the cerulean woven rug. Shrieks of delight coming out of Jude became the unofficial war cry, as he continued to pit horse against horse, while there was her own pit in her stomach, rotting away inside her.

Evelyn stopped in front of the living room, unable to peek her head around the corner to look at Jude. She couldn't bear to look at his face in this moment, not when she was pregnant with someone's child who wasn't Jude's father. The guilt shattered her each time she looked into his deep-set eyes.

Every time she looked at her son, she was reminded of the day when they pulled his body out of the Gulf, limp and tangled in the fishing net they had dragged along the ground. Shrimp trawler after shrimp trawler of Vietnamese fishermen still showed up every morning after Tuấn's disappearance to look for him. She kept hoping the net would just catch nothing more than some stray fish and trash, and for a stretch of time, they pulled up nothing but beer bottles and a few crabs for dinner.

But one morning, almost two years after Tuấn's death, and after the court case had closed, the line became taut—more taut than usual—indicating a big catch. And she knew.

Deep in her heart, she knew that his body—or what was left of it—was at the bottom of the net.

Jude's voice brought her back to reality. He had given up the great horse battle, and had decided to throw his horses against the wall instead. Evelyn caressed her stomach, which only protruded ever so slightly. Though it was just the slightest ridge—it was undeniably a bump of some kind. Men could easily have mistaken her for eating too much; perhaps she was just bloated. But the women at the crab factory knew. They had known before she began to crave the phantom taste of bún bò Huế. They knew immediately when they watched her swallow her saliva a few times in a row, suppressing the metallic taste in her mouth, the scent of a thousand crabs being processed alive suddenly feeling a thousand times more tangible than before. They knew when she had to close her eyes and slowly lower herself down on a chair, her knees buckling, not just from the back-breaking labor, but from the sheer exhaustion of creating life.

Yes, the women all knew she was pregnant. They also knew who the father was.

But they all kept quiet. Not because they were trying to keep it a secret from their husbands, brothers, or uncles—but because they knew that what little joy they had these days, they had to cherish it, even if it was through unconventional means. But Evelyn didn't see having another baby with a different man as joyful. Instead, she saw it as a burden.

Evelyn worked up the courage to peer around the living room corner and began to observe Jude from a distance. She couldn't bring herself to hold him lately; anytime she tried, he felt light-years away in her arms, even the little moments when he fell asleep cuddling her. It wasn't just prolonged postpartum anymore; it was a communal grief. The loss of Jude growing inside of her, the loss of her Tuấn, the new growing baby inside of her. Nothing felt easy anymore, it was only just a continuous struggle. How does one see light when it's eternally midnight?

Jude crawled all over the blue rug, as if he were crossing his own ocean,

just as she had done after the war. His little hands and feet were so coura-
geous and unassuming, finding his way from corner to corner without fear.
She thought of what to do. What to do with the baby growing inside her,
and what to do with the man she had made love to one night, when she
was so overcome with grief, when all she wanted was darkness and a warm
body, and to pretend that she was lying next to Tuấn, one last time.

She couldn't help but feel anger toward Tuấn. What really happened to
him that night on the boat? How could he have abandoned her like this?
She felt too ashamed to go back to her mother in Oklahoma City, and too
ashamed to ask for help from the people around town.

The sound of metal rattling broke her out of her reverie, and she
snapped out of it in time to watch Jude pull something from behind the TV
console. Old clumps of dust bunnies clung to the indents of his palms,
marking topography lines, and he laughed gleefully, throwing the dust up
into the air. It was the cherry on top of an infinite string of bad luck. She ran
forward and yelled at him to stop getting himself dirty. Frustrated with her
lack of peace, and seeing how dirty Jude was, she began to cry. Little tears
fell at first, which quickly turned into big, gasping sobs, the kind of sobs she
hadn't had since she was a child, throwing tantrums. She held Jude's hands
up high to prevent him from getting himself dirtier or anything else dirty.

She wondered what she would do with two children, from two different fathers, one out of wedlock, and if she should just run away before the
baby was born. Or if she should just try to find a clinic that could help her.
She had heard of those clinics and had friends who had gone. Just as her
mind spiraled to an even darker place, out of the corner of her eye, something shiny glistened, under the TV console, where Jude had been playing.
Something peeked out at her, calling her.

Evelyn stopped crying long enough to stoop down toward it. She
couldn't remember ever cleaning behind the console, not in the five years
they'd been living in the house, even when Tuấn was alive. Evelyn squatted,
slid her hand under the small gap, her hand blindly sifting through until it
made contact with what felt like a handle. Her heart stopped, and she got
up immediately, shoving the furniture out of the way. She knew what it was
before she even pulled it out, and upon seeing the rusty green metal tackle
box, she knew it belonged to Tuấn.

The old tackle box he had carried to his boat every morning for years, which held his hooks, lures, bobbers, swivels . . . even an old photo of her, anything he needed to be gone for an hour at sea or for days. Before his death, he'd replaced it with a plastic tackle box, and she didn't ask what he'd done with the old one. Curiosity took over. Why was he hiding his metal tackle box behind the console?

She quickly brought the tackle box to the kitchen sink and wiped it down, her hands covered with dust and grime, discolored worse than Jude's palms. She carefully opened up the box . . . and gasped, almost dropping it. Behind her, Jude had taken over duties as the crier, and his wails bounced off the popcorn ceiling and the small house. Outside, Evelyn could hear her neighbors yelling at one another, one in Vietnamese, the other in Spanish, for once again blocking each other's parking spot. But none of that noise mattered anymore, because staring back up at her were stacks of cash carefully wrapped in faded red rubber bands, presumably from old bánh mì wrappers. Every compartment in the tackle box was stuffed with cash. Jude's wailing became louder and he began to run his blackened palms all over the white walls, transitioning into a human Sharpie, taking his frustrations out.

Evelyn didn't know whether to cry or to laugh as she began to pull out wads of cash, quickly counting how much was in there. Wads of dollar bills, five stacks of tens, and lots of twenties stared back at her. The bills weren't crisp, some even had the familiar smell of rotten fish and cigarette smoke— the two smells that Evelyn had attached to Tuấn. A quick estimate and she could tell that there was at least $20,000.

With trembling hands, she closed the tackle box and slowly backed away from it, as if she'd opened Pandora's box. Tuấn had talked about moving for a while, when things got really bad when the white fisherman was killed. He talked about moving to the city, to Houston, and opening up a family business, something that was just theirs, and nothing that involved fishing. He had talked about opening up a shop of some kind. She had snapped at him one night, telling him that it was all just a dream, and to keep his feet on the ground, how she'd love to run a bánh mì shop of her own one day, but she had to be realistic.

She regretted yelling at him.

Now she fell to the ground, sobbing, shoving her face into her arms.

How wrong she'd been. If only she had had faith that Tuấn always had another plan. She should have had faith that he would always take care of her.

Combined with Jude's vocal strength and her own, she didn't hear the front door open, and in walked Huey, carrying a bundle of sad flowers in his hand, his other hand clutching his wool hat tightly.

"Em?" he called out quietly, hovering near the doorframe, too afraid to come closer to the petite pregnant woman crumpled on the ground. "Are you okay?"

She lifted her head slowly and saw Huey staring down at her. She assessed his face, earnest, young, strong, and the flowers in his hand. He must have known. Someone at the factory must have whispered it to him, or he had overheard. He knew.

There was no doubt in her mind that he was madly in love with her. He'd want her to keep the baby and he'd take Jude in as his own, and he'd marry her in a run-down courthouse somewhere in Texas. It all sounded so easy, perhaps it was a lifeline being thrown to her, and she should take it. There weren't many other options for a pregnant, widowed Vietnamese refugee.

She slowly got up off the floor and threw a glance at the tackle box. She walked into Huey's arms and hugged him hello.

"Marry me, em," Huey whispered into her ear. "I'll always take care of you. I promise. Nothing will ever happen to your family. To *our* family."

She didn't respond right away. They both stood there swaying back and forth, and she closed her eyes, and dreamt about another life. Opening up a shop of her own, somewhere in Houston. Something that was just hers, and no one else's. Maybe even a sandwich shop, a bánh mì shop. It wouldn't be much, but it would be a start.

"Okay, anh," she whispered back. "I'll marry you."

From outside the window, she spotted Duc, patrolling the yard, watching out for the two of them, as he always did, and she closed her eyes and allowed her body to meld into Huey's. She was tired, so very tired.

CHAPTER 43

Duc

Everyone should have known Duc Trần was never going to be sequestered in a Buddhist temple, tucked high up in the mountains in northern Vietnam, praying for world peace. Duc Trần was a man about town, the sentient embodiment of bụi đời—a dust-of-life kind of soul—one who lived for life's hedonistic joys: bar food, gambling, karaoke, cheap beer, even cheaper cigarettes, carom billiards, and the endless hum of magical Sài Gòn nights, which could lead him anywhere at a moment's notice.

The moment everyone landed in Sài Gòn, now known as Ho Chi Minh City, Mr. Ngô led the group straight to Duc's lair, no longer willing to maintain his attorney-client privileges in the face of Connie's wrath. Down an unmarked street, somewhere along the invisible border of District Three and District One, there was a long, winding alley, where the only lights that guided the path were from connecting houses or flashing headlights from motorbikes whizzing past. Faint laughter coupled with drunken insults echoed down the alley, but the laughter was quickly replaced with yelling and beer bottles being thrown about and insults about how ugly one looked. Had it not been for the rich smell of pressed baguette, dripping with honey and enough butter to send you into cardiac arrest, the group would have run for the hills from the explosive argument.

Connie sniffed and clutched her expensive bag close to her. "Don't tell me Duc is down *there*? Why isn't he at the Park Hyatt in District One?"

Mr. Ngô laughed so hard, he nearly sent his glasses flying. "Duc? Duc *Trần* at the *Park* Hyatt?"

"We always stay at five-star hotels!" she exclaimed defensively. "He knows I'm always at any Four Seasons at any given moment, around the world. They know us by name!"

"*You* stay at five-star hotels, they know *you* by name," Mr. Ngô said, raising a brow. "Duc prefers a thin mattress on the ground and at least two or three fans pointed at him at all times."

As if on cue, Duc's distinct voice floated down the alley, along with the smell of his favorite off-brand pack of cigarettes. To rub salt in Connie's wound, Duc started laughing uproariously—it was the kind of laughter that was side-splitting, not only indicative of being three sheets to the wind, but a laughter that carried no weight and no problems attached. Duc was having more than a good time; he was thriving.

Like any wildfire, the probability that the fire was caused by a human is roughly 85 percent.

But Connie had no desire for it to be accidental. She wanted to burn the whole alleyway, the whole street, the whole district, the whole city down. Everyone immediately stepped aside as she shoved her purse into Evelyn's arms and stormed headfirst into the alleyway, screaming Duc's name.

Sheepishly, one by one, everyone else followed her in a snake line, weaving in and out of red plastic stools, people milling about, vendors packing up for the day, delivery motorbikes, loose electric cords, and laundry hung out to dry.

Upon hearing his name screamed, Duc's laughter dried up faster than any water source in Houston on a triple-digit summer day. "DUC TRÂN! You better come out now!" Connie yelled. "Or else I'm going to take you to court!"

"Americans are always the first to be so litigious," Mr. Ngô said.

"Tell me about it," Jane whispered back.

"Listen, if there was universal basic income or people opted for the general strike—" Georgia began whispering. Everyone groaned and told her to please stop, and that *now* was not the moment to solve late-stage capitalism.

A shuffling of chairs screeching across tiles; poker chips clinking against the ground in a rush; whispers from men in shadows telling Duc that he was still ugly and that he still owed them money; multiple feet running away down the opposite end of the alley; and finally a door opening and slamming behind. Out of the darkness, a stout man, similar in age to Mr. Ngô, came shuffling out from behind a curtain.

His face looked nothing like that of Jude, Jane, Bingo, Paulina, or Georgia. Instead, his face was more sunken, his hair greasier, his eyes a bit turned down, like sheet corners that weren't pulled down correctly. He walked out onto the street and as his eyes adjusted to the flickering streetlamp, he began to see eight faces staring back at him, descending from angriest (Connie) to the least angry (Georgia). Everyone in between, he took in stride. His best friend and lawyer (Mr. Ngô), his pretend wife and pretend mother of his children for the past thirty or so years (Evelyn), and then everyone else (his pretend children)—none of these faces fazed him more than Connie Vũ's.

Soon everyone began talking at once, at various decibels. The anger rose and fell—sometimes above sea level, sometimes below—and Duc had no choice but to receive it all. He stood there rubbing his belly, as if he had opened up an employee anonymous feedback box, but unfortunately took the brunt of it all.

"Why did you pretend to be our father for so long?"

"Why did you write me out of the will, you son of a bitch?"

"Anh, it's over, they caught us. Just tell them the truth."

"Is there even an inheritance?"

"Anh, I'm sorry, I tried to explain to them all, but they don't know what it was like for us back then. They were just babies. They don't know what we had to do to survive."

"Are we even legally married???"

"Were you playing Texas Hold'em back there? Do they play that here?" (That was Georgia.)

"Anh, they don't understand the sacrifice you made for us."

"What's your favorite restaurant here?" (Georgia, again.)

"Did you even love us?"

Duc was more than eight beers deep, and all the king's men couldn't have brought him to sobriety more than the last question he heard. *Did you even love us?* Duc cursed under his breath and his stomach rumbled at the same time. He opened his mouth and everyone stopped talking at once, waiting for the infamous Duc Trần of Duc's Sandwiches fame to finally say something profound, to explain the mess that he had laid in his wake for the past year, and for the past thirty-five years.

Then Evelyn pushed through, and she stared at him with vitriol, a haunting in her empty eyes. Decades of pent-up anger welled up in her, and Duc stepped back, frightened for the first time.

"What really happened to Tuấn that night on the boat?" Evelyn asked, anger bubbling in her throat, as she turned to both Duc and Mr. Ngô. "I heard you two. Twenty years ago, outside my bedroom window. Did you kill him? How did he die?"

All the children instantly grew quiet. Even Connie took a step back, shocked by the accusation.

The two men grew pale. Duc instantly sobered up as it dawned on him that twenty years ago Evelyn had walked out on them. He and Mr. Ngô looked at each other, trying to find another way out of this.

"No more lies," Evelyn said. "No *more* lies. I want the truth. Don't tell me that he was a martyr or any of that. I'm sick of your lies and your empty promises."

Only Mr. Ngô stepped forward. "Em, he was drunk, okay? Believe me. He was just drunk that night, and he fell overboard. We didn't realize it until morning. But it was too late by then. All of us were just waiting the night out, you know we were cornered that night. You saw the boat. It was charred to pieces. I'm sorry, em."

Duc managed to swallow his pride and finally stepped up. "It really was just an accident. We just couldn't tell you. You . . . you were in so much pain. What good would it have done if you had known how he really died? Would anything have changed? You went on to have a good life, didn't you? The children were cared for."

Evelyn stared at Duc. "If I had known what had really happened that night, I would have done everything differently. Everything." She pivoted to look at Mr. Ngô accusingly.

"All we've ever done is try to protect you," Mr. Ngô said, with regret, as he turned to all his children. "To protect all of you. I'm sorry. *We* are sorry. We are sorry for lying for so long, but it was the only way. I was scared back then. I still live my life in fear that they'll come after each of you, for being my children, for being my wife, my family."

A steep silence had fallen. As they braced themselves, waiting for Evelyn to react, to show any emotion, Georgia nervously eyed the narrow alleyway, wondering if she should block it somehow in case her mother ran again. But instead, Evelyn hunched her shoulders forward, collapsing from the weight of it all. She suddenly looked smaller than normal, her bones more brittle, and her crow's-feet more defined. Evelyn looked tired.

"I'm hungry," she said finally, her voice hollow, her eyes sunken, resigned to her life of constant grief. "I'm really hungry."

Georgia stepped up, recognizing that it was her turn to make sure her mother ate something. "Should we get some food? Snails and clams?"

"I know a spot," Duc offered up quickly. Everyone soon surrounded and flanked Evelyn, protecting her as if she were the frailest thing on the planet, making sure she got there safely.

....

Which came first—the karaoke machine or Vietnamese fathers?

Duc had never known peace; he just accepted life for what it was—that it was difficult and long, and in order to survive, one needed bad karaoke and snails.

He led them to his favorite local snails and beer spot, next to the Sài Gòn River. All the chairs faced the water as sweaty servers scurried around carrying buckets of beer while simultaneously juggling plates of grilled oysters, mussels, and snails drowning in a coconut milk sauce. The crowd was boisterous, and the sound of beers clinking together seemed to be in rhythm as the night wore on. There were hardly any tourists at this spot, which was becoming increasingly rare in the city. Vietnam had become a tourist trap in more ways than one, the boom caused by young travelers trying to "find themselves" in more cost-efficient ways. But it was strange that these young tourists and expats were doing that in a country that still had undiscovered land mines left-over from the war, hidden in the countryside.

A harried server came by and haphazardly dumped a bucket of snails and plates of razor clams on their table, splashing everyone with a mix of green sauce, butter, and hot sauce in the process. Duc grabbed a toothpick from the table and used it to pull out the snails from their shells, tossing the mantle into his mouth and chucking the exoskeleton onto the riverbank. Mounds littered and piled up on the riverbank, a graveyard of snails, clams, and mussels. Mr. Ngô grabbed a toothpick and joined in, soon Evelyn joined, both their eyes lighting up from the thrill of being able to eat snails again by the water.

Jude, Jane, Bingo, Paulina, Georgia, and Connie watched them eat, their mouths open, chewing loudly. But they all held their tongue, waiting for Duc to speak, even though they were desperate for more answers.

"Anh, eight beers, please," Duc called out to another server walking by. "And keep them coming all night." There was a smile on Duc's face, but the smile didn't travel to his eyes. He could feel eight pairs of eyes on him, waiting for him to address the (many) elephants in the room. The server nodded, and threw up eight fingers to the person in the back, who immediately rushed out, a bottle somehow nestled between each finger, and expertly placed one in front of everyone.

Down at the riverbank, someone kick-started the karaoke machine, an old beat-up projector somehow still standing, and someone began wailing away, singing a lost Vietnamese song from the eighties.

Connie's eyes stabbed Duc through the chest. Her eyes were sharp, angry, and repulsed. She pressed him, unwilling to wait anymore. "Where's the money, Duc?"

Duc groaned, chucked a snail as far as he could throw it, and leaned back into his white plastic chair. He seemed to have aged faster the past year than ever before. He pinched his brows together and began to rub his temples. "Money, money, money," he said, rolling the word over and over in his mouth. "What is money, really? Nothing but funny money."

"Why does that sound . . . disconcerting," Jane said tensely.

"Something a charlatan would say." Paulina laughed nervously.

"Why does that sound like an ABBA lyric?" Bingo whispered to Jane.

"Okay, look. Here's the truth, I lost everything," Duc sighed. "There's nothing left but the stores I gave you all. The ones in Houston, Philadelphia, San Jose, and New Orleans. That's it. We just didn't know how to tell you all so—"

Mr. Ngô shifted in his seat. "—so we planned it in a way—"

"—that you all would each get something and start anew," Duc finished. "That had always been our thought process, that the kids would each get a store, if rough times ever hit."

". . . and that time is now." Mr. Ngô nodded solemnly.

Evelyn was shocked. "You lost *everything*? How? We started the store with Tuấn's money! How could you do this to his memory?"

Connie, nearly bowled over with anger, stood up, knocking over beer bottles and snails. "*Nothing* is left? What do I get, then? If there's only a few crusty stores left?"

"What happened?" Jane whispered.

Duc chuckled nervously. "Mounting debt, inflation, loan sharks, but mostly it was because, well, after your mother left, the food went downhill. People stopped coming. Your mother was the heart and soul of the operation. People didn't want fast and cheap, they didn't like the changes. You know how picky Vietnamese people are. The chain just lost its way. We . . . we just lost our way. It just wasn't making any sense anymore."

"Why didn't you stay?" Jane asked, turning to her mother, her tone becoming accusatory, though that was the wrong choice. "Why did you abandon everything?"

Evelyn watched the drunk karaoke singer on the riverbank, doing his best to follow the lyrics on the screen, but his eyes were turning lopsided, and were dimming lower and lower. Eventually, the singer was booed off and an argument broke out about who should go next.

Her voice was low but still pure fire. "Maybe you'll never understand what it's like to have five kids and never be able to fully recover from it all. Do you know what it's like to give birth to a baby, release it from your body, and then feel nothing but emptiness? I just couldn't live my life in the shadows anymore," she said finally. "I needed to know what it'd be like to be free, and not live a lie anymore.

"Do you know what it's like to have to pretend to be Duc's wife for so long, and hide your real father's identity? Do you know what it's like to have to pretend to go into the bedroom but then wait for night to fall, for your real father to swap places? To pretend in public that I was in love with someone who I wasn't? It wasn't just me the lie was killing, con, it was also killing your father. It killed us."

Mr. Ngô stared at Evelyn, and he reached his hand out to her, and without protest, Evelyn took it. All the Trần children watched with mouths agape as Evelyn's and Mr. Ngô's hands entwined. They were two older Vietnamese people finally stepping out into the light together, so far removed from Seadrift, from Houston, and from watchful, hateful eyes.

Repressed memories of Mr. Ngô began bubbling up. He was always helping Evelyn around the house, helping her when she was pregnant with Paulina or Georgia, running to get her specific cravings. Still, the siblings had never seen Mr. Ngô and Evelyn touch, not even a hug. Now they knew why.

They'd never fully understand how bad it was down in Seadrift, the fearmongering, the racism, the threats to their livelihood that their parents faced. They just had to accept that they had done their best. And maybe, just maybe, that would be enough to quiet the rest of their questions.

"Wait a minute, though," Jude said suddenly. "Why did you want me to get married then?"

Mr. Ngô shrugged as he picked at a snail absentmindedly. "That was Duc's idea. I mean, he was kinda hoping you'd marry *well*. Maybe someone rich? You know? Save the business in a different way. Also, you were lonely, con. What kind of life were you really living before? That *all* of you were living before?"

No one responded, unsure of how wrong they had been about everything and everyone in their lives. The two people they had thought didn't know them had actually known them the best.

There was a loud commotion down by the riverbank, and everyone realized that Duc had somehow escaped the group, found his way down, and wrangled the karaoke microphone out of a drunken stranger's hands.

"What the hell is he up to now?" Connie moaned. Duc tapped the mic, and after setting up the next song, he turned his attention toward all the siblings.

"You all asked me if I had ever loved you?" Duc shouted into the crowd, switching seamlessly between English and Vietnamese. "You may not think of me as your real father, but I am your father, I am *a* father. Just because I'm not one in *your* definition, doesn't mean I didn't do it all for you. I never had children of my own—"

"Thank god," Connie muttered.

"—because you all were enough for me," Duc finished.

All the confused faces in the crowd transitioned into smiles as everyone recognized the familiar opening notes: C, A, A, C, D, G. The universal anthem for all father figures, of all types, across the universe.

Duc, with his heavy Vietnamese accent, pulled out a cigarette and began singing into the microphone, and looked first at Georgia, Paulina, Bingo, Jane, and, finally, at Jude.

Hey Jude, don't make it bad . . .

"Oh no," Bingo whispered. "Please, please, not the karaoke. Someone stop him." Flashbacks of past memories of Duc slurring heavily into a microphone arose for all the children. But Duc sang on, undeterred, off-key, skipping parts of the song to take long inhales of his cigarette.

On and on Duc droned, pitchy and out of breath, sometimes hacking up a lung. Soon enough, the very Vietnamese crowd began singing along with Duc, encouraging him. Everyone raised their beer bottles, clapped along, and pointed at the children. Each of the Trần children looked on, horrified, watching as Duc belted out the most American song ever sung by a British band.

Na na na nananana, nannana, hey Jude . . .

Someone next to Georgia leapt up from their chair and began belting the lyrics as loudly as they could, screaming into the humid Sài Gòn night. Startled, she knocked her beer all over herself.

Huey looked at Evelyn, grateful for the distraction around them as he pleaded with her, their hands still knotted. "Will you come back to us? It's been too long. If you are ready to come home, please. I . . . I miss you. Even if you don't miss me."

She couldn't look at him yet. She just kept watching, bemused as Duc got drunker and drunker and his singing got sloppier and sloppier.

The children did their best to pretend they didn't hear the conversation, even though they were all eavesdropping intensely.

"I'm ready to come back home," she said finally. "But I don't think I can be with you again, anh. You have lied to me for so long. Both of you. It's time for me to be free. I've been on my own for the last twenty years, I need to keep being on my own. For my own sanity." Evelyn let go of his hand first.

Huey's hand fell limp at his side, but he didn't fight back. He just continued looking at her longingly, waiting, as he had done, for most of his life, for her to love him back one day. He would wait forever, and he was okay with that.

Light pollution clouded the skies, and drunken, singing neighbors sloshed beer on all of them. But the Trần family didn't care. The crowd continued swaying along to the song, and Duc was now seemingly howling at the moon.

The children looked at one another. Jude, Jane, Bingo, Paulina, and Georgia. They looked at their parents next to them with renewed eyes, and they looked at everyone around them, watching the crowd swaying along.

Everything that had transpired up until that moment seemed so distant. Under a half-moon, in a country they could never claim as home for themselves, they instead decided to claim each other as family. They all stood up and began belting it as loud as possible, heads tilted up toward the sky.

Na na na nananana, nannana, hey Jude . . .

"To hell with it." Connie sighed as she grabbed a beer, stood up, and joined in on the singing as well.

Na na na nananana, nannana, hey Jude . . .

CHAPTER 44

Diệp

The cicadas had come back to Houston.

Their droning was harmonious, and as more cicadas joined in, it became a nightly concert for the whole city to enjoy. I pretended I was the maestro each night, throwing my hand high up in the air with each crescendo, and throwing it down with the decrescendo. I looked forward to dusk every night, just so I could hear them again. Their humming made me less lonely, or at least, it acted as a Band-Aid. Loneliness, I was afraid, was still something I hadn't gotten used to in my old age. Perhaps it was one of those things no one ever really adjusted to, like getting over your first love. I had forgotten how boisterous the cicadas could be, reminding me of what life had been like as a young mother, with five children under the same roof.

Now life was so quiet, so unnerving. The cicadas also marked the first time my eldest daughter, Jane, had heard them in Houston since moving back a year ago. It was the first thing she had commented on during her visit. There weren't any cicadas in Los Angeles.

We relied heavily on the topic of cicadas for a long time; it was our way to communicate as we started to relearn each other. Like how strangers use the weather to talk to each other, we used the cicadas. Everything else was a learning curve between us. I had told Jane once, over coffee, that the cicadas often signified the beginning of another oppressive Houston summer, guaranteed to make anyone burn for longer than three minutes out in the sun. She had nodded awkwardly as she tried to find a way to keep the conversation going. But we were trying. We were learning. It was a second chance, and I was grateful. Grateful that we could meet in the middle and learn to start over again. It was rare to get second chances, so I held on to the hope, for as long as I could.

I had found a small, quaint apartment near Jane and Jude, and we made it a point to see each other every day. As for the rest of my children, I caught up over phone calls, text messages, and video calls; they were easy to connect with, despite the distance between us. It was Jude and Jane, my two oldest, who were the hardest to understand. They carried the most pain; having memories became their burden. But I tried, I kept trying every day, for a full year. I owed it to them to prove that I wasn't going anywhere this time.

Bingo had moved back to Philadelphia, to try to win a woman's heart again. She said she had to go; she was drawn to this woman and couldn't sleep or think about anyone else. I told her to go, and to not look back. Paulina left for San Francisco, in search of a different type of family. I told her to hold on tight to them, to try to love them in the way that I couldn't. And Georgia, my youngest, had decided to stay in Vietnam and explore the country more. She wanted to see how far she could go before she missed home. Perhaps that was just a marker of youth, to go as far as possible. I told her to go to the edge of the universe, and to do a big U-turn back to me one day.

But the three of them promised me they'd visit several times a year, and I knew they meant it.

One warm summer day Jane called me. I picked up immediately, as I often do now, unafraid to hide myself from them. "Má, are you free now?"

"I'm not allowed to go anywhere without telling one of you, so yes, I am free. But you probably already knew that."

"Can you come by the store now? Duc's?"

I paused. "Con, you know I don't want to be there. It's cursed. You know it haunts me. I can't be inside that store."

Jane paused. I could hear her breathing. "Please, Má? Just stop by for a little bit. Please."

I couldn't say no. Too many missed opportunities had passed us by where I was dumbfounded to see how grown she had gotten. Jane had even started having baby gray hairs appear, and it shocked me to realize that Time was also coming for my children. It broke my heart, when I saw how much time Jane had lost for herself, because of how long I'd been gone. While I was trying to heal, Jane didn't know how to heal without me. "Okay, con, I'll come."

She breathed a sigh of relief. But when we hung up, I suppressed my anxieties as best I could. About seeing the place again that had robbed me of my identity, and of Tuấn's memory. I had promised myself that I would never set foot in any one of those stores. That old-fashioned serif font, the pale yellow menu, and my recipes splayed out there for strangers to gawk at and point to. That store hadn't been my vision at all, nor had it been Tuấn's. We had always talked about a different type of store. Tuấn had wanted something cozier, more homey, to remind him of the street food he had grown up eating in Vietnam.

But I swallowed my pride, pinned my hair neatly back into a bob, and learned to breathe. I grabbed my helmet and headed to my Vespa. Before I took off, I glanced around the small garden I had tended to all year, which grew tall bushes of Thai chili peppers and perilla leaves. Jane had suggested that I learn a new hobby, that perhaps it could help me in moments when I couldn't get out of my own head or whenever I felt extreme bouts of loneliness. She was afraid that I would take it as an insult, but I had simply told her that my own mother had a green thumb, too, and that she was often found in the garden. I said it was a compliment, that I wouldn't be a real Vietnamese woman without knowing my way around a garden.

I started the Vespa up and began to head to Duc's to confront my past.

....

By the time I pulled into the familiar Dakao Plaza, there was a sizable crowd. The usual green signage had been covered up with a crooked gray tarp. No one had noticed my arrival, as there seemed to be some infighting among them.

I spotted my five children immediately. But why were they all here?

They lined up in the order I had always known them: Jude, Jane, Bingo, Paulina, and Georgia. Behind them stood Duc, alone, without Connie, a recent "divorcée" (the paperwork was still never properly filed). Last I heard, Connie had taken whatever money was left and moved back home to New Orleans, to be with her mother. And there was Huey, always watching, observing, also always alone, but in a different way. But it wasn't just them I noticed. It was everyone I had turned my back on twenty years ago. The same faces, still clinging on, the old guard of Dakao Plaza. The plaza had stood the test of time and looked exactly the same as the day I left: the red clay tiles on the roofs, the pylon sign, the cracks in the cement in the parking lot, which looked ready to swallow the plaza whole any minute. It was as if the plaza had been frozen in a time capsule, waiting for my return.

Bác Cai was the only one who noticed my arrival, and she gave me a small smile. I could glean the whole world from that smile. She was welcoming me back so that she could finally rest.

I recognized the neighboring business owners, who were out in full force. Thủy from the nail salon supply store, Duy from the travel agency, Xuân from the sketchy CPA's office, and Linh from the refillable, filtered water store.

I recognized Henry, standing there awkwardly, next to Jane. I remembered him from when he was young, always coming to our house. Jane didn't think I noticed them holding hands back then or sneaking kisses, but I did.

"What is going on?" I asked. Everyone jumped at my voice. I turned to my children. "What are you all doing back here?"

Jane and Jude locked eyes, and then they approached me, each grabbing a hand. They pulled me forward, then spun me around until I faced the store.

"We have something we want to show you," Jane said softly. She glanced at the group behind us. Everyone was biting back smiles.

"You're not about to surprise me with a puppy, right?" I asked suspiciously. "I'm almost sixty, I'm not about to take care of another living thing."

Jane motioned for the sign to be released. Huey and Duc fumbled for a bit with the cord before they yanked it down with all their might on each side. I gasped as the tarp came tumbling down, revealing a new sign, and I covered my mouth. Staring back down at me, in a new font and branding, was the sign Diep's Sandwiches.

"Wait . . . who's Diep?" Georgia whispered to Paulina. "I think we got the sign wrong. It's supposed to say Evelyn."

"That's our mother's Vietnamese name," Paulina whispered back.

"I thought her name was Evelyn?" Georgia began to panic.

"That's her American name. Her real name is Diệp," Bingo whispered back. "You think the woman was born in Vietnam and was named *Evelyn*?!"

Tangled emotions rushed through me. I barely recognized the name my mother had given me. Shock and anger—that was what I felt as I stepped closer to the store. I hadn't thought about my mother in so long.

I used to think about her often, but as the cycle of motherhood hit me, it was my turn to resent my own mother, for all she wasn't able to do, while she battled her own demons. Diệp was my mother's name, and that name had been passed down to me. I had forgotten who Diệp had been, before Evelyn took over. Who was Diệp before it all? Before my children, before Huey, before Duc, and even before Tuấn.

"Oh god," Jane whispered to Jude. "Did we mess up?"

"Trời ơi," Duc said to Huey. "This is your fault."

"But she mentioned this was always her dream. I thought . . ." Huey trailed off.

"I recognize that look in her eyes," Paulina whispered to Georgia. "That looks like a woman who is ready to run again, and this time, she might not come back."

Thủy whispered to Linh as she paused mid-clap. "Typical ungrateful children. Their mother is gone for over two decades, and they give her more work when she comes back. Let the woman rest!"

Only Georgia was willing to be brave and step forward until she was side by side with me. "Má?" Georgia said quietly, her accent having improved since she had moved to Vietnam. "Is everything okay?"

I broke off from staring at the sign and turned to look my youngest daughter in the eye. Georgia, who knew me the best out of all of them, very quickly realized that I wasn't angry at all; instead, she saw how much time had come between us, and how much it had pained me.

"Now, that's a name I haven't heard in a long time," I whispered to her, a smile cracked on my lips.

Georgia began laughing and crying as well, as she took my hand. "*Star Wars*, right?"

"You're finally learning." I laughed as well, and turned to face the rest of my family head on. All seven of them. Huey, Duc, Jude, Jane, Bingo, Paulina, and Georgia.

"We all are," Georgia whispered back, as everyone welcomed Diệp Lê home. I began to cry, finally accepting the long-overdue acknowledgment of being the real breadwinner of the family, as someone who had learned how to survive for them, and had started it all.

Leaving a trail of May rose, jasmine, and a hint of bourbon vanilla behind me, I finally stepped forward.

ACKNOWLEDGMENTS

The journey toward this novel has been full of anxiety. The sophomore slump is real, I fear. But luckily, I continue to have a beautiful support system to yell encouragements at me.

To my editor, Loan Le, who gave me a second shot at this life. Cảm ơn, em. (I fixed it this time, Loan!) This career is unforgiving and nebulous; thank you for continuing to be a familiar face. Atria! Elizabeth Hitti, you're a gem. Gena Lanzi and Maudee Genao, the women you two are. Dana Trocker, Abby Velasco, Davina Mock-Maniscalco, Shelby Pumphrey, Lacee Burr, Paige Lytle, Liz Byer, Vanessa Silverio, Libby McGuire, Kitt Reckord, Nicole Bond, Sara Bowne, Rebecca Justiniano, Joel Holland (for bringing this cover to life), and Lisa Nicholas, I am humbled and thankful.

I am grateful to Jordan Hill, my literary agent, who is a very patient woman with impeccable grammar. Thank you for always telling me to stop apologizing anytime I apologize. To the other folks at New Leaf, who read early (horrible) drafts, Suzie Townsend and Sophia Ramos, and gave the kind of feedback writers dream of. To everyone else, Tracy Williams, Keifer Ludwing, Joe Volpe, Donna Yee, Gabby Benjamin, Kim Rogers, Hilary Pecheone, and Eileen Lalley—my lifelong gratitude.

To Laura Reddy, manager extraordinaire, and the person to call during an apocalypse, thank you for asking me to meet up at that Thai restaurant all those years ago and asking me "What's the worst that could happen?"

I won't lie, this book was hell to get through. I wanted to do the historical fiction part justice and knew I was in way over my head. I owe many people for their expertise, time, and research. You all came before this book and continue to do the work toward community care and social justice.

First and foremost, to Dr. Thao Ha, for your patience, sensitivity read, and your early consultation. I'll forever laugh about that Zoom meeting we had about an entirely different topic, which escalated into a deeper conversation. Thank you for consulting on this book, for being a beacon for the incarcerated, for being my friend, and for showing me and Jes Vu how to properly eat crawfish in Houston.

To Judge Denny Chin and Kathy Chin (by way of Grace Tran and Kimberly Han—Mexico City was serendipitous) and the Asian American Bar Association of New York. Thank you for sending over all the research and for all that AABANY has done to preserve and maintain AAPI history that has been lost to time. Other notable works I pulled inspiration and research from were Kirk Wallace Johnson's *The Fishermen and the Dragon* and Tim Tsai's *Seadrift* documentary (which Dr. Thao Ha also produced). Two extraordinary works that I was able to filter through the lens of fiction.

One of the best aspects of being on this journey has been meeting all the incredible people along the way. I have been searching for community my entire life. It's rare to find, rarer than waiting for lightning to strike twice. I've been lucky to have been struck a million times over. To my fellow authors, readers, librarians, booksellers, independent bookstores, and all the Viet book girlies who I've met along the way . . . I cherish you all. It never ceases to amaze me how far my words have traveled, to resonate with souls like yours. Amanda Khong, Viviann Do, Trinity Nguyen, Grace Tran, Jes Vu, Michelle Quach, Julie Tieu, Suzanne Park, Hannah Sawyerr, Diane Brown, and many more. May we always be able to get dinner on a whim and discuss books ad nauseam in rapid-fire texts.

To my family, though our ties are fragile, may we continue working to move closer back to each other. I await that day eagerly.

Finally to Charles, my squire, best friend, and, I guess, husband (if we must be technical). Thank you for marrying me on our patio that one random summer day and for loving me and Pili, just two chaotic girls.

And finally, dear reader, thank you for all the support. Until next time.

ABOUT THE AUTHOR

Carolyn Huynh loves writing about messy Asian women who never learn from their mistakes. After living up and down the West Coast, she now resides in Los Angeles with her husband and her chaotic dog. When she's not writing, Carolyn daydreams about having iced coffee on a rooftop in Ho Chi Minh City. *The Family Recipe* is her second novel.